A Victorian Marriage

Muriel Canfield

BETHANY HOUSE PUBLISHERS
MINNEAPOLIS, MINNESOTA 55438
A Division of Bethany Fellowship, Inc.

Credit: Albert Deutsch, *The Mentally Ill in America* (New York and London: Columbia University Press, 1967).

Published by Bethany House Publishers
A Division of Bethany Fellowship, Inc.
6820 Auto Club Road, Minneapolis, Minnesota 55438

Printed in the United States of America

Library of Congress Cataloging-in-Publication Data

Canfield, Muriel, 1935-
   A Victorian marriage.

   I. Title.
PS3553.A494V53   1986   813'.54   86-14776
ISBN 0-87123-880-2 (pbk.)

To Gene

To Donald MacDonell Hansen and Audrey Hindon Hansen, my parents, who inspired my love for Chicago.

MURIEL CANFIELD was born in Oak Park, Illinois, and raised in suburban Chicago. She married in 1956 and has three children. She and her husband were converted to Christ after seventeen years of marriage. A full-time writer for the past seven years, she has a degree in English Education from Miami University. This is Muriel's third book. Her other books are *I Wish I Could Say I Love You* and *Anne*.

Chicago

For thousands of years the wild onion laid its brilliant pink flower on the prairie at the foot of Lake Michigan, from horizon to horizon. In the first heat of summer the flower burned and withered on the ground and the air was pungent, initiating the Algonquian name, Chikaugong, the place of the powerful wild onion. The Indian occupied Chicago then.

In 1803 the white man built Fort Dearborn at Chikaugong, and he plowed up the prairie, the wild onion, and the Indian. He renamed the land Chicago, because the Indian name was difficult to pronounce.

By 1871 Chicago had a population of 334,000. It was the country's fastest-growing city, a distribution center for grain, drygoods, and livestock. Yet some looked nervously at the many wooden buildings it contained, the wood sidewalks, wood streets, thinking it like an artificial forest waiting for a match.

One

Chicago: October 9, 1871

*J*ust before dawn Julia and David Gerard stood in Lake Michigan while Chicago burned. The freezing water covered Julia's knees, numbing her legs. She was glad, at least, for that. Hundreds of people endured the cold water with them. Thousands more were on the beach, their backs hunched against the flames reaching from the city. Hot wind scorched Julia's back. Brands of fire sailed overhead, and she felt the horrible night etching itself in her memory. Most of all, she thought, she would remember the awful orange and yellow sky. How the color blotted out the sun, moon, and stars.

Everything Julia had ever owned was gone. The daguerreotype of her mother. The family Bible. The baby's cradle. Everything! Julia's tall frame shook. She dreamed of hot chicken soup the way their family servant made it, with big chunks of chicken and so hot that steam rose from the bowl for a long time. She pressed against her husband David for comfort, and he wrapped her and Nelda into his coat.

"David, will we die? Will we make it through this?"

His dark eyes were reassuring. "We won't die."

Recently, though, Julia had wanted to die.

She and David had been married only six months, and most of that time had been troubled. Remembering those months, she shivered from more than the cold water lapping around her knees.

On the morning of Julia Adam's marriage to David, white cabbage butterflies fluttered through the trees, an unusual event for early April.

But cold was predicted for tomorrow and they would die. One lighted high on the bud of an elm twig outside the window, so near that Julia saw the down on its wings. She chose the butterfly as a symbol of her happy future with David, though she felt uneasy that her symbol would die so soon. She raised her window, hoping the butterfly might enter and she could save it in a jar. She recalled, though, that butterflies seldom flew through windows as moths did; butterflies had an excellent sense of direction.

"Close the window—I'm freezing," her sister Melinda called.

"It's not cold."

"It is. You always like it too cold."

Julia shut the window. Certainly Melinda had no physical stamina or fortitude, she thought, and was comfortable only if the room were in the midseventies. Melinda's figure and face were as soft and plump as the bonbons she gorged on. It was a wonder her face bloomed with color, Julia thought, considering her pasty diet.

Melinda popped a yellow bonbon into her mouth and shoved the candy box under the bed, apparently hiding it from herself.

"Please grab hold of something so I can lace your corset," Melinda said. "We're due at the church soon."

Grasping the bedpost, Julia braced herself. "Pull hard! Remember, I need an eighteen-inch waist."

"I can't pull that hard. Why did you have your wedding dress made so small? Why do you have to have an eighteen-inch waist? It's too small for you, really."

"Pull, Melinda!"

Melinda tugged ineffectually on the laces. "This is tight enough if you ask me. If I hurry, I've got time to let out a seam, and I'll take orange-blossoms from the veil and pin them over the seam to hide it. You're silly to ruin your insides for an inch or two. Accept a twenty-inch waist. You always did. I'd be glad for it. Have you considered that you might faint at the altar? You—"

"Pull! Please!" Julia said. "Trina had an eighteen-inch waist."

"David won't be thinking about Trina. I'm surprised you are."

Julia choked up. "Oh, Melinda, I'm trying not to. But it's terrible to be a second wife. David hardly knows me compared to Trina. He was married to her for ten years, and he's known me six months. David's never gotten over Trina's death."

"How do you know that?"

"Because he never talks about her. If he had recovered, he would talk about her."

"He's over her. She died three years ago."

"Two," Julia corrected.

"I wish you'd be more relaxed about David. Sometimes I think you'll get hurt."

"How could I be hurt? I love him too much. When you sincerely love someone, you can't be hurt at a deep level. You overlook things."

"Then overlook Trina."

"I am! I'm trying."

Julia grasped the bedpost again and Melinda jerked, tugged, and gasped. "There!"

Carefully, so as not to muss Julia's hair, Melinda guided the wedding dress over her head. Julia smoothed down the sleek silk overskirt, touching the lovely scallops of tulle and Valenciennes lace on the skirt. The bodice was tight enough to display her well-shaped bosom, she thought, but not as tight as she wished. Of course her sister Edith had prevailed in the fitting.

Melinda turned Julia to the bureau mirror. "You've never looked more beautiful."

Julia didn't think so and her green eyes widened anxiously. Her red hair was pinned up in a loose chignon, frizzed at the forehead, a simple style she had thought would flatter her high-boned face. But now she realized the style made her cheekbones stick out too much. Her face looked stark and she reminded herself of a baby bird. Furthermore, the Taylor's Moth Patch and Freckle Lotion that she had applied all week hadn't worked. Her freckles were as pronounced as ever. She should have asked Edith to do her hair, she thought. Edith had talent in hairdressing, but Julia had hated to cope with her abrasive personality today. Nonetheless, Julia made a fast decision. "Put the iron in the gas. I'll have Edith put a few curls around my ears."

"You don't have time," Edith said, entering, her long-boned fingers gesturing in all directions, threatening to knock her pince-nez from her thin nose.

Edith Chapman and Melinda Adams were bridesmaids, and Julia thought it a pity that Edith's angled arms canceled the feminine effect of her dress. Melinda's and Edith's dresses were identical, apple green satin with white lace flounces. The color helped Edith's sallow complexion and pale eyes, but drained Melinda's bright face. Edith had insisted on the color, of course.

Edith plucked Julia's veil from the armchair and shook it, rattling all the delicate orange blooms on the wreath. "Look at it heaped on the chair! How dare you let it wrinkle after I ironed it for you? You know I have little enough time."

Julia granted that Edith was busy, having to constantly know where her husband Morton was, even to which room of their house he traveled through. Then, too, she had to graph her little Freddie's physical progress and record his daily diet. These records were consulted to determine causes of illness and for items of conversation. Julia thought Edith was a possessive, silly woman.

Edith studied Julia. "You don't look too bad, though I don't like your hair. We leave for church in exactly seven minutes, and Miss Nancy sent me to be sure you aren't fiddling around. She would come up herself, except she's mending a moth hole in Father's suit coat. Father's having a fit because he found a hole. Of course he's careful about his clothes and he's upset that he hadn't noticed the hole before this. Though I don't believe it, Miss Nancy swears she stored the suit in cedar chips last summer. Miss Nancy simply forgot to, I say. She's too old and forgetful to be a servant, and Father should let her go. I say—"

"Miss Nancy does her best," Julia interrupted. "No servant could please you."

"Don't be snippy, miss."

Julia thought Edith should be grateful to Miss Nancy. Miss Nancy, with the aid of various servant girls, had loyally cooked and cleaned for the family all of Edith's life. Miss Nancy had helped nurse Julia's mother during her final illness. Mrs. Adams had died of consumption when Julia was a young child. Julia remembered her mother as a pale woman with thin but surprisingly soft arms. Julia wished that Edith hadn't assumed the role of mother for Melinda and her. Edith probably had done so because she was twelve years older than Julia, nine years older than Melinda. Certainly Julia wouldn't choose to have Edith as a mother. *Neither would Melinda*, Julia mused.

Edith straightened Julia's bustle and folded the long court train over her arm. "Watch you don't fall on your face coming downstairs. You know I don't approve of this marriage. David is *not* religious like Morton, nor is he affectionate to you. I say that a man who can't show affection will not make a good father, as Morton is."

Julia turned away.

"David's too old as well. He's twelve years your senior—my age. He's been married before and, of course, he had that—that—well, that business with Diane. One thing is sure, David has a peculiar past, if you ask me."

"Who is Diane?" Julia asked in a strangled voice. She had never heard of Diane.

"Never mind. It's nothing—a slip of the tongue."

"Leave Julia alone," Melinda said. "It's too late to make the comments you're making."

"It's never too late. I believe Julia *is* acting foolishly in not marrying Arthur, and everybody would understand if she came to her senses and cancelled this wedding. Everyone at church adores Arthur. I admit my mistakes, which is to my credit, and I'm teaching my Freddie to do the same."

Melinda retorted, "I'm glad Julia and Arthur broke up. He's not Julia's type. He's too perfect—he's too nice and I think he's artificial. He shakes everyone's hand as if he wants them to do business at his bank. Plus he's peculiar. Anybody that's read all twenty-two books of the *Encyclopedia Britannica* is peculiar."

She'd certainly never tell Edith why she and Arthur hadn't married, Julia thought. Melinda was the only one who knew that. And Arthur's mother, Mrs. Newton. Julia recalled the horrified expression on Mrs. Newton's face when she had discovered Julia and Arthur embracing in her elegant parlor. Arthur had lived with his mother then. What an evil conclusion Mrs. Newton had come to! Julia felt shame all over again; for there had been some reason for the assumption. It was the one time she had surrendered to Arthur to that degree, and that only after he had pressured her. Of course Mrs. Newton used the incident to force a breakup. She hadn't approved of Arthur marrying below his social class, and Julia believed Mrs. Newton had been searching for an incident. Julia had told Edith that she and Arthur were incompatible.

Edith said, "It's shocking that you've had just a three-month betrothal. You hardly know David. Why, you only met him last fall at a charity ball. It's as if you have to—"

"She *doesn't* have to!" Melinda cried. Her face was flushed with anger.

Looking startled, Edith stepped away. "I suppose not—now hurry downstairs."

Edith left and Melinda embraced Julia. "What a prune! Don't let her ruin your day."

"She drives me mad!"

"Forget her."

"I can't. Oh, Melinda, who is Diane?"

"I don't know. Forget it!"

With David there was such exhaustive forgetting to do, Julia thought. There were probably many facts she didn't know that she must one day forget. "Edith's wrong that David isn't affectionate," Julia said. "He *is* affectionate."

"I know that."

"It's just that we're seldom alone. Either we're in a crowd or in the parlor, and Miss Nancy's in the next room."

"Julia, forget what Edith said!"

Melinda carefully folded the veil into the box she took from the bureau. Julia hung her beaded reticule over her wrist and tucked a handkerchief of Melinda's into it for luck. Moving toward the door, Julia looked around the room she had shared with Melinda all her life. She choked out, "This is the hard part—leaving you."

Melinda nodded. "I'll hate the room with you gone. I'm not coming back to it. I'll change rooms with Miss Nancy."

"You know Miss Nancy won't budge from her room—she's got her things placed just where she wants them."

"I wish—oh—" Melinda broke off.

"You wish what?"

"Oh, nothing—just nothing." Tears ran from Melinda's round blue eyes.

"Melinda!" Julia insisted.

"I—I wish I were getting married too. I hate myself—I must be jealous."

Julia was incredulous. "You? No!"

"I'm almost an old maid, and I have no prospects. Heaven knows I attend every event in the world to find a man, and who do I find—nobody! Nobody looks at me. I'm the person who sits with the old ladies in the corner at every ball. The only man in two years who's called is that nasty, selfish little butcher with the pocked face, and I loathe him. He smells like meat, and he's missing three fingers. I despise my fat body. I—"

"You've got a lovely personality," Julia interrupted. "Men would court you if you didn't always belittle yourself."

Melinda shook her head, throwing her sausage curls into disorder. "I don't want a lecture. I've decided to take drastic action. I'm consulting with Madame Trudeau, that clairvoyant on Randolph . . . by the river. If she doesn't predict a husband for my future, then I'll give up hoping."

Julia straightened Melinda's long curls. "She'll simply fabricate a nice-looking man for you. I don't put any stock in prophecy of that kind."

"You can't judge. You've never been to a clairvoyant."

"Neither have you."

"Come . . . now!" Edith screeched from the bottom of the stairs. "The carriage is here, and Father is in it—waiting."

Julia hesitated. Her father was a dentist with a busy practice. Because he prided himself on keeping appointments, he hated to wait. But she had to finish their conversation. "Melinda, clairvoyants are evil—like witches."

"Madame Trudeau is legitimate. She's advertised a one thousand dollar reward to anyone who equals her skills in prediction."

"Fiddlesticks! She couldn't pay out one thousand and you know it."

"Ezekiel and Isaiah knew the future," Melinda said.

"Because God told it to them. They didn't charge for their information either."

"Well, I'm going!"

Julia heard Edith's slippers storm up the stairs, and Melinda and she fled. Melinda almost collided with Edith at the head of the stairs.

"I'm sorry. We—" Melinda said.

"Tardiness is a sin," Edith interrupted, her thin and angry features protruding like signs on a storefront.

"Everything's sin to you," Melinda said. "Breathing is a sin!"

Edith pulled up the watch chain at her waist. "I hope we don't run into heavy traffic. We always run into busy traffic. Have you brought your smelling salts, Julia?"

"No—I've never fainted."

Edith unearthed a crystal vial from her reticule.

"I won't need it!" Julia protested.

"Take it! Brides are very unpredictable."

As Julia dropped the vial into her reticule, she noticed her hand trembling. She hated her weakness in always complying with Edith. Thankfully, today she would be independent from Edith and all she expected. Julia only had to please David and herself from now on, and pleasing David would be simple compared to pleasing Edith. Edith had told Julia it was her advice that kept others from failure. Julia thought that sounded a little presumptuous. Yet, Julia did have to admit that Edith had been concerned and interested in all aspects of Julia's life. For that she was grateful.

Julia ventured, "Will you please remove that watch from your waist at church? It looks out of place with your dressy gown."

"Yes, of course."

Edith believed that to be precisely on time was to be Christian, and Julia was relieved that at exactly 11:45 the wedding group lined up in the narthex.

Julia's hand was on her father's arm. She looked into the sanctuary, a familiar place to her. She usually attended Sunday morning, Sunday evening, and Wednesday evening services. She was proud of her church, with its exquisite stained-glass windows and carved pews with soft spring cushions on the backs and seats. There were even fans in the pew racks for the women on warm days.

Mrs. Pratt, the organist since the church was built thirty years ago, was at her bench, looking even more frail than usual. Her music had grown erratic, along with her health, and the uneven beat of "Christ, from Whom All Blessings Flow" filled the sanctuary. David was to the right of the organ, in front of the pulpit. Julia saw him look toward her, his face appearing hazy through her veil. She had been waiting for this moment for three months, imagining it in detail.

David wore a pale-blue frock coat, dove gray trousers, and a blue necktie to match his coat. The light colors contrasted with his olive skin, producing a striking effect. Julia wished she could see his eyes clearly, for she believed they were his best feature. They were very dark, and quite heavily lashed. But his eyes were also a problem for her: they reflected little of his feelings and thoughts. Of course she hadn't known him long, and she would learn to read his feelings. Julia thought his face was too heavily-boned to be considered handsome. But he was tall enough and large enough to make an imposing figure. Melinda, however, thought David looked like a king, talked like a saint, and she practically worshiped him like a god. But Melinda tended to get carried away when she admired a man, Julia realized.

She fought the urge to run to him.

Mrs. Pratt announced Julia's entrance with Handel's *Occasional Overture* as Melinda and Edith stepped forward, their dresses rustling. Wearing a pince-nez in public wasn't considered fashionable, and, though Edith usually wore hers in spite of this, she had removed it. She had also taken off the watch as she promised Julia she would.

Julia and her father entered the aisle. They weren't close; he had been so occupied with his dental practice and fraternal organizations that he had little time for his daughters. When he squeezed her hand quickly, she was surprised.

"Well, my dear—"

"Yes, my wedding day," she said, smiling.

When Julia approached the third pew from the front, her steps flagged. She was shocked to see Arthur Newton sitting in his pew, his blond head nodding genially above his expensive suit. Though his eyes were pleasant, they narrowed as they observed her gown, and she knew he estimated the cost, judged the workmanship. *How dare Arthur come and wreck my wedding!* she thought. She had courteously invited the congregation, but she hadn't once thought Arthur would include himself as one of the invited!

She supposed he came out of guilt, to assure his conscience that she was happy. He was just the kind who had to have a clear conscience to be able to figure profitable interest rates. She looked away from him—she wouldn't let him upset her. She was thankful, at least, that Mrs. Newton wasn't here.

Julia slipped in beside David. He smelled faintly of the pine and cedar in his lumberyard. He didn't smile; his expression was somber, his face a little pale. She didn't smile either.

Melinda whispered. "You're breathing funny. I told you not to—"

"Hush—" Edith said.

"I'm all right."

"Hush!"

Julia pressed close to David and her dress crushed against him. Having the dress lie smoothly wasn't important now.

The Reverend Dr. Portor began the marriage ceremony. " 'But from the beginning of the creation God made them male and female. For this cause shall a man leave his father and mother, and cleave to his wife; And they twain shall be one flesh: so then they are no more twain, but one flesh. What therefore God hath joined together, let not man put asunder' " (Mark 10:6–9).

The ceremony passed in a concert of scripture, scents, and feelings, with David standing solidly at her side. He looked intently at the minister, his lips pale, compressed. His forehead was damp; the church was warm. Julia's skin was damp as well. She noticed that Edith's eyes were moist. Either Edith was moved or the scented candles on the chancel wall bothered her; Edith was sensitive to certain perfumes.

The Reverend Dr. Portor raised his arms in blessing. " 'The Lord bless thee, and keep thee: the Lord make his face shine upon thee, and be gracious unto thee: the Lord lift up his countenance upon thee, and give thee peace' " (Num. 6:24–26).

David looked at Julia. His expression dazzled her. So there it was! For the first time, she could read David's feelings. Julia's heart beat faster as she realized it was David's love for her that was shining in his eyes. Oh, it was bright! Brighter than the sun on the edge of a cloud.

Why hadn't she seen it before?

Two

*B*eneath the privacy of her skirts Julia kicked off her shoes. Her feet ached from standing so long in the receiving line in her parlor. China and silver clinked in the dining room, where guests were serving themselves to the wedding breakfast (by rights a luncheon, Julia thought, but the term breakfast was in vogue): galantines, mayonnaises of fowl, chicken salad, oyster and turkey patties, fruit salad, breads. The meal was catered, but Miss Nancy had baked the bridal cake, a lovely creation of three tiers with piped borders and live daisies. Julia couldn't dissuade the elderly servant from the difficult project. Miss Nancy said she had baked Edith's bridal cake, as she would do for all *her* girls.

Julia had invited Miss Nancy to eat in the parlor, but she had stationed herself in the kitchen in case the caterer might need something. At one end of the dining table stood a bowl of nonalcoholic fruit punch. Edith believed drinking indicated weakness of character, and Julia thought it best not to irritate her. However, it was the custom to drink healths with champagne, and Julia would have preferred to include some in the punch.

A female classmate from Chicago High School took Julia's hands. "Well, Mrs. David Gerard!"

"Yes!" Julia said.

"How does it feel to be married?"

"Just wonderful." Julia glanced at David, and he smiled quietly at her.

As the last guest passed through the receiving line, David's mother

18

sighed, "Julia, I'm tired, and if you don't mind, I'll sit down and eat. You really don't need me anymore, do you?"

Alma Gerard wobbled and grabbed Julia's arms for support. Alma's dress was shorter than was fashionable, and Julia noticed that her feet were small. Julia wasn't surprised the little feet had difficulty supporting Alma's large frame. Now set aright, Alma smiled. Her mouth over her tier of chins was shaped like a rosebud, and her eyes were warm and held a childlike innocence. To Julia, Alma seemed but a child set in an old frame. "Please go ahead," Julia said. "David and I will eat too. If anyone else comes, a friend of mine will be at the door to greet them."

"You are hungry, aren't you, Edgar?" Alma's eyes nervously sought her husband's approval to eat. "We had an early breakfast and it was skimpy."

"Fine—let's eat," he said brusquely. He was taller and heavier than his wife, his facial features were large and unattractive. The few times Julia had been with him he had been curt. David and Edgar owned the Gerard Lumber Company—a rather antagonistic alliance, David had said.

"You're sure you don't need me anymore?" Alma said, blinking nervously.

Julia remembered that David said his mother seldom left the house and was nervous in crowds. Therefore it was her practice to take a chloral tablet, a mild sedative, before leaving home. Julia thought Alma had probably forgotten her pill. "No, really, please go ahead."

"As soon as you get back from your honeymoon, you must come to dinner," Alma said. "I haven't invited you because I've had some problems. I'm really sorry. I do look forward to getting to know you."

Julia had been so preoccupied with David that she had hardly noticed. David had mentioned that his mother often cared for a troublesome cousin, and Julia wondered if the cousin were the problem she alluded to. "I've been busy too—getting ready for the wedding and all, Mrs.—"

"Just call me Mother Gerard," Alma said, "or Mother, or Alma if you would like."

"Mother Gerard is fine. I haven't called anyone mother for a long time."

"I don't know what you should call Edgar. Edgar, what should Julia call you?"

"Edgar will be fine. I don't court sentimental titles." He then left for the dining room.

His abrupt exit didn't offend Julia. She had learned one couldn't fight another's personality.

While Julia slipped back into her shoes, Edith addressed David. "I would suggest you take your luggage out now. It's best to be ready.

When it's time to leave, you can simply go. Then people won't detain you while you walk back and forth with valises and make you miss your train."

"All right," David said agreeably.

David left, and Melinda and Julia drank a cup of punch. "It infuriates me how Edith is already ordering David around," Melinda said.

"She does the same with Morton. David already planned to take the luggage out early. I think it white of him not to tell Edith that. By the way, did you see Arthur at the wedding?"

Melinda's troubled eyes indicated she had. "Julia, I told you to forget him."

"I only mentioned it because I can't believe he came."

"I'm not surprised—nothing he does surprises me."

When David finished carrying out the luggage, he and Julia ate. Afterward, Julia found Melinda in the dining room. Edith's Freddie was nearby, fingering the hem of the tablecloth, and Julia kissed his forehead. "Don't, Freddie." Then turning to Melinda, she said, "David and I have to leave soon—will you help me change?"

"Yes."

Suddenly Melinda's hand shot out toward Freddie. It was too late. Freddie had tugged the edge of the tablecloth, and a galantine of fish was sliding to the carpet. Julia and Melinda jumped back, but gelatin splattered on their skirts.

"You brat!" Melinda exclaimed.

"Mama . . . Mama!" Freddie wailed. He was tall, precocious, with long arms for a two-and-a-half-year-old. He looked deceptively charming in kilts and boots with pretty black tassels.

While Edith rushed from the other side of the table, Julia and Melinda wiped their skirts with napkins.

Edith addressed Freddie. "What happened, sweetheart?"

Freddie pointed to the floor. "It fell itself."

Melinda frowned at him. "It did not, Freddie. You did it. Admit it—it's terrible to lie."

"I didn't . . . do . . . nothing," he wailed.

Edith caught Freddie up in her arms. "There, there, of course you didn't. Freddie doesn't lie. He simply made a slight mistake."

"He yanked the dish to the floor, and I saw it," Melinda said angrily. "The child needs spankings, not moral dissertations on mistakes."

"Hush, hush, you'll upset him. Don't be vindictive, Melinda," she ordered. "You have no tolerance or understanding of children and will make a terrible parent someday," she predicted and stalked off.

Melinda's eyes dimmed. "Maybe I *will* make a terrible parent.

Maybe it's good I've never married. I was too hard on Freddie. He's just a baby."

"That's silly," Julia said. "You know better than to listen to Edith. Let's go upstairs and finish wiping up."

In the bedroom Melinda stated emphatically, "I don't like Freddie, and that's why I'm so hard on him. I might as well admit it. It seems awful not to like a two-year-old, but I don't."

"It *is* awful, Melinda. But most of the time I don't either. The poor thing can't help how he's being raised. I guess we just shouldn't expect too much from him. In a way I don't blame Edith for being overprotective. I've heard that half the children under six in Chicago die. If I were a mother, I'd be careful too."

Julia changed into a pink poplin traveling dress with a scalloped overskirt pulled into a large bustle. Melinda buttoned the back buttons. "Julia, have you asked Edith about prevention yet?"

"No." Julia had told Melinda that David wished to delay having children. Trina and her baby, a dark-haired boy, had died in childbirth, and David feared going through another like experience. He realized his fears were irrational, yet he needed time to overcome them. In addition, his lumberyard required long hours, and he didn't have time for fatherhood. David had asked Julia to discuss prevention with Edith, but Julia hadn't found the nerve. Julia said, "Melinda, you must know something about prevention—you've read a lot."

Melinda's face turned bright red and she stammered, "I haven't read about that! You had better speak to Edith before you leave."

There was a rap on the door, and Julia admitted her father, Raymond Adams. He handed her a white envelope. The austere-looking man with white hair, mixed with a few strands of red, seemed exhausted from his long hours at work and the strain of the wedding. Julia, like her father, was tall and had sharp-boned facial features. Because they weren't close, Julia always addressed him formally. "Hello, Father," she said quietly.

"Here's a little gift," he stated, "something extra for you. You could, as one of my Jewish patients might, consider it a *knipl*."*

Julia removed ten twenties from the envelope, surprised to find the gift so generous; her father wasn't rich by any means, and she knew this meant a sacrifice for him. She put her arms around him, saying, "Thank you so much!"

"I hope you weren't hurt because I worked this morning." His voice was hesitant, looking for understanding.

I was, Julia thought.

"I couldn't cancel the appointments with my patients," he contin-

---

*A Yiddish term meaning a small knot. The knipl is a knotted handkerchief containing money a woman has secreted.

ued. "There were several emergencies—Mrs. Emery had an abscessed tooth."

"I understand," Julia responded. She couldn't hurt him outright.

He looked relieved, kissed her quickly on the cheek and left. Shortly after his departure, Edith sailed briskly into the room. "I hope you're ready!" she stated officiously. "The hack's downstairs. Have you packed extra shoes? You'll get muddy at the Des Plaines River and will need them. Why are you and David going to the Whitfield Inn? Nobody at church has ever heard of it. There are much nicer spots in Wisconsin or Michigan—where everyone else goes. Nobody goes for a holiday in Joliet. Why, that's where the state prison is!"

"I told you before that David chose it," Julia returned sharply. "He stops there sometimes when he's traveling south to purchase lumber. He thinks I'll like it. Besides, you shouldn't judge it when you haven't been there yourself."

"Worthy places gain reputations, you know; they don't bask in obscurity. Your shoes?"

"I have enough shoes—plenty!" Julia answered, irritated at her sister's dominance.

"Well, hurry on then," Edith said.

As Edith started for the door, Melinda turned to Julia and said, "Ask her."

"No!" Julia responded.

"What's this all about?" Edith asked, looking at them quizzically.

"Nothing—really nothing at all," Julia stated, scowling at Melinda.

"Well, you must get going," Edith said and swished out the door.

"Oh, dear!" Melinda wailed, "what will you do?"

"It'll be all right," Julia answered. She wondered, though, if it would.

Melinda placed Julia's money in a handkerchief and knotted it. "You know where to keep a knipl, don't you?"

Laughing, Julia tucked the handkerchief under her corset top.

"What will you spend it on?"

"I don't know—maybe something special for David."

The sky was clear and dark, and the moon deeply curved when Julia and David arrived in Joliet via the Chicago, Altow & St. Louis Railroad at 9:40 p.m. The Whitfield Inn sent a side-seated platform wagon to pick them up at the station. The wagon had a jaunty fringe on top, yellow wheels, and open sides. It was cooler now, and Julia buttoned her coat. Three older women sat opposite them, giving them curious glances. Julia supposed they guessed she was just married. She felt embarrassed, and blushed. Julia felt happy, but nervous and tired from the trip. It had been an emotional day. She needed a good night's sleep, but she doubted she would have it.

Julia had had a sheltered upbringing and wasn't sure about the wedding night. Novels, though, hinted the nuptial night was romantic. In one novel she had read, the bride, wearing a fine white dress and white kid gloves, strolled toward the bedroom on the arm of a confident groom. She appeared serene, but her heart pounded with love and fear. In strokes of authorial magic, the two then faded into obscurity.

Julia regretted not asking Edith about pregnancy. Now she had that to worry about—among other things.

Then that silly adage popped into her mind: "Marry in Lent, live to repent." It would have been wise to wait, she thought; after all, Easter was only eight days away. Certainly she shouldn't have married on Saturday! "Monday for wealth, Tuesday for health, Wednesday best day of all, Thursday for losses, Friday for crosses, and Saturday no luck at all."

Shaking off the depressing thoughts, she tucked her arm through David's.

At the Whitfield Inn they pulled up under a porte-cochere. Because the area behind the building wasn't lighted, the Des Plaines River wasn't visible. Julia thought the architecture of the inn was lovely, appropriate to a honeymoon. *Edith should see this!* she mused. Like a fruit basket, the inn spilled towers and lacy trim from every surface. The windows, with shutters with heart-shaped cutouts, were particularly charming.

David jumped down and helped Julia, then turned and assisted the three older women as well.

The smaller of the women spoke. "Thank you," she said. "You appear to be just married, if I may be so bold as to say."

Julia turned crimson.

"Yes, just," David said, amused.

"A lovely bride, very lovely."

"Yes," he stated simply.

"Congratulations, and have a fine time here. It's very nice."

"Thank you. I'm sure it will be."

"My husband and I—he's dead now—often stayed here," she stated.

David nodded, then turning, he took Julia's arm and led her into the inn.

The lobby was a mishmash of potted plants scattered throughout, with pictures and bric-a-brac hung everywhere. After the women registered, David addressed the clerk at the counter. "I'm David Gerard. I have reservations for five days. I requested a room overlooking the river.''

The clerk nervously fingered the pencil behind his ear while he flipped through his reservation book. His checked suit coat was worn at the elbows, and Julia thought he looked tired and old, weary of his job. "We don't have an available room with a river view—I'm sorry. But I can give you a room in the front on the second floor. It's bigger than the ones by the river, and I think you will prefer it. It has two armchairs and a bath alongside. Not all of the river rooms have private baths.''

Julia could tell from David's tight expression that he was supressing irritation. "I am *not* happy about this. I made reservations a month ago.''

Julia stepped back from the counter. She hoped David wouldn't announce that they were on their honeymoon and must have a river view. Or that the clerk could keep his room, and they would take the next train to Chicago.

"I'm sorry, sir. The clerk on duty before me made an error. The rooms on the river were filled when I came an hour ago. If you'll take a room in front tonight, I'll move you to a river room tomorrow.''

To Julia's relief, David agreed and registered. The clerk handed David a key, saying, "Breakfast is between seven and nine.''

The clerk rang for a boy, who carried their valises to their room. The room was pleasant, decorated in pink, ecru, and white, and it was as large as promised. Julia breathed in the fresh scents of lemon furniture oil, and pine from the fire in the grate. A feather mattress puffed up from a four-poster bed, which was covered with an embroidered eiderdown, much like the one on her own bed. Julia liked the familiar look of home.

David tipped the boy and closed the door and the draperies. "I'm sorry about the mix-up,'' he apologized. "We'll change rooms after breakfast. I'm anxious for you to see the river. It's lovely—crystal clear—and probably banked with wildflowers.''

"The room is fine. If you don't mind, I'd like to stay in it. It's our first room together.'' She smiled at him warmly.

He returned her smile and said, "Of course, if you wish.''

He kissed her lightly on the forehead, then gently touched her shoulders; his expression was pleasant but preoccupied. She hoped he would embrace her, but he simply kissed her cheek. He lifted Julia's valise to the top of the bureau and unbuckled it. Then he looked into the bathroom. Julia supposed he was checking for towels and soap. She had not traveled much, only north to a watering place on holidays and east to Indianapolis. Occasionally, the hotels had not provided soap and towels.

Julia removed her coat and bonnet, hanging them in the wardrobe.

She observed the closed draperies and her heartbeat increased. She turned as David returned from the bathroom. He was smiling faintly, searching her face with his eyes. *Surely he will kiss me now*, she thought.

Instead he asked, "Would you like something to drink—coffee, something cold? I can ring for service."

"I'm not thirsty."

"Are you tired? You must be. It's been a long day for you."

"Yes."

"I'll smoke a cigarette outside while you change."

"How long will you be?"

"Not very. Why?"

"If there's time I might bathe—I'm rather dirty from the train." She wouldn't take a bath if he were likely to return when she was in the bathtub. She would feel embarrassed and awkward coming from the bathroom in her nightclothes.

"Of course you have time."

"How much?"

"As much as you need."

"Maybe I won't bathe."

"Julia, you just said you wished to. Why are you acting so strange?"

Julia flung herself into his arms. "Because I'm nervous."

Holding her close, he smiled and kissed her lips gently. "There's no reason to be nervous," he reassured her.

When David left, Julia rang for a maid to unlace her, then quickly bathed and changed into a nightgown. She liked how the tight bodice and low neckline highlighted her figure. She spun around, pleased that the gown was short enough to reveal her ankles. She put on her wrapper, though, too shy to outright display herself. She unpinned her hair and brushed it until it sparkled like fire from her crown to her back. She opened the window and looked down to see if David were under the porte-cochere. He wasn't. A carriage pulled up, dropping off a large group. Laughter floated up from the happy couples. Lamplight played on the group's bonnets and top hats, and she enjoyed the pretty picture they made. Then David strode toward the porte-cochere, a cigarette glowing in his hand. He dropped the cigarette and stepped on it. He glanced up. She waved and closed the window.

Oh, he was coming!

Her heart beat wildly. She stepped back and wondered, *Should I sit on an armchair or stand where I am?* She had never been so uncertain about what to do. Nervously she paced—from the door to the window. Her nightgown and wrapper billowed out behind her. As she turned from the window, her wrapper caught a nail and she heard the dull rip of material.

"Oh no!" she cried.

Bending, she pulled her wrapper from a nail in a baseboard, leaving behind an inch-long piece of material. Lifting the skirt, she studied the hole and wondered what stitch would best repair it. *Of course I didn't bring thread,* she thought; Edith would have. But surely she didn't have time to sew, even if she had the means.

Then hearing a boot strike the hall flooring, she forgot her torn gown and ran for an armchair.

When David opened the door, Julia was heaped in the armchair, the silky wrapper tumbled around her. She supposed she appeared all eyes— big, round, green, nervous circles. She straightened her gown. "Did you walk by the river?" she asked timidly.

"Yes. I wanted to get away from the guests. I prefer being alone sometimes. At the lumberyard I deal with people, and my father, all day, so I welcome a minute alone. But I don't want to talk about work tonight."

"Did you see any wildflowers?"

"Yes—though it's too dark to see much."

David hung his coat on the bedpost and untied his necktie. When he looked at her, his intent gaze seemed a physical touch. "You look beautiful, Julia—very, very lovely."

"Oh!" she said, pleased, breathless.

He unbuckled his valise and removed a nightshirt. "I'll bathe and be out in a minute."

That casual remark, as much as the marriage ceremony, announced her marriage. The intimate things were now everyday events. Tomorrow she would tell him she had ripped her gown and think nothing of it. Tomorrow she would casually bathe.

Julia listened to the hollow sound of water on the metal tub. Then there was silence, followed by a splash as David entered the tub. She walked to his valise and touched the shirts that were on top. She wanted to examine the contents, but felt that would be meddlesome. If she were bathing, she doubted he would disturb her valise. Yet a wife often packed for her husband; she would probably pack David's valise when they left the inn. She lifted the shirts and other clothes. The ordinary materials felt extraordinarily rich because they were his. At the bottom was a folder of papers. She opened the folder and recognized lumberyard reports, disappointed that David brought work. She wondered if he had worked on his honeymoon with Trina. Of course the lumberyard hadn't been as busy then, she thought. David had told her he and Trina had spent their honeymoon in New York City. He hadn't offered the information; Julia had asked. Julia would dislike a honeymoon in New York City. It would probably be much like Chicago, with its heavy traffic and soot and grime from factories. On the other hand, it might have been fun to compare New York to Chicago.

But Julia didn't wish to think about David's other honeymoon.

She heard water draining. She replaced the folder and arranged the contents of the valise in their original order and sat again in an armchair. Water sounded on the metal tub, and she supposed David was rinsing it. She liked that he would do so. It was considerate of him to leave it clean. Arthur wouldn't have rinsed the tub, Julia thought.

David opened the bathroom door with a characteristic quick movement. He was damp, with beads of water clinging to his dark hair and mustache. His nightshirt adhered to his chest. He didn't wear slippers or a dressing gown. He stopped beside the bed. She wondered if he would continue to her chair. She had the sensation of being light, and she felt her body temperature rising. He said, "I hope I wasn't too long."

"No."

"You haven't moved."

"I have."

He smiled. "You're lovely."

"I hope I didn't use all the hot water."

"No, it's a central system."

"Oh." She couldn't think of conversation—not now.

He folded back the eiderdown. He lifted her by the hand and led her to the bed. He smelled like soap and water, she thought, and he was very warm.

In the morning Julia brushed her hair with long, luxurious strokes. She loved brushing with David watching from an armchair. Her hair crackled around her shoulders, full of electricity. The room was warm and she hadn't put the wrapper over her nightgown. How lovely it was to be intimate with David, not worrying if she were entirely covered. Marriage was so free and perfect. She felt several feet off the ground. Last night was wonderful. "Our life together will be perfect," she stated firmly.

David laughed. "Nothing's perfect, Julia."

"Of course—but I *am* happy." The only wrinkle was that he hadn't once told her that he loved her. But he certainly had expressed love. She excused David because he was reserved. He would be able to declare his love soon, she thought.

"Are you done brushing?" he asked firmly.

"Yes. Why?"

"Then come here," he ordered gently, his eyes smiling.

She sat on his lap and he held her, kissing her softly, warmly. After a while he said, "I'll leave for a cigarette if you don't mind."

Julia disliked the bitter smell of cigarettes, and she wished David didn't smoke; nonetheless she decided to accustom herself to the smell. "Please smoke it here. I'd rather have you smoking with me than leaving me alone."

He found his box of cigarettes in his frock coat, lighted one, and sat in the other armchair. She sighed. She had waited long enough to reveal her omission. "You won't be happy with me. I—I didn't speak to Edith about . . . about prevention. She's too difficult to approach. It's not a subject I'm used to discussing." She watched his eyes for a sign of his reaction, but she couldn't read them.

His voice sounded irritated. "This isn't something to have neglected," he said evenly. "You could be in the family way."

"I just said, I couldn't talk to Edith."

"She *is* your sister. I would think you could have managed a talk. Edith is stuffy, but she's not unapproachable. You should have told me last night. I could have taken care of things for us. I've told you it's important that we don't have children for a while." He measured his words. "Do you understand that, Julia?"

"Yes, yes! But what could I do? I was nervous last night!"

He inhaled smoke and his eyes softened as he looked at her tense face. "You have certain safe times of the month—that's what I wanted Edith to define for you."

"I told you, I couldn't!"

Julia jumped up. She was hurt, she had to be alone. She planned to run to the bathroom and cry. He came to her and wiped her eyes. "Don't cry, Julia," he said gently. "Just talk to Edith when we return home."

She nodded.

"I didn't mean to upset you—I'm sure you're not in the family way, and no damage has been done."

But damage has been done, Julia thought. She felt horrible. She resented Trina. It was Trina's fault that she and David had argued. If Trina had never existed, this discussion wouldn't have occurred. Julia could have had a baby right away then. She wouldn't have had to be careful!

"I hope you don't mind waiting just awhile."

"No." *Oh, why couldn't she state the truth?—that she longed to have his child.*

Three

The honeymoon over, Julia and David returned to Chicago. On the train David read a lumber report, while Julia watched rain beating down on mile after mile of dry, dead prairie weeds, remnants from last summer. The endless expanse of gray clouds indicated to Julia there wouldn't be many dry weeds standing tomorrow.

There was no visible change in Julia, except for a slight look of anxiety, where before there had been just anticipation. She thought fatigue caused the anxiety, for she was always somewhat nervous when she was tired. She hadn't slept well all week. David had fallen asleep the minute he closed his eyes, but the noise of guests coming and going kept Julia awake. She had listened to conversations. One wife had reprimanded her husband for wearing a yellow cravat with a green suit, and Julia pitied the husband. She wouldn't nag about such a trifle. For hours, she had watched David sleep. He lay on his back most of the time, breathing heavily. She watched the sheet rise and fall. She laid her hand on his chest and felt his heartbeat. She kissed him softly without waking him. She didn't tell him she watched him sleep. She wished she wasn't too timid to ask if he ever watched her sleep.

On the several occasions he worked on lumberyard business, she read. She didn't mind him working, because he was genuinely sorry for it and kept his sessions short. There was ample time to walk along the river, drive in the countryside, and linger over excellent meals. She thought she had pleased David as a wife; certainly she had tried.

It was late afternoon when they arrived at David's house. Rain sheeted over the umbrella David held above Julia. The hack driver carrying their luggage and David's dog, Chester, splashed behind them. Chester was a Great Dane, a particularly large member of his breed. They had just picked up Chester from where he was kenneled, and in his joy at being home he pranced and splashed mud on Julia's dress.

"Watch out!" David said to Julia.

It was too late. She had stepped into a water hole where several bricks were missing. Water seeped between her shoe buttons, filling her shoes. Her feet turned icy cold. She would have worn overshoes, but it had only been drizzling in Joliet and she had thought the weather would improve.

Through the rain, Julia observed David's house, a small two-story with shuttered windows and a mansard roof fenced with wrought iron pickets. Rain washed the wood into a dreary mustard color. Julia tried to ignore the dismal effect of the rain, and she admired the handsome fencing around the roof. She liked how the side porch balanced the bay window from the dining room. The house was on Illinois Street on the North Side, one of the better sections of Chicago. Julia had been raised on the North Side and liked the area. She would rather have a small house in a fine area than a fine house in a plain area. She would enjoy the landscaping and metal statuary on the wide lawns around them, the elegance of the houses constructed of local limestone, a marblelike stone.

David unlocked the door and told Julia, "Wait under the roof here, please." He tipped the driver, and when the driver had left, David scooped Julia into his arms and carried her inside. Chester bolted ahead and bounded through the house.

She laughed. "I didn't think you would."

"Why?"

"You're so serious—I've never seen you frivolous at all."

"Then perhaps I'd better change."

He set her on her feet. "I'm sorry I couldn't have taken more time for our trip, but I had a terribly hard time breaking free for five days."

The vestibule was dark, and the house smelled musty. David lighted the gas fixture on the ceiling. "The house isn't as I want it for you," he apologized. "I didn't think it would be so musty. We can stay at the Tremont House until the new servant girl airs it."

David's former servant had married and moved east a few weeks ago, and rather than struggle through housekeeping or training new help, David had moved into the Tremont House. He had asked Julia to arrange for a servant. In the morning Bridget Boland, the servant girl whom Julia had hired through the Shamrock Benevolent Society, would arrive.

"I'd rather not move to a hotel," Julia admitted. "Bridget's coming early, and it would be easier not to have to hurry over in the morning. I don't mind the smell."

After David picked up their valises, Julia followed him upstairs. She remembered the floor plan from her tour of the house last month. Their bedroom and David's study faced the street, with two smaller rooms in the back. Julia planned to give Bridget the bedroom above the sitting room. The other room would be for guests, and eventually a child. The house was decorated in strong yellows and greens, colors that overpowered Julia. Julia would have chosen sedate colors—pale blues and creams. She wondered if David liked bold colors, or if they had been Trina's choice.

David placed the luggage on the bed, a four-poster with bright yellow lilies on the quilt and tester. Julia hadn't slept under a canopy, and she looked forward to doing so. But someday she hoped to replace the bright coverings with a lacy, cream-colored comforter and canopy.

David indicated the wardrobe that had drawers. "My clothes are in there. You can have the other wardrobe and the bureau. If you need more room, I have an extra bureau in the cellar."

While they were away, a workman from David's lumberyard had delivered Julia's possessions, and she saw her trunk and boxes in the corner. "There should be enough room. I don't have that much."

"I have a few things to take care of downstairs—call me if you need anything."

She glanced at his valise. "Should I unpack for you?"

He smiled. "Yes—thanks."

Julia changed her dress and shoes and unpacked their bags, placing her knipl in the top bureau drawer. *Maybe I'll spend some of the money for bed coverings*, she thought. Taking a sheet of her stationery, she started a list of chores for Bridget and herself:

—Unpack my trunk and boxes.

—Unpack wedding gifts. (Edith had said Morton would deliver them, and Julia was sure they were downstairs. Edith never broke a promise.)

—Clean and air entire house.

Julia lifted the quilt to check if the bedclothes were clean. They didn't look as crisp as Miss Nancy's freshly laundered sheets, but possibly this was limp material. Julia was reluctant to ask David if the bedding was fresh. He might have taken special pains to change it. Or his servant might have changed it before she left. It was better to just have Bridget wash the bedding, she thought.

—Do laundry, including changing blankets and sheets.

—Shop for groceries. (David said there were only a few staples in the house and the icebox was empty.)

—Plan menus.

Julia knew little about cooking. Miss Nancy had offered to teach her, but her father had refused permission; it would make extra mess for Miss Nancy, who had plenty of work to do already. Julia had read a cookbook, but felt confident of only the basics, such as laying a fire, seeing that nothing burned. Because she had often watched Miss Nancy bake carrot pudding and apple crisp, Julia thought she could manage them. She hoped Bridget was an accomplished cook.

She heard David downstairs and joined him in the sitting room. He was leaning over the sofa, removing a watercolor of Lake Michigan from the wall. It was a storm scene; sea gulls huddled on pier posts, foaming waves slamming into the beach. Julia was impressed with the attitude of the gulls. "Don't take it down. I like it," she said.

David lifted the picture from the wall and set it on the sofa. He turned the hammer and pulled out the nail. "It was Trina's. I'll replace it with the landscape Mother gave us."

"Trina was an artist?"

"Yes. Landscapes and seascapes were her specialty."

"Did she sell her work?"

"Yes."

"Where?" Julia asked.

"In Chicago and New York mainly. She was well-recognized."

"You never mentioned that. Only that Trina was a horsewoman. Did she have a studio in the house?" Julia thought Trina probably used David's study as a studio as the study faced north.

David hesitated, as if reluctant to answer. "No. She worked away from the house—I rented a studio downtown for her."

"She worked hard at her painting then?"

"Yes." David's eyes searched Julia's. "Julia, why so many questions about Trina?"

"Because you've seldom talked about her, and of course I'm curious. Being in the house she lived in makes me wonder about her."

"I don't like talking about Trina. That's the past. Our life is now. I had hoped to have this picture down before you came, but I was too busy at work. This house is your house now. I realize the difficulties in being the second wife here. I'll rearrange the furniture any way you want it. There are still knickknacks out that were Trina's. I had asked my servant to pack them, but she didn't. She was excited about her wedding and was almost useless. Would you pack away the things you don't want—and put out wedding gifts wherever you'd like?"

David placed Trina's picture under his arm. "I'll store this in the study closet with Trina's other paintings. Trina's trunks are in the cellar. Sometime soon I'll sort through them and give what I don't want to charity. There are a few things I'll keep—a shawl, a photograph. I'm giving the photograph to Trina's mother. She asked me for it. The shawl is an heirloom from my family, my mother's grandmother's. I'd like you to have it—and someday our daughter."

"Did Trina wear it?"

"Yes."

Julia didn't want it. "I . . . thank you," she said lamely. "Do you have a photograph of Trina for yourself?"

"No—I only have the one."

Julia thought it was unusual for David to give his only photograph of Trina away. She was glad, however. She supposed it was his way of forgetting the past.

"I'll commission an art dealer to sell Trina's paintings."

"You should at least keep one," Julia suggested. "You might regret later that you have nothing of Trina's. I do like the picture you just took down."

"I suppose you're right," he acknowledged. Then picking up the hammer, he pounded the nail back in and centered the seascape on the wall again.

They left then for dinner with Julia's father. He had invited them before they left on their honeymoon.

Because rain caused Miss Nancy's rheumatism to flare up, she went to bed after serving dessert. Melinda was out for the evening with the butcher, which surprised Julia. Melinda had left a note stating that she would see Julia later—either here or at Julia's house. So there was just Julia, David, and her father for dinner.

After dinner the men sat in the back parlor while Julia cleaned up. Edith arrived and joined Julia in the kitchen. She had just been to a church meeting; Morton was calling for Freddie. Edith looked around with displeased eyes, and Julia spoke before Edith questioned her. "Miss Nancy's in bed. You know she can't walk well when it rains. She didn't ask to go to bed. I told her to. I know she doesn't expect me to do the dishes—I'm doing her a favor."

"Miss Nancy's undependable—I intend to urge Father to let her go with a pension."

"Edith, please let Miss Nancy be. This isn't your house."

"Oh, all right. I suppose it's none of my business."

"What was your meeting for?"

"We were marking prices for the spring clothing bazaar—it will benefit the half-orphan house. Don't you remember? You were there when I announced it."

Julia remembered now. The half-orphan house was the latest charitable project of the Women's Mission Society, of which Edith was president.

"I hope you can help Saturday in the booths," Edith proposed.

"Bridget Boland comes tomorrow, and I have to see how she works out. She might still need supervision on Saturday. She's new in the country and it might take her awhile to get on to American ways."

"You've hired the Irish girl!"

"Yes."

Edith's eyes snapped, and she folded her arms over her chest. "You've made a terrible mistake. You should have listened to my advice not to employ her. The Irish are despicable people, and I mean that in a Christian sense. They believe the priest is God and they trust in saints and holy water to save them. They're wild and ignorant and terrible drunkards. Most of them don't even wear shoes and stockings to church."

Julia sighed. "Because they're poor. Ireland is a very poor country. They would wear shoes and stockings if they had them. Besides, Edith, most of the Irish are not like you say at all. They are decent and orderly. You really have no right to judge them—or anyone else for that matter."

"They live in sod hovels with pigs and chickens. They—"

"Edith! Bridget has landed and been through immigration. It's too late to cancel her. I wish, just once, you'd approve of something I did."

Julia turned on the water cocks and filled the dishpan. She remembered her promise to ask Edith about prevention. Edith's sour mood didn't eliminate the task; David knew very well she had the opportunity to inquire. "I . . . I need some advice," Julia said hesitantly. "David wants to wait . . . for children. What times are safe in the month?"

"Wait! Why, David's thirty-four! It's unnatural for him to wish to wait. Morton wouldn't. Why, Morton and I would have three children by now if nature had permitted!"

"You forget David lost a wife and child in childbirth. He's naturally afraid something will go wrong. Please just answer my question. If you won't, I'll ask Dr. Scott."

"All right. Read the Bible. It covers the subject."

Julia's eyes widened. "That subject is in the Bible?"

"Leviticus, chapter fifteen. You would know that if you read your Bible like you ought. The scripture directs the woman to the most fruitful time of the month. Do some interpreting, and you'll figure out which is the least fruitful time."

"Thank you—I'll read it."

Edith found an apron in a cupboard drawer and rolled up her sleeves. She moved Julia aside and beat the soap in the dishpan to a froth. "I'll help with dishes for a short time, but I won't stay and do them all. Morton can't be left forever with Freddie. He just doesn't understand our son as I do. Not that Morton isn't a wonderful father, but he tends to read periodicals and ignore Freddie. This is what causes a nervous disposition in a child." Edith paused. "What was the Whitfield Inn like?"

"It was lovely—you would have thought so yourself."

"What did you do?"

"Walked a lot along the river and in the woods near it. There were many wildflowers out—skunk cabbage, hepatica, snow trillium—"

"It's a bit unusual to find snow trillium," Edith interrupted. "It's very local. Are you sure what you saw was snow trillium?"

"Yes."

"Well, I don't know." Edith rinsed a glass and set it on a towel. "Morton told me he wishes to see David. He's expanding his store, and he'll need a good price on lumber. I advised Morton to stock more sewing machines—they're in demand and he will sell all he can stock." (Julia recalled that Edith was Morton's unofficial advisor, a position Julia wouldn't dare attempt, or wish to attempt, with David.) "David should think about selling sewing machines."

"He likes the lumber business."

"I suppose one becomes accustomed to what one does, but you must inform him of the excellent possibilities in sewing machines."

Edith washed half the dishes, then dried her hands. She faced Julia squarely. "I have to leave now, and I don't have time to mince words. I'm asking your forgiveness. I shouldn't have mentioned Diane Hastings to you before the wedding. I've regretted it. I was concerned about how Freddie would cope with crowds, and I wasn't myself."

Julia felt miserable; she had been trying to forget that name. "Who is Diane Hastings?"

"That isn't important."

"Edith—for heaven's sake! The other day you made Diane sound like David's mistress."

"Look, forget her! She was a high school acquaintance of mine, and of course you don't know her. You were twelve years behind me."

"Edith—who is Diane?"

"After Trina died, Diane and David were in love, you might say." Edith's eyes flashed. "I've said all I intend to."

"What does Diane look like—what is she like?"

"She has black hair, very black, like coal, and one never forgets it. It's blacker than David's."

Edith unrolled her sleeves, removed her apron, and marched from the kitchen.

Julia collapsed against the sink. She tried to be objective. At David's age it was normal to have experienced many women. Diane was just one of those women, that's all. If she dwelt on Trina and David's other romances, she would become depressed. David had probably long forgotten Diane. Edith had the memory of an elephant and remembered much that others forgot. Julia was surprised that Edith had apologized, though. Indeed, she had never done that before.

Shortly after Edith left, Julia and David drove home.

Then, while Julia packed Trina's knickknacks in the parlor, David worked on lumberyard business in his study. Julia hoped David would finish in time to help unpack some of their wedding gifts. It would be fun doing this with him.

Because the parlor was cluttered with bric-a-brac, it took Julia some time to clear it. When she had gotten to the point of unpacking the first wedding gift, a set of little china birds, Melinda arrived. Melinda hugged Julia, then sighed elaborately and gulped down a chocolate from the box on the table. "Those are probably stale," Julia warned her. "They were here when I toured the house. I planned to throw them out." Julie wondered whose chocolates they were; David did not like chocolates.

Melinda took another. "I don't care. Forgive me for coming so late—I should've waited until morning. I saw the light and I had to take a chance."

"I expected you—I would have been disappointed if you hadn't come."

"Where's David?"

"In his study—he needs to catch up on work."

Melinda dropped onto the sofa. "I'm just a wreck. What an awful night! But I'll tell you all about it after you tell me how the honeymoon was. I missed you terribly. I thought about you all the time."

"I missed you, too. The honeymoon was fine—perfect. I loved getting to know David. He's reserved, Melinda, but he opened up some about his business, and it was interesting. Of course, no man discusses much business with his wife, except Morton. Edith wants me to advise David to sell sewing machines—can you imagine *me* telling David that!"

"No—only Edith would suggest that," she said sarcastically.

Julia looked at Melinda with concern. "Melinda, what's wrong—is it Charlie? I was surprised you were out with him tonight."

"I hate to talk about me."

"Please—I care about you."

Tears welled up in Melinda's eyes. "I got so lonely while you were gone I started seeing him, though I swore I never would. I dislike him more than ever. We went to a lecture after dinner, and I'm sure they could smell meat in the rows around us. I'm so desperate for a husband that I'm afraid I'll marry him."

Melinda sniffed and Julia handed her a handkerchief. "Nothing goes right for me," Melinda mourned. "I didn't go to see Madame Trudeau— you scared me off that. I suppose that was best. Oh, Julia, I can't accept a future of being Miss Nancy's helper! I don't mean Miss Nancy isn't all right; but I can't exist without a husband."

"Melinda, you'll be married someday."

"I won't. Look at me!" Melinda looked down at her plump figure, tears dripping on her lap. "I'm a mess. No one wants me. I could hardly squeeze into this dress, and it's my favorite. I'll be lucky to get Charlie."

"It's a person's character that is important."

"You can say that because you're slim!" Melinda cried.

"Melinda, please don't start comparing us like that," Julia urged.

Melinda wiped her tears with the handkerchief. "I'm sorry, I won't."

"I certainly wouldn't see Charlie again if I were you. He makes you too miserable." Julia wished she didn't have to protect Melinda. It made her feel too much like Edith.

"Maybe I won't." Melinda managed a slight smile. "I don't want to drive you mad with my problems. I have some good news. I wrote a rather good poem yesterday—at least I think it is."

"Did you bring it?"

"No."

"I wish you had. And I wish you'd try to get your poetry published." But so far Melinda refused to show it to anyone except Julia.

"I have enough rejection from men without having it from publishers too."

Julia sighed. "You don't know that periodicals would reject you. You should try. It would lift your spirits if you had a poem published."

"Well, maybe I'll mail this last one to *Godey's Lady's Book And Magazine*."

"Good."

Melinda looked around the parlor. "I see you haven't put your gifts out yet."

"I had to pack up Trina's things first."

Melinda's voice was hesitant. "It would bother me . . . living in another woman's house."

Julia nodded. "It's the little things. Like there's a photograph of

Trina in a trunk in the cellar. I was thinking about it before you came. I had to make myself stay upstairs. It will haunt me if I know what Trina looks like. Edith told me Diane's hair is black and that's all I think about."

"For goodness' sake, don't look!" Melinda commanded her.

Miss Nancy had given Julia rolls and ham to take home for breakfast, and Julia served the rolls with only jam as there was no butter. Julia planned to shop after Bridget arrived. It had stopped raining, but it was foggy and chilly. When David left for work, his buggy disappeared into the fog halfway down the driveway.

Julia was washing the breakfast dishes when the doorbell rang. She quickly dried her hands and removed her apron. She patted her hair, hoping she looked neat and genteel. Edith said it was imperative that Julia immediately gain the respect of her servant girl; otherwise the girl would be lax.

Julia opened the door to Bridget Boland and her agent from the Shamrock Benevolent Society, a stout and pleasant-looking woman. Not only had the agent arranged for Bridget's position with Julia, but for Bridget's lodging last night.

"Mrs. Gerard, may I present Bridget Boland."

Bridget huddled in a swirl of foggy air. She was thin and pale with limp dark hair and brown blotches on her face that must have been the exhausted remains of freckles. Her blue eyes, wide as saucers, were staring at the front door. She shivered beneath a thin cape that was no more than a rag. She wore no gloves and her dress, though clean, was shiny from wear. Her trunk was battered, announcing a rough voyage across the Atlantic. The trunk was small; she hadn't brought much.

"I'm so glad to meet you," Julia acknowledged.

"Aye," Bridget whispered in a barely audible voice. She then lifted her little shoulders and looked at Julia. "It's glad I am to be meeting yourself."

"If you have any questions or problems, just contact us," the agent told Bridget.

"Aye."

The agent shook Bridget's hand and left.

Julia helped Bridget carry the trunk into the vestibule. She hung Bridget's cape on the hatrack. "Would you like some hot tea?"

Bridget spoke in a thick brogue. "No, I should be starting to work, surely."

"But you're chilled. You need something hot first."

"If yourself is saying it—Mrs. Gerard . . . madam . . . me lady."

"Mrs. Gerard will be fine. You can leave the trunk and I'll help you upstairs with it later."

"I'll be taking it with me. Itself is all that I have in the world."

Julia again helped Bridget with the trunk, bringing it in the sitting room, where Bridget perched on the edge of the sofa with the trunk at her feet.

Chester walked up and thrust his tongue toward Bridget's hand. Bridget looked alarmed and clasped her hand to her breast before the tongue touched it. Julia reassured her. "He's big, but he won't bite. Mr. Gerard wouldn't own a mean dog."

"Aye," Bridget said. But she pressed against the sofa nevertheless.

While the water for the tea heated, Julia chained Chester in the yard, deciding to leave the dog out today for Bridget's sake. She returned with the tea and said, "I'm glad you've come to work for me. I read the report from the Shamrock Benevolent Society, but it was incomplete. I know you're just eighteen—"

Bridget's hands clutched her cup and her eyes widened in panic. "I'm eighteen and a half, I am! I'm the strongest girl in County Kerry, surely. I'm even stronger than Molly Emmet, and herself twice as big as myself! I'm the smartest girl in Dunquin and I can reason out anything. I can read and write better than Molly or anybody. I helped raise me eleven brothers and sisters. I'm the oldest now . . . and I can cook almost as good as Mama. I don't hike downstairs backward like those country girls—themselves not knowing any like but the ladders to their turf lofts. I don't know much about the big city, but I'll learn."

Bridget gulped at her tea.

The impassioned defense touched Julia. She understood Bridget's fears; she was young, underqualified—likely to be fired. Julia said gently, "Of course you will. Tell me, what is Dunquin like?"

"It's a wee fishing village on the Dingle peninsula in County Kerry. Me mama and papa don't be having any room so lovely as this. Ourselves has just a kitchen and a bedroom. The cow is kept in the kitchen and me mama's rocker, surely. Me papa takes a poor living from the sea and our rough bit of land. We don't have much and we're often hungry, but ourselves is happy. We keep the faith. Even when ourselves is starving, we don't convert for a bowl of soup. The 'Soupers' is the worst lot of all."

"The 'Soupers'?"

"The Protestants is always trying to get us Catholics to convert for a bowl of soup. The 'Soupers' are like that convert. The Protestants own the government and the land and they is starving the Catholics.

They charge ourselves terrible rents for plots of land the size of me hand."

Bridget looked aghast. "Saints, yourself is a Protestant, I'm afeared."

"I am, but I don't judge another's religion. I think one should believe as one chooses. Everyone goes to heaven if he is good, and it doesn't matter by which faith he gets there."

"Holy mother!" Bridget cried. "In Ireland only the Catholics is going to heaven."

"Well, it's different here." Bridget's ignorance amazed yet appealed to Julia.

Bridget placed her cup on the table. She reached into her skirt pocket and pulled out a little box. Looking miserable, she turned it in her hand. Julia looked curiously at the box, and Bridget said, "It's dirt, it is, and from the floor of me parents' house."

Bridget's thin face twisted as she fought for control, but tears splashed on the box. "Oh, but I've got no call to be crying, surely."

Julia handed Bridget her handkerchief. "It's all right to cry. I'd be homesick too. Was the voyage difficult?"

Bridget wiped her tears. "Not so bad I didn't make it! Mama packed myself a big basket of Indian meal bread and salted mackerel, so I never was hungry when there wasn't much food. But I worried about me family going without for me. Me papa had arranged for my virtue and he slept me with a good Catholic family. I slept with the two daughters, but they were big as elephants! Themselves must have weighed two hundred pounds, at least. And ourselves all squeezed into a bunk that was six by six. I measured the space with me hand, which is five and three-fourths inches long from me palm to the top of me long finger. I couldn't turn over unless the daughters turned. I like to move from this side to that, but themselves were bricks when they slept. Twice I thought I'd go mad from lying there. The noise was terrible in steerage where myself was, and the ship rocked all the time. Everyone was getting sick all the time, and there wasn't a drop of air to breathe. The trip took only eleven days though, and nobody died."

"I'm sorry. I wish it hadn't been so awful."

Bridget jumped up. "I'll be starting work now."

Julia thought there was little danger Bridget would be lax. "This afternoon's time enough for that. You need to get settled this morning. I'm leaving soon to shop for groceries and have lunch with my sister. There's hardly any food in the house. We just returned from our honeymoon last night. When I get back I'll go over the housekeeping details with you."

Julia led Bridget upstairs to her room, and she opened the door to a stripped, dismal place. Fog pressed on the window, hiding the green grass in the laundry yard. The curtains and bedding were folded on the bureau and the rug was rolled up. Julia lighted the gas, but it didn't dispel the depressing atmosphere. "I'm sorry the room isn't more cheerful," Julia said. "I think the sheets and curtains are clean—that's probably why they're folded. But you might want to wash them to be sure. I would have put the room in order for you if I had had the time."

Bridget turned around, studying the room, then turned around again. She looked at Julia and smiled. "Itself is the prettiest room I ever saw."

"Let me help you roll out the rug."

"Saints, no! It's heathen, it is, having the lady of the house working!"

"Oh!" Julia exclaimed. Then she smiled.

When Julia left, Bridget gingerly touched the mattress, awed to have her own bed—and one so large as to hold four people her size. She had never slept by herself, and she wondered what it would be like. At home she slept with Maury and Nell. Tears came again as she thought about her family. She reminded herself that it was necessary to come to America. There were no well-paying opportunities for service back home. Her parents had urged her to stay home, but Bridget refused. She had two strong arms and she had to help her family! Why, she would send home almost all the money she made! Her family would never be hungry again!

Opening her trunk, Bridget decided she would unpack her clothes, then do up the room.

She liked Mrs. Gerard, she decided. She'd do everything perfectly to please her. Why, herself was so pretty and stately, she was like a queen. She'd not regret having the likes of Bridget Boland in her house.

I don't know much, but I'll learn fast, Bridget thought.

Four

As she was about to fix breakfast the next morning, Bridget encountered a problem that rattled her determined little frame to the core: Chester, the Gerards' huge Great Dane. "Get the likes of you out of me kitchen and go sit yourself in the sitting room so a body can do her work," she bawled.

Chester's mouth parted to reveal teeth that seemed the size of pickets to Bridget's frightened mind. She shook all over. She feared Chester more than she feared the devil. She remembered how in her childhood a rabid dog had driven her to the roof of her house, where she screamed until her father captured the animal in a dragnet. Since then, just the sight of a dog set her trembling.

"Get, get—and you holding me up while themselves are hungry for breakfast."

Chester placed one tremendous paw in front of the other and backed her into the sink.

Sure, Mrs. Gerard was wrong in saying that Chester didn't bite! But she'd fight the dog until one or the other died. She broke from the sink and ran for the broom in the corner. She waved it wildly at Chester. "Off with you—I'm not afeard to knock your head off!"

Chester opened his mouth wider.

"Out, out!"

Chester flexed his muscles and the fur on his powerful body rippled for action.

"Away with yourself!"

He cast a mean look, but he stalked to the sitting room. *That fiend will be planning his revenge*, she worried. She had to be on guard night and day. With wary glances in his direction, she set about making breakfast.

In her parents' sod house in Dunquin, she had cooked on an open fire, fueling it with turf from the turf loft above the kitchen area. She had not seen a cookstove in all of Dunquin, and she hoped she understood Mrs. Gerard's directions for this one's use. The thing resembled a monster, having clawed feet and protrusions on it that Mrs. Gerard called "modern cooking conveniences": a roaster, baking cover, and hot water reservoir. She didn't think she needed that equipment for pancakes, so she set it aside. She remembered to check the firebox, and seeing that the coals still burned, she placed the coffeepot on the burner. Mrs. Gerard had requested fried eggs and pancakes, and Bridget set her hands on her hips, pondering what American pancakes might be. Sure, she thought finally, they are being like Mama's oatmeal and bacon pancakes.

Bridget hadn't dared ask Mrs. Gerard to describe American pancakes. *Saints! already herself thinks I'm too young to be a servant girl,* Bridget mused. *Why else would Mrs. Gerard mention me age? If Mrs. Gerard thinks I can't cook right, herself will send me back to the Shamrock Benevolent Society!*

While the bacon fried, Bridget beat together flour, oatmeal, milk, eggs, and salt, making a batter like thick cream. After frying four large pancakes, she filled each with a slice of bacon, a little mustard, then folded it in half. *The pancakes are just like Mama's*, she thought with pride—*perfect half moons and nicely browned.* She straightened the lappets on her white cap, poking under a strand of flyaway hair. She brushed down the uniform Mrs. Gerard had provided, a lilac print with deep pockets in the skirt. She loved the uniform. It was too large at first, but she had altered it last night. It was only the second new dress she had owned, the other dress being the one Mama made for her first communion.

After carrying the breakfast tray to the dining room, she wondered whether to set it on the long cabinet or the dining table. Because the Gerards had eaten their meals out yesterday, this was Bridget's first meal to serve. She looked at Mrs. Gerard for direction, but Mrs. Gerard simply smiled. *It would be quicker to serve from the dining table, surely,* she thought. *But saints! the tray would look queer in the midst of the pretty silver and dishes.* She decided the cabinet was a more likely tray stand, so she set her tray there. Bridget was tense as she looked to Mrs. Gerard for approval.

"You serve me first, then Mr. Gerard," Mrs. Gerard instructed her.

"It's sorry I am that I kept yourselves waiting, but you'll not be waiting on me again," Bridget apologized.

"It's your first meal, and of course it took extra time. Did you find everything you needed?"

"Aye."

Mr. Gerard smiled, but he didn't speak. He reminded her of Father Brady, her quiet, dark-eyed priest back home. Bridget thought Mr. Gerard was one of the biggest men she had ever seen. His size didn't scare her, surely, because he had kind lines in his face.

Bridget had to be honest. "It might be a different kind of pancake than yourself eats, but I'm thinking you'll like them."

Mr. Gerard tasted his.

"They are different," he agreed. "Though as you say, they're very nice. Perhaps Mrs. Gerard can teach you to make the American kind. But of course this mustard type is nice for a change."

Bridget was delighted that he loved them. "Has yourself enough?"

"Yes, quite enough," he affirmed.

"Should I be staying by the table, I'm wondering, or should I go in the kitchen?"

"You can go. We'll ring if we need anything," Julia replied.

Bridget left. She rolled up her sleeves and started wiping the stove. Happy with her success, she couldn't keep from singing "Kitty of Coleraine." She sang softly, not wishing to disturb the Gerards.

> As beautiful Kitty one morning was tripping,
> With a pitcher of milk from the fair of Coleraine,
> When she saw me she stumbled, the pitcher it tumbled,
> And all the sweet buttermilk water'd the plain.
> "Oh, what shall I do now? T'was looking at you, now!
> Sure, sure such a pitcher I'll ne'er meet again!
> T'was the pride of my dairy: O Barney McCleary,
> You're sent as a plague to the girls of Coleraine."

She wondered if there were a Barney McCleary for her in Chicago. Sure, she was a silly girl to be thinking of that when other things must be thought of. She dried her hands and took Mrs. Gerard's list of chores from her pocket. Yesterday she had washed her and Mrs. Gerard's sheets. Today she would wash dirty clothes from the honeymoon; Mrs. Gerard said they couldn't wait until Monday, which would be her regular washing day. Next week she would clean the house from top to bottom. Bridget understood the house hadn't been cleaned recently, but she didn't mind being critical of the last servant. Saints, she was an awful cleaner! Why, she left grease on the fancy cookstove, and mud on the cellar floor!

Suddenly the responsibility of caring for the newly married couple overwhelmed her. They counted on her for meals, clean clothes—everything! Holy mother, their happiness was in her hands!

After washing the breakfast dishes, Bridget collected the laundry and scrubbed it in the cellar tubs. She carried two heavy baskets of wet clothes to the laundry yard. The sky was clear, and a warm wind swelled the clothes, promising to dry them quickly.

"Hey," someone called.

Bridget turned as a youngish woman in a uniform much like hers approached. Her cap was in her hand, and Bridget supposed the wind had blown it from her head. She was plain, and the bright sun highlighted her bad complexion and squinty eyes. Her golden hair sparkled in the light though, and it would have been a glory but that it straggled around her face. Five sleek cats with jeweled collars pranced around her feet. The woman pushed through an opening in the hedge and the cats followed.

"I'm Mary Monahan. I saw you out yesterday hangin' sheets. I work next door for Mr. and Mrs. Cullen, and let me tell you they're mean. I hope you don't mind Mrs. Cullen's cats coming. I can't leave them while I'm airing them. They run off."

Bridget hoped it would be all right with the Gerards. "Make sure themselves behave. I'm Bridget Boland, from Dunquin, County Kerry, Ireland."

Mary leaned on the laundry post and regarded Bridget. "You sound like you just got here—a real greenhorn."

"Aye. Myself went through the immigration at Castle Garden. I came on a boat and a train, and I didn't sleep much, surely. I miss me mama and papa and family, and I still don't sleep much."

"You'll get used to it here. I did. I came over from County Cork ten years ago. I don't hardly have no brogue no more. What room did Mrs. Gerard give you?"

"Itself is in the back, and it has a bureau and wardrobe and beautiful yellow curtains, the like of which I've never seen."

"That's the room the other servant had. I've got a room in the garret, and it ain't so nice. Mrs. Cullen's too refined to sleep servants on the main floors. I'm hot all summer and cold all winter. Well, I ain't a complainer. I'm just saying, I'm a good worker and I deserve better. All the other servant girls has got better."

Bridget had promised her mother she would attend mass daily, so she asked where the Catholic church was.

"It's real close," Mary said. "I can take you."

"Will Mrs. Gerard be letting me go to mass every morning?"

"Most of us servant girls can attend mass whenever we want. Our employers think we'll work better if we do. Herself, Mrs. Cullen, lets me go when I want and, like I said, she's mean."

Bridget smiled. "Then, surely, I'll be going, and Mrs. Gerard being so kind."

Mary's mouth puckered. "You don't hardly know her. But if you're really so fond of her, you've got some reason to worry for her sake."

"Like what, surely?"

Mary looked around to see that the cats were all present. The eyes she then turned on Bridget were bright with knowledge. "Mr. Gerard married Mrs. Gerard suddenly, and us servant girls think he still loves the beautiful lady that visited him here. She was veiled up like a mummy she was, but you just know'd she was something special. He adored her with his eyes . . . never took 'em off her. Why, I saw that lady here one week before he married Mrs. Gerard! I don't lie neither. I ask you, why did that lady come just before he married Mrs. Gerard? I say there was monkey business. Of course, he was married before too, and he adored that wife. I say that he's married this new Mrs. Gerard for some bad reason—such as money."

"That's gossip!" Bridget cried, aflame with loyalty. "Let it not be said that Mr. Gerard doesn't love Mrs. Gerard!"

Mary's chin thrust forward. "I said I ain't a liar!"

"Well—"

"I ain't."

"It's hard pressed I am to think yourself would be lying, and you a good Catholic. Maybe that lady is a cousin."

"She was *no* cousin," Mary said. "Like I said, he married her for money."

"Myself won't be gossiping anymore," Bridget said.

Chester barked from the kitchen. "You'd better tie him outside," Mary advised.

"Let you not think I'm responsible for that dog! Mr. Gerard put him out this morning, and Mrs. Gerard put him out yesterday."

"The other Mrs. Gerard didn't care for him, and neither will this Mrs. Gerard. You can't expect a lady to do that. You'll have to take care of him, just like the other servant did. Mark my words!"

Mary's little eyes glared. "You keep him from the Cullens' yard. He gets into the trash all the time. Mr. Cullen will shoot him if he does that again. Chester teases the cats too—gets them howling and running all over. Keep him away!"

A high voice shouted for Mary. "There—Mrs. Cullen's calling. I'll stop by for you tomorrow for mass. It's Sunday, so I don't leave until ten-thirty."

So, it was Chester or her job, Bridget realized. Bridget found a leash on the back porch and inched the kitchen door open. Chester's nose pushed through the opening. Frightened, Bridget stepped back. Chester bounded out, and Bridget ran for the porch door. "Get back! I'm not afeard of your like!"

He stopped a few feet from her. She grabbed the doorknob. If he came one step closer, she'd run. If only she could call Papa. "I'll throw yourself down the stairs!"

Chester stared at her, his eyes challenging.

"Myself can do it! I'm stronger than Molly Emmet!"

The dog continued to stare. She was about to run when he suddenly flopped to the floor, laying his head down. Then he crept forward on his belly and gently nosed her foot.

She stared at him in amazement. "Saints—what is yourself doing?"

He made a whining sound.

"Holy Mary! Is yourself apologizing? Sure, yourself ought to!"

Her hand dropped from the doorknob as she felt a sudden sympathy toward the dog. "I forgive you," she conceded.

He licked her shoe. His affection overwhelmed her. Saints, she'd been a fool to be afeard of dogs all these years. Bridget knelt and tentatively touched his tawny head. "Yourself is very soft for a dog."

He licked her hand.

She ran her hand over his heavy body. The ribs were buried in fat and his stomach was flabby. "Yourself is too fat, and you'll not be eating so hearty when Bridget Boland feeds you."

He laid his head on her knee.

"Yourself will be minding your manners, too. No more of those tempers, I'm saying."

She leaned over and hugged the dog's neck.

Five

*J*ulia's bedroom smelled like lilac.

Bridget knocked on her door, and Julia dropped the packet of letters and string into David's wardrobe drawer, slamming it shut. Her hands were shaking. To hide them from Bridget, she shoved them into her pockets. A couple of minutes ago, she had accidentally discovered the letters. She had been sewing woolen dresses into brown wrapping paper, planning to store the packages in cedar chips as a protection from moths. Edith had told her about using wrapping paper. Julia had been looking through David's drawers for sharper scissors; she had left her good scissors at home, and the ones she brought were too dull to easily cut the paper. The letters had been under David's shirts, tied in string. Diane's return address was on them. She wrote boldly in purple ink, her letters vertical, tall, commanding attention. The latest envelope was dated March 26, 1871, only days before her wedding. It was lavender, several shades lighter than the ink.

"Come in," Julia called, answering the knock on the door.

"Let me not be interrupting yourself," Bridget said.

"You're not."

"I'd like to go to mass every morning. Would yourself let me? I'll rise up early to catch up the time."

"Of course you can go." Julia believed her face must be pale. Surely her distress showed in her eyes. She hoped that was all Bridget wished to discuss, for she was anxious to examine the letters further.

Bridget glanced at the sewing project on the floor. " 'Tis you wanting some coffee while you work? Itself is just made."

"No, but thank you."

Bridget left, and Julia had no sooner retrieved the letters than she heard Melinda greeting Bridget. Julia returned the letters to the drawer and opened the door for Melinda. "I just came from church," Melinda stated. "Edith sent me to ask you to come help with the bazaar. There's quite a crowd."

"I can't. I'm busy. I've been to every bazaar since Edith's been president, and I don't feel guilty missing one."

"Edith won't understand."

"Well, she'll have to."

"I've only a minute, or Edith will complain." Melinda removed a piece of paper from an envelope. "Here's a copy of the poem I told you about, 'Reflections.' I sent the original to *Godey's*. I'll read it aloud."

When Melinda finished reading, she looked at Julia for her reaction. "I love it!" Julia declared. "It has depth and vitality. It's wonderful. I'm sure it will be published."

"You really think so?"

"Yes, I do."

Melinda smiled and returned the poem to the envelope.

"Wait one more minute," Julia said. She closed the bedroom door and opened David's drawer. Being accustomed to sharing everything with Melinda, she handed her the letters.

"I found these in David's drawer just before you came. They're from Diane Hastings. There must be fifty of them. Why has he saved them?"

Melinda shook her head as she leafed through the letters. "I suppose David forgot about them. You said he's busy. He probably forgets many things."

"They're all tied together. They are obviously important to him."

"Nobody but David knows why he saved them. There's probably a simple reason. Some people just don't like throwing out letters. You saved Arthur's letters."

Julia remembered Arthur's love letters carefully boxed in her bureau. In the same drawer were the pressed remains of his bouquets to her, and the heart-shaped locket he gave her, among other gifts. Why had she kept them? They had no sentimental value. Were the items a historical record of sorts? "I left them at home, though," Julia reasoned.

"This *is* David's home." Melinda was gazing steadily at Julia. "Why did you keep Arthur's letters?"

"I don't know. But next time I'm home I'll throw them out." Julia pointed at the postmark on the top envelope. "Look at that date! Why did Diane write so recently? Why did David save one so recent?"

"He did it out of habit."

"That doesn't explain why *she* wrote."

"Don't read them," Melinda advised. "You know all the reasons why you shouldn't."

Julia nodded.

"I have to go. Edith will be furious."

When Julia was alone, she studied Diane's handwriting on the March twenty-sixth envelope. The letter D was particularly tall and dominant. She wondered if Diane's personality was as authoritative as her writing. Julia formed an image of a tall woman, who wore her hair severely pulled back from her head; who, like Cleopatra, charmed men with her bold personality. Julia had to know.

She opened the envelope flap. The scalloped edges of the paper showed. The paper was the same shade of lavender as the envelope, a fashionable shade this year. It was heavy paper, very expensive. Julia started to pull out the letter, then hesitated. She wanted to forget Diane, didn't she? Reading this would reinforce Diane in her mind. Then, too, these letters were David's, not hers. If he found her love letters, he wouldn't read them. She knew she would regret it forever if she removed the letter. She had to trust David. She had to believe that he had kept the letters from habit, as she had kept Arthur's.

Julia returned the letters to David's drawer. For a moment her decision gave a feeling of satisfaction. Then, smelling lilac in the air, she opened the window wide.

That evening David arrived home an hour and a half late for dinner. It was their one-week anniversary. To celebrate it Bridget had cooked roast beef and oven-browned potatoes—with the aid of a cookbook. The food was dried out now. The only dish that held up was the apple crisp Julia had made. Of that she was proud; it looked almost as crispy as Miss Nancy's and smelled as spicy.

David's eyes were red. Realizing he was exhausted, Julia first kissed him and then took his hat from his hand and hung it on the hatrack.

"Forgive me," he said remorsefully. "I was at a factory, estimating a large order for their expansion. Time passed from me."

"I'm afraid the dinner is dry."

"I *am* sorry."

"Will you work this late every night?"

"No, but often enough."

"David, I don't need a lot of material things."

"Tell Bridget I'm here—I've more to say on this subject, but let's sit first."

At the table David explained, "The main reason I'm pressed is that

Father isn't working a full week anymore, and I have to make up the difference. He thinks only about his retirement in September and his newspapers and periodicals at home. We need to hire more sales help, but he won't permit it. Father won't permit improvements or expansion—any expenditure that risks the money he counts on for retirement. He owns seventy percent of the business, and of course his word is law."

David expected to purchase his father's share of the lumberyard, and Julia remarked, "Well, soon the company will be yours."

He looked troubled; he shook his head slightly. "I shouldn't press my business concerns on you."

"If there's more, I'd like to hear."

"Well, I'm having problems working out a purchase. To buy out Father I need ninety thousand dollars, and I don't have enough collateral for a loan. Father has refused to finance me. He thinks I'm a poor business risk, but has no basis for his opinion. I don't understand it."

David lowered his eyes and Julia realized how hurt he was. "I have an inheritance of ten thousand dollars from my grandmother. I wish you would use it. Father has it invested in bonds, but I'm sure he can easily cash them in."

"I can't take your money."

"But it's really ours now."

"Thank you, Julia, but I can't take it. I hope to work out some other arrangement."

Bridget served the shriveled roast, not taking her woeful eyes from it.

"Don't worry," Julia said to her; "it's not your fault."

Casting one last sad look at the roast, Bridget scurried away.

David didn't begin eating. "There's one last bit of troubling news. I might as well get it said. Today Father announced he won't travel any longer. He hates the soot and delays involved in train travel . . . well, so do I! This means I'll have to travel to New Orleans next month to purchase yellow pine. He had promised to make this trip. He's quite aware I hate to leave you so soon. I've taken four out of the last six trips, and he's hardly being fair."

"David, won't he reconsider?"

"No." David's expression showed sympathy for Julia. "At least it will only be ten days."

"Ten days!"

"That isn't so long."

Ten days was long—forever for her. If it wasn't his job, it was his past: Trina, Diane, shawls, photographs, letters. "Could I come with you?" she pleaded.

"No, it's all business and traveling. It would be boring and difficult for you."

It wouldn't! she thought. She had loved traveling north for holidays. Perhaps he simply didn't wish to have her with him. If that were so, she didn't want to know; she changed the subject. "Morton is expanding his company. Edith wants you to give him a price on lumber."

The next morning was Easter, and the bright sun sparkled on the tableware in the dining room. Because Sunday was Bridget's day off, Julia cooked breakfast. She set a bowl of watery scrambled eggs and a platter of fried ham before David.

"I messed up the eggs. I'll ask Edith how to do them when I see her at church. She does them just right."

"They'll be fine."

"Would you say the blessing?"

David muttered, "Thank You for this provision, Father."

Julia was accustomed to her father's eloquent blessing. "Would you like to have my father's blessing to say?"

"No. We didn't have a blessing at home and I'd rather not have one at all if you don't mind. I'm uncomfortable praying aloud. I prefer we just silently bless the food."

"I'd miss having a blessing."

"Then you say it."

"It isn't my place."

David spoke with irritation. "Form certainly isn't as important as heart."

Julia flushed in disappointment. Though she knew David wasn't a church attender, she didn't know he was impious. "All right—we'll forego the blessing. I'll say it silently."

David filled his plate. He looked at her and his eyes sought understanding. "Julia, you know I wasn't raised in a religious home. Father's an atheist and he never prays. Of course Mother respects his views, and she never prays either. We seldom attended church—I have no interest in religion."

Julia could *not* understand him missing church on Easter. "Won't you at least go today?"

"No. I'm not an atheist like Father—I've always believed in God— but I find church boring. I can worship God better in the out-of-doors."

Sometimes church bored Julia too, but she would never admit it to David or anyone else. Why did she go? she wondered, questioning her religion for the first time. Habit? To learn right moral principles? Because Father or Edith would be upset if she didn't go? No, it wasn't that, she thought, for there was a sense of God's presence in church that she felt nowhere else, and she loved knowing He was there, listening to the prayers of the minister and congregation. But she didn't wish to appear overly religious to David, so she decided upon skipping the Wednesday and Sunday evening services when he was home.

At church, Julia sat in the pew her father rented, near the back, where he didn't have to meet the minister's eyes. Julia was early, and Mrs. Pratt was just arranging her skirts over the organ bench, preparing to play.

Their church was considered one of the more liberal ones in Chicago. The stone building was formidable, with tall stained-glass windows that colored the sunbeams and dropped them like jewels on the congregation. Julia's father was an evolutionist, and because the minister supported his views, Raymond Adams worshiped contentedly. The women wore lovely bonnets of velvet, topped with flowers and feathers; extravagances a servant girl would have to save for months to own. The elegance of dress inspired the women congregants, Julia believed. She suspected that even Edith was inspired, as she wore attractive hats. Julia had her own lovely hat, of course. The minister was fifty and dignified, the epitome of a man of God to Julia. Even though obscurity marred the heart of his messages, his sentences at times held enough truth that Julia felt purer after Sunday service.

Raymond Adams and Melinda were already seated. Melinda wore a yellow hat with a feather that touched her cheek, and her face was bright, even eager. "I thought David was coming," Melinda whispered. "Father and I could have picked you up, had we known."

"David doesn't care to attend church. He offered me his phaeton, but I wanted to walk. It's lovely out."

"I feel a thousand times better about Charlie," Melinda continued. "His mother invited me for dessert last night, and I had a nice time. She's crippled and has difficulty walking. Charles lives with her and does everything for her. He said he made the dessert. Isn't that kind! I'm really impressed by his kindness and I've decided to give him a chance."

"I can't keep up with your opinions on Charlie."

"As I said, I've changed my mind. I want you to know him better. I wonder if you'd have him to dinner?"

"All right. Will next week be soon enough? I'll be all settled by then."

Melinda nodded.

Morton and Edith rented the pew in front of Julia's. After they were seated, Edith handed Freddie a crayon and notebook and turned, showing displeased eyes above her gold-framed pince-nez. "You would think that once a week David could spare time to worship God. I certainly expected him to, now that you're married."

"He isn't interested in church."

"Perhaps Morton could talk to David about the importance of church."

"We have enough trouble without making church an issue." Edith's gray eyes were riveted on Julia's, and immediately, Julia regretted mentioning trouble. "Just normal problems that any newly married couple has. Like what to do about dinner when David's late. Just simple things."

"Oh—really?"

"Yes!"

"Then surely Morton could talk to David."

"No—please."

Edith didn't comment further. If Morton accepted the mission, not much damage would be done, Julia decided. Morton was too mild to be offensive.

Edith's gaze traveled forward to Arthur's third-row pew and rested on his blond head. *No one is more worshipful in church than Arthur*, Julia thought. "Edith, I know what you're thinking. Arthur isn't what he seems. David is."

"That sounds spiteful to me."

"I'm not going to discuss Arthur," replied Julia, changing the subject. "Edith, how do you cook scrambled eggs? Mine were watery."

"Beat together your eggs, then pour them into a pan of sizzling butter. Stir them continuously. That's the trick."

Edith turned. The quartet of cultured voices hired to sing Easter music stood before the congregation.

Julia arrived home as Bridget sprang down the back steps. Several of Julia's dresses were out of style and she had given them to Bridget. Bridget wore the blue cotton with sprigs of white flowers, and she looked quite pretty. Her dark hair was brushed up, her cheeks were flushed, her blue eyes sparkling with anticipation.

"I'm stopping by for Mary and we're meeting Michael O'Keefe downtown. Michael is showing us the sights of Chicago. Himself is the janitor at me church, and a good Catholic, surely."

"Is he Mary's beau?"

"No, but Mary's hoping he'll be. She says every unmarried girl in the parish is hoping. But Mary says he'll not notice the likes of her. Mary is thinking herself is plain. I'm thinking Mary has a chance."

"Michael must be exceptionally handsome?"

Bridget bristled. "Why, you won't find me looking at himself with Mary liking him! And himself not even a native-born Irishman!"

"It sounds like you talked to him awhile this morning?"

"Aye."

Bridget continued down the walk, and Julia smiled after her. *So Bridget likes Michael*, Julia mused.

Julia found David asleep in an armchair in the sitting room, his feet propped on an ottoman, the *Chicago Tribune* lying on his chest. He wore slippers and a smoking jacket, and his box of cigarettes was on the table. Sleep relaxed the heavy lines of his face, and he looked as if he dreamed of something pleasant. She leaned over and kissed his lips. They tasted bitterly of nicotine. He didn't wake up.

She went to the bedroom and changed from her Sunday dress to a beige cotton gown. While she clasped her dress pin, she noticed that David's shirt drawer was slightly open. She doubted he had changed shirts.

Opening his drawer, she reached under the shirts. The letters were gone. She looked in his other drawers and on the wardrobe floor, but they weren't there. She was frantic. Feeling she had to find them, she ran to the kitchen to check the trash. There was nothing in the container except yesterday's newspaper. Of course Bridget had burned the trash last night. David, then, had either burned the letters or hidden them where she couldn't find them. Oh, how utterly foolish not to have read them! Julia realized now that she had planned on reading the letters all along.

Six

"Saints! Me food is being fearful bad," Bridget exclaimed the next morning in the kitchen when Julia mentioned she and David would eat dinner at his parents'. "Mr. Gerard isn't forgiving myself for the dried-up roast."

"It wasn't your fault Mr. Gerard was late. Your cooking is coming along fine. We will eat out occasionally, that's all."

"Aye."

"Have you had trouble finding the supplies you need for cleaning? Are there any cleaning solutions I can buy to help you?"

Bridget raised her chin. "Myself is needing nothing."

Of course the girl was too uncertain in her position to admit to any need, Julia realized. She would ask Miss Nancy for a list of supplies that would help Bridget.

That evening the dusty pampas grass in tall vases waved as the servant opened the door of the elder Gerards' dining room. He was serving the roast pork. Dust filtered through the air, and Julia sneezed. She hoped Mother Gerard didn't notice her sneezes each time the kitchen door opened. The house was dilapidated, a narrow two-and-a-half story in the downtown district. Edgar, who hoarded money for retirement, refused to repair it. The house was built in 1837, the year Chicago was incorporated as a city. A house so run-down in the young city was unusual. The dining room was cluttered, dirty, and depressing to be in, Julia thought.

"Pork is one of my favorite dishes." Julia tried to sound cheerful.

"Is it, dear? I'm so glad." But Alma didn't look pleased. Her heavy face was pleated with worry, and she kept glancing back at the vestibule as if expecting another guest.

When the servant left, Alma continued. "We're lucky that Bretta is here tonight. She doesn't come to work half the time—and she's a horrible housekeeper." Alma nervously addressed Edgar. "Couldn't Bretta live in? That way I could depend on her."

Edgar's reply was immediate. "No. I need my privacy."

Edgar concentrated on eating his pork. Seeing how heartily he ate during the preceding courses, Julia wasn't surprised at his enormous paunch. Though he had an abundance of flesh, he had a paucity of hair— a slim half circle around his scalp and a thin little goatee. When the Gerards were in the same room, Julia thought the combination of their bulk lent them each a certain grandeur.

Alma continued. "But I'd keep Bretta out of your way. I really need her. Everything has piled up because of . . . because of all the extra work there is now."

"Then hire someone reliable."

"But Bretta likes working here."

Edgar kicked out his feet, striking Julia's ankle with his boots. She muffled a cry of pain. That was the third time he had kicked her, and she longed to tell him to be careful. She pressed her feet back under her chair.

"Fire Bretta," Edgar suggested. "Hire another woman. Hire someone that will remember to come. Furthermore, get this situation with Nelda settled. This place is a madhouse."

"Edgar! You promised Martha you wouldn't say a word," Alma scolded.

"Nelda's here again," Edgar informed David.

Julia hadn't met David's cousin Nelda, or her mother Martha Wilson, a widow of three years. Martha had written to decline Julia's wedding invitation for herself and Nelda, giving no reason for doing so. David had told Julia that Nelda was an eccentric spinster in her early thirties. Because Nelda was difficult, she exhausted Martha; in order to recuperate, Martha often sent Nelda to Alma. Edgar tolerated Nelda in the house only because Martha was his sister, his closest living relative.

Alma sipped nervously from her water glass.

"Why are you being so secretive?" David asked his mother.

Alma put down the glass. "Oh—well, certainly I must tell you. Nelda's finally gone mad. We all expected it, except Martha. She always hoped Nelda would improve. Martha asked me to keep Nelda's condition a secret until she decides what action to take."

"What exactly is Nelda's condition?" David asked.

"She's irrational and excited—she doesn't sleep, except in snatches. She jabbers about buying gowns, jewels, and carriages for investments. Of course, she hasn't any money."

"Considering Nelda's state, I'm surprised Martha would inflict her on you."

"Martha feels I can handle Nelda better than she can."

Alma glanced up at the ceiling, and Julia heard the noise that had caught Alma's attention. It was high laughter, continuous and unsettling. It sounded as if it came from the rear of the long house.

"There, hear that!" Alma shrilled. "Oh, dear! I feared Nelda would ruin dinner." Alma's black eyes sought Julia. "I shouldn't have had you here . . . yet I had to or you would feel rejected. I've been occupied with Nelda—that's why I haven't invited you until now. I hate having you learn about our problems in this manner. I should have told you sooner."

"David did tell me you occasionally had problems with his cousin."

David pushed back his chair. "Where is Nelda?"

"In the back bedroom—where she always sleeps."

"I'd like to see her," David stated. Alma started to rise and David touched her arm. "Just finish your dinner—you need to relax."

Julia didn't offer to accompany David. That she was frightened of people with diseased minds made her reluctant to meet Nelda. Perhaps her fear stemmed from her own case of nerves when she was at the Riverview Young Ladies' Seminary in Indianapolis, Julia reasoned. That incident linked her too closely with the fearful world of lunatics.

When David returned, Bretta served apple dumplings. "How is Nelda?" Alma asked.

"She was excited, pacing the room, pounding on the wall. I'll board up her window after dessert. I think her eyes look very odd—feverish. I persuaded her to lie down—she's quite exhausted. I think she might even sleep."

Alma looked at Julia. "David always has a soothing effect on Nelda. Neither has sisters and brothers, so they're very close."

David's eyes met his mother's; his voice was deliberate. "Nelda belongs in an asylum."

"Martha won't consider that."

"She's at a point where she must."

Alma's voice to Edgar was pleading, nervous. "Edgar, you heard David. Will you speak to Martha?"

Before answering, Edgar spooned the last of the dumpling into his mouth and wiped his face with his napkin. He gave Alma an irritated look, and Julia disliked his lack of concern. "Let David. Martha will be emotional, and you know I don't like displays of emotion."

"I'll talk to Martha tomorrow," David promised.

When Edgar excused himself to do some reading, David went after boards and nails. Julia and Alma remained at the dining table. Alma's hand shook while she sipped her coffee. "You just don't know how awful it is! Martha is too exhausted to help, and Bretta is afraid to go near Nelda. Edgar won't do a thing. He eats, then goes to his study. Everything is up to me. Of course, I shouldn't criticize Edgar. He's my husband and he's all that I have."

Julia's heart went out to her in sympathy. "I'd like to help. Could I come tomorrow?"

Alma had a dazed look on her face. "Oh, how kind; how really nice of you. Why, I'm so touched and—" She began to cry.

Julia feared Alma's nerves were about to snap. If Julia knew Alma better, she would offer to fetch her chloral tablets. "How can I best help tomorrow?"

"Ah—oh, yes." Alma was pulling herself together. "By doing housework. My mind's clearer after lunch. Come then, please. You're so kind—I really can't get over it. Trina wouldn't have offered. Neither would Diane Hastings."

There is that name again, Julia thought. Her head felt peculiar, airy.

Apparently surprised at herself for mentioning Trina and Diane, Alma hastened to explain. "Diane is *not* kind natured. She's extravagant and cold, quite selfish. I wasn't for the betrothal at all. There was something false about Diane. She seems nice enough on the surface, but underneath she's poison. Only a poisonous person would marry for money like she did. Yes, she jilted David to marry one of Chicago's wealthiest men."

Julia's voice was weak from the shock. "I didn't know David was betrothed to Diane!"

Alma stammered, "Oh—didn't you?" Her hand covered Julia's— it was hot, like pudding from a pan. "My! I should never have mentioned it—and I wouldn't have, except I'm so wrought up."

"When did Diane break her engagement with David?"

"Just before he met you. Please, David wouldn't like me talking about it. Now tell me, dear, how are you? What are you doing with yourself? How are your sisters and father?"

Julia was unable to speak. She had heard of these marriages on the rebound.

Alma clasped Julia's hand in both of hers. "Please forgive me for speaking so recklessly. I pointed out the contrast between you and Diane and Trina because I like you. I do want us to be close."

"Yes, of course," Julia finally managed.

The air had chilled while they were at dinner, and when Julia entered David's phaeton, she tucked the blanket around her legs. The phaeton was a light, four-passenger vehicle with side curtains and green leather upholstery. David needed a four-seater to transport customers. He tapped the horse with the whip, and as they entered the street, Julia spoke. She was direct; Alma's comments had removed her past hesitation. "Why didn't you tell me you were betrothed to Diane Hastings?"

The curtains were up, and in the light from a street lamp Julia saw David blanch. "Mother?"

"Yes."

"I'm sorry you learned that way. Mother talks about things she shouldn't. She isn't a gossip—she's just thoughtless."

Julia persisted. "David, *why* didn't you tell me?"

"I thought you had enough to deal with concerning Trina."

"Oh . . ." Julia's voice faded. She could understand that. It was true, of course. Yet she would rather he had been candid. But, then, she wasn't always candid with him. Julia fought against crying out, *Oh David! Do you still love Diane?* "Well," Julia finally said, "did you give Morton a price for his lumber today?"

"Yes—he has to check it with Edith. She has him under her thumb, I must say. Yet I like her directness and force. She missed her place in being born a woman."

"Yes, she did." Julia paused. "I'm doing some housework for your mother tomorrow."

"Thanks, I appreciate you for helping." He pulled her close, his eyes were loving. Julia laid her head on his shoulder and closed her eyes, allowing him to think she slept. *Diane!* she moaned inwardly. *Diane!*

Early the next morning Julia walked to her father's house and received a list of cleaning supplies Miss Nancy considered indispensable. On returning home, Julia found the industrious Bridget fluffing bed pillows. She handed Bridget the list, saying, "We probably have most of these cleaning items, but if there are any you'd like to try, I'll buy them."

"Thank you."

Julia pointed to the list. "The use of each item is given. Occasionally I'll be busy and you'll need to shop. Mr. Gerard has an account at Smithy's Market. We just charge items there. I'll take you with me next time so you can learn how it works."

Bridget looked amazed. "Yourself would be letting me buy things itself? Sure Bridget Boland will be buying the best bargains!"

Julia smiled. "I'm sure you will. Is your work going all right this morning?"

"Grand itself!"

Later in the morning David picked Julia up and they drove to Aunt Martha's. His aunt was emotional and David was hoping Julia's presence would soothe her. Mrs. Wilson seated them in what Julia supposed was like a nest to her—a darkened parlor with containers of candy all around and books piled carelessly on the table. Martha's little frame was weighted with jewelry, including a silver broach the size of a biscuit. Her blue eyes were dreamy, as if her mind were on the events in her books. Though her skin was wrinkled and liver-spotted, her violet eyes and bow-shaped lips indicated she was once beautiful.

"I see you enjoy books," Julia observed. "So do I."

"I like romances the best. They take my mind off Nelda. She looked knowingly at David. "I suppose you've learned that Nelda is mad. Alma never keeps anything quiet."

David's voice was gentle. "Nelda needs to be in an asylum—neither you nor Mother can manage her. Neither of you should even try."

"No, no, I won't hear of that! Alma can manage her—she told me she could."

"She can't. She only agrees to because she can't say no. She's having a terrible time. In fact, Julia's going to help Mother this afternoon. Something needs to be done—and quickly. Mother is about to collapse."

Martha started shaking her head, then cupped it in her hands. "Oh, dear," she wailed, "I hate making decisions on my own. If only Wilbur were still here!" She looked at Julia. "He always knew what to do about Nelda. It's all up to me now. The decision's too big for me. If I put Nelda through a trial, she'll imagine she's committed a crime and lose her mind permanently."

Julia recalled that in Illinois a person had to undergo a trial by jury and be judged a lunatic before he could be committed to an asylum.

"There are private homes in Chicago that keep lunatics," David stated. "If Nelda were placed in one of those, we could avoid a trial."

"Oh, do you think that would be possible?" she asked hopefully.

"Of course the disadvantage is that she can come and go as she pleases," David warned. "She won't be legally restrained, you know."

"I don't think Nelda would run off. She has threatened to, but they proved idle threats," his aunt said.

"I understand that Wilbur left you a comfortable income."

"I can manage to pay Nelda's keep."

"Then shall I check around for a place for Nelda?"

Martha looked relieved. "Yes, please do. I'd be so grateful. I realized, of course, that I couldn't leave Nelda with Alma much longer, but I just couldn't decide what to do."

David asked Julia to inform his mother of Martha's decision.

Not long after David drove Julia home in his buggy, Melinda dropped in. She flopped into an armchair and brushed down her skirts. Irritated, Julia said, "Really, you ought to learn how to sit properly."

Melinda sighed. "I know I'm not graceful. Coming over, I tripped on a curb and fell. It was so embarrassing. A man lifted me up"—she smiled—"I must say he was rather good-looking."

Julia laughed. "You're accident prone, Melinda."

"I *am* not!"

Julia recited the catalogue of mishaps. "You fell out of a tree and broke your arm. You tripped over a box and broke a leg. You fell off the porch and broke your ribs."

"That was years ago."

"I suppose," Julia conceded. "Will you stay for lunch? I'm going to Mother Gerard's afterward to help her with housework." Julia filled Melinda in on Nelda's history. "Why don't you come? She would appreciate your help."

"All right." Melinda was facing Trina's seascape. "That really is good. It captures the mood of the lake in a storm."

"I told you that Trina painted it, didn't I?"

"Yes."

"I wish I had asked David to store it with Trina's other paintings."

"Why?"

"It reminds me of Trina. I can't tell him to take it down now, though. He'd think I was jealous."

It was a relief to have admitted her jealousy to Melinda. "I *am* jealous, Melinda! All I think about is Trina and Diane. I think about Trina's photograph in her trunk. At least the photograph won't be here long—David's giving it to Trina's mother." Julia's eyes were stark, her voice a whisper. "Yes—I wonder if Trina is prettier than I am. Yes—I do want to see it!"

Melinda's eyes were alarmed. "I think you'll be sorry if you look."

"I have to."

"Julia, you don't!"

Julia stood up.

"Then I'll look too, if your mind is made up," Melinda yielded.

Julia and Melinda found Trina's three trunks against the wall of the coal bin. The window nearby was small and dirty, not giving much light, so Julia lit an oil lamp and handed it to Melinda. "Stand right here—close by," Julia directed.

Julia opened the lid of the outer trunk. She reached into a pile of silk and satin dresses. Most of the dresses were spotted with dark mold, and they felt cool and damp from the cellar air. They would be ruined, she thought, if they remained in the cellar much longer.

Julia said, "The photograph's not in here."

"Then let's go."

Julia opened the middle trunk. It was filled with boxes, books, shoes. She lifted them out quickly. Near the bottom she found a photograph.

"Hold up the light. I've found it."

The frame was expensive, gilded wood. Julia polished the glass with her dress sleeve, and Melinda pressed close. Julia caught her breath. Trina was beautiful, her face heart-shaped, her eyes large and luminous. She and David stood apart, with her dainty, white arms on his waist, and his strong ones around her. Their bodies didn't touch, but their rapturous gazes bound them like ropes. *David never looked at me like that*, Julia thought, feeling the barbs of jealousy again.

"Oh, Melinda, look at her!"

"It's my fault!" Melinda cried. "I should have stopped you from finding that photograph. Put it back and let's go!"

"He doesn't love me!" Julia wailed.

Melinda's eyes were wide and frightened. "He does! Julia, of course he does. A man can love many women."

"Oh, Melinda!"

"You must forget the photograph."

"I will. I'll try never to think of it again. He's married to me now—not Trina, not Diane."

Julia's tears began to flow freely.

Melinda handed Julia the lamp and took the photograph and returned it to the bottom of the trunk. As she packed the boxes and shoes on top of it, she asked, "Do you think I have them in right?"

"It doesn't matter," Julia replied disconsolately.

Melinda blew out the lamp and guided her sister toward the cellar stairs. Julia walked up the steps, her emotions a mixture of remorse and despair.

"Let's have lunch now," Melinda said, obviously trying to encourage her. "Then we'll tackle your project for this afternoon. It will help to keep busy." Melinda put her arm around Julia, saying, "Try not to think about the photograph. You knew you would always wonder about it. Now that you've seen it, put it out of your mind. Remember, *you* are David's wife. He *does* love you. Give him time."

"Thanks, Melinda. I'll try," replied Julia.

They were served a lovely lunch of chopped whitefish and pickle sandwiches. When Bridget served the coffee, Melinda, trying to lighten the heavy atmosphere, said, "That sandwich was delicious! Did you learn to make the spread in Ireland?"

Bridget smiled. "Aye. Papa's fish was almost our only meat, and we cooked it every way we could be thinking of."

Julia ate only a few bites of her sandwich. Choking down the last morsel, she stated tearfully, "I can't get Trina from my mind. Let's go as soon as you're done—I *do* need to get busy, to concentrate on something else, so I won't think about her."

Since neither Julia nor Melinda owned buggies, they took the horse-car to Alma's. They stepped carefully across Alma's sagging porch to avoid tripping on a loose board. Julia knocked since the clapper on the bell was missing. As she waited she noticed the paint peeling from the door. Julia wondered again how Edgar tolerated such shabby living quarters.

It took some time for Alma to answer, and when she did she peered at Julia and Melinda with surprise. Alma appeared to have just dressed hurriedly; her bodice buttons were lined up wrong, and her salt-and-pepper hair was pinned into a messy pile. "Oh, won't you come in?" Alma invited, motioning them into the vestibule.

"Did you forget I was coming?"

"It's terrible, inexcusable, of me to forget when you've come to help."

"You remember my sister Melinda Adams. She's has offered to help, too."

"Oh, how nice of you, Melinda! It's been difficult today. Bretta, my servant, has just quit. I talked her into carrying up Nelda's breakfast, and Nelda threw a plate at Bretta's head causing quite a lump. I don't blame her for quitting."

"Is Nelda still disorderly?" Julia asked apprehensively.

"Yes. I've had to padlock her door to keep her confined. She's been banging on it for hours now. It's like living in a drum. Can't you hear it?"

They were some distance from Nelda's room, but Julia could faintly hear the beat. "Well, at least I have some good news," Julia announced. "Aunt Martha has agreed to admit Nelda to a private asylum."

"When?"

"As soon as David finds one—this week probably."

"Thank heavens! Just knowing the end is in sight is a relief."

Alma supplied Julia and Melinda with aprons, feather dusters, and brooms. She pointed out the cloths for washing the kitchen oilcloth and other areas. "Just do what you can," she suggested. "Don't worry about what you can't get to and don't go in Nelda's room. I appreciate your helping me."

Four hours later Julia and Melinda had dusted and swept the house and washed the kitchen floor. Perspiring, they dropped into chairs at the kitchen table. Nelda's room was overhead and her pounding reverberated throughout the kitchen. "You'd think her hands would be raw," Julia sighed.

Julia was relieved that Alma had excused them from cleaning Nelda's room. She wasn't eager to meet Nelda. Nelda's condition brought back vivid memories of her our painful experience when she was a student at Riverview Young Lady's Institute in Indianapolis. Her tuition had been paid by a wealthy aunt in that city. Julia was her favorite niece, and the only one to whom the aunt offered schooling. Julia hadn't wanted to leave home, but since the school had high standards of deportment and scholarship, her father insisted she attend.

Julia recalled the grinding schedule: 5:30 rise; 6:00 study in the parlor; 6:30 meditation in her room; 7:00 breakfast and tidying up the room; 8:00 more study in the parlor; 9:00–12:00 in class with only a 15-minute recess; 12:30–2:00 dinner and study; 2:00–5:00 in class with a 15-minute recess; 5:00–8:00 recreation, tea, and supper; 8:00–9:00 study and meditation on religious principles; 9:15 bed, with no talking allowed—except in an emergency. Chores and study periods consumed Saturday morning and evening, leaving just Saturday afternoon for un-structured recreation. Sunday should have been a day of rest, but she was expected to attend church, study the Bible, and prepare an abstract of the sermon—pure slavery! Adding to the torture, the abstract had to be read aloud to the headmistress before supper. The headmistress al-ways faulted Julia's written and oral expression, which caused Julia to perspire and shake each time she read aloud.

Finally, her nervous system reacted, making her pale and jittery. She would jump when a book dropped or a door slammed. She slept poorly and had difficulty concentrating on her studies. Then one morning the walls of her room seemed to close in on her and the floor to lift. She tried to run to a safe place, but her arms and legs held her fast, paralyzed. Following a doctor's advice, she was transferred to Chicago High School, where she slowly recovered, though she couldn't forget the trauma.

Julia hadn't told David about Riverside, nor would she. To her it was a shame, and she resented Nelda for reminding her of it. She won-dered if she would have suffered Nelda's fate had she been left at Riv-erside.

Alma entered the kitchen and surveyed the shining floor. "You've done too much," she protested. "I can't tell you how I appreciate it." Her eyes filled with tears. "Nobody's ever helped me like this."

Julia said. "I'll come tomorrow, too, if there's more I can do."

"No, no! This is quite enough. My neighbor just found a servant for me, a girl from Germany. I've always liked the Germans' work and diligence, despite how they annexed Alsace at the end of the Franco-German War. My family's from Alsace—I try not to be bitter. Helga will start in a few days."

Alma poured glasses of sweetened raspberry vinegar, and while they drank they noticed how quiet it was upstairs. "I'd better check on Nelda and bring her a drink," Alma stated. "Since she seems quiet, perhaps this would be a good time for you to meet her."

"It's late . . . it . . . ." Julia tried to postpone the inevitable meeting.

Melinda broke in eagerly, her expression curious, interested. "Oh, I'd like to do that."

The dingy wallpaper in the long upstairs hall and, the closed doors along both sides, created a gloomy atmosphere. As they approached Nelda's door, there was an uneasy silence. Alma cautiously turned her key in the padlock, while Julia nervously stood by, clutching a lamp and hoping Nelda was asleep. "Nelda, it's Aunt Alma," she called soothingly. "I have guests I'd like you to meet. I've also brought your favorite drink." There was no answer.

As they entered the room they saw Nelda hunched on an iron bed, staring miserably at the floor. She didn't look up or acknowledge her visitors in any way. She wore a jacket and hat as if ready to escape. Her homely, long-shaped face and nose were red from crying—or cold, Julie couldn't tell which, for the room was like an icebox. Nelda's large-boned frame looked strangely frail, Julie thought. Her bed was heaped with blankets, with the pillow crumpled on the floor. Julia picked up the pillow and set it on the blankets, keeping her eyes fastened on Nelda.

"Hold on to the lamp," Alma advised Julia. "Nelda might grab it, setting fire to us. We can't have any fire around her. That's why the stove isn't lit. I know it's terribly cold, but it's necessary for her safety."

Melinda handed Nelda the raspberry drink while Alma locked the door again. Going over to Nelda and touching her on the shoulder, Alma introduced Julia and Melinda to her.

"Hello," Julia said, smiling stiffly.

Nelda gave no response.

"It's quite chilly for spring, isn't it?" Julia said, trying to draw her out.

Nelda silently drank from her glass, then looked at the floor. Julia couldn't think of another comment. Melinda sat beside Nelda and touched her hand, saying in a warm voice, "How are you, Nelda? I'm really glad to meet you. I hope we can be friends."

Nelda finished her drink.

"I hope to visit you often," Melinda continued, taking Nelda's glass. "I don't live far away, and if you'd like I could read to you."

Julia noticed Nelda sneak a look at Melinda from the corner of her eye.

"Nelda won't talk," Alma informed them. "She talks constantly when she's excited, but not when she's melancholic. Her moods change just like that. I can't keep up with them."

Seeing that Nelda's hands were scraped and bruised from banging on the door all afternoon, Julia asked Alma where she kept ointment and bandages. When she returned with them, Melinda offered to treat Nelda's hands.

Julia was relieved. Though Nelda didn't disturb her nearly as much as she had expected, she would rather not touch her.

Nelda showed no interest in her treatment, but at one point she glanced again at Melinda. When Melinda had finished, Alma suggested, "We'd better go." Then turning to Nelda, she said, "I'll be up soon with dinner. You look exhausted. Why don't you rest until I come back."

"Do come again," Alma told Melinda downstairs at the door.

"Yes, I'd like to help Nelda," Melinda responded.

Riding home in the horsecar, Melinda confided, "It made me feel worthwhile to get Nelda to respond even a little. I think I'd be happier if I helped others more."

"I felt that way too. Just going to see her made me feel better."

Julia ate dinner alone in the dining room. She hadn't seen David since morning. As vice-president of the Chicago Lumberman's Association, he had gone from work to the monthly board meeting at Henrici's restaurant. She picked at her piece of chicken, then put down her fork. This was her first dinner alone since her marriage, yet it was far from the last, she thought glumly. But she had better accept David's busy schedule, or be miserable. He worked to provide for her; therefore, not only should she be accepting, but appreciative.

When Bridget carried in a bowl of bread pudding, she looked unhappily at Julia's full plate.

"It was delicious," Julia assured her. "But I'm just not hungry. I can't eat the dessert either. You can save it for dinner tomorrow."

"Aye. Then I'll be doing the dishes and going to Mary's. I'll be bringing Chester in. Himself is after barking at me to come home when he knows I'm at Mary's. Michael O'Keefe is stopping by Mary's to visit. It's a grand thing that himself is liking Mary. Michael asked me to be there for the visit. He's shy with Mary, I'm thinking."

"Or maybe it's you that he wants to see." Julia's eyes twinkled.

Bridget's blue eyes reflected horror. "Saints no! Myself would keep away if that were true."

After Bridget left to visit Mary, Julia worked at arranging the parlor to her taste. She held a blue tablecloth, a wedding gift, against the yellow wallpaper. Deciding it didn't clash, she laid it on the center table, a lovely piece of rosewood furniture. Julia thought the table looked best uncovered; nonetheless, she left the cloth on. The parlor needed blue— her color. She placed her grandmother's Bible and her mother's daguerreotype, both treasured possessions, on the blue cloth. Last of all, she added an oil lamp for reading. Then, stepping back, she surveyed the room, satisfied with the effect.

Remembering some pans in the cellar Bridget could use for cooking, Julia lit a lamp and went to retrieve them. She had not forgotten Trina at all. Her memory of that lovely face grew clearer with each downward step.

When the light from Julia's lamp revealed the storage shelves, it fell on Trina's trunks nearby. She couldn't take her eyes from *the* trunk. She had to look at Trina's photograph again. Perhaps Trina's beauty was only superficial, with no radiance or character shining through. If that were true, then Julia could accept her.

She found a chair to serve as a lampstand and unpacked the trunk. An apprehensive nervousness grew inside her and spread quickly. Her fingers tingling, she removed the photograph and held it under the light. Since the picture was shadowed she turned up the wick. There was Trina—her face bathed in golden light, glowing with a delicate beauty. Radiant! Julia's hand trembled as she touched her own cheek. She could almost feel those ugly freckles. Even by touch, one would know hers wasn't the face of a beauty. With her fingertips she traced Trina's heart-shaped face. Ah, there was beauty—sheer beauty. A surge of jealousy swept over Julia. She hated Trina. Hated her beauty. Hot, angry tears spilled down Julia's face. She didn't have a chance against Trina's memory. *Why on earth did David marry me?* she wondered. It had been a mistake; one he bitterly regretted but decently endured in silence. She hated his decency. Why couldn't he openly tell her of his feelings for Trina?

But she had the power to destroy David's remembrance of Trina's beauty. Like God . . .

Julia looked over at the furnace, tears streaming down her face. David had started a fire that morning. Though the draft was open just a crack, the coals were probably hot enough, she concluded. As she opened the door, the hot air struck her, making her feel dizzy. *If the picture is destroyed, then Trina is too!* she decided, her thoughts now irrational. She didn't try to stop her hand, but flung the picture from her and watched it land on the coals, glass up. The glass cracked first, then the portrait turned brown and burned. Now Trina was destroyed. She wanted to laugh. Soon no one would remember Trina's face clearly. She hadn't seen her aunt's face in Indianapolis in years and she had almost forgotten it. She could remember the square shape, the large features, that was all. The fine details were lost. So it would be with Trina.

Julia clutched her sides and laughed and laughed, the hollow sound reverberating throughout the cellar. She had done the right thing! Oh, she felt light, free, happy!

Then she panicked, and her hands trembled as she closed the furnace door. What she had done was unforgivable. She had overlooked the importance of the photograph to Trina's mother. David would be furious, she thought, and justly so. Now he would know she was wildly jealous. He would lose all respect for her—he would *never* love her!

Yet, if he were in her position, wouldn't he be rash? Yes, yes! she concluded, justifying her action.

Julia heard the cellar door opening. Her knees went weak. Was David home early?

To her relief Melinda called, "I let myself in with my key. I came to get that book about Africa you borrowed from Father. He wants to read it tonight."

Julia struggled to speak normally, but her voice was reedy. "It's on the table by my bed."

"Where's David?"

"At a meeting. Don't come down. I'll be right up."

Julia repacked the trunk and picked up the lamp. She didn't remember the pans until she was halfway up the stairs. However, she didn't go back for them; in fact, she wondered if she had really come for them in the first place.

When Julia entered the sitting room, Melinda was sitting with the book on Africa in her lap, an unhappy expression in her eyes. "Charlie stopped by awhile ago. I invited him to your house for dinner, but he declined. He feels inferior to David because he's just a butcher and David owns a lumberyard. Charlie is looking to purchase a meat market, though. When he does, he'll come to dinner. Isn't that the silliest thing you've ever heard?"

"No."

Julia started to cry and Melinda hurried to her. "Melinda, I just did a terrible thing. I burned Trina's photograph in the furnace."

"Julia! That wasn't yours to burn! You shouldn't have done it."

"I know. What should I do?"

"Tell David."

"I can't."

"Tell him!"

"You're right. I have to—I want no secrets between us. I can't tonight, though. I have to give our marriage time to develop stability, then I'll tell him. He's busy now. He can't go through Trina's things for a while anyway. I have time to wait."

Melinda nodded, but her eyes reflected the worry she felt.

Seven

*J*ulia tried to look relaxed as David walked into the sitting room after his board meeting. He wore the fashionable Newmarket frock coat with the double breast and shorter front skirt, and a dark green silk waistcoat. He kissed her and removed his box of cigarettes from inside his coat. "Do you mind?"

Her voice was forced. "No."

After he lit the cigarette, he looked at her. To her relief, there was no indication from his expression that he saw guilt on her face; in fact, his eyes looked tired. She relaxed then and her voice sounded normal. "How was the meeting?"

"Long—and boring at times. I thought of how I'd rather be with you."

She was surprised. "Oh!"

"Thanks for helping Mother today. Did you meet Nelda?"

Julia nodded. "Melinda went with me. Nelda was depressed, but Melinda got a slight response from her.

"I found a place for Nelda today. I took Aunt Martha there this afternoon and she approved. We can probably admit Nelda Thursday."

"What's it like?"

"It's a private home, but it's managed much like a state asylum. The owner isn't a doctor, but he's been working with mental patients for twenty-five years. He's independently wealthy; therefore concern, not money, motivates him to cure them. He keeps fifteen patients, which is quite a few for a private place. The owner is efficient in manner. He calls himself a superintendent, as they do in state asylums. He doesn't

71

keep the extremely violent since he doesn't have the security for it."

David crushed his cigarette in the china dish provided for ashes and went to the cellar to bank the fire. Julia listened nervously as the shovel hit the metal walls of the furnace. She imagined David peering at the coals as he worked. *Of course the photograph is burned*, she thought. There might be some glass, but David would think nothing of that, Julia consoled herself, straightening out her tight fists in her lap.

When he entered the room, her face drained of color. She waited tensely for him to speak. "We shouldn't have to bother with a fire before long," he said.

"No," she murmured.

"I'm looking forward to warm weather," he added.

"I am too," Julia agreed, relieved that her offense had not been discovered.

David sat down beside her and put his arm around her shoulder. "Is Bridget here?" he asked.

"No, she's at Mary's."

"I have some news for her. I hired a friend of hers today as a loader, Billy Williams. He asked if I knew Bridget Boland. He met Bridget on the ship. Bridget had told him she would be working for the owner of a lumber company."

David smiled. "Bridget said I was a grand man, rich and famous in Chicago. Billy came on my lumber company by chance—he didn't have my name. Mine was the sixth one from which he sought employment. He's brash and I can understand why he wasn't hired. I hired him only because he's Bridget's friend. We badly needed another loader, but of course I had a hard time convincing Father of that."

Julia smiled. "Bridget will be pleased."

David continued. "I suppose I've been saving the bad news for last."
Somehow, he knows, Julia thought, turning cold.

"It's business. I hope you don't mind."

She breathed a sigh of relief. "No—not at all."

"I doubt I'll have the opportunity to buy Father out. Alvin White-head, a friend of Father's, offered Father ninety thousand cash, and Father is giving me three days to meet the offer. Of course I can't—I haven't enough collateral for a loan. So I'll be stuck with Whitehead. I don't trust him. I just can't imagine working with him."

Julia heard Bridget entering the kitchen with someone, probably Mary, and it was a few moments before Julia responded. "That is unfair! If that happens, will you sell out?"

David spoke with emotion. "I love the business. I've given it my all for sixteen years—almost sixteen years—I had that year and a half fighting in the Southern Rebellion. Even then I fought almost as much for the lumberyard as the Union. But, yes, I will sell if Whitehead buys in."

"David, please take my inheritance."

"Thank you, Julia, but I won't risk it."

"Would it give you enough collateral for the loan?"

"I think so, but it's your emergency fund."

"This is an emergency."

He didn't speak for quite a while. He sat stiffly, silently. She understood how much it would hurt his pride to receive her help; she willed him to have the humility. Finally he said, "Thank you, Julia. I'll repay you, of course."

Bridget brought Mary to the kitchen to show her the wonderful appliances she had for cooking—especially the cheese grater and grid-iron. Mary stopped suddenly in the middle of the room and strained forward to hear the voices in the sitting room. She tugged at Bridget's arm, her eyes knowing.

"See, see it's as I told you," Mary whispered. "He married Mrs. Gerard for her money. You heard them!"

Bridget felt miserable. "Himself is repaying!"

Mary hopped back and forth. "Maybe!"

Bridget refused to discuss it or judge the Gerards. In Ireland the rich married the rich for money and themselves were always happy, Bridget thought. Bridget whirled at Mary. "Let not a word be gossiped to the servant girls or you'll answer to Bridget Boland."

"I ain't no gossip."

Bridget wondered.

Mary seemed determined to make at least one point. "You flirted with Michael tonight. I never saw nothing like it."

"It was yourself throwing your eyes all over Michael."

"You better not be going after him!"

Bridget shoved her hands on her hips. "Me! Bridget Boland is no siren!"

Mary sighed and hung her head. "I ain't so pretty, and I forgot it. Michael has a way of making a body forget it."

Bridget threw her arms around Mary. "Why, himself is liking you very much. I could tell that."

"You could?"

"Why, surely." She would always encourage Mary and Michael's romance, she thought.

At breakfast, when David told Bridget he had hired Billy Williams, she responded with a shocked look and no comment. Julia supposed that Billy wasn't so much a friend of Bridget's as David thought. Later in the morning Edith and Freddie paid Julia a surprise visit. As Julia opened the door to admit them, the warm air, blue sky, and blazing forsythia made her feel good. The snowball and lilac were just blooming, perfuming the air. It was a pleasant contrast to a possible disagreeable visit.

"I hope you don't mind us dropping in," Edith said. "We were in the neighborhood visiting Mrs. Johnson from church. She is not feeling well. I'm taking Freddie to lunch and he's starving—so we won't be long. I'd like to see the house," she stated in her usual blunt manner. "You haven't shown it to me, and I don't understand why."

"I wanted to have it in order first," Julia replied.

Julia gave Edith a tour of the house, ending with the parlor. "Well, the house is in good order," Edith conceded. "It's very clean, in fact."

"Because Bridget is keeping it clean."

"I was wrong about her—don't press it."

Freddie was impatiently tugging Edith's skirt. "I'll see you in church tonight, Julia," she stated pointedly, pulling on her gloves.

Determined to stand up to Edith, Julia nervously clasped her hands. "I won't be at church tonight. I'm staying home Wednesday and Sunday evenings—unless David is out. He's not religious and I don't like to appear overly religious to him. I want to fit in with his way of life."

Edith's facial muscles contracted. "Mark my words, you'll regret it! You'll slip in your conduct and your attitudes. Furthermore, you should set an example for him."

"I'm not reconsidering. I'm not changing my mind," she responded, unmoved by her sister's demand.

Edith looked around the room. Julia suspected that Edith was searching for some way of attack, so when her gaze settled on the center table, Julia supposed she had found an object worthy of her frustration. "I don't like that cloth on the center table. I can tell by the legs it's made of rosewood. It's improper to cover good wood."

"I had my reasons," Julia responded evenly.

"What, if I may ask?" Edith inquired haughtily.

"I want my food!" Freddie interrupted, whining. "I'm hungry—I want my food!"

"Yes, yes—in a minute. Julia, just why are you covering good wood?"

Julia's face turned hot. She was weary of Edith's attacks. Why should she hide the truth from her? Let her hear! Let her figure out what she would do in Julia's place! She felt bold; having faced Edith before, she could do it again. She dropped her hands to her side as she began her tirade. "Everything is as Trina left it in this house. I put the cloth on the center table because it's *Trina's* table. I was trying to make it *my* table. How would you like being Morton's second wife? How would you like living with another woman's things?"

"That's jealousy," Edith admonished.

"Yes—I'm jealous! You'd be jealous too. Tell me, how would you feel if your husband never talked about his first wife? If he grieved night and day for her? I'll tell you! You'd be jealous! You'd burn her photograph in the furnace too!"

Looking aghast, Edith punched her pince-nez higher on her nose.

Hearing someone in the vestibule, Julia looked over Edith's shoulder to David. He was by the hatrack, staring at Julia with a tight look around his mouth. He must have entered through the back door, she thought. Surely he had just walked into the vestibule. But then she saw his coat on a peg. "Why—why are you home?" she stammered.

"I came for lunch—I wanted to make up for being out late last night. Hello, Edith, Freddie. I'll wash up and tell Bridget I'm here."

Edith collected Freddie's little tam and her parasol.

Julia stopped Edith at the front door. "I'm sure he heard."

"I would say you're in trouble. If I were you, I would discuss your feelings about Trina and your destructive action with him. I am always straightforward with Morton. I'm sorry for you, though, very sorry. Yes, you *are* in trouble."

Julia choked out, "Yes."

"Though if you need Morton or me, we'll help."

"I don't really. And, Edith, please don't send Morton over to talk to David about this."

"Morton won't come. He even refused to talk to David about church attendance. Morton hates to intrude."

At the dining table, Julia waited while Bridget served ham sandwiches and fruit salad. Bridget had cut the crusts from the bread as Julia liked. The salad contained oranges, bananas, strawberries, and apples—all shipped in on refrigerated railroad cars. Julia's wedding ring reflected the light from the window beside her as she nervously twisted it. She wondered how much Bridget had heard. Because of her quick intelligence, Bridget probably observed quite a lot, Julia surmised.

"The salad looks lovely," Julia complimented Bridget. "I'll ring if we need seconds." But she had no appetite.

"Aye."

They served themselves, and David unfolded his napkin. His hands were on the table; he didn't move to pick up his fork. He looked steadily at her. She was thirsty, but she feared she would drop her glass if she picked it up. "So you did hear," Julia said miserably.

"Yes. I'm amazed you interpret my silence in regard to Trina as grief. I thought you understood it was tact. You were aware I wish to focus on our future, not my past. I'm shocked. Did you really burn her photograph?"

Julia's emotions exploded. "Yes! I can't help it. Everything of Trina's is still here—her trunks, her paintings. It's like you can't part with anything. This is not my house. Very few things in it are mine. It's not as I would decorate it. If you must know, I don't like yellow at all. I hate it!" The ring turned around and around, and Julia noticed David's eyes on it. "I . . . I, yes, I am jealous! I purposely burned Trina's photograph—because . . . because of the love the photograph expressed!"

Feeling as though she deserved his hate, Julia lowered her eyes. He didn't speak immediately. When he did, his voice was angry. "I didn't want you to see the photograph. It wasn't out for you to see."

"Oh, David! If I had thought of Trina's mother, I wouldn't have burned it. I'm so sorry!"

Julia looked up. His expression turned from anger to compassion. "Trina's mother has a smaller photograph. I don't long for Trina. I grieved and I'm over it. That *is* the past. Trina and I had a happy marriage until a year before her death. She became absorbed in her art; she talked of nothing else and painted constantly. Throughout her confinement, she entertained artist friends; they drank liberally—it wasn't pleasant. Her style of living might have contributed to her death and the child's. This is why the boy's death hit me particularly hard—it might have been prevented."

"I—I didn't realize."

"I married you—you should have known I care."

But his eyes reflected some inner turmoil. Julia felt a mixture of relief and despair: he no longer loved Trina, but he didn't say, "I love you—only you, Julia." She feared that he never would.

He added tenderly, "I'll send a loader from the yard for the trunks and Trina's paintings this afternoon. I have an agent who will sell the paintings on commission. If you would like, I can donate her trunks to your church."

"That's fine. Do you want to leave the seascape up?"

"Yes. I would like to keep one painting, as you suggested. Would you please find the shawl? I don't have time to search for it, and I want you to have it. Furthermore, we will redecorate. I don't like yellow that well, either."

How could he sound so loving when he loved her so little? she wondered. "I like soft colors," Julia managed to add.

"So do I."

"I think blue wallpaper would look nice in the parlor."

"Pick out what you'd like and I'll hang it."

"But do you have time?"

"I'll make time." David handed her ten dollars. "I applied for the loan this morning, and the loan officer expects my application to be approved. Will you ask your father to cash in your bonds?"

"Yes, while I'm out this afternoon."

After Julia spoke to her father, she bought wallpaper with bluebells on it and spent some of her knipl on a cream-colored comforter and canopy. The store promised delivery late that afternoon. She arrived home to find a young man on the back steps in work pants and a coarse, drop-shouldered shirt rolled to his elbows. The beak of his red cap was pulled over his dark hair. His squat legs were planted in a wide V as if he owned the place.

"I'm Billy Williams," he said with a cockney accent. "I work for Mr. Gerard, and I came for the trunks and paintings."

He looked her over from head to toe, making her blush. "I'm Mrs. Gerard. The things you came for are in the cellar and study. I'll take you in."

"Wait." He lifted a bouquet of forsythia from the step. The stems were unwrapped and of various lengths, suggesting to Julia he had just plucked them from her bushes. "These are for Bridget. I know she works here. I'm a friend of hers from the boat."

Julia let Billy in the kitchen and called Bridget from the parlor; she came running in with her housemaid's box of cleaning utensils in her hand. Bridget frowned on seeing him and reluctantly accepted the flowers he shoved at her. "For you."

"Thanks," she said shortly.

"That ain't much of a welcome."

"It's all your like will be getting from me. I told you on the boat not to be calling."

"I ain't calling. I'm getting trunks for Mr. Gerard. I work for him."

"Well, be after them," Bridget said sharply, dismissing him.

"I just said I work for Mr. Gerard. I'd think you'd be glad."

"That wasn't me idea, surely. Though I wouldn't begrudge yourself work, even though you're an Englishman and a liar."

"Liar!"

"Sure, and didn't yourself brag on the boat that the English is better than the Irish? Me family is in misery because yourself stole our land and charged us terrible rents. Me two big brothers died in the potato famine, they did! Saints, I'll give the boiling pot to the Englishmen!''

"I ain't got nothing to do with the government!" Billy snapped. "I ain't responsible for the potato famine."

"Yourself is an Englishman!"

"I ain't a killer."

"Sure yourself is!" Bridget shook her finger at him.

"You're a lunatic—a real crazy girl!"

"Myself isn't!"

"Well, I ain't here to see your royal highness anyhow!"

Bridget clutched the flowers to her breast. "Oh, I'm not meaning to hurt your feelings, surely. The flowers is pretty and I am thanking yourself. I don't mean to be mad. It's no harm I'm wishing you in this country. I hope you do well at Mr. Gerard's, but I'll be thanking you to keep off from me and bring your next flowers to another girl."

Billy whisked the flowers from her hand. Startled, Bridget and Julia watched him open the porch door and toss the bouquet over the railing. "I've got my pride," Billy declared loudly.

Bridget stomped indignantly back to the parlor with her housemaid's box swinging.

Billy carried the trunks upstairs, and Julia removed the shawl. After he left, she posed before the pier glass in her bedroom with the shawl draped over her shoulders. It was black, stitched in an intricate fillet pattern. Yes, it did look pretty on her as it draped softly around her shoulders. David's great grandmother had so expertly crocheted it that the stitches were still tight. She supposed it had looked lovely on Trina, too. It was strange not to mind, not to be jealous, to have grace to wear what Trina had worn.

Bridget approached Julia as she left the bedroom. "Myself is apologizing for shouting at Billy. But I can't be trusting himself. Me mama said I should quit off Englishmen on the boat—and in America."

"Well, Billy won't be back—you don't have to worry about that."

After dinner Julia showed David the comforter, canopy, and wallpaper. "I bought the items for the bed from money Father gave me as a wedding gift."

"I hope you have some money left," he responded anxiously.

"I do," she assured him.

"Please save it for personal things. I would rather buy our household furnishings from my earnings."

"But do you like everything?" There was a touch of anxiety in her voice.

"Very much," he declared.

David decided to hang the wallpaper right away. He placed a board for cutting and pasting across two sawhorses in the parlor. As he worked, Julia read. She had checked out *Lunacy: History and Treatment* from the Chicago Library Association. She realized she would be more comfortable with Nelda if she better understood lunacy.

After reading awhile Julia looked up from the book. "Would you like me to read some of this aloud? It's interesting."

He stopped rolling out paper for a moment. "Yes, go ahead."

Julia read. " 'One of the first lunatic asylums in Europe was Bedlam in London. There, for a small fee, the public viewed caged maniacs and goaded them until they raved like beasts. For a larger fee, the public was shown those who believed they were Jesus Christ, John the Baptist, Muhammad, and other notables. Occasionally, inmates were released to beg!' " Julia looked up. "Here's a quote from Shakespeare about these 'Toms o' Bedlam':

" ' "Poor Tom; that eats the swimming frog, the toad, the tadpole, the wall-newt and the water; that in the fury of his heart, when the foul fiend rages, eats cow-dung for pallets; swallows the old rat and the ditch-dog; drinks the green mantle of the standing pool; who is whipped from tithing to tithing, and stocked-punished, and imprisoned; who hath had three suits to his back, six shirts to his body, horse to ride, and weapon to wear;

" ' "But mice and rats, and such small deer,

" ' "Have been Tom's food for seven long year." ' " (King Lear, Act III, Scene IV).

David glanced from the strip of paper he was pasting. "I hadn't heard that—or if I had, I must have forgotten."

Julia read from another chapter: " 'In this country, until recently, doctors usually diagnosed lunatics as suffering from demon possession or from excess black bile. Usually the lunatic was left untreated. But if he were treated he was bled, blistered to draw out suppressed fluids, purged, and drugged into insensibility.' "

Julia turned to a list of court records from 1676 to 1756 of judgments concerning lunatics and read: " 'Jan Vorelissen of Amesland, Complayning to ye Court that his son Erik is bereft of his naturall Senses and is turned quyt madd and yt, he being a poore man is not able to maintaine him; Ordered: yt three or four persons bee hired to build a little block-house at Amesland for to put in the said madman.'

"Here's one where funds were granted to Samuel Speere, who 'should build a little house 7 foote long & 5 foote wide & set it by his house to secure his Sister good wife Witty being distracted & provide for her.' "

"What a terrible time those creatures had!" David commented vehemently.

"Not all of them," Julia asserted, "There were many lunatics in decent poorhouses as well as at home."

David brushed the wrinkles from a strip of paper he had just placed on the wall. "You're rather special, taking all this interest in lunacy for Nelda's sake."

He stepped back from the wallpaper. He had finished half of the wall opposite the windows. "I like it quite well," he stated, pleased with the new look.

It made her happy to think she had pleased him. If she continued to do so, he might someday love her, she speculated.

Eight

One morning near the end of May, Julia rose from her bed for the second time and swung her feet to the floor. She had returned to bed immediately after David left for work. Now the sun had long since burned off the early haze, and the heat of the day was upon her. The air was filled with the calls of the seventeen-year locust, which had just arrived in the area. She stood, wobbling a bit on unsteady legs. It had taken fortitude to remain with David at breakfast while the greasy smell of sausage initiated waves of nausea. She might have excused herself but she was so eager to see him; he had just returned from his eighteen-day trip to New Orleans the previous evening. Perhaps, though, even if he had been home for days, she would have sat at the table— for she dreaded telling him, "I might be pregnant."

She pressed her abdomen. Her skin seemed more sensitive to the touch, but it might be her imagination. Julia studied her face in the mirror; it was pale with dark smudges under the eyes, even though she had slept well last night. Equivocal or not, the signs pointed to pregnancy. She felt happy for a moment, imagining the tiny form of a boy with minute hands and fingers and soft, downy hair. She pictured him nursing, his little nose pressed into her, so dependent on her. His name would be David, of course.

If she was pregnant, conception had probably occurred on the honeymoon. David would blame her for not being careful. Furthermore, throughout her pregnancy he'd be in agony, worrying she might miscarry. He'd hate her for putting him through the trauma. He'd watch her figure change and wish he had never met her. *Oh, God, please don't let me be pregnant!* she prayed silently.

That evening word arrived informing them of a bed available for Nelda. The patient in the bed previously designated for Nelda had had a relapse, so Nelda had remained in Alma's back bedroom for another three weeks. During that time Nelda had plummeted from mania to melancholy, the melancholy proving a great help to Alma, who could easily manage the docile woman. Nelda's melancholy was a help to both Julia and Melinda as well, for it allowed them to build some rapport with Nelda. As Julia helped care for Nelda, she became less nervous and more sympathetic toward her.

The next morning Julia accompanied Nelda, David, and Alma to Lakeside. Martha did not go with them because she couldn't bear to see Nelda "put away." Melinda had become fond of Nelda and wished to be with them, but she had to shop for Charlie's mother, she said.

Lakeside was set well back from the street and surrounded by a tall iron fence with a locked gate. The building was larger and more sprawling than Julia expected. The center section was inspired by the Greek form, having a small portico with plain columns. Two one-story wings bracketed the main building. It had once been a residence, and the wings were obviously added for the patients. Sweeping grounds gave way to Lake Michigan, tinted with gray even in the bright sunlight. Gulls soared over the lawn, their cries mixing with the murmur of the waves. The only off-key elements in what seemed a tranquil lakeshore retreat were the barred windows on the wings and the high-pitched shriek of a woman.

Julia worried about Nelda, huddling by the buggy like a scared rabbit, her eyes almost closed, her thin lashes fluttering on her long face. Taking Nelda's hand, Julia led her up the stairs. It was abhorrent to Julia that Nelda, like a stick in a river, was at the mercy of the current—her mind dominated by her madness, her body by others. Nelda dragged one foot before the other.

"Nelda, you'll be all right here," Julia encouraged. "You'll become yourself again."

"She doesn't understand, Julia," Alma said.

"I think she does," David declared. "Perhaps her problem is that she understands too much."

"You're close to home," Julia assured her. "We'll be near you and will come to see you often."

A tear slipped between Nelda's lashes.

An attendant led them to George Huntly, the superintendent of Lakeside. He stepped from behind his desk and briskly shook hands with them all. Then, he indicated that they should be seated. His office was pleasant, with high windows overlooking the lake, with books lining the paneled walls. Mr. Huntly was tall and pale. Julia doubted he spent much time on the grounds. Behind his gold-framed spectacles, his eyes were intense, as if results were paramount to him. That boded well for Nelda, Julia concluded. But there was no warmth to his countenance; his nose was pinched and narrow; his manner, businesslike. His gray-blond hair, the bags under his eyes, the lines around his mouth all indicated he was near fifty.

Dipping his pen in ink, he began gathering and recording Nelda's history as David and Alma answered his questions. Except for briefly greeting Nelda, Mr. Huntly ignored her. When he had finished, he closed his journal and rose to his feet. "Come, Miss Wilson. We'll have a short examination. It won't be uncomfortable."

Seeing Nelda looking so dismal, Julia asked hopefully, "May I come too?"

"No," he stated brusquely. "It's better that Miss Wilson and I be alone. Come, Miss Wilson," he said, leading her into the examining room.

After Nelda had left, Alma lamented, "This is no good! I'm so glad Martha isn't here. Mr. Huntly is too cold and uncaring. He's not good with Nelda. I'm so worried for her, David. Let's take her home. Maybe we can manage."

David spoke gently but firmly. "No. You can't handle her. You're barely hanging on now. You manage only by taking tablets for your nerves. We have no basis for disliking Mr. Huntly yet. I find him efficient and competent, and Lakeside appears clean and well run."

"Isn't there another place we could take her?" she urged.

"Not that I'm aware of," he answered. "There are two smaller homes, but they are full. We can't send Nelda out of town. Martha hates traveling of any kind; consequently she would never see Nelda. Here Martha can drive or walk to Lakeside for a visit anytime she wishes. Think how you'd miss Nelda if she were farther away. Besides, you may have gotten a wrong first impression. Let's try it for a while."

Julia, too, wished George Huntly were warmer.

When Nelda emerged from the examining room, she shuffled mechanically to a seat near Julia. Julia reached out and clasped her hands, trying to rub warmth into them. As she stroked Nelda's hands, Julia wondered how God could stand by and do nothing while this waste of humanity wandered blindly through life.

Mr. Huntly resumed his seat behind his large desk, creating a distance from his audience. He enunciated each word carefully. "Miss Wilson has circular mania, a condition characterized by cycles of melancholy and mania—high elation. Like most circular maniacs, Miss Wilson is usually in the melancholic phase. Lunacy is caused by physical and moral agents. Physical causes are blows on the head, epilepsy, small pox, accidents to the body, sexual abuse, sexual excess, and so forth. Moral causes are immoral behavior, jealousy, anger, pride, sloth, excess religion, overwork, domestic difficulties, excessive ambition, faulty education. Some lunacy is inherited, of course. It's my opinion that some races, such as the Irish, are highly susceptible to lunacy. Miss Wilson has a highly sensitive nervous system and her lunacy stems from reading stimulating novels. Her bout of small pox as a child may also be a contributing factor."

Alma looked alarmed. "I warned Nelda's mother to stop her from reading those romances! Can Nelda be cured?"

He looked surprised at the question. "Yes, of course," he stated confidently. "I cure ninety percent of my patients." (That seemed a grandiose claim to Julia.) "I will employ both medical and moral therapy. My medical regimen consists of diets and laxatives—and tonics to strengthen the body. I use opium or morphine to control attacks of violent or irrational behavior. Moral therapy is my primary method of cure. I will re-educate Miss Wilson in a proper moral atmosphere so she can manage when she returns home. Some methods of moral treatment I will employ are religious worship, lectures, classes, manual labor, recreation, amusements, and kindness. We have a well-equipped diversion room."

"Do you use any type of restraint or physical punishment?" Julia questioned nervously.

"I never use a strap or other instrument of punishment. When it's clear that a patient will harm himself and drug therapy isn't in order, I confine him in a tranquilizer. This is the only method of restraint I use. I employ it because there are times it benefits a patient to consider his actions—one can't do that when drugged. I don't keep severely violent patients; therefore, I don't often have violent behavior."

Julia recalled the picture of a tranquilizer she had seen in *Lunacy: History and Treatment*. It was a chair, designed by Dr. Benjamin Rush, an authority on the mind. It confined the patient's hands and feet in boxes and gripped his head in a three-sided box. The purpose was to reduce the pulse and excitement by restricting activity. Julia had read that the cruel-looking devise was used only occasionally today.

"I don't want Nelda restrained," David said emphatically. "We've never restrained her at home, and I don't think it is necessary. If you ever feel Nelda is a candidate for the tranquilizer, please contact me first."

"Of course. But you must understand there are times when I must act quickly. I need written permission for that option, or I cannot keep Miss Wilson."

"All right. But if possible, you must contact me. I would rather have Nelda drugged if she becomes unmanageable."

Alma addressed Dr. Huntly. "I'm embarrassed to tell anyone that Nelda's in an asylum. Would you advise us to tell people she's in England."

Julia was concerned about the open discussion in Nelda's presence and wondered if Nelda felt ashamed. "I think we should be honest," Julia asserted.

"Whatever the family wishes," Mr. Huntly said dispassionately. "That isn't my province."

Julia disliked his neutrality. But she didn't mention her view to David until they had dropped his mother at home and were parked in their own driveway.

"I think Mr. Huntly should have advised your mother to be honest," she stated. "I think Nelda felt ashamed. I'm surprised Mr. Huntly remained so neutral."

"Mr. Huntly is right in leaving this to the family's discretion. If Aunt Martha and Mother are more comfortable telling others that Nelda is in England, then I feel they should. After all, this is very hard on them too. But I'm glad you brought this up. I'll ask Mother and Martha to be careful how they speak in front of Nelda."

When David left for work, Julia walked around the house, trying to ease her mind from the morning's activity. She decided to check the peonies in the backyard. If they had bloomed, she would cut some flowers for the dining room table. As she turned from the side yard, she noticed a wagon parked in front of the stable. Bridget was on the porch steps, glancing nervously at the driver, a blond giant with strikingly kind blue eyes. His work shirt, stretched across his broad shoulders, revealed a strong muscular frame. His boots, Julia noticed, went some distance to cover his large feet. He smiled at Julia, and his eyes lit up like the lake on a sunny day. Julia knew at once he was Michael, the church janitor.

Julia paused to check the peony bushes along the foundation. There were no flowers, but the buds were full. When she joined the chatting couple, Bridget introduced her to Michael O'Keefe.

"Pleased to meet you," he said, clutching his cap and smiling shyly.

Bridget plunged into an energetic explanation of Michael's visit. "Himself has stopped by on his way to the store. He's buying a trowel for the church. He's planting petunias and himself broke the handle right off his other one. Mary isn't home, or 'tis there Michael would be passing his time, I'm thinking. I saw Mary leaving to walk her cats some time ago. Herself will be coming back soon."

"Are you from Chicago, Michael?" Julia inquired.

"I was borned here twenty-four years ago, and my parents were borned in Ireland," he said. "My mama and papa and two sisters live on the West Side."

Bridget's eyes shone on Michael. "It's proud themselves must be, and you working for a priest."

"I didn't always work there. I was in California for a while, lookin' for gold."

Julia was curious. "Did you find any?"

"Enough to get by on, but no great amount. It's a different place out there. I seen trees with trunks as big as a man's house. They stretch right up to heaven."

"Saints!" Bridget exclaimed. "Myself would be giving anything to see such a tree."

He smiled down at her. Julia couldn't help noticing the affection in his eyes—a protective look, as if he felt responsible for Bridget. "There were whole forests of them trees."

"Saints!"

"Why did you leave the West?" Julia asked.

"I had an experience with Christ and wanted to come back and serve the church. I ain't got much training, but I can be a janitor and serve God."

Julia was curious about his experience, but said no more. Perhaps it was too sacred to discuss. Instead she asked, "Do you live at the church?"

"Yes, in a little room. I take my meals with Father Purcell. I've got a good bed, and Father gave me a glass-covered bookcase. I ain't too educated, but I like to read."

Michael looked over at the peony bushes. "I saw you checkin' them. They'll be out anytime. When the buds get real full and sticky like that, it's about time for them to burst open."

Bridget looked at him, trying to hide the admiration she felt. Julia noticed and excused herself.

A few minutes later Bridget stormed into the kitchen, Chester at her heels. The dog, having transferred his allegiance from David to Bridget, followed her everywhere. Chester was a thinner, sleeker, handsome animal now—and more obedient. Since Bridget's arrival, he had scattered the Cullens' trash only once. "It's mad I am," Bridget declared. "Michael O'Keefe is bolder than an Englishman!"

"He seemed quite civil, very pleasant, I thought," Julia responded.

"Holy Mother— himself is a devil! Mary is loving him and himself is having the nerve to ask me to the park next Sunday. I told him to keep off me. Invite Mary when herself is back with the cats, I said. Let it not be said he came to invite Mary, he said. I told him that Bridget Boland is no siren. I'm a good honest girl from Dunquin, I am. Himself said Mary shouldn't be liking him. He never led her on a bit, he says."

The sparks left Bridget's eyes, and she gave Julia a helpless look as she twisted her apron in frustration.

"Do you like him, Bridget?" Julia asked.

"Mary is me friend," Bridget whispered softly.

"But you said he doesn't care for her," Julia stated.

"Herself will be thinking I'm stealing him. Sure, she won't like being me best friend."

"Then you won't accept Michael's invitation?"

Bridget didn't answer. Instead she turned from Julia, opened the flour bin, and prepared to bake a cake. Julia didn't press her for an answer.

The next morning Julia was amazed at how distracted Bridget seemed. Her bread ballooned beyond the sweet stage and became sour. Attempting to sweeten it, she kneaded in saleratus and created a mess— five loaves with green streaks. Neither Julia nor Chester could eat it. Dust coated the furniture because she forgot to cover it before sweeping the parlor. Her shoulders drooped as she went about her work. When her sleeve ignited on the cookstove, she told Julia it wasn't because she was thinking about Michael O'Keefe. When she dropped the iron on the kitchen floor, Julia heard her exclaiming to Chester, "I like himself, I do! Oh, God, forgive me for caring for him!"

Later that day Bridget looked up from the stove as Julia entered the kitchen. Chester was at Bridget's heel, where he had been since she'd confided in him. "I won't be walking in the park with Michael O'Keefe," she declared emphatically. "Bridget Boland is not a traitor! I'll be after keeping off from him, I will!"

Julia sat with her feet propped on her old bed as she visited Melinda a few days later. Melinda was searching for a dress to wear to dinner at Julia's house. Charlie had finally accepted Julia's dinner invitation and would be there at six. To Julia it appeared a unique coincidence that the closings on David's lumberyard and Charlie's butcher shop occurred the same day. It seemed to connect Charlie and Melinda's family, and Julia wondered if it presaged a further connection of marriage. Melinda had said Charlie's favorite foods were a joint or roast of beef cut by himself and bread spread with fresh butter. Melinda had delivered Charlie's meat, seven pounds of beef wrapped in white paper, to Bridget earlier that afternoon. Bridget planned to bake bread, and Julia had asked David to buy dairy butter on the way home. She had also asked him to buy some arsenic. Rats had gotten into the grain bags in the stable. They bred under the wood sidewalks and were a constant nuisance to Julia.

Melinda turned from the wardrobe. "It really angers me that Charlie charged you for the roast. After all the cooking and shopping I've done for him! I know the meat is for you, but that makes no difference. He's eating it too! He did sell it at cost—and, would you believe, he smiled at his generosity!"

"I don't mind paying," Julia assured her. "What are you going to wear?"

"I don't know yet."

"How about the gray silk dress with the lilac piping and fringe? Gray looks good on you."

"I suppose," Melinda said glumly. She looked ruefully at Julia and attempted a smile. "Look, I have to be cheerful. I want dinner to go well. After all, I asked you to invite Charlie. I just won't think about the beef, or my feelings for him. I'm anxious to hear your opinion of Charlie—later."

Julia laced Melinda in her corset and adjusted her overskirt, positioning the bustle correctly. Then lifting the curling iron from the coal box, she rolled up a strand of Melinda's hair. "Don't make the curls too tight," Melinda cautioned. "I don't like that tight look anymore."

Melinda was facing Julia's old bureau. "I know I shouldn't have, but I looked in your bureau to see if Arthur's letters were still there. I thought you planned to throw them out."

"I couldn't. I suppose I'd feel lost without them. They're a comfort—security. I don't read them . . . I just like knowing they're there."

Melinda's brow creased. She didn't say anything and Julia appreciated that. Julia wished she understood herself better. Of course Arthur wasn't security to her; he had, in effect, abandoned her. But the words in his letters were eternal and—she didn't have a love letter from David.

Julia finally broke the silence. "What do you think David did with Diane's letters?"

"I think he burned them."

"I think so, too."

When Julia finished Melinda's hair, she retrieved Arthur's letters from the bureau and began placing them in a box. Working methodically and unemotionally, she finally dropped the last letter in, picked up the box, and carried it to the fire pit in the alley. As she held a match to the letters and watched the flames consume the content, for some inexplicable reason she felt great loss and she sobbed. "There," she said through her tears, "I've done it. I must cut all ties to Arthur." Returning to the house, she sighed with relief. She knew she had done what was right.

Melinda accompanied Julia home, bringing a satchel with her, for she planned to spend the night. Charlie was prompt, but David was two hours late. Julia had been frantic.

Julia, wild-eyed, met David at the back door. When she saw he wasn't ill, didn't appear hurt, and the buggy wasn't damaged, she exploded. "How could you forget Charlie's here for dinner! Bridget's cooked scalloped oysters for the second course. Now they're ruined—tough as leather! She's been crying. Melinda's in the parlor trying to entertain Charlie while Bridget and I salvage the dinner. The roast is dried out too. The potatoes are a mess. David, what happened? Where were you? Did you bring the butter? Or did you forget that, too? Charlie is awful, just awful! Wait until you meet him."

"Haven't I met him?" he asked, dismissing her tirade.

"No!" she sputtered, her eyes flashing.

Julia wiped her hot face with her dress sleeve and studied him minutely. He looked lost in another world. The collar above his beige cravat was damp and limp. "I forgot the butter," he said vaguely.

"David, what's wrong? Did the closing go badly?"

"I'm sorry, I'm late. The closing—" He paused. "Father signed the deed and bill of sale. He questioned my ability to manage the yard in front of the bank officers . . . a very difficult experience for me. I left the bank immediately after the closing and went to my office. I tore the calendar prints off the wall. You've seen them, Chicago scenes. Those prints were markers. They reminded me of my Father—how I had endured working with him, trying to please him. I ripped up each print and threw them all in the trash. I thought I'd feel better, but I didn't feel the freedom I had expected. I'll be bound until I earn my father's respect, I guess."

"Oh, David!" Julia cried, putting her arms around him. "I'm sorry! How horrible I've been! I'll understand if you want to skip dinner. We can manage—really." She felt the heavy beating of his heart as she held him close.

Placing his hands on her shoulders, he looked into her eyes and said quietly, "It's all right. I'll have dinner with you."

"Where have you been?" she asked.

"Walking."

"Where?"

"I . . . I've just been walking," he answered hesitantly.

"David, don't you know where?" She studied his face, perplexed.

"Yes, but I'd rather not talk about it now," he responded.

He stepped back from her, the lost expression still on his face. She almost hated his father. "I'll wash up and be with you in a minute," he stated.

When Julia and David joined their guests in the parlor, they found Charlie speaking rapidly. Melinda's eyes sparked with relief at seeing them.

Julia introduced Charlie to David. Charlie jumped up and pumped David's hand. "Please to meet ya!" He was a plump young man with dark hair and a full beard, wearing a suit that fit him like a sausage skin. His cheeks were puffy, initially giving Julia the impression of softness until she saw his hands. They were wide, strong; even though three fingers were missing, they were instruments suitable to his occupation. A faint odor of meat hung about him.

Before Julia left the parlor to help Bridget, Charlie had related butchering and meat market information to her, leaving no details to the imagination. As she left, Julia heard Charlie remark, "I'll have a pork-cutting business on the side as well."

Bridget served the salvaged meal with proper grace, in spite of its condition. Surprisingly, Charlie didn't comment on the shriveled roast, but he did give Bridget an accusatory look.

"I closed on my market this morning and opened up this afternoon," Charlie informed David. "I'm located on State Street, near the bridge, one of the best locations in town. Already I've had fourteen customers. I'm offering free pickles to customers, as a business promotion. I'll deliver to any area of town. The lady of the house doesn't have to be home. I'm having a service where my driver will leave meat in an icebox on the porch. We'll give credit if necessary—it's giving credit that made Potter Palmer one of the richest men in Chicago. I have the best meat in town; nobody trims off more fat and bone. My scales are honest and I don't hold my finger down. I sell nothing but healthy meat; you'll find no rotten or diseased carcasses in my shop."

Julia looked sternly at Charlie, trying to warn him to keep unpleasant details from his dinner conversation, but his eyes swept brightly past her. Charlie continued. "I've got my knife collection in the store window, and I think it makes an attractive display. I became interested in knives through working with them in butchering. I have several machetes from Mexico which are, by the way, quite handy for quartering chickens and geese." He raised his arm and sliced it down. "One good swipe across the breastbone and you've got her in half—then another through the breast and thigh and she's in the neatest quarters you've ever seen. I suppose you're wondering why I won't quarter pigs with a machete to save time. You see, they have a strong backbone and the machete bounces—"

"Charlie," Julia interrupted, when she noticed Melinda turning green, "you must tell us about your family."

Switching from one subject to another, like pressing a button, Charlie replied. "It's just my crippled mother and me. She had an accident downtown—a cornice fell off a bank building and crushed her foot. She sued, but we had a bad lawyer and got practically nothing. She was left with a dragging foot. It's getting worse now that she's older and arthritis has set in. Before Melinda started helping, Mother was always after me to shop and cook. I would have moved out except I've got my sense of responsibility. I don't know what I'd do without Melinda."

Julia frowned, unhappy that Charlie's mother had prevailed on Melinda's kind nature to do much of her shopping and cooking.

Charlie avoided Julia's apparent disapproval and smiled appreciatively at Melinda, but she looked away, seemingly embarrassed at his uncouth manners. From then on she avoided his eyes, and adjusted her position so her arm wouldn't touch his. She obviously wished Charlie were somewhere else.

After dinner Charlie soon left, saying he needed to sweep out his market. Melinda, frustrated, refused his invitation to accompany him.

Later David worked in his study while Julia and Melinda visited in the guest room where Melinda was staying. Slipping a nightgown over her head, Melinda let the soft material swirl around her legs. It was lovely, but her mood was not. Turning abruptly to Julia, she snapped, "I know you despise Charlie! It was written all over your face!"

"Despise is the wrong word."

"He was crude. I was embarrassed. He's never been that loud—and boring. If I'd known he'd be like that, I wouldn't have inflicted him on you."

Melinda put on her wrapper and sat on the bed. She fished a bonbon from her satchel and swallowed it in one hard gulp. "I think Charlie's about to propose. It seems as if he's been hinting at it for days. I suppose having the market will give him the courage. I know he lacks propriety, so it really wouldn't occur to him to ask Father's permission." She stopped a moment. Then looking seriously at Julia, she asked, "What should I do? Should I marry him? Father would probably be pleased to have me situated. I long to be married. I guess I'll just accept if Charlie proposes."

Julia stared at Melinda in amazement. "What!"

Melinda licked a piece of chocolate from her lips, her eyes displaying misery and confusion. "His poor mother needs me. With his new business, Charlie won't have time to help her much." Then she broke down and began to cry. "Oh, Julia, I can't lie to you. Charlie's mother is a tyrant. She drags around the house and hounds him to do this and do that—mostly things she could do herself. She's not *that* crippled. She's very demanding to me too, and I really hate being around her."

"Melinda! If she needs extra help, Charlie can hire a servant!" Julia exploded.

"He needs his money for his business," Melinda replied, trying to justify Charlie.

"Well, he can just let some of it go! I'm amazed you feel so responsible." Julia stopped, musing over the situation.

Although any marriage was possibly preferable to spinsterhood, Julia hated to advise Melinda to accept Charlie. Julia feared Melinda would be destroyed if she were constantly subjected to Charlie and his mother's selfish demands. "You can't marry Charlie," she stated firmly. "He doesn't behave as if he loves you, and you don't love him, either. How can you marry someone you don't love?"

Melinda stared miserably into space. Finally she agreed. "I know you're right. I can't."

Turning from Melinda's problem to her own, Julia was conscious of her tight corset. It seemed tighter than usual, making breathing difficult. She doubted it was the dinner; she had eaten little of it. In reality, her waist wasn't larger, simply more sensitive to the binding corset.

Her mind dwelt on her number-one dread: her probable pregnancy. She thought she'd give heaven and earth if by some miracle it were not true. Should she be pregnant, she would even welcome a spontaneous miscarriage. The blood rushed to her head as she realized she might help a miscarriage occur. She had heard that tight lacing could cause a miscarriage. She could lace herself up like Nancy Smith at church, who pulled herself in until her waist was abnormally small. She was ashamed of the direction her thoughts were taking, for they amounted to contemplating murder. But was a fetus such as hers, surely no larger than a fingernail, human? Her hands trembled. Desperately needing to share her thoughts, she sat on the bed beside Melinda.

"Melinda, I think I'm in the family way. It must have happened on the honeymoon."

Melinda hugged Julia exuberantly. "How wonderful!"

"Melinda! You've forgotten that David doesn't want children now. I'm afraid to tell him. I don't know how he'll react."

Melinda didn't appear worried in the least. "Just tell him. Of course he wants children. Why, he'll be delighted!"

"He'll blame me."

"No—David's not like that."

Julia looked doubtfully at Melinda. Melinda's admiration for David blinded her to any fault he might have.

"When are you going to tell him?" Melinda queried.

"Maybe I won't have to," Julia whispered.

Melinda's eyes flashed in dismay. "What are you talking about?"

"I don't know!" Julia cried.

"Julia, something's going on in your mind. Tell me!"

"I was thinking I could be laced very tightly. I've heard—"

"Julia! A child is created by God!"

Julia sobbed. "I know that—it was just a thought. I don't know why I said it—I wouldn't hurt the child. Oh, God! What's wrong with me?"

"Nerves," Melinda responded. "You'd better tell David tonight. I'll be here—if you should need me."

Julia shook her head uncertainly. Then, having come to a decision, she kissed her sister and said decisively, "All right, I'll speak to David tonight."

Later that night Julia lay in bed staring blankly through the moonlit window. David was breathing heavily, about to doze off. If she was to tell him, she must speak now.

She bent over and kissed him, continuing the kiss until his warm lips responded to hers.

"Hmm," he murmured, putting his arms around her.

"David, I need to talk to you. But I don't—I don't know where to start."

"Just say it," he mumbled sleepily as he held her closer.

"I'm—I'm probably in the family way."

David didn't answer her, but she felt the snap of shock in his arms. *Speak!* she thought. *Say something!* She shouldn't have followed Melinda's advice to tell him. She should have let her shape reveal her pregnancy. Oh, what a fool she was! She could have used the next few weeks to win his love. Now she would have no chance to win it—there would only be tension between them. Her heart pounded. Her voice burst from her. "Say something! I just told you I'm in the family way!"

"Then you weren't careful," he said tightly.

Crushed, Julia sat upright and looked straight ahead. Tears fell, and she let them stream without wiping them. Didn't he care about her at all? If there were a way to end this conversation now, she would. One thing was certain, the moment it was over, she would join Melinda in the guest room. "I marked the calendar—nobody could have been more careful. It probably happened on our honeymoon. It's your fault," she added defensively. "You shouldn't have left everything to me. You should have taken some responsibility. Anyhow, these calendar records aren't foolproof, I'm sure."

"Have you been to the doctor?"

"No, but I've got good reason to think I'm pregnant. I've missed my menses, and I haven't felt well."

"Maybe you're indisposed."

"I'm *not* indisposed! If I thought I were, I wouldn't have brought up this subject," she sputtered. "David, this is the last news on earth I want to give you. I remember how upset you were over losing your child—I know how you'll worry that I'll miscarry."

"When are you due?"

"January, I think."

"When do you propose to see a doctor?"

She couldn't stand another minute of this matter-of-fact conversation. She wanted to shake him and tell him to accept the child happily. She wanted to be pulled in his arms, to be surrounded by his joy. She faced him, hoping to see his expression despite the dim light. But the moonlight outlined only the rims of his dark eyes, giving them the appearance of black holes. "Soon," she said. "I'd see Dr. Scott right now if I could."

She started to cry again, moving to the edge of the bed.

His words came softly, swiftly. "Forgive me, Julia. Past feelings were confusing me. I'm pleased about your pregnancy."

"I want to believe that."

He reached for her hand. "I really am—come here." He pulled her down to him. "I hadn't thought I'd be pleased—but I feel responsible for the child. The child I lost is no longer the consideration."

Julia settled against his shoulder, her tears flowing harder now. He touched her cheek. "Don't you believe me?"

"Yes—I'm just happy."

"I'd like a boy," he said softly. "What would you like?"

"A boy—it would make up for not having a brother."

"Perhaps the boy will go into the lumber business with me."

"Oh, yes!" Julia cried, putting her arms around him. "I never thought we'd be planning like this—I'm so happy."

"But be careful, Julia. Promise you'll be very careful."

"I will."

"You'll see the doctor tomorrow—follow his advice?"

"Yes. But please don't worry. I feel certain our child will be born healthy."

The next afternoon Dr. Scott said Julia was probably pregnant. He prescribed a healthy diet, rest, a light corset.

That evening while Julia was reading in the sitting room, Melinda stopped by, her cheeks flushed and her eyes frantic. She paced the room, her beaded bag swinging from her wrist. "Charlie's at the meat market having a fit! He's hacking up chickens with his machete and might have an accident. He says he's all right, but I don't believe it. He's upset because I refused him. He's taking it harder than we thought. What should I do?''

"We'll send David over. He went to the office after dinner to work on books with his bookkeeper—let's go after him.''

"No, don't bother David.''

"He won't mind.''

"Oh, I suppose Charlie will be all right. He's a very experienced butcher.''

"So he proposed.''

"Yes—at his meat market. He said he was most comfortable there.''

Noticing her reticule swinging dangerously near a vase, Melinda sat down. "Charlie was nervous about proposing, but he was also in poor spirits. He had just received two carcasses of bad beef he has to return. He says there's no excuse for that with so many packinghouses in town. Oh, Julia, then he went into this horrible story about packinghouses— telling me how they kill pigs. I supposed he was nervous about propos- ing—stalling for time.'' Melinda looked horrified. "I've got to tell you. I have to get it out of my system. They hang pigs by their hind feet from two long rods and slit their throats—bang, bang, bang, one after the other, a dozen just like that. Some packinghouses slaughter a thousand hogs daily in the winter. They boil out a yellow lard for grease from the innards. Oxen are—''

"Melinda,'' Julia interrupted, "that's enough!''

"I'm sorry,'' she said crying "I'm just upset. It was awful when Charlie proposed. He took a diamond ring from a box, and I almost fainted when I saw it. You know how easily I become speechless. He was putting the ring on my finger before I found words to refuse it. He started crying on the counter when I told him no. He really loves me. I don't know if I can go through with this. He threatened to sell the market and try his luck in the West. He says his mother feels like I'm a daughter to her and her health will decline if I don't marry him.''

"That's a nasty threat, Melinda. He's trying to maneuver you.''

"I almost took back the ring. I'm afraid I might still break down and accept.''

Julia hugged Melinda. "Melinda, you don't love him. You'll be over this in a few days—but if you marry him you'll suffer all your life.''

Melinda raised her head, her eyes filled with tears. "I couldn't be strong if it weren't for you.''

Julia would rather Melinda hadn't said that. "You did what you had to do. It'll be all right.''

Nine

That morning as Julia and Melinda walked along the circular drive to Lakeside to see Nelda, the air and earth seemed filled with locusts, now at their peak. Brushing a locust from her arm, Julia turned to Melinda and remarked, "You seem happier today."

"Oh, I am! I was feeling so bad about rejecting Charlie's proposal, but yesterday I received a letter from a publication." She went on to share that *Godey's Lady's Book And Magazine*, the leading women's periodical in the country, had purchased her poem "Reflections" and scheduled it for publication in August. "I think of nothing else than being published!" Melinda exclaimed.

"Oh, Melinda, I'm happy for you," Julia responded joyously, squeezing Melinda's arm.

"You still have your subscription, I hope?"

"Yes. I'll buy extra copies, though."

"I hope Nelda will respond to us today," Melinda said, changing the subject. Disturbed over her transfer, Nelda had been comatose on their previous visits and hadn't so much as blinked to acknowledge them. Julia suffered over Nelda's condition.

Finding the attendants occupied, Julia and Melinda sought out Mr. Huntly. He was on his way to see Nelda, so they followed him along the north wing to her room. There were six women patients in this wing, nine men patients in the other. The heavy, metal-lined doors along the hall each contained a small barred hole for viewing. Through one door, Julia could hear the lovely lilting sound of a soprano voice. It broke off abruptly, and she wondered who sang it, and why. Through another door she heard muttering and thumping. *Poor thing!* she thought. Mr. Huntly strode quickly, his large key ring rattling in his hand. Melinda's full-length corset and tight lacing caused her to take sharp little breaths as she sought to keep up with him. Julia managed better in her lighter corset. In fact, she hadn't breathed so freely since she was sixteen, when she began wearing the heavier one.

Mr. Huntly stopped at Nelda's door. "Nelda has not improved," he stated, "but she hears you, and I must warn you to guard your conversation. Make remarks of a general nature—about the weather, the lake, her room. Don't mention her mother or aunt, as she will become further melancholic. But don't be discouraged. It's natural for patients to have difficult adjustments."

"I brought Nelda some candy. Is that all right?" Melinda asked.

"Yes, but she probably won't eat it. We're still having to force feed her." He unlocked the door, removed a key from his ring, and handed it to Melinda. "Please lock up afterward."

Melinda stared after the tall, stiff frame moving quickly down the hall. He looked quite fashionable in his two-button frock coat and Albert watch chain. "He's rather interesting looking," Melinda said. "I like the authority in his eyes."

"I think he is a bit too authoritative," Julia said.

"But he seems kind too."

"Yes," Julia agreed.

Melinda and Julia entered Nelda's room. It was cheerful but plain. Julia knew from reading about other institutions that Nelda had a superior situation here. The walls were painted soft yellow and the floor was of polished parquet. Mr. Huntly had explained that carpeting was impractical for this type of care. Julia was glad the barred window was covered with a bright cotton curtain. On the wall hung a landscape of a wheat field, which Mr. Huntly said was donated by a women's society. There were no gas fixtures. At nightfall an attendant brought in a lamp while she readied Nelda for the night, then removed it when she left.

Nelda was tightly curled in a fetal position and still comatose. Her simple dress was carelessly arranged, revealing her blue-stockinged calves. For a moment Julia looked away from the pathetic sight.

Melinda adjusted Nelda's dress and sat down beside her. "Nelda, it's Melinda. I've brought you candy—chocolates from Winton Confectionary. They have the best candy."

Nelda remained stonelike.

Julia sat on the straight-backed chair. "Nelda, it's sunny outside," she said. "Open your eyes. Don't you want to see the sunshine?"

No response.

Julia and Melinda continued to carry on a one-sided conversation with Nelda until the effort exhausted them. "Let's go," Julia finally suggested. "She probably wishes we would leave. I can stand this only so long." Julia kissed Nelda's cheek where the sun fell on it; it felt warm and alive. Then she touched the shadowed skin on Nelda's forehead; it was icy.

Julia started for the door, then turned back to Nelda. She touched her shoulder and pleaded, "Nelda, please, please open your eyes. You can get well. We'll help you, but you need to try."

Again there was no response.

When they returned the key, Mr. Huntly invited them for coffee. Julia stirred in cream and asked, "When will Nelda come out of this? It's very difficult to see her so."

"I'd say in a few weeks, more or less, you'll see a difference. Then her moral therapy can begin."

He turned to Melinda and seemed to be studying her. His expression was somber, unsmiling. Julia hadn't yet seen him smile. Melinda blushed and lowered her eyes. "But you must both visit Nelda often," he advised. "You have compassion, and that will help her. I wonder, Miss Adams"—he hesitated—"I'm quite behind in my correspondence. My secretary left several weeks ago, and I haven't found a satisfactory replacement. The last time you visited, you mentioned writing poetry, and since you're experienced in writing, I wonder if you would consider secretarial work. It would require about twenty hours a week. I could offer you a salary."

"Why, yes!" Melinda responded eagerly. "It's the kind of work I'd love doing. Of course I couldn't take a salary. You have volunteers—just consider me a volunteer. When shall I start?"

"If you could come tomorrow, I would appreciate it."

"I can."

After Julia and Melinda left the building, they raised their parasols to protect them from the sun. Melinda leaned back against a column supporting the portico. "Oh, Julia! I'll love helping Mr. Huntly. I think I have good penmanship. You've heard of the new typewriters, of course. I hear they're difficult to use, but maybe one day I'll learn to operate one."

Julia smiled. She hadn't seen Melinda so enthusiastic for months. "I'm pleased for you. It would be good therapy for you now." Julia thought Charlie was too much on Melinda's mind. She knew Melinda often hurried past the meat market and glanced in to see how Charlie was doing. He seemed to be managing. He looked animated while serving customers, and his store was clean and well stocked. Julia had warned Melinda that Charlie would catch her spying. Now she hoped this new occupation would keep her from Charlie's market.

"Do you think Mr. Huntly's married?" Melinda wondered aloud.

"Somehow he doesn't seem the marrying kind. Most married men aren't as efficient and exacting as he."

"I think he's a bachelor, though that doesn't seem possible. Any woman would set her cap for him—he's so intelligent. His eyes are so bright and alive."

"Are you attracted to him?"

Melinda turned red and started down the walk, her parasol tilted forward. "Of course not! After all, he might be married. How old do you think he is?"

"Fifty or so."

"Why, I doubt he's over forty-five!"

"Maybe not. It's hard to tell with him. He looks as if he has an ageless face."

Melinda sighed. "Well, he's probably married."

Sunday afternoon Bridget entered her bedroom seemingly in shock. She was clutching the Bible Michael had just given her. When he offered it to her, she had been too dumbfounded to refuse. But it wasn't just the Bible that confused her; it was himself towering over her and looking so handsome.

"I'd like you to have one like mine," he had said. "I was hoping you'd like it." Studying the astonished look on her face, he added, "Forgive me if I'm giving you something you don't want."

"Thank you," she had said, reaching out her hand. *Saints! Why had herself done that?*

"Will you go boatin' with me this afternoon?" he had asked quickly before she had time to regain her composure.

She had thought: *Myself will never go anywhere with you, Michael O'Keefe! Quit off me!* But she heard herself say, "Aye."

"I'll be by for you at two," he promised.

Then he had shocked Bridget. "I read my Bible every morning and night," he confided.

Bridget untied her bonnet and sat on her bed. How dare Michael O'Keefe give her a Bible! Bridget Boland was a good Catholic girl and she didn't attempt to understand Scripture on her own. Father Brady back home discouraged the laity from Bible reading. She read her prayer book every night, as she ought. She said the five decades of her rosary every day, taking a full ten minutes, never slighting one decade. She would return the Bible to Michael when he called. And she'd tell himself to take Mary boating instead.

She touched the smooth, black leather and the gold-edged pages. She had never owned such a beautiful book. In fact, it was her first book. She sighed. "'Tis not harming a body to read one verse," she reasoned aloud.

Opening the pages to Matthew, she began reading chapter one, continuing until halfway through chapter four, where Satan tempted Jesus Christ.

She jumped from the bed in excitement. What a grand thing it was to read the Bible herself! Why it was like having Jesus Christ in her room. Let it not be said reading the Bible was a sin! Sure, itself was only a wee transgression.

Then she remembered Father Brady's position on Bible reading. She also remembered the Bible she dusted every other day on the center table in the parlor: itself wasn't read; it was always in the same position. The Gerards thought Bible reading was sinful, surely! Yet Michael read his Bible. To reconcile the differences, Bridget compromised; she would finish Matthew, then return the Bible.

When Michael rang the bell, Bridget hurried to open the door. She was dressed in a powder-blue lawn dress, her favorite of the hand-me-downs from Mrs. Gerard. It didn't have two skirts and a bustle, as was the fashion, but she was accustomed to plain dresses and loved it as it was. She opened her mouth to send him to Mary. But there himself was, his smile taking up her heart and his eyes sending sunlight into her mind. His suit of sooty broadcloth was neatly pressed, but shiny at the elbows and knees. He was strong, tall, kind, perfect. Bridget said, "Yes, myself is going, and that is that."

He stepped in, looking puzzled. "I never thought you wasn't."

"But Mary won't be liking it. Herself is waiting for you to court her."

"Mary ain't my kind of girl."

"Herself is thinking she is."

"We'll figure that out later. Take a light jacket. It's sometimes cold on the lake."

Bridget ran upstairs for a jacket, giving herself a quick look in the mirror before leaving her bedroom. She had a heap of freckles from hanging the laundry, but saints, she didn't look too bad!

They rented a rowboat at the Michigan Avenue Boathouse. Determined to enjoy herself, Bridget suppressed her guilt feelings about Mary. The water was choppy, but being a fisherman's daughter fit her for rougher water, by far. The sky was overcast, and the gulls gave the dimension that separated the gray lake from the sky. Bridget watched a herring gull skim the water, either scavenging or searching out a marine animal. Tall granaries, the Illinois Central depot, and an anchored schooner with its sails furled were behind her. Before her was a thin line of smoke from a steamer on the horizon.

"Is it big fish the fishermen be catching on this sea?" Bridget asked.

"They catch lake trout and whitefish—many other kinds."

"Me papa caught sea trout and I'd like to be tasting these lake trout. I never will though, because Mr. Gerard isn't liking most fish. Himself only eats oysters and shrimps. Mrs. Gerard is liking fish, but she respects his tastes."

"You could come to dinner at my parents'. My mama would cook lake trout for you."

"Wouldn't that be grand!"

He smiled; in all Ireland she hadn't seen a smile like that. The only thing wrong with Michael was his birthplace. She would far rather he were born in Ireland, preferably County Kerry.

"Do you like being a servant girl?"

"More than anything in the world, except I miss me family. Me sister Maury just wrote she'll be going into service here when herself is eighteen. Me mama won't let her go afore that. Mama is sad us girls is immigrating, but we have to be helping her and Papa. I'm living for the day Maury comes."

Michael balanced the oars on the gunwale, and while they drifted, Bridget's concern suddenly manifested itself. "Is Father Purcell knowing I have a Bible?"

"Yes—I asked his permission. He doubts you'll read it much. He don't think anyone but priests can understand it. He don't think I understand it, but I do. He ain't happy to have Catholics reading Bibles too much. He's afraid they'll get heretic ideas—like Martin Luther."

She heard the splash of fish jumping nearby, but kept her concerned eyes on Michael. "In Ireland no Catholics is reading Bibles."

"If you don't want it, I'll understand," he said gently.

"Myself is wanting it!" Sure as long as Father Purcell gave permission, it was best to keep it, she decided.

Michael rowed parallel to the shore, pulling leisurely on the oars, while Bridget ran her finger through the cold water. He was quiet, his eyes thoughtful, and when he spoke his voice was hesitant. "I ain't liking to be personal, but I need to ask. Are you a Christian?"

"Since I was born."

"That ain't possible. A person ain't born Christian."

"Let it not be said that Bridget Boland isn't Christian! The Bolands is being Catholics in Dunquin all their lives, and not one of them is a 'Souper.' "

His eyes looked disturbed—blue-gray, picking up the tint of the lake. Bridget no longer felt comfortable with him. He said, "The Bible says I can't court a girl that ain't Christian."

"Myself is a good Christian, I am. All good Catholics is."

"Some Catholics ain't Christians."

"Holy Mother! It's wrong you are!"

"I guess you think Protestants can't be Christians."

"Aye." Finally Michael O'Keefe was sensible, she thought. "Though it's sorry I am for Mr. and Mrs. Gerard. I'm hoping themselves convert."

"Protestants can be Christians," he stated firmly and quoted the Bible. " 'For there is no difference between the Jew and the Greek: for the same Lord over all is rich unto all that call upon him' " (Rom. 10:12).

"I never heard the like of it!"

Michael continued. " 'Behold, I stand at the door, and knock: if any man hear my voice, and open the door, I will come in to him, and will sup with him, and he with me' (Rev. 3:20). 'For God so loved the world, that he gave his only begotten Son, that whosoever believeth in him should not perish, but have everlasting life' " (John 3:16).

Bridget thought Michael was in danger of excommunication. She grasped the gunwale to keep from leaping to her feet as she spoke. "Saints! The 'all' and 'whosoever' yourself is naming is the Catholic."

He quoted the Bible again. " 'As it is written, There is none righteous, no, not one' (Rom. 3:10). 'For all have sinned, and come short of the glory of God' " (Rom. 3:23).

Michael explained, "Everyone has sinned; everyone needs Christ to save them—the Catholic, the Protestant, anybody in the world."

The sky darkened and the wind picked up, rocking the small craft. Michael rowed quickly toward shore. *Saints*, she thought in dismay, *if only Michael were a regular-thinking Catholic man!* She could die, herself wanting to love him so. "You're a heretic, you are!" she declared. "Let you be living through the potato famine and see if you'll be thinking Protestants are Christians! Let you be hungry like me family. The Protestants starved me two oldest brothers to death, and me family is still grieving."

"I'm sorry about your brothers, but that don't change God's truth. I apologize for takin' you boating. I thought you was a Christian—there's just something about you."

Bridget forced back tears. Himself was crazy, he was. Let Mary have him! Let the other girls in the parish have him! Let Mary marry him!

"Don't be telling Mary I was with yourself. I won't be losing me best friend over you."

When she returned home, Bridget met Julia in the kitchen. Julia was fixing tea, and a pillowcase she was embroidering lay on the worktable.

"Itself is a pretty thing," Bridget complimented her. Then she could no longer stop her tears.

"What's wrong?" Julia asked tenderly.

"Oh—it's upset I am because of Michael O'Keefe. Himself is saying I'm not a Christian, and myself is!"

"Of course you are. You're a good person and a hard worker—you're doing a lovely job here. Be patient with Michael. After all, he works in a church and is likely to have strong views. Try not to discuss religion with him. Mr. Gerard and I seldom do. It only causes trouble."

The advice came too late, Bridget thought sadly.

That evening David started building a cradle from specifications he had drawn, and Edith arrived to invite Julia to church.

"I can't go—please stop inviting me. I told you before I won't go to evening services when David is home."

Edith had left the front door open and Julia waved at Morton and Freddie in the buggy. David had asked Julia not to tell Mother Gerard she was pregnant; because Alma tended toward overexcitement, it was best she didn't long anticipate the child. Julia decided to tell Edith, for Edith would be miffed if she weren't informed immediately. "I have good news. I've been to Dr. Scott. I'm probably in the family way."

Edith folded Julia in her arms and pecked her cheek. "Well, I must say I'm glad you took my advice to have children. Obviously things have finally quieted between you and David. Now, drink lots of milk. Don't move any heavy objects or stand on ladders. Eat strong meat, but not too much of it. Don't sit in stuffy rooms or breathe vitiated air. Keep an even temper and give David his way in everything, as I do with Morton. Otherwise he'll be jealous of the child and cause you no end of trouble. Well, I must go."

Julia waved after the buggy, smiling.

David called Julia to the cellar. He was wearing an old pair of railroad trousers, a muslin shirt, and his face had a stubble of beard. He looked content and rather eager. To have good light, he had lit two oil lamps. There was a stack of top-grade walnut in the corner. David held up a piece he had cut for the side of the cradle. "It's three feet long. Is that long enough for the baby?"

"Yes, I think so."

"She'll rock smoothly. I'm cutting it out carefully. It'll be well crafted—I'll peg the slats and sides."

"I think the cradle will be beautiful—an heirloom, like the shawl," Julia assured him.

"You are being careful, Julia?"

"Very."

He laid his hand over her abdomen. "You won't feel the baby for months," she told him.

"I know, but this gives me a sense of him somehow."

Julia moved, planning to leave, but his hand caught her arm. His voice was so quiet that she strained to hear. "I—there is something that needs saying."

His expression was serious; his eyes sought her understanding. "It has been on my mind since our dinner with Charlie. I need to be honest with you, Julia. I was late for dinner because I was at Diane's."

Oh, God, help me! Julia prayed. The air grew hot and close.

"Father's remarks at the closing wounded my ego; Diane is considered rather outstanding by some and my association with her was once a source of ego satisfaction. I thought I needed her. I stood before her house for an hour. Her marriage was as profitable as she had hoped; her house is one of the largest on the North Side. I did a lot of thinking. She is so grasping, so materialistic—very different from you, Julia."

His hands grasped her arms so hard, he hurt her. *No! Did he want a divorce?* She couldn't control her ragged breathing. She wanted to run, unable to bear hearing more; but she didn't have the strength to free herself.

He didn't speak for a while. Then he said quietly, "I never really loved her—I needed her because of Father. *I love you, Julia.*"

There it was—suddenly! Not as she expected, but in the cellar with a stack of wood on the floor, the cheap oil lamps, and her not even thinking of love. His lips covered hers, warm and expressive.

He whispered in a voice heavy with emotion, "I think I've always loved you—though I didn't consciously know it. I remember the impact you had on me the first time I saw you at the charity ball in the Opera House. You were dancing the German with a wheezing old fellow. You looked brave and determined. You were like a breath of fresh air after my breakup with Diane. I regret that I haven't expressed this to you before. I didn't really understand my feelings until tonight. I know these last months have been difficult for you. Forgive me, darling."

He cupped her face in his hands. His eyes were open, alive; she saw the depth of his love in them. It didn't matter that he had married her on the rebound. She didn't even mind that he had gone to Diane's. She didn't care that he had waited until today to say he loved her. The only important thing was that he had actually said it. She felt lightheaded, miles from earth, and weak all over. Finally, he loved her. He loved only her! He didn't love Trina or Diane! He loved her—Julia!

She pressed closer and kissed him.

That night Julia lay awake thinking after David slept. There was a cool breeze blowing through the window, and she pulled a blanket over her. If it were not that David liked circulating air, she would close the window.

Her arm touched his arm, her leg touched his leg. How wonderful it was to feel him next to her. Her heart almost burst with happiness. His tender words of love rolled over and over in her mind. Finally he loved her!

But she had to guard David's love, she decided, for love wasn't necessarily permanent. After all, Arthur had stopped loving her the night she had compromised her standards. Then, too, David had stopped loving Trina and Diane. Their fates could befall her. She had to seek, earn, win more of David's love continually, for what did not progress, regressed.

She kissed him; his lips were warm and soft, but he didn't wake up.

In the morning at breakfast, Julia noticed that Bridget looked strained. Afterward Julia stopped in the kitchen to encourage her. Bridget was at the sink, up to her elbows in dishwater. What struck Julia most wasn't Bridget's long face but her silence; Bridget always sang "Kitty of Coleraine," or "The Battle of the Boyne," or some Irish air while she worked. The window was in front of the sink and Bridget was staring vacantly through it. Chester had his head on Bridget's feet. Rather than upset Bridget by mentioning Michael, Julia said softly, touching Bridget's arm, "Everything will work out."

"Did yourself hear me leaving for mass earlier?"

"Yes."

Tears escaped from Bridget's eyes. "At church Michael waved at myself from the churchyard and never came over. Himself let me walk into church all by myself."

"Give him a day or so to soften."

"Aye. Sure but itself is a queer hard day. Mary wouldn't walk to mass with me this morning. She heard I was boating with Michael from some servant girls who gossiped about seeing us. Herself will never speak to me."

"Would it help if I talk to Mary?"

"Would yourself?"

"Yes." Julia decided to share news that would cheer Bridget. "Bridget, I've been to the doctor and he thinks I may be in the family way."

Bridget wheeled around, patting her hands dry on her apron. Her face was radiant. "It's happy I am for yourself. Me littlest sister is two and myself has been longing to hold a wee one."

"The doctor isn't positive."

"Myself is."

"How?"

"Your eyes is after looking like me mama's when she is having a little one."

Julia saw Mary shepherding the cats with a broom, and she hurried outside. It was a golden morning, the grass sweet smelling from a bath of morning dew. The locusts weren't as loud or thick as they would be in the heat of the day, but there was a sufficient quantity to keep the cats pouncing and swatting. Mary told Julia she must watch that the cats didn't eat the locusts. "Mrs. Cullen only lets them eat table leavings. She says cats get indigestion from locusts, though I ain't sure of that. Sometimes they eat locusts before I can stop them, and they ain't been sick. It ain't right I've got to look after five cats. No other servant girl's got such work."

Julia nodded sympathetically. "Mary, Bridget's upset that you're angry with her. She considers you her best friend."

"She don't act like it."

"She didn't encourage Michael—in fact, she hoped he would court you. She waited a long time before accepting an invitation from him."

"Bridget talks all the time until she's got every man at church noticing her."

"She deeply regrets hurting you."

"Oh . . . well . . . I ain't mean or nothing, not like Mrs. Cullen. Oh, excuse me, Mrs. Gerard. It ain't fitting to talk against Mrs. Cullen— she'd have my job. But I'm mad at Bridget—I can't trust her."

"Bridget would like to explain."

"I ain't ready to hear her yet."

"Please give her a chance."

"Maybe—I don't know."

One of the cats had a locust between its teeth and Mary raised her broom and ran after him.

That night Bridget sat at the kitchen table, her eye on the back door, hoping Mary would come. To pass the time, she searched for the scriptures Michael had quoted. She found only one of them: John 3:16. After reading it several times, she admitted reluctantly that "whosoever" was any person. It was a fearful hard thing, she thought, that she couldn't share her opinion with Michael. But himself would never speak to her again, surely.

The evening, and the week, passed without Mary calling; Mary refused to look at Bridget across the back hedge, or at mass. Bridget continued to read her Bible nightly at the table with Chester's head on her feet. "Sure," she told Chester one night, "Jesus Christ is becoming real to myself. It's like himself is in the kitchen, I'm thinking."

The Sunday after the boat trip, Bridget stopped Michael in front of the church after mass. He was shining as usual, his red hair like copper and his eyes like blue stars. Her nervous hands would not stay still and she clasped them together. *Oh*, she prayed, *let me have the courage to be speaking*. "Sure it's nice today," she ventured.

"Yes, ain't it."

Saints, himself would think her forward, but she had to ask. "I . . . could yourself stop by me house? I've been studying me Bible and I'm having questions."

It was out; she held her breath, waiting for his answer. "Will two o'clock be all right?" he asked.

"Aye." She wiped a bit of perspiration from her forehead.

Bridget didn't change to her favorite blue dress, but kept on the brown striped dress with the high ruffled collar she had worn to church. She couldn't mar this serious occasion with vanity. In her bureau mirror, she noticed her eyes seemed dark and worried, and her skin looked as hot as when she ironed Mr. Gerard's shirts. She started to leave her room, then stopped to splash on just a bit of the rosewater Mrs. Gerard had given her.

She was waiting in the kitchen with her Bible when Michael arrived. She poured him some lemonade, then opened her Bible to John 3:16. She felt humbled, but had to be honest. "I looked over some pages in me Bible and I'm afeard I'm not finding any Catholics." She read John 3:16 with a thick brogue. " 'For God so loved the world, that he gave his only begotten Son, that whosoever believeth in him should not perish, but have everlasting life.' "

Bridget lowered her eyes. "Yourself is right. 'Whosoever' is anyone, not just the Catholic."

He smiled gently; she was grateful his expression contained no self-satisfaction. She continued with her question, certain he had the answer. "How does myself believeth on Jesus? I've been wondering all day."

"You ask Him to forgive your sins. You ask Him to take over in your life."

"Will himself do that?"

"Yes."

Bridget began crying. "Myself has too many sins. Jesus won't be wanting me. I've been hating Mary all week because she's mad at me.

Myself talks back to people and myself isn't always kind. I'm full of pride because I'm smart and quick."

Michael looked at her; he didn't smile. She feared she had shocked him, but couldn't take her eyes from his face. "Jesus died for you, Bridget. He died for all your sins. It ain't the righteous Pharisee Jesus justified, but the humble tax collector."

"What should myself do?"

"Just pray what's in your heart."

"Please forgive me for hating Mary and for being so prideful. Me life isn't worth much, but I would be pleased if yourself would have it."

Bridget looked up to Michael; his eyes were moist and shining. The house was quiet—like Chester's soft breathing at her feet. Yet she felt God's presence in the kitchen; she had never felt so close to Him, surely. "Is himself here?"

"Yes—in you."

He stood and lifted Bridget to her feet. He pressed her quickly to him, a brotherly hug, and she felt his wide chest against her cheek only for a moment. "I guess you'll need some Bible teaching," he advised.

"From yourself?"

"Yes," he agreed.

"Oh, yes!"

"Are you free most evenings?"

"Every evening, surely!"

Ten

hester was gone. On the last night of spring, just before the worst storm of the season, Chester had snapped his lead from his wire and left, taking three feet of chain with him. David, Bridget, and Michael had been searching for Chester over an hour. Julia stared out the sitting room window into the backyard. She watched the flame from the gas jet draw wavy images in the water sheeting down the window. Lightning forked, thunder crashed, and the wind howled around the house, rattling the shutters. The air in the room was oppressive, making Julia's head throb. This was no night to be out searching for a dog, she thought. Julia prayed that Mr. Cullen hadn't shot Chester. She would have checked there now, except, worried for her baby's safety, David had forbidden her to leave the house.

Thunder clapped, followed by the sound of footsteps in the kitchen. Julia met David, Bridget, and Michael at the back door. They had left their shoes on the back porch and were in their stocking feet. Strands of Bridget's hair dripped from beneath her soaked bonnet. She looked at Julia with worried eyes as she removed her waterproof cloak.

"Was Chester at the Cullens'?" Julia inquired anxiously.

"No," David replied. "We checked where they keep their trash, and the barrels weren't disturbed."

"It's me own fault," Bridget moaned.

"Mr. Gerard says it ain't your fault," Michael corrected her.

Bridget looked bleakly at Michael. " 'Tis me fault, I'm saying. Myself should have heard Chester leaving. We were studying the Bible by the back door, and it was near Chester, we were."

"You can't hear a chain snap," Michael insisted.

"Sure himself is tangled up somewhere."

Michael spoke firmly. "He's a strong dog—he'll pull off anything."

Bridget held her head in her hands and rocked back and forth on a chair near the table. Julia served coffee to David and Michael, but Bridget was so concerned about Chester that she wouldn't take any. As the others drank their coffee, Chester was the center of conversation. When Michael rose to leave, it was still storming, so David offered him a waterproof cloak to protect him while driving.

"You'd better go to bed," Michael advised Bridget. "I'm sure Chester will be here in the morning."

"No. I'll be listening for himself right here. When himself comes home, sure I'll be letting him in."

"Well, at least make yourself a bed on the sofa so you'll have some rest,"Julia suggested.

"Aye."

Bridget gathered her bed coverings and fixed a bed on the sitting room sofa. Finally, after a sleepless night, she saw the first gray light dawn. The sky was low, the air misty—silent. Bridget quickly dressed and borrowed Mrs. Gerard's umbrella from the hatrack. Slipping on a waterproof cloak and overshoes, she closed the kitchen door behind her. *There was only one place Chester was being—the Cullens'.*

Bridget slipped through the hedge to the Cullens' yard. It was cool, drizzly, the sky steel-gray. The house was dark. There were no trees, as Mr. Cullen liked open space, so Bridget had a clear view of the grounds. There was no sign of Chester.

She walked around to the back of the stable and found barrels lying on their sides with debris scattered all over. Bridget forced her eyes to look beyond the litter. Oh! There he was! She saw Chester's paw, stretched out as if he were sleeping. She dropped her umbrella and threw herself on his neck, but he didn't respond. He just lay stiffly on his side, his chain still on his neck. "Chester!" she cried. Then she noticed a small hole in this temple, like a harmless wound. She buried her face in Chester's wet, smelly fur and screamed, "Wake up, Chester! Chester, wake yourself up!"

Bridget didn't know how long she lay on Chester. When she finally stood up, the sky had lightened, though it was still overcast and drizzling. She looked around the side of the stable. The lights were now on in Mary's room and the kitchen.

The porch door opened and Mary walked toward her. "Bridget," she called.

Bridget couldn't answer.

Mary, under an umbrella, sloshed through the puddles in her over-shoes. The cats ran ahead, rounded the stable, and leaped at Chester. They sniffed and pawed at his fur. Bridget kicked at them. "Get those cats off me dog!"

Mary stepped up. "Cats don't stay off dead animals."

Bridget booted a cat and it flew through the air. "Get, get!" she yelled.

"I told you to keep Chester chained," Mary blurted. Mary's eyes begged Bridget to understand. "I warned you! Oh, Bridget! Last night I seen Mr. Cullen headin' across the yard with a lantern and a gun. I was at my window. Thunder had woke me. I can't see behind the stable from my room, but I was scared Chester was there, rummaging in the barrels. I almost know'd he was."

"Why didn't you come after myself?"

"Sure there wasn't time."

"Mary! There was being time!"

"It was late—the middle of the night. I was too tired to think. There was thunder all the time. I didn't know if a gun went off. I kept hoping Chester was all right."

The cats again nosed Chester. "Saints—if yourself isn't moving those cats, I'll be killing them."

Mary scooped up the cats and set them on the back porch. When she returned, she was weeping. "I'm—I'm sorry, Bridget. I'm sure Chester died right off and didn't suffer. I've been scared to come out. I was laying in bed, just scared."

"Oh, Mary, I'm not blaming yourself. It's me own fault."

Mary's eyes fixed on something behind Bridget. Following her gaze Bridget saw Michael. He looked sorrowfully at Chester and gathered Bridget to him. His arms pressed her tightly; needing the comfort of his strength, she clung to him, pressing her face into his shoulder. "Oh—oh," Bridget sobbed. "How did yourself know?"

"I ain't sure."

Bridget didn't hear Mary leave. But when she looked up she saw Mary's thin frame marching off. Mary turned for a moment, her face pinched and angry. Bridget knew the embrace had cost Mary's friend-ship, and that, along with losing Chester, was too much to bear. She hardly found the strength to say, "I'm going home, Michael. Would yourself be carrying Chester?"

Bridget hated Mr. Cullen. *Mr. Cullen hasn't heard the last from the likes of me,* she determined. *I'll get even with himself!*

Michael couldn't neglect his morning duties at church, so he left after bringing Chester home. Bridget and Julia watched while David buried Chester under the cottonwood tree behind the stable. Bridget stood rigidly staring at David's shovel. When he had laid the last clod of earth on Chester's grave, she took a little box from her pocket. Julia didn't realize what it contained until Bridget sprinkled the contents on Chester's grave. It was the sod she had brought from Ireland. She really loved that dog, Julia thought.

Julia led Bridget inside, brewed her a cup of tea, and sent her to bed. When the doorbell rang, Julia was surprised to see the Cullens standing there. Reluctantly, she invited them in. "Could we talk to your husband?" Mr. Cullen asked stiffly.

He was obviously nervous. He couldn't meet Julia's eyes, nor did he step any farther into the vestibule than was absolutely necessary. Mrs. Cullen was equally nervous. She clasped her hands together and cleared her throat. The couple appeared to be in their sixties.

Julia called David. When he entered the room, Mr. Cullen began. "I'm sorry I found it necessary to shoot your dog," he said. "But I had warned you about his behavior and I feel within my legal rights."

David looked levelly at Mr. Cullen; Julia realized he wasn't angry and had accepted the situation. "You were within your rights," he agreed. "I'm sorry he bothered you so often."

"I'm glad you understand." Mr. Cullen looked relieved.

"I do hope this won't affect our relationship," Mrs. Cullen addressed Julia.

Julia thought they had little relationship to affect; they had only shared an occasional greeting. "No, not a bit."

There was a shuffling sound at the head of the stairs. And as they all looked up, they saw Bridget. Her eyes were red and swollen.

"Could myself be saying a word to Mr. and Mrs. Cullen?" she asked.

"Yes," Julia agreed hesitantly.

The Cullens stared at her, surprised. Julia read their expressions: *Why is the servant girl wishing a word with us? Of course we've seen her in the yard patting the dog, but we aren't responsible to her.*

"I'm . . . I . . ." Bridget clasped her hands tightly. "I understand why yourself killed Chester."

The Cullens looked blankly at Bridget, neither comprehending her comment.

"Oh . . . well . . . I'm glad. Thank you," Mrs. Cullen finally said.

Bridget backed away and returned to her room.

As soon as the Cullens left, Julia hurried upstairs and knocked on Bridget's door. "Bridget, it's Mrs. Gerard."

"Aye, come in."

When Julia entered, Bridget was standing by her bed, ready to lie down. Her teacup was on the bureau, and Julia was pleased to see that she had drunk the tea. "I know it was difficult to say what you did,"Julia offered.

"Aye, but myself was wanting to," Bridget said slowly.

"Why?"

"Jesus asks us to forgive," she stated simply.

"Oh—well, yes." Julia was awed by the simple explanation. "But it *is* your own kind nature that prompted you, too."

Bridget's hand nervously played with the coverlet on the bed. Julia didn't pursue the subject any further, but her love went out to the servant girl. Julia knew Edith would disapprove of what she was about to do. Simple kindness toward servants was one thing, Edith would say, but affection, brotherhood—why, they were taboo!

"Bridget—"

"Aye?"

Julia spoke softly. "I'm very fond of you. You are special to me." Bridget blushed.

"If you would, I'd like you to call me Julia."

Amazed, Bridget stared at Julia. "In Ireland we never call our mistress by herself's first name."

"We don't here either—but I would like you to."

Bridget's eyes became round, moist. She said it hesitantly. "Julia."

During the next week, Julia noticed that Bridget tried to be cheerful; she sang Irish airs and greeted Michael brightly when he came for Bible study. Julia was surprised at their interest in the Bible, for she believed Catholics generally didn't read it.

Bridget had told Julia that Mary wouldn't speak to her, though Bridget had tried to make peace. Mary called her a man-stealer, a cheat, a loose woman, and refused to accompany her to mass—and looked the other way whenever Bridget was near.

One morning while Julia and Bridget made blackberry jam, Bridget told her she had seen Mary and Billy Williams airing the cats out back. "Saints, her eyes were fastened on Billy," she said. "Herself is in for trouble with his like. Sure there's one happy thing, though. With Mary liking Billy, she might forgive meself for having Michael."

"You like Michael a lot?"

"With all me heart."

"Where did Mary meet Billy?"

Bridget shook her head.

"He's not Catholic," Julia said. "Mary couldn't have met him at church."

"Himself gets around," Bridget said knowingly.

"David told me he had to fire Billy because of his belligerent attitude."

Bridget vigorously stirred the jam. "It's hard set himself will be to find another job, and him so cheeky."

"It's the bold that achieve," Julia asserted. "Like my sister Edith."

Bridget looked up from the jam pot and shook her head, withholding comment.

That same week Dr. Scott confirmed Julia's pregnancy. David and Julia celebrated the good news by going out for dinner.

Hours after the dinner, Julia lay in bed, frightened. An uncomfortable feeling in her back had awakened her. Now her lower back ached steadily and her nightgown felt damp. The lights of a ripe summer moon shone on the cradle that David had just finished and placed in the corner. Julia stared at it, thinking desperately, *Oh, I can't be miscarrying! It's only that I'm hot and perspiring.* But she didn't feel warm; rather, the night breeze was cool and refreshing. She determined to lie quietly and just wait. If she did, the pain would pass, she tried to convince herself.

Finally the pain subsided, and she no longer felt the dampness. She arose quietly so as not to disturb David and went to the sitting room and turned up the gas in the fireplace fixture. She saw a dark stain on her nightgown. *No,* she told herself, *I'm not miscarrying. The pain is gone and I feel fine.* This episode must be from bumping the wheelbarrow handle today while weeding the flower bed. She turned the gas fully up and examined her skin for a cut. The skin was clear.

She was fine—just fine! She tried to convince herself. Then she began to cry.

However, she remembered Edith had suffered a complaint during her pregnancy and, under doctor's orders, had been in bed four days. Because Edith never discussed female problems, she hadn't defined the complaint. Nonetheless, it was possible Edith had the same problem as she. If so, no harm had come of it. Julia felt reassured.

She didn't mention the episode to David in the morning, nor to Melinda that afternoon as they walked the few blocks to Lakeside. She wanted to forget it. The day was balmy, the sky blue, the clouds puffy— the sun a blast of golden light from heaven.

Today was Melinda's day off; she worked three eight-hour shifts a week. Mr. Huntly had invited them to swim any time they wished, so Melinda carried a satchel of swimming clothes. Julia had declined, however, since she couldn't swim while pregnant. She planned to visit

Nelda while Melinda swam. Melinda had learned that Mr. Huntly wasn't married, so had taken pains with her appearance. Today she wore a coral walking dress with lace on the bodice and open sleeves. Her hair was tied back in curls and frizzled at the forehead, a becoming style. "Do I look all right?" she asked anxiously.

Julia smiled. "Absolutely lovely."

"Not too fat? Does the lace widen me too much?"

"Not at all."

"I'd like to stop at Mr. Huntly's office first—before I'm mussed."

"Of course."

Mr. Huntly's office door was ajar, and Melinda tapped. Looking up from behind his desk, he waved toward the circle of chairs. The sun glaring on the lake through the window behind him strained Julia's eyes and it was difficult to see him clearly. His expression, though, was cool amidst the light, his smile mechanical. "We walked over," Melinda began.

"Ah, good."

She seemed lost for conversation after that. Julia was surprised he had asked them to sit down, for he, too, had nothing to say. He didn't even seem to notice Melinda's appearance.

Opening his desk drawer and removing an appointment book, he quickly leafed through several pages, then looked at Melinda. "You're working tomorrow, I see. There's a minstrel at Hooley's Opera House tomorrow evening. Would you have dinner with me after work and accompany me to the show?"

Melinda flushed and her eyes widened. "Yes—yes, I'd love to," she answered eagerly.

"All right. I'll pick you up at seven." Then glancing at Melinda's satchel, he said, "I take it you're swimming today."

"Yes, but we're visiting Nelda first."

"I'm about to leave for a meeting downtown. Alert an attendant before you swim, and he'll keep male patients from the beach." He handed Nelda's key to them. "Be sure and lock up and return the key to my office. You'll find that Nelda's doing much better now."

Melinda waited to speak until they were down the hallway, out of Mr. Huntly's hearing. "I never expected he'd ask me out, did you? What will I wear? My bright pink dress, I think. It's tight on me, though. But if I don't eat anything until then, it may fit better. You do like Mr. Huntly, don't you?" she asked anxiously.

"I hardly know him," Julia returned.

"But what do you think so far?"

Julia wished she could wholeheartedly endorse him, but his cool manner prevented it. In addition, he was too old for Melinda, she thought. Yet she did prefer Mr. Huntly to Charlie; and Melinda *was* happy—that was the only consideration. "I think I like him. But it does take time to know another person, Melinda."

They found Nelda sitting in her chair, dressed in a plain dress in the style of the sixties, without a bustle or the copious trimming that was now the fashion. Her hair was pinned in a simple bun. She stared at the floor and didn't look up at Julia or Melinda when they greeted her.

"I'm so happy you're up," Melinda said cheerfully.

"Yes." Though the response was almost inaudible, Julia was delighted. It was the first word she had heard from Nelda in this room. Nelda looked up and Julia noticed a bit of light in her eyes.

"I'm glad to see you're doing better," Julia encouraged her.

"I want to go home."

"You will. You must be well first. Melinda sees you often. That is helpful. Your mother and aunt come—I come."

"I want to leave. I don't like this place."

Julia changed the subject. "What activities are you doing?" .

"Nothing."

"There are many activities in the diversion room—cards, bagattele, chess. There are handicrafts—embroidery, painting."

"Why can't I go home?"

"Nelda, you aren't well yet," Melinda stated firmly but kindly.

Nelda pursued that subject, and when they left her, Julia felt depressed. But she reminded herself to judge Nelda against her former debility. Speech was a triumph! Movement a victory!

While Melinda changed in the bathhouse, Julia dipped her fingers in the water. Even in the hot sun it was cold. To Julia there was something foreboding about the lake: the cold surface water pictured the lake as a heart of ice. But the pale creatures of the sea swam in her, and the ships cut her cool surface, and the birds devoured her frosty food.

Melinda stepped out in a blue shirtdress worn over pantalets. The dress was piped in white and cinched with a white belt. Flung around her shoulders was a long cape to wear to the water's edge. Melinda tucked her hair under a net and pulled on swimming slippers.

Melinda was an expert swimmer; she had received instruction in Michigan on family vacations and had been a star pupil. Nonetheless, Julia said, "Don't go out as far as usual. You don't have to swim until you're out of breath."

"The lake is calm—don't worry."

"Why can't you swim parallel to shore?"

"Because I enjoy making distance."

Julia sat on a bench and held her parasol over her head while Melinda struck out in an even overhand stroke until her head was a dot in the distance. Julia felt the usual relief when Melinda turned toward shore. Stepping out of the water she removed her net and shook out her hair. The water had chilled her skin to a pale color. Julia handed her the cape and towel. "Will you *never* listen!" Julia scolded.

"I know what I'm doing. I've swum hundreds of times and I've never had a problem. I'm comfortable in the water. You're not, and so you don't understand."

"No, I don't!" Julia snapped.

When Julia returned from Lakeside, she entered the house through the kitchen door. Bridget was at the stove, and the rich odors of beef soup and freshly baked bread wafted through the air. Bridget lifted the kettle lid and peaked in the pot. Her face was hot and steamy. "It's hard set I'll be to make a better soup, I'm thinking," she said, pleased.

"It certainly smells good," Julia agreed.

"It's me mama's way of doing it," she smiled.

David entered the kitchen a few minutes later, home early. He smiled as he walked over to Bridget and handed her a wicker basket he was carrying. His expression was expectant.

Bridget moved aside the loaves of bread on the worktable and set down the basket. It wiggled and emitted scratching sounds from its depths. "I hope the gift doesn't come too soon after Chester," David said gently.

Bridget tentatively raised the lid. She lifted out a sable pup with silky hair and long, drooping ears. His coat was wavy, his ears curly. He stared at Bridget, his tongue hanging down. Bridget's eyes were wide and round. She held the dog out from her and stared back at it with delight. "Is yourself a spaniel?"

"He's a cocker spaniel," David affirmed.

"Myself never saw the like of a black cocker in Dunquin. Himself is a queer-looking thing, he is. But sure I am liking himself."

The pup licked Bridget's wrist, its tail whipped the air. Julia felt tears coming. "What are you calling yourself?" Bridget asked the dog.

"You're to name him," David told her.

"Then it's Patrick Boland yourself is being."

"That's a good Irish name," David commented.

"It's after me papa."

"Is it too soon for you?" he asked.

Bridget started to cry. "No, and I'm thanking yourself, Mr. Gerard. It isn't fitting you should be so kind to myself."

"Quite the contrary."

The pup nipped Bridget's finger, and she spanked his nose, glaring at him. "We'll have no more of that like! Let it not be said me dog is having bad manners. You'll be a proper dog or it's to the stable with yourself!"

Bridget tucked the dog in her arm and marched to the sink to pour him a bowl of water.

Julia followed David to the vestibule and put her arm around him after he hung his hat. "Darling," she said, "I've never loved you so much! That was a lovely thing to do."

June 30 was a Friday, a shining summer day with the scent of sweet grass and roses in the air. Melinda had just stopped by to rave about the minstrel and dinner at Henrici's: buffalo steak, a favorite of George's—she called him George now—and the most wonderful buttered clams in the world!

"Then you've stopped worrying about Charlie?" Julia asked.

"Ah, yes. Charlie will be all right. He has reserves; it requires backbone to buy and manage a meat market. It's doing well and he'll be happy—though of course I occasionally pass by to be sure."

The bell rang and a loader from the lumberyard handed Julia an envelope from David. Julia held it a moment, wondering why David had sent it.

"Open it!" Melinda coaxed.

Julia read aloud. " 'Father had an apoplectic stroke at work. Dr. Scott is treating him and we'll drive him home when we can. Will you meet us there? Mother will need you.' "

Julia was shocked. Edgar, though heavy, looked healthy—invulnerable.

"Oh, dear!" Melinda exclaimed. "Shall I come?"

"No, but thanks. Mother Gerard is so nervous, it might be best if only David and I are with her."

"I thought Mr. Gerard had retired."

"He has. But David said he often visits the yard. He watches the traffic on the river and walks around the piles of lumber. David thinks Edgar wishes he had part-time work, but it hasn't gotten to the point of Edgar asking. David understands his father's boredom, but he won't hire him. He couldn't work with him again."

Julia didn't have to wait long for a horsecar and she arrived at Alma's before David. *Everything seems so tranquil and lovely,* Julia thought, as she hurried up the front walk. The bright sun lighted the house and gave the peeling paint and sagging windows a cheerful facade. The front windows were open, and the tinkling noise from Alma's music box drifted out; it was Alma's treasure. Julia lifted her hand to knock, then hesitated. She hated to shatter Alma's world. Edgar was difficult, but Alma had said she loved him. If only she knew what Edgar's condition really was; she was reluctant to alarm Alma more than was necessary. Should she wait and have David tell his mother?

David arrived then, resolving her problem. She ran to meet him. Edgar and Dr. Scott were in the backseat of David's phaeton, and at once Julia realized Edgar's attack was severe. Edgar was slumped against the side, his face ashen. His eyes were open, staring blankly. The set of his mouth frightened Julia. His lips were pale, drooping on the left side. Saliva dribbled from his mouth and spotted his frock coat.

Alma came running from the house, leaving the front door open. Her eyes didn't leave Edgar's figure. Julia feared Alma would trip on the broken walk but she arrived at the buggy intact—and breathless. She leaned over Edgar and plucked at his lapel abstractedly. David placed his arm around her shoulders. "What!" she gasped. "What's wrong, Edgar!"

His speech was slurred, but understandable. "I've a headache—I'm weak. Get me inside."

"What happened?" Alma asked.

Edgar stared at Alma. He cursed.

"Father collapsed on the dock at work," David informed her.

While Dr. Scott drew Alma aside and explained Edgar's condition, David removed a wheelchair from the front seat. Then setting his father in the chair, he wheeled him into the house. Because Edgar was too heavy to be pulled upstairs in the wheelchair or be carried, David moved Edgar's bed to the back parlor. While David undressed his father, Alma sank in a heaving mass at the dining room table. Julia brought her tea and a chloral tablet. "Oh, Julia!" she cried out desperately.

"Try to be calm. Edgar's resting fine," Julia encouraged.

"Will he live?" Alma asked, almost frantic with fear. "Oh, Julia, will he live?"

"Yes," Julia assured her. She thought so anyway. But even if she didn't, she would say yes to calm Alma.

"His retirement caused this attack. He just hasn't been himself since then. After he quit working, he lost his will to live," she moaned, clasping her head in her hands. "Will he be paralyzed, an invalid? Most people with apoplexy are," she stated.

"He'll be fine," Julia assured, searching for other words of comfort. She had experienced no tragedy in her life, except her mother's death. She didn't remember the words of consolation, only the coffin in the parlor, the strange feeling of seeing her mother so still and white. "He'll be just fine," she assured again.

Dr. Scott prescribed continuous nursing care for Edgar, and suggested Alma's German servant Helga live in, which was arranged. He then left to secure nurses. He soon returned with two—Mrs. Reatherford, a sturdy woman in the prime of life, for the day shift; and Mrs Harper, a pale, timid woman, for the night shift. After giving the nurses their instructions, he talked with Julia and David.

Dr. Scott, an energetic man of about sixty, spoke solemnly. "We need to watch your father closely for a few days. There's danger of pneumonia, kidney trouble, heart complications—another attack of apoplexy. Be positive around your mother, and try to keep her from depression. Your father is losing muscular power and sensation on his left side, and I expect he'll suffer a degree of paralysis. I don't look for any aphasia—loss of speech. And I expect him to live," he finished reassuringly.

By nightfall Edgar had difficulty swallowing and could only sip water. His left side was becoming increasingly paralyzed, making any movement of his fingers difficult. His eyes were filled with fear.

That night in bed as Julia lay thinking, she knew David was awake, too, by the way he was breathing. In the darkness of the room, she whispered softy, "David."

"Yes."

"You must sleep."

"I should have hired Father," he said. "Mother says his retirement caused the attack."

"Of course it didn't! You know how your mother is. She says things from emotion that she doesn't mean at all."

His voice was rough. "Julia—when I said goodbye to Father today, I almost broke down. I thought of all the years I've sought his respect. This attack has given me an automatic superiority that I don't wish to have. I'm a man my father can envy because *he's* lost everything. It is grim to me. I've fought for nothing."

Julia clasped his hand. There was nothing she could say.

"Father wasn't always bitter and angry. I remember him as warmer when I was young. Mother said his first business partner swindled him and that is what changed his personality."

David doesn't realize, Julia thought, *that he loves his father.* She put her arms around him.

After a while he said, "I want you to be careful, darling. Don't be over at Mother's all the time. She has nurses to assist her. Remember you must save your strength for the baby's sake. We don't want anything to happen to him."

"All right, I will," Julia promised. She hadn't had any more problems since that first scare. Should she tell him about the bleeding? But then he'd wonder why she hadn't told him at the time. He would remember her secrecy after burning Trina's photograph and conclude she was never honest with him. Then, too, it was best he didn't know; he had enough to worry about now.

"I appreciate your concern for my parents," he said lovingly.

That was what was important—helping David, enforcing his love for her through her actions.

Edgar didn't die; he was a victim, he said, of his strong heart and constitution. He was partially paralyzed on his left side, his left eye was almost sightless, but he regained the ability to blink, swallow, and scream for attention.

On a bleak morning five days after his illness, Julia read a periodical to Edgar. The sky was milky-white, uncertain whether it would rain or clear up. Yesterday, the Fourth of July, had been a fine day and the fireworks had gone off magnificently at the baseball grounds. Julia saw rockets and heard bomb shells from Edgar's home. David offered to wheel his father to the window, but he declined, saying, if he couldn't walk to the window, he wouldn't be brought to the window. This morning as Julia read to him, he looked depressed and she doubted he was listening to her.

"I will *not* be an invalid," he said adamantly.

Julia lowered the periodical and looked questioningly at him.

"Alma is out of the room for a change—she clings like a shadow—" he stated, a wild look appearing in his eyes. "My pistol is in my bureau upstairs—it's loaded. This is a dangerous area of town and I have it ready for prowlers. Bring it to me, then leave me alone," he ordered gruffly.

Frightened, Julia shook her head. The periodical slipped from her lap, unnoticed. What should she do? Run for help? But she couldn't leave him alone. *Oh, David!* she cried inwardly.

Perspiration appeared on his forehead. "I said bring my pistol!" he yelled. "Set it on my lap. Leave the room and close the door!"

"No!" she declared firmly.

He lifted his head an inch from the pillow—a tremendous effort. "I am no longer a man, nor will I ever be! I will *not* be like this. You try and live with a paralyzed body. You look through my blind eye! You lie here day and night thinking. You try remembering how it was to walk and know you never will again. Try it, I say! It's fortunate I don't believe in God. If I did He'd hear from me! He'd not need another enemy!"

Julia stared at him in shock. She was surprised at her firm answer. "If you use that gun on yourself, you will kill your wife also."

He gave Julia a hard, steady look. He didn't speak for a while. Finally he conceded, "Finish the article."

As Julia read, her voice shook. She could *not* understand why God allowed Edgar to suffer. Was God indeed so impersonal that His universe was governed by cause and effect? No . . . she had to believe God cared; when man suffered, God suffered. But if God suffered, why didn't He intervene for Edgar? And for Nelda? She hardly knew God's character, she realized, even though she had attended church all her life. She didn't even know how to impart hope and faith to Edgar.

Then she remembered Bridget. She had faith.

"There is someone I'd like you to talk to," Julia said hopefully.

That afternoon Julia discussed Edgar's condition with Bridget and invited her to see him, to impart some hope. Bridget was outside beating the parlor rug. Leaning her wire beater on the laundry post, she looked nervously at Julia. "Sure myself will be going," she said slowly. "It's sorry, I am, himself is ailing, but himself is scaring me. 'Tis little I want to blacken himself, but when he ate dinner here, he looked big and mean."

Julia couldn't promise that the encounter would be pleasant. Then realizing she had imposed on Bridget, she stated, "You needn't go. I shouldn't have asked. He's the family's problem, after all."

"Myself will be going," Bridget declared.

That evening Bridget wore a dainty dress of pale yellow, another hand-me-down from Julia. It was a walking dress, raised to the ankles in front and long in back. Its sunny color flattered Bridget's fair skin. Julia noticed Bridget had filled out, and her figure, though still thin, was more feminine and attractive. Bridget carried a satchel in which she had put a loaf of Irish soda bread and her Bible.

As they entered the house, they saw Edgar propped on pillows, a light shawl around his shoulders. Alma sat in an armchair, knitting him another shawl. He had mentioned that a shawl gave the proper warmth, and Alma had determined to knit him a sufficient supply. She jumped up before Bridget and Julia could enter the room, ushering them to the front parlor. "Edgar said you were bringing someone, but he doesn't want to see anyone. Is Bridget the person?"

"Yes."

Alma had spoken slowly, as if considering the pronunciation of each word. She was exhausted, her eyes dazed behind the pillows of flesh her cheeks made. She hovered over Edgar, fearing he would need something the nurse would not or could not provide. During the night she repeatedly checked on him. Julia hadn't told Alma that Edgar was suicidal; she hoped Edgar hadn't either. "Edgar needs hope," Julia told her. "And I think Bridget can help him."

"I know he does."

Julia took her arm and led her to the sofa. "Please rest. We won't be long."

"Don't tell Edgar I gave you permission," she begged.

"I won't," Julia promised.

They found Edgar staring angrily at the doorway. His nurse was in the kitchen preparing a poultice, and he hated being left alone. Bridget stepped up to the bed and offered her hand. Julia couldn't detect any nervousness in her manner. "Mrs. Gerard asked myself to be visiting you. So myself is here."

"Get me some water!" he barked, glaring at her.

Bridget poured him a glass of water and held it toward him, but his right hand remained on the bed. Alma appeared in the doorway. "He doesn't like to hold anything," Alma explained. "We help him."

Bridget held the glass to his lips, and when he finished drinking, she asked sympathetically, "When did yourself get struck down?"

"I do *not* prefer to discuss my health with a stranger!" he snapped. "I'm a sick man, leave it at that. Sit if you must stay."

Bridget pulled a straight-backed chair up to the bed. Then taking the bread and Bible from the satchel, she said cheerily, "I baked this for yourself."

He looked miserably at her and the bread. Julia was losing faith that anything could touch his heart. Finally he said, "What did you bring a Bible for?"

"To be reading yourself something from God's Word."

"I don't believe in God; therefore I don't acknowledge the Bible."

Bridget stared at him in astonishment. "Saints! Sure God believes in *you*!"

Bridget opened her Bible to 1 John 4:9 and began reading, " 'In this was manifested the love of God toward us, because that God sent his only begotten Son into the world, that we might live through him.' "

"Poppycock! Get that Bible out of my room!" he screamed.

Bridget closed the Bible and placed it in her satchel. Then she stood up, ready to leave. He stared angrily at her. Suddenly the anger left and he looked pensive. "Do you really think God believes in me?"

"Aye."

"Poppycock!"

Julia and Bridget quickly left. Julia hired a hack, and while they rode she apologized to Bridget for the difficult visit. Bridget said, "If it would be all right, could myself be returning? Himself is no atheist, I'm thinking.''

"You saw how religion upsets him.''

"Aye, but himself might be needing upsetting.''

Perhaps she was right and certainly a relationship with God would help Edgar out of his depression. "Yes, if Alma will permit it, you may visit him anytime.''

Later that evening, hearing David's buggy when he arrived home from a business dinner, Julia quickly finished brushing out her hair. She had changed for bed, putting on a nightgown that David liked on her, and a silky wrapper. When his feet sounded on the stairs, she ran to meet him at the bedroom doorway.

He closed the door with one hand and embraced her with the other. While she helped him off with his frock coat, she asked, "How was the dinner?''

"Fine,'' he answered. "I'm hiring the man I ate with as a sales agent. He should work out well—I certainly can use him. This month business is up ten percent beyond the normal summer increase. I'm stocking more lumber than Father did and my ability to fill orders quickly accounts for the rise. Father had refused to tie up money in inventory; he didn't believe we could move it.''

Julia knew, considering Edgar's condition, David couldn't comment further on his father's mistake.

"I've decided to try to interest my father in estimating for me. He could do that from his bed. He needs an interest beyond himself.''

Julia realized the personal cost to David. "Yes, he does, if only he will do it,'' she agreed softly.

She then told David that Edgar had asked for his gun. David's face registered no surprise. "I might have done the same thing.''

"You? I can't believe that!''

She wouldn't believe it; David had to be strong. She counted on him to remain a strong refuge for her love. She didn't like to think that place of refuge was vulnerable. The thought of David being struck down appalled her. Would she love him then? *Yes—yes!*

But she couldn't follow this line of thought any longer. She didn't understand the implications, the path, the destination. "I suppose there are some things that can't be accepted,'' Julia added quietly.

Julia related Edgar's response to Bridget's scripture reading. "I don't think he's an atheist,'' David speculated.

"Neither do I.''

Eleven

*O*n Monday morning when Julia rang the brass bell on her night table for Bridget, the sound seemed strangely musical. She had slept alone. Last night David had boarded the Michigan Central Express for Grand Rapids. He would return Wednesday evening. She hated to be without him. Maybe that was the cause of her physical symptoms. She pulled the sheet up to her chin, soothed by the feel of the cool linen on her skin. It was not hot yet, though the bright sun and still air promised a scorcher. Bridget entered. "I won't be down for breakfast—I'm tired, a little indisposed," Julia explained.

Bridget looked concerned. "Can I bring yourself some hot broth?"

"No. I'll ring if I need anything."

" 'Tis better I'm not doing the laundry then. I wouldn't be hearing yourself from the cellar or yard."

"No, go ahead. I'm not exactly sick. If I lie here a while I'll be all right."

The door shut quietly, and Bridget's small feet tapped down the stairs. Julia wondered if she should call her back to have her fetch Dr. Scott. She had suffered cramps since midnight. However, she wasn't bleeding and the pain wasn't severe. This was a milder attack than the last, she reasoned. It too would pass. She thought about David again. The train wasn't due in at Grand Rapids until nine. She imagined him looking out the window at Michigan's flat, wooded landscape. He was probably tired. David didn't sleep well on trains; the berths were too short for him. Was he wishing she were with him? Was he thinking of her?

125

Julia stared at the cradle across the room. The open grain contained no knots or defects. It was an attractive addition to the room, but she wished David had left it in the cellar. *What if we never use it?* she thought, terrified.

An hour later pain was stabbing her in the back, striking so hard she felt disoriented. She rolled to her side and doubled her legs. "Bridget!" she screamed. "Bridget!"

She grabbed the bell and rang and rang it, willing Bridget to come.

The pain bored into her, and Julia dropped the bell on the bed. The sun struck her body, hard and bright. Perspiring, she threw back the sheet. Then she felt the other dampness.

"Bridget!" she cried again weakly. Julia forced herself to stand, her nightgown falling around her legs in bloody folds. Holding onto the bedpost to steady herself, she realized she had waited too long. *Oh— not this—not this!* she thought desperately.

Was Bridget in the laundry yard? In the cellar?

Bridget's room overlooked the laundry yard, and Julia staggered down the hall toward it. She prayed Bridget was hanging laundry. She didn't have the strength to go downstairs to the cellar door. She thought of David. Oh, how she wanted him with her! Oh, how she needed him! He would help her. *Oh, David, please, please come now!* she pleaded silently.

Finally she reached Bridget's room. She leaned on the windowsill. With relief, she spotted Bridget in the laundry yard, pinning a dress to the clothesline. "Bridget!"

Bridget looked up.

"Come, hurry!"

Bridget started running.

Julia returned to her bed. When Bridget entered, she looked pale, frightened. Running to Julia's side, she cried breathlessly, "Julia! What's wrong with yourself?"

Julia admitted the truth. "I'm miscarrying."

"Saints!"

Bridget quickly checked her and raised shocked eyes to Julia. "Yourself is bleeding bad. Should myself be getting Dr. Scott?"

"Yes!" she screamed as the pain intensified. Then, suddenly, it ceased.

Now the pain in her mind began, even worse than the physical pain she'd been through. "Oh, Bridget," she moaned, "I've lost his child!"

Bridget's eyes were dark and troubled. The evidence was there— only the size of her finger, and yet a complete human being with all the potential for greatness. A tiny life was ended almost before it had begun.

Tears ran down Bridget's cheeks. She covered the mass with the sheet. "Myself will be finding rags to clean up. And I'll be after something to bury the little one in. I'll send Mary for Dr. Scott, I'm thinking."

Julia held herself together with effort so that they could deal with her situation. "Let's clean up first."

After Bridget had cleaned the room and Julia was settled in bed again, Julia began to cry. How could the sun shine just as it had before—and the blue sky endure with the clouds scurrying across it as they always had, and always would? Had nothing changed? However, she touched her abdomen; she had never felt so empty.

Bridget touched her hand. " 'Tis a terrible thing what happened, but sure the little one is being in heaven."

"But—Mr. Gerard will wish him here."

"Aye."

"It's my fault I miscarried. I've had symptoms before. I should have gone to the doctor."

Bridget shook her head. "Let that not be said! Me mama had three miscarriages, and it wasn't her doing."

"I'm not telling David about it yet," Julia decided. "It would hurt him too much."

Bridget was bent over picking up the buckets, but she quickly straightened up with surprise at Julia's pronouncement.

"He lost his first wife and child in childbirth," Julia explained. Then suddenly Julia began to shake so hard the bed vibrated. Everything—the impact of the whole thing on David—struck her. "Oh, maybe I'll never tell him! Maybe I'll never have to. I can't hurt him. He'll think it's my fault. He'll wonder why I didn't see a doctor. I can't tell him. I won't!"

Bridget's eyes were round and troubled. "Himself should know."

"No!"

Bridget shook her head slowly, but didn't object further. "Should myself be burying the child?"

"Yes, please."

"I should be going for the doctor first, I'm thinking."

"Go yourself; don't send Mary. Don't tell her this. No one must know."

Bridget placed the fetus in a tin and wrapped it with her kerchief, the best pall she could manage in her haste. She set the package atop the cupboard and went after Dr. Scott. He found Julia in good condition, but exhausted; he ordered bed rest.

After Dr. Scott left, Bridget retrieved the tin, and it wasn't until she was outside that she realized she hadn't asked Julia where to dig the grave. She wondered if she should return and ask. No, it was hard set Julia would be to choose a burial site, and her so upset and weak. Bridget surveyed the backyard and picked the area behind the forsythia bush. Next spring when the bush bloomed, it would be a pretty bower for the grave.

It was a terrible thing that Julia wouldn't tell Mr. Gerard she miscarried. Things weren't right between themselves, Bridget thought. Bridget had heard fighting over Mr. Gerard's first wife that made her cry. Then, too, there was Mary's gossip about Mr. Gerard's veiled lady and Mary's opinion that Mr. Gerard married Julia for her money. But she mustn't judge the Gerards' marriage. She was just their servant girl and no more, even though she loved themselves. Her place was to guard Julia's secret, and to be praying for the Gerards.

Yet Julia's figure would eventually reveal her secret, Bridget mused. Surely herself realized that.

She picked up her shovel and began her sad task. She dug a small hole. While Bridget patted the dirt over the grave with the back of the shovel, Mary spoke from behind her. Bridget hadn't heard Mary approach and she wheeled around. "'Tis you wanting to scare a body to dying, sneaking up on them?"

"Why are you digging around the bush?"

"Myself just is."

"If you ask me you're burying something that silly dog of yours wrecked. Right! Ain't I right! I've seen that yappy little thing. He never stops chewin' on sticks. He looks like trouble to me."

"Me dog is a proper dog."

"Where'd you get him?"

"From Mr. Gerard."

"Oh." Mary lowered her eyes. Bridget thought Mary had suddenly remembered Chester.

Bridget hoped this visit meant Mary wished to resume their friendship. Nonetheless, Bridget couldn't pursue that right now; Julia might be needing something. "Myself is—"

Mary interrupted. She held her head up prouder than a strutting bird. "I've got a suitor—Billy Williams, your friend from the train. He likes me a lot. He don't speak well of you, that's for sure."

"Be careful of his lies. He's an awful liar." Bridget immediately regretted her comment. She stared at Mary and hoped this wasn't the end for them.

"Ain't you full of sour grapes! Billy's doing fine since he left Mr. Gerard. He's the gardener for a rich family—and let me tell you they treat him good. He hates Mr. Gerard for firing him. Mr. Gerard is a tyrant, Billy said. Mr. Gerard didn't have no reason to fire Billy. He just took out after him for not doing things his way. Billy says he'll get him for it. Billy sticks up for himself, he does. I'm sure glad I never took up with Michael O'Keefe. He's no prize."

"Where did yourself meet Billy?"

"At the place where he works. I was delivering a note from Mrs. Cullen to the owners. The Cullens is friends of Billy's people."

"Sure myself has to leave. Can I be walking to mass with you in the morning?"

Mary studied Bridget, taking her time in answering. Bridget held her breath. "I suppose. Come by at the usual time."

It was a hot afternoon two days later—even the flies on the side porch lacked energy. As Julia watched the insects dismally, she shifted in her chair, trying to find a comfortable position. The chair back was forged to resemble twisted roots and impossible to rest against. It was one of a suite consisting of a table, settee with rockers, and two chairs. She dipped a cloth in a bowl of ice water and covered her face.

David was due in from Grand Rapids tonight, but she didn't want to see him. Or anyone. Fortunately, no one had visited her since the miscarriage. Everyone seemed occupied with his own life.

The porch abutted the outside wall of the parlor, where Bridget was cleaning. Through the window Julia heard Bridget singing her favorite air:

> As beautiful Kitty one morning was tripping,
> With a pitcher of milk from the fair of Coleraine,
> When she saw me she stumbled,
> The pitcher it tumbled,
> And all the sweet buttermilk water'd the plain. . . .

Julia longed for Bridget's uncomplicated life. Bridget worked, studied the Bible with Michael, attended mass. *Oh, how I would love such a simple life!* she thought.

She began to cry. She should have consulted Dr. Scott at the first sign of trouble. Why hadn't she been able to face the meaning of her symptoms? If she had sought treatment, the child might still be alive. Probably the reason Edith had delivered safely was that she received treatment for her problem. Julia would never forgive herself. Neither would David; he'd charge her with negligence; and he certainly would love her less, she thought, as she began to tremble.

She remembered Jennifer Cummings at church. She had miscarried, but had become pregnant again immediately. How delighted Mr. Cummings had been when he announced his wife's second pregnancy. What if Julia followed the same course as Mrs. Cummings? Then when she informed David of the miscarriage, he wouldn't be bereft; he would have a child to anticipate. He would be tolerant of her negligence. He wouldn't love her any less.

Did she dare wait until she was pregnant again to tell him of the miscarriage? Was it the kind thing to do, or was it inexcusable deception?

She lifted the cloth from her head in time to see Melinda walking toward the porch. Melinda's parasol bounced above her head. She smiled, her cheeks flushed, looking as jaunty as her parasol.

"Would you like a drink?" Julia asked after Melinda was situated on the settee.

"No, thank you. I had iced tea at Lakeside."

"Did you see Nelda today?"

"Yes. She's doing much better, and is taking part in some of the games in the diversion room. I think she's more settled now because she's not asking to go home so often. I've just started working every day, doing bookkeeping as well as correspondence, so I'll see her as often as possible. Because it's so hot today George sent me home early."

Julia thought the work schedule would exhaust Melinda. But she realized her foolish managing of her own health made her a poor advisor, so she kept quiet. "Have you been out with Mr. Huntly?"

"Oh, yes! Last night we had dinner at the Tremont House. We had a wonderful time. He talked about his family—his grandmother. She was wealthy and it was her inheritance that enabled him to establish Lakeside. He's devoted himself to Lakeside, and that's why he hasn't married. He told me he was mistaken in not marrying—that a wife would have been a helpmate." Melinda turned crimson, asking, "Why do you think he said that? He also said he had his grandmother's engagement ring—why would he mention that? I don't dare think he's falling in love with me, but his comments lead me to hope. Julia, what should I think? David proposed to you after a short courtship. Is George about to propose?"

Melinda looked eager, nervous, her head tilted forward. "Oh, but he can't love me!" she wailed, shaking her head. "I forget how fat I am. He's often expressed his admiration for small figures. And he's never touched me—not even on the arm or hand. Of course, he isn't accustomed to touching anyone. Because he has to be authoritarian to his patients, he's had to develop an untouchable personality." She paused. "Look how David loves you now, and he wasn't so affectionate at first. Oh, Julia, there is so much to consider!"

Melinda moved forward on her chair, eyes round, worried. "Julia, give me your opinion. Will he propose?"

Melinda had presented too much for Julia to cope with today. She simply said, "I don't know. I do want you to be happy. Don't let yourself be hurt."

"I'm not—I'm dreaming, but I'm realistic too. Do you think he feels he's too old for me? He shouldn't—he's very vital, very progressive in his thinking and attitudes."

"I don't know," Julia answered, finding it difficult to concentrate.

"Edith likes him," Melinda continued. "She was at the house one evening when he called, and was quite cordial to him."

"That is a benefit."

They were quiet for a while with Julia lost in thought: *Tell Melinda what's happened to you; seek her advice as to when to tell David.* But Julia knew what Melinda would advise, so she kept quiet.

A few hours later Julia drove David's phaeton to pick him up at the Illinois and Michigan Central depot. The depot was on the lake, but the odor of cinders and smoke overcame the scent of water, the train whistles outcried the gulls. Julia was glad for that; she wanted noise and motion— anything to distract her from thinking about the miscarriage. It was difficult for her to look at him as he stepped from the train. His three- piece suit was rumpled, his boots polished. His eyes looked tired, so puffy, shadowed. He ran to her and caught her in his arms. He smelled like tobacco and cinders from the train, and she wept as she buried her head in his shoulder. Then silently they walked toward the phaeton.

"I missed you," he said as they were riding home. "At night espe- cially." There was such love and tenderness in his eyes, it made her throat ache.

She twisted her handkerchief. This was her chance to state why she had particularly missed him. *No, no!* she thought, as the dull clop of the horse marked time, *that is not best.* "I missed you, too," she said solemnly.

"Darling, you look lovely," he murmured.

"Oh, thank you, David." She found it difficult to look him in the eye.

"Did Father do any of the estimating?" David had left his father several plans to estimate, even though he refused the work. Invalids didn't perform work, he had said resignedly.

"I don't know. I didn't stop by," Julia replied.

He looked surprised at that, for she had been visiting frequently. "Can we stop on the way home?" Julia suggested.

David changed course, then said, "I'm continuing to build a sales staff. I hired a sales agent to do traveling—a man who will move down from Grand Rapids. This gives me two inside agents and two outside. Business is excellent and I expect to have quite a profit this month." He smiled. "Very soon I'll buy you a buggy for your own use. I don't like your relying on public transportation."

Look how he loved her! she thought. She was correct not to risk losing his love. "Thank you, David!"

He lit a cigarette and inhaled it deeply, the lines of his face easing as he continued to smoke. With alarm Julia noted his increasing dependence on cigarettes. She believed the stress of business caused it. Why did he drive himself so? For her? Himself? He wasn't particularly materialistic; was it that he still sought the respect of his father? Was it impossible for one to stop seeking what one had long sought? Perhaps, she thought, that was her problem too. "Will you always have such long hours?" she asked with concern. "I think you work too hard."

"I do—and I certainly hope that changes someday. But for now I must establish the business." He looked closely at her. "How are you feeling? Are you still sick in the morning?"

"No. How was the trip?" she returned, diverting his thoughts. "Where did you stay? What did you eat? Oh, darling, how I missed you! Does having this new salesman mean you'll travel less?"

He put his arm around her shoulders and looked fondly at her. "Yes, I believe it will. I should be able to spend more time with you. Oh, Julia, I'd love that. You've made me so happy."

Edgar's sickroom looked less like a parlor each time Julia visited. In the place of the sofa and armchair were his bureau and wheelchair. There was a table containing tonics for his stomach (which had bothered him since his attack), a jar of cotton balls, a stack of cloths. Edgar had completed the estimating and he evidently considered that a contretemps, for he mumbled the admission.

"Would you consider estimating on a regular basis?" David asked hopefully.

"I suppose I could," Edgar muttered.

"Thanks—it will be a great help," David stated. It was obviously not just a comment. He really did want his father involved.

"That foolhardy doctor was in again today, telling me I can learn to walk—if I work at it," Edgar sputtered. "He suggests I buy some kind of device to practice on."

"I hope you do."

Edgar's eyes bulged. "I will not! It's ridiculous to think I can walk— pure poppycock! I refuse to hope for naught. Look, it's late and my stomach is upset. Come back some other time. Bring Bridget. There is something appealing about her. As long as I'm glutted with visitors, I might as well have one of my choice."

The next afternoon Julia invited Bridget to visit Edgar, asking if she would encourage him to walk. This time Bridget packed a Bible, a lemon cake, and Patrick; Julia had suggested that perhaps the dog might cheer Edgar up. They met Alma and Martha on the Gerards' front porch in the midst of an argument. Alma stood ·pressed against the wall, her hands behind her. "I'm not going, Martha! I'm not! I've changed my mind," she said adamantly. "Leave it at that! Look, here's Julia and Bridget. I must stay."

Martha looked beseechingly at Julia, her eyes distraught. "Julia, tell her she needs to come!"

"Edgar insisted Martha and I have tea out," Alma explained, her eyes filling with tears. "It's the first time he's been concerned for me in years. I want to go, but I can't get myself to leave him. I'm glad you're here, Julia. Please make Martha understand."

Julia looked from one woman to the other. "We've come to visit Edgar, so you aren't obliged to stay. Could you try to go, Alma? You can return any time you wish. Just *try*. You need to get out."

Alma's hands fell to her sides and she stepped from the wall. "I suppose I could try," she admitted. "But be sure the nurse gives Edgar his three o'clock medication. Be sure she sits Edgar up for it—it's necessary for his circulation. She must also rub his arms and legs. She—"

"Oh, Alma, let's go," Martha said, leading her off.

Julia entered the back parlor and Mrs. Reatherford excused herself to prepare Edgar's afternoon medication. Bridget waited in the hall with Patrick. "I've brought Bridget," Julia greeted Edgar cheerily. "I asked her to bring her dog, Patrick. Is that all right?"

His head snapped up from his pile of shawls and pillows. His eyes found Bridget in the hallway. "Get that dog out of here!"

"Aye," Bridget called. She had hooked Patrick in her arm and was nervously playing with his ears.

"I hate dogs—all animals!" Edgar exploded.

Julia was about to take Patrick to the porch so that Bridget could visit when Edgar said, "Never mind. Bring him here. Let's see what he looks like." He fell back on the pillows.

Bridget stepped up to the bed. As she held Patrick near Edgar, the puppy began licking Edgar's hand and nuzzling into his fingers. Edgar gave the dog a moment's look, then flicked his hand to evict the dog.

Julia took Patrick, and Bridget pulled a chair to the bed. She removed the Bible from her purse and set the cake on the night table. "Thank you," he said, looking at the cake.

"Itself is a lemon cake."

"I like lemon cake."

"How is yourself feeling?"

"That is not a question to ask a man in my shape. I see you have the Bible. Why? I don't recall requesting Bible study. Do you carry that thing wherever you go?"

" 'Tis just one scripture I'm wanting to say." Bridget turned to 2 Tim. 4:7 and read, " 'I have fought a good fight, I have finished my course, I have kept the faith.' Paul was saying this about his life."

Bridget paused. She looked troubled, as if her next comment would be difficult. "What will your family be saying when *your* course is finished?"

He stared at her, his right cheek twitching in anger. "Nurse!" he yelled. "Mrs. Reatherford. Where is that woman?"

"I hear her coming now," Julia said. Bridget tended to be too pointed in her religion, Julia thought; it was best to lead Edgar to God, not push him.

Mrs. Reatherford entered. She moved the cake to the bureau and set her tray of medications on the table. Julia noted it was precisely three. Mrs. Reatherford turned patiently to Edgar. "Yes, sir?"

"Get ahold of Dr. Scott. Ask him where to buy one of those contraptions on which to practice walking."

Julia looked at Edgar in amazement. Bridget's eyes widened, and she too looked surprised. The nurse moved to the bedside and helped Edgar sit up so he could take his medicine.

As Julia and Bridget walked to the door, Edgar called, "Come again, Bridget—and bring the Bible."

Bridget turned and smiled. "Aye."

Outside on the porch Julia said, "How did you know that scripture?"

"I read itself one morning. I read me Bible every morning before mass."

Julia thought of the family Bible in the parlor, decades old, but probably less read than Bridget's. Someday she might read it, she decided.

Twelve

t the beginning of the next week, Edgar stood in his walker, a frame with a floor and parallel bars, and took one step. Alma immediately hurried over to Julia's to inform her and Bridget in person. Alma could hardly contain herself as she paced Julia's vestibule. "I can't stay—I hate to leave him long. But you should have been there! I think he was pleased. He might have smiled—it's hard to tell. Bridget, it's all due to you. Oh, please visit him often!" she finished, giving Bridget a hug.

"Himself will be taking two steps soon," Bridget declared optimistically.

"Oh, yes, I'm sure he will. But now I must go."

"Could myself and me friend Michael O'Keefe visit Mr. Gerard tonight?"

"That will be fine."

"I'm glad you've gotten out of your house," Julia said. "Is it getting easier?"

"No! I took two nerve pills just before leaving. The tea with Martha was a horror, as I told you before."

Alma hurried out the door. Julia leaned out and waved after Alma's buggy. There was a blue sky with puffy clouds scudding across it—a perfect setting for Edgar's first step.

By that evening the weather had changed. Julia was on the settee on the side porch, waiting for David to return from a lumbermen's gathering. She had a clear view of the street to the front, but a trellis of roses walled the side and back. The sky was overcast and heat lightning flashed on the horizon. The dull lightning and rumbling air disturbed her, but it was not that which caused her real turmoil.

She had decided she must tell David she had miscarried. That she hadn't been open with him was more serious than neglecting to seek medical aid. Why hadn't she realized that sooner? Now certainly he would love her less, trust her less, have no faith in her. Oh, what on earth was wrong with her? She would never purposely hurt their relationship.

She rocked nervously on the settee, hoping he would return soon. Now that she had made up her mind to tell him, she had to do it quickly. To soothe her dry, scratchy throat, she reached for her lemonade on the floor, then drew back her hand. She was too upset to hold liquid.

Finally she saw his buggy turning into the driveway and she jumped up to greet him. "I'd like to sit out with you a while," he called. "I'll stable the horse and be right there."

In a few minutes his boots sounded behind the trellis—that deliberate, strong sound which usually gave her a sense of security; now the sound intimidated her. He looked tall and broad-shouldered in his dark suit as he stepped onto the porch and sat with her on the settee. Putting his arms around her, he held her close and kissed her warmly. Her emotions responded. Then she abruptly pushed him away before she lost her nerve. "No one is passing," he said. "Even if they were, I doubt they'd notice us."

"It isn't that. I need to speak to you. I—I have something quite serious to tell you. David, I just—I don't know how to start."

"Nothing can be that serious, darling."

She spoke quickly, rushing to have it said. "I miscarried while you were in Grand Rapids. Bridget helped me through it. I was planning to get pregnant again and then tell you. That way you might not be so grieved. I—I—" She paused, not knowing if she should tell him everything. Yes, she decided—everything! "I had some symptoms before I miscarried. I didn't go to the doctor—I couldn't face what he might tell me. It's my fault I miscarried. Dr. Scott might have helped me." There, it was out.

He didn't speak for a moment. The silence was deadening. Did he hate her too much for words? When he did speak, his voice was barely audible. "Was the child a boy?"

"I couldn't tell."

"My God, Julia!"

"Oh, David! I'm so sorry!"

The street lamp threw dim light on the porch. She could see his dark eyes—dull, throbbing, moist with tears. "David, please understand!" she begged.

"I don't—really, I don't, Julia. Did you take care of yourself? Did you rest? Did you eat properly? Did you—?"

"I did everything I knew I should do," she interrupted. "Everything! No one could have done more! I'm so sorry. If—oh, I am sorry!"

She heard laughing as Billy Williams and Mary passed under the street lamp. *Let them go by quickly*, Julia prayed silently. *Oh, please don't let them see us.*

"You should have told me before."

"I said I was sparing you."

Mary and Billy passed.

David asked, "Were you in much pain?"

"Yes, it was very bad. It was horrible. I thought of you all the time. I worried about grieving you, don't you understand? Oh, David, this is the worst thing that's ever happened to me. If you stop loving me, I don't know what I'll do."

"I shouldn't have gotten angry. I'm sure you watched your health, and I doubt that medical attention would have prevented the miscarriage."

She clung to him. "Then you forgive me? I was afraid you wouldn't. Darling, we'll have other children." She felt his muscles stiffen. She clung harder, tighter. Not this again, she thought—no, don't let him say he can't go through it. "You do want children?" she whispered.

For a moment he didn't answer. Finally he said, "I had looked forward to the other child."

"Then you mean you anticipate another?" Hope rose in Julia's heart.

He shifted, and seeing that he didn't wish to hold her, she released him. His foot restlessly pushed the floor, and the squeak of the rocker on the boards hammered into the silence he created. "You aren't straightforward with me," he said flatly, "and I don't appreciate it. There was that deception over Trina's photograph. You will do anything to please me, to create an atmosphere that you think I want. I find that unpleasant—and yes, it disturbs me a great deal. Frankly, I wonder if you've told me everything about this miscarriage."

"Of course I have! The only thing I didn't say was that Edith sought medical attention when she had a problem in her pregnancy and she went on to give birth to Freddie. That's all!"

"You always hold back something."

"You've held things back from me," she countered. "What about that night you went to Diane's? You said nothing about it for quite a while. I'm as open with you as you are with me."

He stood, facing the street, flinging tight, angry words back at her. "You don't know what you're saying. If you knew what actually occurred in my heart that night, you would regret that comment. The things you hold back are mean, vital. I had been working through our relationship that night—that is a far different matter."

"If you loved me, you'd trust me! You've never loved me! You've just said it because it's expected. I know that now."

He turned and stared intently at her, his eyes like black spaces. So she had stunned him, she thought. She had said more than she meant to and didn't know how to recant. Oh, God, why was marriage so difficult? She had been through such agony. Didn't he understand that she'd do anything for him, that every breath her body took was for him? She loved and adored him. But everything she tried to do for him he rejected. Perhaps she had been wrong to be honest, though she believed in honesty. She should have lied, told him it happened suddenly—then he would pity her pain, her loss; he would express his love. He was correct that she would do anything to please him, but he misunderstood why. If he would totally accept her, she wouldn't be forced to try so hard.

"I'm sorry," she sighed. "I shouldn't have said you didn't love me."

"No, you shouldn't have," he replied, wiping the tears from her face. "Just be yourself, darling," he whispered. "There must be no more secrets."

Just then Michael's wagon entered the driveway. "Michael and Bridget have been to see your father," Julia explained. "Your mother stopped today and told us Edgar took a step."

"He did? Wonderful!"

David and Julia walked out as Michael parked by the porch. Bridget leaned down from her high perch, saying, "Sure it was a grand thing to see your papa. Michael read himself John chapter one and two, and your papa loved hearing about Jesus. Michael reads good, too, and your papa is loving Michael!"

David smiled. "Well!"

"Ourselves is going back tomorrow," Bridget went on. "Your papa took another two steps tonight and was so proud."

"Father needs you more than any treatment. I'm amazed, though, that he likes the Bible."

"That he does, surely."

Michael jumped out and swung Bridget down from the rough board wagon, making her laugh with unrestrained joy. Julia envied her. How she wished David would swing her through the air, make her laugh, bring that joy to her heart!

Julia told Edith and Melinda what had happened. After the emotional trauma Julia had gone through, she wasn't sure she wanted children right away, though both Edith and Melinda encouraged her.

In all the turmoil, Julia had neglected Nelda. She arrived after breakfast on Monday to visit her, stopping first at Huntly's office to get the key.

Melinda was seated at a little working table, too small for her elbows, account manuals, ledgers, pencils, ink pots, and pens. However, her table faced the lake, giving her a view she loved. The air was hot, causing little tendrils of damp hair to cling to her face. She capped the ink pot and smiled at Julia. Melinda's eyes looked strained, and Julia hoped that, in her eagerness to please George, Melinda didn't strive for impossible standards of work. "Doesn't George have a larger table?" Julia asked.

"A larger table would cramp the office. I'm fine. I just happen to be working on many things today."

"I hope you're not working too hard."

"Julia, don't worry." Then changing the subject, she asked nervously, "I suppose you've come to visit Nelda?"

"Yes."

"You . . . you can't today," she said hesitently. "I wish George were here to explain, but he's at a meeting in town. Julia, he was forced to put Nelda in a tranquilizer. I realize he promised David he would try to inform him before doing so, but he couldn't today. It was vital he be at his meeting on time, and since Nelda was in a frenzy, it had to be done before he left."

Under no circumstance could Julia agree to having Nelda restrained, and she shook her head.

Melinda nervously rolled a pencil. "Nelda started becoming maniacal two days ago, just after Martha visited. George says it's typical of her condition to fluctuate between melancholy and mania. She won't sleep and she's been writing a romance novel nonstop, hoping to become wealthy and start her own lunatic asylum. When she had written on all her stationery, she started on the walls and floor. Then when her pen was removed, she used her finger, writing invisibly. I haven't seen her today because George asked me not to. I did see her manuscript though. It's badly written—unrealistic and incoherent. Nelda needs restraint in order to rest, but drugs aren't the answer. George says Nelda needs to think through why she writes obsessively and understand that she must learn to write in moderation, not compulsively, which is the problem."

Melinda's eyes pleaded for understanding. "If Nelda's obsession isn't stopped, she will become suicidal, Julia. George would only do what's in Nelda's best interest and plans to see David after his meeting."

"Let me have the keys," Julia demanded quietly.

Melinda jumped up from her seat. She was so nervous she trembled. "I just said I can't see her myself."

"Melinda—take me!" Julia asserted impatiently.

"I don't know. I just don't know," she stated, confused, but reluctant to give in.

Julia felt like shaking her. "Melinda!" she demanded.

Unable to persuade her sister, Melinda unlocked George's desk drawer and removed his key ring. Together they walked to Nelda's room.

The picture Julia had seen in *Lunacy: History and Treatment* didn't prepare her for the shocking sight. The tranquilizer chair had a board back several inches higher than Nelda's head, flat board arms, and a padded seat. Nelda looked as if she had been crated. Boxes on the chair arms and extending from the chair legs held her arms and legs fast. A three-sided box enclosed her head. Her hair was tucked under the box, framing a gaunt and pathetic-looking face. Her skin was mottled and fragile.

"Oh!" Nelda sobbed when she saw them. "Oh—oh—!"

Melinda's back pressed against the door in unbelief. Julia turned toward her. Melinda's eyes, wide with shock, flinched at Julia's hard look. "So what do you think now!" Julia demanded.

"I—"

"Tell me this is right!"

Melinda's face struggled for composure. "It is if George believes it is! He wouldn't do it if it weren't absolutely necessary. It's shocking and I don't like it either, but I trust George. Nelda isn't being hurt; you can see that. She's only restrained. Please, Julia, understand this: drugs aren't the answer for her."

The boxes holding Nelda's hands and feet rattled as she jerked her body to free herself. "Get me out! Get me out!" she screamed.

"I will," Julia promised. "Just as soon as I can."

Nelda's expression suddenly changed from despair to exaltation, and she shrilled, "Find my manuscript. Bring it. I've an idea for Netta that can't wait." She turned bright, mad eyes on Julia and explained, "Netta is grieving over the death of her child, who is dying a lingering death in her arms. I can cheer Netta with a gift from an anonymous sender. Netta will shake the package and smile as she wonders about it. What is the gift? Ha! Ha! I won't tell you. Don't ask—merciful heaven, don't ask!"

"See—" Melinda challenged; "see how mad she is!" She stood trembling by the door. Melinda didn't approach Nelda, Julia thought, because if she did, she would break down. Julia knew that Melinda did not agree with this treatment either. "Please understand," Melinda whispered.

"There," Nelda ranted. "Netta is tearing off the last shred of paper and finding a little pile of dried buttercups. This has a significance to Netta—"

Melinda stared at Nelda, gave her one last desperate look, then hurriedly hung the keys on the doorknob and rushed from the room.

Julia touched Nelda's skin; it was hot and pulsing. "Hush, Nelda."

"Get me my book, get me my book, get me my book—"

"Hush—hush."

Nelda wailed and pleaded for her manuscript, her face dripping perspiration from the effort. Julia could listen no longer. She left Nelda and locked her door with shaking hands and returned the keys to Melinda without comment. On the way home, Julia stopped at David's office. He was at a client's factory, and she left a note describing Nelda's situation.

When David arrived for dinner, Julia met him in the backyard. He gave her a warm hug, then held her hand as they walked the horse into the stable. It was hot and dry. Because there was no breeze off the lake, the flies were thick on shore and the horse's tail constantly flicked at them.

"Did you meet with George?" Julia asked.

"Yes, Martha and I did. Neither Martha nor I agree that obsessive behavior constitutes grounds for restraint—though we understand restraint is sometimes necessary. We believe Nelda should be under drug therapy. But George doesn't agree, so we're moving her. I hadn't realized how bad the tranquilizer was until I saw Nelda in it."

"This will break Melinda's heart. She's fond of George and will take this as a personal affront. I don't want any bad feelings between Melinda and me."

"I understand your concern, but I'm at an impasse with George. He refuses to consider any treatment but the tranquilizer for Nelda. I hope to find a bed in one of the other private asylums in Chicago. If not, I'll find a place out of town."

"David, perhaps if you speak to him one more time."

"I'm sorry, Julia, it would do no good."

David finally found a private asylum located on Rush Street, which had just opened. It was operated by Dr. Sutton, a retired physician, and his wife, a former choir director in Julia's church. Including Nelda, there would be only four patients since the Suttons believed in individual care. Their treatment was quite different from Lakeside, employing drug therapy rather than restraint for obsessive behavior. Julia liked the Suttons, who were warm, dedicated people, and she believed Nelda would be helped in their home.

On the day of Nelda's transfer, while David and Aunt Martha prepared Nelda for the trip, Julia stopped to see Melinda. Melinda looked coolly up from her worktable. Julia couldn't recall her relationship with Melinda ever having been so strained. Melinda's hair was pulled back from her face, giving her face a taut appearance. "Good morning," Julia began tentatively.

"Good morning," she returned indifferently.

Julia hurried over to the table. "I only have a minute—Nelda is almost ready to go. Melinda, don't be upset with me. Please don't take our moving Nelda as a personal affront to George."

"How else can I feel?" she replied angrily. "You've rejected George's method of treatment, and that's a rejection of him, no matter how prettily you might phrase it."

"I can disagree about George's methods and still be friendly with him."

"You've never cared for him—admit it!"

"I . . . I . . ." Julia did think he imposed on Melinda in permitting her to volunteer so many hours. Furthermore, Melinda wouldn't behave so coldly without his influence. Yes, he was turning Melinda into a cold person like himself.

"Admit it—come on!" Melinda demanded.

An attendant looked in and said Miss Wilson was waiting in the buggy. "Just a minute," Julia said. Then turning to Melinda, she replied, "I do admire George's dedication to his patients." She meant that at least. "I wish I could stay longer. We need to talk."

"Oh, Julia, I don't like this situation any better than you," Melinda said, softening. "I just don't know what to do. I know my feelings are involved and I believe my loyalty should be to George. Just give me time to work it out."

Julia nodded and left.

Nelda's new asylum was neither titled, as was Lakeside, nor as impressive. It was a narrow house on a busy corner with a plain wood facade and a small piazza. But the piazza furniture looked comfortable and Nelda's room was attractive, even rather homey, with mottos and scenes Mrs. Sutton had embroidered for the walls. One motto, "ALL WILL YET BE WELL," Julia thought inspirational for Nelda.

Nelda resumed writing *Trouble on the North Side* the moment she was installed in her quarters, and she seemed to hardly notice the transfer. Opium and bromides were given to reduce her nervous activity, and in a few days her output of words had decreased markedly.

On Sunday, a steamy day when Julia's petticoats and two-skirted dress retained almost more heat than she could bear, she sat in her pew and fanned herself. She would indeed prefer to be home with David. She was the first of the family to arrive, and while she listened to Mrs. Pratt's erratic version of "When All Thy Mercies, O My God," she nervously looked back for Melinda. She hadn't seen Melinda since Nelda left Lakeside a few days ago.

Edith arrived and after settling Freddie, she turned to Julia. "Isn't it nice that Melinda is bringing Mr. Huntly to church?"

"I didn't know she was. When did she tell you?"

"Last night. I had her and Mr. Huntly over for dinner. I would have had you and David too, but Melinda said things are tense between you. Frankly, you were wrong to disregard Mr. Huntly's expertise by transferring Nelda. Of course, the damage is done."

Julia looked away from Edith. Her eyes filled with tears. Didn't Edith realize it hurt to be excluded? Didn't she remember Julia and Melinda did everything together? Julia realized Edith usually wasn't included in her and Melinda's activities, but that was different. Edith had not wished to be included.

"What's wrong with you?" Edith asked irritably.

"Nothing—nothing." Julia changed the subject. "How is Freddie?"

"Fine. I've added an ounce of red meat to his daily diet, and he's gained a pound over the month."

Melinda, Mr. Adams, and George Huntly arrived next. George wore a cool-looking tan suit and a claret silk waistcoat and cravat. The diamond in his stickpin was the size of Julia's dress button, and it occurred to Julia that his appearance would be an asset if he joined the church.

Melinda sat between her father and George and nodded quickly at Julia. There was no emotion on her face. Each Sunday the service began with a selection from a quartet of cultured voices, and this Sunday's group now stood before the congregation. Julia felt miserable. To still her hands, she picked up her fan and began to cool herself rapidly. She couldn't tolerate the strain; she would have to repair her relationship with Melinda—or leave. She leaned over George and pleaded, "Melinda, forgive me. I can't—I just can't go on like this."

Melinda didn't hesitate; her eyes became moist. "Neither can I."

"I'm so sorry," Julia whispered.

"No, it's my fault."

George looked in bewilderment from one woman to the other. Julia doubted he was aware of the strained relationship. Edith turned and flicked her fan. "Hush, please."

Late in the afternoon, Melinda joined Julia on Julia's side porch. Melinda moved restlessly around, sipping at a glass of lemonade. She didn't take her gloves off. Her former cool and crisp-looking dress was now rumpled and damp. "Julia, I should have apologized first. I was the one out of line. George isn't upset about Nelda's move. He realizes Nelda may very well be cured somewhere else. It's just that he's convinced his methods are best. I hope Nelda is happy and I plan to visit her whenever I can."

"Let's forget it happened."

"Yes, it's forgotten. Oh, Julia! George is the most marvelous person! He'd have come, but he had to check the patients."

Melinda smiled joyfully and somewhat mysteriously. She set her glass on the table and impatiently tugged at the glove on her left hand. The glove flipped off, and Melinda fluttered her hand before Julia. A large diamond sparkled brilliantly on her ring finger. Melinda's eyes were vivid.

"You're engaged! How wonderful!" Julia refused to be anything but happy for her, as she jumped up and put her arms around Melinda.

"It's three carats, at least," Melinda claimed proudly. She removed the ring and handed it to Julia, pointing out the entwined initials on the inside of the band. Julia read the date of George's grandparents' marriage: 1799.

"It's lovely."

"We won't be married until March. George needs time to have his affairs in order. He has to train the assistant superintendent to manage Lakeside while he is gone—George has never left him in charge for an extended period of time. We're going to honeymoon in Saint Augustine, Florida, for two weeks."

Melinda looked bedazzled. "I never believed I'd marry. Imagine a man of George's stature loving me! He says he loves my dedication to his work. Lakeside is like a religion to him—he lives for it. He hopes to find a cure for lunacy—in fact, he treats his patients with that in mind."

"That would be quite an accomplishment."

"Yes, but he'll do it."

Melinda returned the ring to her finger and stared at it.

"Is it insured?" Julia asked.

"Yes, of course. But it's an heirloom and I certainly hope I will never have to use the insurance."

Melinda sighed and fell back into the settee. "George asked me to lose forty pounds before the wedding. I don't know if I can. I've never lost more than fifteen pounds at once."

"Melinda, I should think—" No, Julia wouldn't say it. Perhaps George was correct to insist on a thin wife. If David were asked, he would probably state the same preference.

Melinda looked nervously at Julia. "You do like George?"

"Yes, I'm fond of him."

The next morning Julia felt tired and too nauseated to eat her breakfast. These were the same feelings she had suffered when she was pregnant; she didn't like to think she was in that condition again already, for she wasn't sure David would welcome a child. But she refused to worry at this point.

"Why aren't you eating?" David asked.

"I just can't. I've never had a big appetite in the morning, and it's unusual for me to eat a lot." That was the truth, at least. Changing the subject, she asked, "Do you think Melinda and George will be happy?"

"I think so. Melinda loves him, and she is dedicated to him and his work. I doubt she will ever see a fault in him."

"That's how I look at it."

Bridget entered with a china coffeepot. She had been silently slipping in and out of the room. While serving, Bridget spoke only if spoken to, or if inquiring about service or food. Julia appreciated Bridget's silence, for it gave her and David a degree of privacy. Bridget poured Julia's coffee and lifted the pot. Her other hand passed slowly in front of Julia's eyes, displaying a silver ring with diamond chips. Julia took Bridget's hand and exclaimed, "Oh, from Michael!"

"Aye, myself is being engaged since last night," she said, smiling and bouncing on her feet, her blue eyes sparkling with delight. " 'Tis hard set I am to wait any longer to tell you."

Julia stood up and hugged her while David offered congratulations.

"When is the wedding?" Julia asked.

"The ninth of September."

"That's so soon!"

"Michael is older than me and himself has waited long enough for marrying. The ninth is being a Saturday. Could you do without me working that day?"

"Of course. But you must take a week's honeymoon," Julia offered, "and with your regular salary."

Bridget stared at Julia with troubled eyes. "Why, Mr. Gerard's shirts will need ironing, and the dust will be rising—"

"I insist. We can hire temporary help."

"Sure, 'tis thanking you, I am."

"Will Mary be your bridesmaid?"

"I'm hoping so. When herself goes to mass with me, she's not very friendly. She's been seeing Billy Williams a lot, and himself sets Mary against me. If Mary won't be me bridesmaid, I'll have Margaret. She works for Mrs. Powers down the street. I like herself, but not as good as Mary."

"I hope Mary will accept," Julia said.

"Oh—" Bridget sputtered and tears fell. "I wrote me mama and papa about me engagement last night. I only wish themselves could be here for me wedding. But let myself not be thinking of sad things, surely. Why, it's the luckiest girl in the world, I am! Michael has been paying regular on a little cottage on Taylor Street, and it will be ours next month. Saints! Here myself is rambling and your food is being cold." Bridget scurried off.

"It's quite possible Mr. and Mrs. Boland will be here," David said.

"What do you mean?"

"I'll send tickets today. If the Bolands can't come, they can return them to the shipping line in Ireland. But don't say anything to Bridget—unless we hear her parents will come. She's excitable and I don't want her greatly disappointed."

"All right. But, David, why would you do this for Bridget—you don't know her that well?"

He sipped his coffee and looked embarrassed. "I don't know. There are just some things one does."

"No, that *you* do, darling," Julia said softly.

That evening Julia nervously paced the parlor, waiting for David. She hadn't seen him since breakfast. Where was he? He hadn't notified her he would miss dinner. Or had he? she wondered. She had been through so much lately, perhaps she couldn't remember everything. But hadn't his last words been, "See you at dinner, darling"? She looked out the open window. Moisture-laden clouds bulged in from the lake, spreading a thick layer of fog in the yard. The light of street lamps diffused into a row of hazy little moons. Fog erased the passing carriages, except for the sound. Branches on the trees, roofs on the houses, and the street nearby—all had disappeared, seemingly leaving half a world.

If David didn't return soon, should she go out looking for him? Since it was improper for a woman to be alone on the streets at this hour, who would accompany her? She didn't know where to search. But what if David had been injured? Then the police would notify her, she thought. She admitted her greatest concern: David was at Diane's. The last time David was late without word, he had been there.

Finally, she heard David's horse in the driveway, and she ran to the kitchen door. When he entered, he kissed her dutifully, not warmly as he usually did. He mechanically set his hat on the table and loosened his yellow cravat. She had the chilling feeling he would rather have found her asleep. "David, where were you?"

He looked at her, but didn't reply.

"I've been worried. It's after ten."

"I'm sorry. I didn't mean to worry you."

"Were you working late? Were you at some meeting?"

He looked off into space, and she began to think he might be drunk. But she smelled no liquor, only tobacco.

He finally said, "I worked late and I've been walking. Let it suffice at that. I've had a difficult day, and I don't wish to burden you with it. I'm very sorry I worried you, darling."

"But—" She stopped. What she wanted to say was, *Aren't we to be open with each other? Come, tell me! Where did you walk!* He was certainly more secretive than she. He lifted her chin and looked in her eyes. She could not read his eyes clearly. There seemed to be a mixture of grief and love in them. Just as long as he loved her, that was all that mattered, she reasoned. Certainly business problems had caused his difficulties.

"Would you like some tea or coffee?" she asked calmly.

"Yes, thanks, whatever is easier. I *am* sorry I'm late. I should have sent word."

The next morning the sun shone in an almost cloudless sky. The fog had left the air sweet and clean and had shined the grass to mirror the sun. Bridget saw Mary sweeping the back walk with listless strokes. Mary was doing a terrible job, leaving debris that Bridget would dispose of in one lick. Pushing through the hedges, Bridget approached her. Mary leaned on her broom handle and blinked.

Apprehensive about Mary's reaction, Bridget had stalled in telling Mary about her engagement. "I missed yourself at mass," Bridget began. "I knocked at your door but you didn't be coming."

"I didn't hear. Billy and I was out late last night, and I was sleeping."

Bridget held out her hand. "Myself is engaged to Michael O'Keefe, and I'm wanting you to be me bridesmaid. The wedding's September ninth at church and the reception's at Michael's papa and mama's."

"Me!" Mary's hand flew to her mouth. "Nobody's never asked me to be a bridesmaid."

"I'm asking." Bridget hugged Mary.

"I ain't always been so nice to you."

"I don't care one bit. Yourself is me best friend and that is that!"

"What should I wear?" Mary worried. "I ain't got no gown."

Bridget stepped closer and looked searchingly at Mary. "Then yourself really isn't being mad about Michael anymore?''

"No. I never liked him much.''

Bridget smiled widely at that. "Mrs. Gerard has a sewing machine, a real fancy one, and herself told me to use it whenever I want. So myself will make your dress.''

"I just love blue—could I have that color? Ain't I awful to be asking, but I'm so excited I could die!''

"Then we'll be having blue. I have a piece of lace from a dress of me mama's that would look lovely at your throat, surely.''

Mary started to cry. "You'd give that lace to me! I seen it in your box and it's the nicest thing you've got.''

"Yourself is after forgetting you're me friend.''

"Bridget, can Billy come to the wedding? I've fallen bad for him. I've got to stay with him all the time—he's got a quick eye. He looks at girls when we're out walking, and I'm scared. Maybe if he sees me in a beautiful dress, I'll win him for good.''

Not about to risk their friendship, Bridget assured her, "Himself can come. Sure I'll be surprised if he does, though. He isn't liking myself.''

"Billy will be there. He likes party food. He gets his room and board where he works, but he's sick of the bad food they give the help. Land!'' Mary interjected. "You can quit working! My, you're lucky.''

"No—the Gerards need me, and I need to send money home to me family. I can be working until I have a baby, Michael is saying.''

Mary spoke confidentially. "You know the queerest thing happened. Billy came by last night kinda late and said he had some real good gossip about Mr. Gerard that he had to keep quiet. He flashed fifty dollars under my eyes. He said it was from Mr. Gerard. Did Billy ever grin! Have you heard anything?''

"Myself doesn't listen for gossip.''

"Well, tell me if you hear anything. I'd better finish the sweeping or Mrs. Cullen will be after me.''

Thirteen

The beach at Lakeside was hot, and the brilliant sun reflected such glare on the sand that it made Julia squint. Melinda tied on a bathing net and pulled on rubber slippers. Because George correlated strong bodies with strong minds, he encouraged Melinda to swim daily. Though his slim frame bore no signs of enlarged muscles, he daily lifted weights and performed a half hour of calisthenics. He provided Melinda with a female attendant as a swimming guard—and a skiff, should the attendant need it. The attendant, an athletic woman who was proficient at rowing and swimming, sat under an umbrella on a camp chair. She occasionally peeked over her reading glasses to check if Melinda were ready to swim.

Julia had stopped on her way to the Women's Mission Society luncheon at church. "This is the first meeting you've missed in years," Julia told Melinda. "Edith won't be happy."

Edith considered attendance at mission society a virtue for members, an obligation for sisters. In Edith's three years as president, attendance was up one hundred percent. She was an excellent president, and though not exactly loved, she was respected. Julia supposed Edith would be re-elected yearly until she died, as was the preceding president.

Julia walked to the water's edge with Melinda. "Edith will say, 'If Melinda can take time to swim, she can take time for mission society.' "

"Then don't tell her I swam."

"Edith hopes George will attend the bazaar Friday night. David's going. I'm surprised—and it was his idea. Will George go?"

"Yes, if the assistant superintendent can work that night. Please tell

Edith I haven't had time to make anything for the bazaar. I don't have the nerve to tell her."

Fancy work, painted china, and various handicrafts would be sold to earn money for missions. Julia had stenciled roses on several china plates and teacups. Painted china was popular and she thought her dishes would sell. "I already told her. She expects, at least, that you'll work at a booth."

"Then I'll work in Mrs. Pratt's booth again."

Melinda handed Julia her cape. "Arthur will probably be there. David hasn't met him—you might have to introduce them."

"I don't mind; both of them would be polite. What bothers me more is seeing Mrs. Newton. She treats me coolly whenever we meet. I know she remembers the day she found me with Arthur. I worry that she'll gossip and ruin my reputation."

"She won't. That would put Arthur in a bad light. Forget about her."

"Sometimes I wonder if Arthur will marry. I haven't heard any rumor of a girl in his life."

Melinda stepped close to Julia. "How would you feel about that?"

"Wonderful!" Julia had never considered the possibility before. Her response had been the expected; she wondered how she actually would feel.

"Do you and David ever discuss Arthur?"

"No. David doesn't question me much about my past. He knows Arthur and I were engaged—that's about all."

The attendant turned her book over on her lap and asked Melinda if she wanted to swim. The woman was evidently hot and wished to leave the beach soon.

Melinda plunged into the cold lake.

Because Julia was decorations chairman for the bazaar, Edith placed her at the head table. The lunch included chicken salad and fresh fruit and rolls. Most of the one hundred mission society members were present—except Melinda, which upset Edith. "Melinda is only a volunteer at Lakeside. She should be able to come and go as she pleases," Edith declared angrily.

"George has prevailed on her to work full time," Julia replied.

"I don't believe that—he's not the type! Mind you, she established the extreme schedule."

"She didn't," Julia defended.

"Don't contradict me!" Edith snapped.

Julia gave up the argument. Dominating and opinionated, Edith would never change.

After a moment of silence, Edith asked, "Shall Morton and I pick you and David up Friday night? We're delighted David is going."

"No—but thanks. You need to be there quite early; I'm sure earlier than David would wish."

Edith placed her fork on her plate and tapped her fingers nervously in her lap. Looking closely at her, Julia noticed for the first time that she seemed strained. Perhaps she felt the responsibility of the bazaar, Julia thought. "Is—is David always attentive to you?" Edith asked hesitantly.

"Yes, when he's home. He's away a lot. Why?"

"I . . . I, never mind. It was a simple question that's all." Edith picked up her fork and stabbed a piece of cantaloupe. Julia didn't press her; when Edith closed a subject, it remained closed. She wondered, though, if Edith had noticed the tension in her marriage.

The night of the bazaar the air was hot, motionless; the curtains hung limply beside the open bedroom window. Julia's drawers and petticoat clung hotly to her. The weather would upset Edith, Julia thought; Edith said people unable to stand the heat left bazaars early without many purchases.

Julia completed her dressing by donning a dress with a green grenadine upper skirt and silk underskirt amply trimmed with lace. Liking the effect of black with her red hair, she put on her jet earrings, necklace, and bracelet. She studied herself critically in the mirror. Her hair was pulled back from her forehead and pinned with a small bow; it then rose to a high crown and descended in a waterfall. She liked the waterfall effect, but the high crown seemed to emphasize her angular features, making her cheekbones appear higher than normal, the hollows in her cheeks, deeper. To soften her features, she pulled a few tendrils of hair to her forehead.

David was at the washstand shaving. He wiped his face with a towel and looked appreciatively at Julia. "You look lovely," he smiled.

"My hair?"

"Perfect."

As long as she pleased him, she was content. "I haven't been so eager to go to a bazaar in a long time. It's because you're going, darling."

He hung his towel on the washstand rack. "How many people do you expect?"

"Edith hopes for three hundred. Can we leave soon? I should be there a bit early to replace any wilted flowers. I have some cut flowers in the icebox." That afternoon Julia had festooned the walls of the social hall with ivy and set bowls of garden flowers on the refreshment tables and booths.

"Then while I put on my shirt and collar, would you please get my gray-striped coat?"

Julia removed his coat from the wardrobe, and while she shook it to remove wrinkles, she noticed a bulge in the pocket. She reached in to remove the object and found an envelope folded into a small square. She thought it strange that he had folded it that way.

She moved forward, intending to give him the letter. Then she smelled the scent of lilac and noted the lavender color. She pressed the envelope in her hand, and dropping the coat on the bed, she ran downstairs to the parlor. She unfolded the envelope with icy and fumbling fingers. She held up the creased wrapping, staring at the straight, commanding handwriting. That purple ink! That hand! That arresting, dominating hand!

The envelope contained no postmark; obviously it was hand-delivered. *When?* she thought frantically. *Not recently—no!* She couldn't bear that Diane still corresponded with David. It must be an old letter, placed in his pocket last summer and forgotten. *No!* Julia amended; *he wore this suit frequently and would have noticed such an apparent bulge. He must have received the letter and put it in his pocket the last time he wore the suit. When was that?* She couldn't remember.

She flushed, and her eyelids began to burn.

This letter she would read.

"Julia, where are you?" David called.

She heard his footsteps in the upstairs hall and quickly shoved the letter under her corset top.

On the way to church, a buggy struck a dray at an intersection, and Julia and David were delayed. They arrived at the social hall late, preceded by scores of people. Julia waved to Melinda at Mrs. Pratt's booth. She noticed the booths were doing a fair business. Her decorations looked in good shape, except for a few wilted flowers. The air smelled of flowers and perfume, and rosettes on the toes of women's shoes laid a flower garden on the floor. Gaslights cast a soft glow. The sight was pretty—probably uplifting to all but her, Julia speculated.

Edith appeared and after greeting David pleasantly, she attacked Julia. "Well, I should think you would arrive on time! The decorations need attention."

"We were behind an accident."

Edith passed her hand over her eyes as if about to faint. Julia wondered if her clothes were too tight. Instead of her usual looser and drab apparel, Edith wore a bright dress with a tight bodice and large bustle.

Her hair was elaborately tiered over a tortoise-shell bandeau. Her appearance amazed Julia. "Are you all right?" Julia asked.

"Fine, just hot."

"You look lovely," Julia complimented her.

"Thank you," Edith smiled.

"I don't see George," Julia observed.

"He couldn't come—he had to work. Hurry now and fix the decorations!"

When Julia returned to David, he was talking to Nancy Smith, a friend of Julia's from high school—a small woman known for her tiny waist and her large intellect, verified by a college degree. Julia liked Nancy, but found her difficult to communicate with. All Nancy cared to discuss was the Chicago Historical Society, where she volunteered her time. Nancy wasn't yet married.

Julia hugged Nancy. "It's about time you brought David to church—we've all been anxious to know him better. We have several new volumes in the library at the historical society, about which I've been telling David. The library contains sixteen thousand bound volumes now."

"That's quite a number," David said, politely impressed.

"Were you aware we have the original manuscript copy of the Emancipation Proclamation—written in President Lincoln's own hand?"

"Yes, I've seen it," David said.

"Nancy and I went through Sunday school together and sang duets for our class," Julia informed David.

"Julia and I were in the high school choir too. In fact, we always seemed to be in the same singing group, except when you missed the cantata that time you were in school in Indianapolis."

David looked quizzically at Julia. "You went to school in Indianapolis?"

"I'll tell you about it later." Julia wasn't eager to explain that episode, and she hoped he would forget the matter.

Nancy left and Julia and David walked to Mrs. Pratt's booth to greet Melinda. Featured were hundreds of little birds that Mrs. Pratt had crocheted through the years. Though they were pretty, there wasn't much one could do with a bird except pin it on a dress. One bird was quite enough to own, as they all looked alike. Over the years, as the church members purchased their bird, Mrs. Pratt found her supply far surpassed the demand. She relied on new members and visitors.

"Perhaps we could buy one for your mother and Nelda," Julia suggested.

David bought the two, and several for the wives of his office staff as well. Mrs. Pratt began a conversation with David, and Julia thought it an opportune time to read the letter. "Excuse me," she said. "I'll be right back."

She walked along a short passageway and turned into a long, vacant hallway. At the end of the hall she entered a Sunday school room marked "Fourth Grade Class." She turned on the gaslight, shut the door, and unfolded the letter. She couldn't stand the smell of lilac, and to her chagrin, it was now on her dress. Her hand shook. She should toss the letter into the trash basket and trust that there was a justifiable reason for its place in David's pocket.

But she couldn't resist. As she began to read, the words jumped before her eyes. Oh, if only she had never seen this!

> You're always in my thoughts. How I miss you! I remember especially our walks on the beach at the north point at night. Warren is no companion to me. He travels most of the time, and when he is home, he is uncommunicative. It has been very difficult for me. I need to see you for a little while tonight—Warren will be at the Chicago Club. Will you meet me at the north point at eight? I just must see you.

"Must see you!" Julia gasped. *Had David met with Diane?* She looked at the date on the letter: July 31, a Monday. She thought back. Oh—that was the day David had been late without an explanation. Now she remembered when he last wore the gray-striped frock coat! That day! He wore a yellow cravat with it. She remembered it clearly!

Julia imagined Diane on the beach with David, walking under a black sky, a thousand stars pulsing for them. Suddenly the air in the room became thin. She thought she'd suffocate. What should she do? She had to think coherently. She had to believe David had refused that invitation. David loved her! He had stated that over and over. He was an honest man, not a hypocrite! She frantically reconstructed that Monday: David had received the letter, put it in his pocket, forgotten it. If he had met Diane, he would have destroyed the evidence. *But where had he been walking that night?*

Nowhere important, she rationalized. He hadn't met Diane—that could not be. Nothing had happened that night. If she showed David the letter, he would confirm that. He would look surprised and say, "Darling, you know I love you—why do you doubt? I had a disturbing day and I was walking it off. Of course I didn't meet Diane. We are not having an affair."

She feared someone would check out the lighted room. She didn't wish to be found gasping for air, so she replaced the letter, turned off the gaslight, and left.

She turned into the passageway to the social hall, a dimly lighted area. There were people milling around the entrance to the hall. A blond man of some height broke from the others and approached her. She immediately recognized Arthur's poised frame.

He pressed her hand for a moment. She had forgotten how soft his hands were, how much like cotton. She felt ill-at-ease, but he looked composed, his complicated banking affairs being more difficult, she thought, than meeting her alone for the first time in months. He leaned on his gold-headed cane, an accessory that must have cost him dearly. He was dressed in a dark navy suit and a conservative waistcoat. She recognized the spice scent of cologne, which he had worn for years. "Well, what are you doing down here?" he asked.

"I needed a little air."

He smiled in a friendly fashion. "I suspect you'd find more air outside."

"I preferred not to go out."

"There is quite a crowd—it does get close."

"Edith is hoping for more—but it's hot and many will stay home."

"What did you make?"

"I stenciled flowers on cups and saucers—I usually do something simple like that. I'm not very talented with handicrafts."

His blue eyes were genial. Julia twisted her hands and could not stop. What was wrong with her? It wasn't he that was her problem, David was. "But painted china does sell well," Julia added. *Oh, what an inane conversation!* she thought.

"I still have some of yours."

"Really!"

"How are you, Julia?"

"Fine—just fine." Why couldn't he have asked on a better day? She supposed he knew she was upset. Julia could think of nothing more to say. She bitterly recalled the night he broke their engagement, with little more explanation than that he and his mother thought it best, considering the circumstances. How cheap she had felt! How abandoned. How wounded her pride was. What if David now left her, as Arthur had! She fearfully wondered. She felt herself turn white, clammy.

Arthur looked at her with concern. "Let me take you out."

"No—I'm all right. It's been a difficult day."

"Then let's go to a window—a breeze has started up."

Julia looked at the window down the passageway. "No—no!" She didn't wish to be aside with him.

He stepped near her. "Is it me you're reacting to?"

"No."

His eyes were fixed on her. She doubted he believed her. "I've wanted to speak to you for some time," he admitted. "I didn't handle that incident between us wisely. I've regretted canceling our engagement."

It was her chance to strike back. "It's too late to be sorry. It worked out for the best—I love David."

Sharp lines of pain formed on his face. "I did care for you," she said, not wishing to hurt him further. She liked the bright, burning look he now gave her. It helped soften Diane's devastating letter.

"I'd better get back," Julia murmured. To her surprise she was reluctant to leave him.

Edith met Julia just as she entered the social hall. There was a line of perspiration above her lip. "Where have you been? David's been wondering. I would think you'd pay some attention to him. After all, this is his first time at a church function and we must make sure he likes it. You want to interest David in church, don't you?"

"Yes, yes! Edith, leave me alone."

"What's wrong?"

"Nothing—I needed time to myself."

"I must talk to you now." Edith moved Julia to the corner, away from the crowd and booths. "What do you think of my dress and hair?" she asked urgently.

"I said earlier you look attractive and I meant it."

"I'm trying to be more feminine for Morton. I've noticed you're quite feminine for David, and I've seen him express appreciation. Oh, Julia, I'm at my wit's end! Morton has been so distant lately. He's not interested in Freddie's care as he once was, or in my advice. He hasn't joined me at all tonight, but has been fixing various things on the booths. It's entirely unnecessary—everything's in good order." Edith's back was to the crowd and she turned to glance at Morton, who was hammering the side of a booth.

Julia was thunderstruck; Edith never discussed personal concerns with her.

"To what do you attribute Morton's attitude?" Edith queried.

"He's trying to help you. After all, you're the president of the society."

Edith's long fingers circled Julia's arm. "Julia, please listen more attentively. It isn't just his actions tonight. I worry that he doesn't love me. He didn't comment on my appearance and, Julia, I spent hours!"

"Morton loves you. He's probably preoccupied over work. David often is—I should say usually is."

"I'm an organized woman. Do you think that bothers Morton?"

"Maybe a little."

"Of course if it weren't for my prodding, he wouldn't be half the success he is."

"Morton is placid. Perhaps he has as much business as he wants. He might wish to feel less strained about work. He might like less advice."

Edith stared at the wall, deep in thought. "You're right," she finally conceded. "I'll keep that in mind. Marriage and family are of utmost importance, and nothing must ruffle the equanimity of the home. I would prefer you don't mention this to anyone—even Melinda. It's rather personal."

"I won't."

To have Edith confide in her was rather pleasant, Julia realized. Seeing that the booth with wall hangings had received an influx of customers, Edith left to help the manager. Julia stared after her, amazed.

On the way home Julia leaned against the comfortable seats in David's phaeton, refreshed by a breeze from the lake. The stars, blazing in the clear sky like countless candles were crossed by a delicate slice of moon. The clop of the horse was musical, hypnotic. The externals were lovely, Julia reflected. "Did you enjoy the bazaar?" she asked after a thoughtful silence.

"Yes. I realized tonight how important your church is to you. I'll be attending Sunday service with you. I've cut myself off from a big part of your life in not doing so."

"Oh, good," Julia said flatly. The desired commitment was untimely.

"What was this about going to school in Indianapolis?" David asked.

"Nothing much. The school didn't suit my temperament. It was too strict. I worked hard on my studies and I failed to make it. I . . . I tend to try hard, and it's very upsetting to fail." There—that was enough said. She was under no obligation to reveal facts that would lower his esteem of her.

"In what way was it strict?"

"Too many rules—that type of thing. I hated it, and I want to forget it."

"Fine."

Averting any further discussion, she asked, "Will we rent our own pew or sit with Father? Each 'slip' seats five, so we could sit in Father's."

"Would you prefer sitting with Melinda?"

"Yes."

"All right. By the way, I was introduced to Arthur Newton tonight. He's the one you were engaged to, if I remember correctly?"

"Yes, for five years. I wish that he didn't go to our church—it keeps our past open." It would serve no purpose to tell David that Arthur probably still cared for her. He would think it petty of her to state it. What did it matter what Arthur felt anyway? Only David was important.

Arriving home, David stabled the horse, while Julia greeted Michael and Bridget on the back steps. The post lantern illuminated the yellow in Bridget's bonnet and her flushed cheeks. She stepped down to the walk and excitedly moved around.

"What is it, Bridget?" Julia asked.

"Michael and myself was walking downtown. We heard Mr. D. L. Moody speaking outside the courthouse and we stopped to listen. What a grand-speaking man himself is!"

"The jail's in the cellar and he preached where the prisoners and the people outside could hear," Michael added. "After he finished speaking, he walked up and asked if we was Christians."

"I told himself my name was Bridget Boland and I loved Jesus with all me heart," she said excitedly. "I asked himself if he minded me listening to him, and me being a Catholic. He's stout, and my can himself laugh!"

David joined them as Bridget continued. "Mr. Moody said when he first came to Chicago he had Sunday school meetings. Some Catholic boys broke his windows and called him fearful names. Themselves ruined his meetings. Mr. Moody asked the bishop to stop the boys. The bishop and Mr. Moody prayed together, and the bishop kept the Catholic boys from disturbing Mr. Moody from then on." Bridget turned her head from Julia to David in amazement. "For truth, Mr. Moody was telling us this. In Ireland, no Catholics is praying with Protestants."

Julia marveled at Bridget's capacity to accept everyone, from Mr. Moody to Mary.

"D. L. Moody is impressive, but he's a little too fervent for me," David offered.

Julia noted the troubled look on Bridget's face as she looked at David—but she didn't try to contest his statement.

In the house, while David read the *Chicago Tribune*, Julia changed into a cool nightgown. As she undressed, she removed the letter and placed it in the bottom of one of her bureau drawers. She would *not* return it to David's coat tomorrow. Let him worry about where he had left it.

Fourteen

The next day the wind lifted the heat from the stalks of blazing star, compass plant, bush clover, and tall grass in the prairie to the west and dumped it on Chicago. Julia and Melinda were having a snack at the Arcade Dining Hall, a downtown restaurant renowned for its platter lunches and shortcake. The Arcade's stand-up bar was busy, though it was closer to dinner than lunch. Businessmen on break bolted down a snack, and no sooner had one finished than another man took his place.

Melinda took a sip of water. "Well, how was Nelda?"

Julia had just visited Nelda. Dr. Sutton had provided Nelda with a desk and two periods a day in which to write. Her manuscript was a tangle of unrelated and unresolved situations.

"Nelda's on a light dosage of drugs and she's become somewhat maniacal again. There's a peculiar light in her eyes. Yet she has short periods when she seems almost normal."

"Is Martha back?" Melinda asked.

Last week Martha's sister-in-law in Virginia had died, and Martha had gone there for the funeral. "No. She'll be back in a few days. Nelda hasn't missed Martha, occupied as she is with her story."

"George says I must return in an hour—so hurry with your peaches. You know he's against my leaving for a break."

"I think he's being too strict."

"No, he's not. We're busy. We're correlating the effect on patients of having two periods of recreation a day rather than one. George aims for a higher cure rate than any other asylum. The other superintendents

159

make grandiose claims of cure based on opinion. We plan to document our cures."

"You're more than a volunteer then?"

"Yes. I'm like a partner; though of course I'm under George's authority. I'm very happy, Julia. I've always wished my life to count. Perhaps that's why I want my poetry published. I guess I'm egocentric."

"For heaven's sake, no! You're creative and you need to create."

"I suppose. The difficult part is meeting George's standards for me. I want to, but I'm so weak. Julia, last night I was reading in bed, and I had such a craving for Miss Nancy's chocolate cakes. I fought going to the kitchen. But I went—and ate them all, every last one. This morning I had two stacks of pancakes and six sausages. I'm sure I've gained back every pound I lost. What if George should stop loving me over this? I'd do anything for him. Why can't I stay away from food?"

"It's over six months until the wedding. You have plenty of time to lose forty pounds."

Melinda shook her head. "The weight has to be lost before the wedding gown's made. I have three months, that's all."

"Explain your difficulty to George."

"He won't understand. He's a rigid disciplinarian. He must set an example for the patients, and he's never impulsive. He never eats a bit more than he needs. That's why he looks so trim. Would you talk to him for me? Tell him I want to be thin, but I can't stand being hungry. Ask him if fifteen pounds will be all right. I could manage that."

Melinda sipped her coffee while Julia thought. "I don't know. Won't he be angry that you sent me?"

"I think it'll show him how worried I am."

"All right then, I will."

Julia told Melinda about Diane's letter and David's late homecoming the date he received it.

"I can guess exactly what happened," Melinda said. "David was late because he met Diane. He met her face-to-face and discouraged her in strong terms. He had to make sure she wouldn't contact him again."

"I don't know that—nor do you."

"Yes, I do—I know David."

"Perhaps you're right. That would explain why David looked so disturbed that night."

They were quiet while the waiter filled their coffee cups.

"But why didn't he tell me about meeting Diane—why?" Julia absently stirred cream into her coffee.

"He didn't want to hurt you—after all, jealousy has been a problem for you."

"No, it hasn't."

"You have a short memory."

"I know, you're right," Julia admitted reluctantly.

"Throw the letter out today," Melinda advised.

Julia met Melinda's eyes and nodded. She then told Melinda about her meeting with Arthur at the bazaar. "I wonder if my life would be calmer if I had married Arthur," she mused. "I never loved him as I do David, so I wouldn't have suffered over him. I think I love David too much."

"I understand that," Melinda said quietly. "I have the same problem regarding George."

"For me, it's good to have the distraction of Nelda and David's parents."

"Then maybe you understand why I'm occupied with work."

Julia nodded. "When shall I speak to George?"

Melinda lifted her gloves from her lap. "Now, if you would. Hurry up and eat."

"I'm not hungry." Julia felt mildly nauseated. She decided not to confide in Melinda about her growing fear that she was pregnant. Julia didn't wish to think about that subject. "Let's just go."

George was at his desk, the light from the window shining on the back of his gray-blond hair. Julia was surprised he didn't arrange his desk to have a view of the lake. Instead, the seasons passed behind him while before him passed the titles he added to his bookshelves.

Melinda stood before his desk, suddenly speechless. She flushed and cleared her throat. Then losing all nerve, she ran from the room, leaving Julia to initiate the conversation about Melinda's weight problem. He looked at Julia through his spectacles, his eyes narrow with irritation. He wasn't accustomed, Julia realized, to Melinda's flitting off without his approval. Julia fanned herself, feeling hot and nervous about this confrontation.

"I hope Melinda returns immediately," he declared stiffly. "We're in the midst of an important study."

"She'll be right back. She asked me to speak to you."

"Yes?"

"She's having trouble losing weight. She tends to be nervous, and half-starving herself is too difficult. Could you relent a little? I think she could lose fifteen pounds by the wedding, but forty is too much."

"Melinda hasn't told me she's having difficulty."

"She doesn't want to disappoint you. She would do anything to please you."

His hands formed a tent under his chin. "Melinda must be an example of discipline to the patients. We cannot expect them to discipline their minds if we don't set an example of physical and mental assiduity."

"But Melinda can't change her nature."

"We *are* in the business of changing natures here."

"Yes, sick ones. But Melinda is healthy and happy." She worried about her sister's future. This man bloomed in a soil of ideals that might bury Melinda.

"I'm quite wealthy, Julia. I can hire what help I need. I could hire a hundred secretaries if necessary. I could allow Melinda to gorge in our apartments when we marry. But I prefer having Melinda work with me. She inspires me."

"But, Melinda—"

"We lead a disciplined life here," he interrupted. "A place for everything and everything in its place. A time for performance of duty and duty performed. A place of cleanliness and cleanliness observed. A place of order and order maintained."

Julia couldn't understand the subtleties of George and Melinda's relationship, but given George's regulations, she understood what Melinda must do. "I see," Julia said. "Yes, I see. I'll speak to Melinda."

"And do send her back to work."

Julia found Melinda in the diversion room, playing chess with a patient. Melinda excused herself and called a melancholic-looking woman to take her place. The woman shuffled to the table and dropped in a heap in the chair. She looked at the board with a dazed expression.

"The important thing is that they are kept busy," Melinda pointed out, moving a knight for the woman. "This will count as one recreational period."

Melinda took Julia aside. "Well, what did George say?"

"I think you will have to lose forty pounds before you have your dress fitted. I don't think there is any other way. You'll violate George's ideals and rules if you don't diet strictly."

Melinda blinked rapidly. "Then I will—somehow."

At home, Julia stood before the brick fire pit in the alley, clutching Diane's letter in her hand . The bricks were coated with soot, blackened in what seemed a thick layer from countless burnings. Dropping the letter into the pit and lighting it, she watched the tiny flame dance on the burned debris, a far smaller flame than Arthur's letter had made. She felt disappointed; her mind had envisioned a bonfire.

But the relief was momentary. When the letter had burned, she still wondered if David were having an affair with Diane.

In church Sunday morning, along with the caroling call of robins and the harsh "jeeah" of blue jays through the tall windows, there was a faint stirring as heads turned to view David in the Adam's "slip." Julia was relieved there would be no more comments, such as, "I do hope your husband will join us next week." Or, "My, we would like to see Mr. Gerard in church." Or, "Does your husband attend another church?"

Morton was staring at Edith as if fascinated. Edith wore a delicate dress of sea-foam green and a matching hat. The crown was depressed like a basket and piled with fruit and flowers. Because Morton was such a quiet, bland man, Julia thought it a triumph that Edith had fascinated him. It was strange about Morton, Julia thought. When she was with him she noticed his blue eyes and regular features and wide, rather flat face; but away from him, she forgot his features and imagined him sharp-faced like Edith.

Morton turned. "Glad to have you, David. Yes, quite glad—wouldn't you say, Edith?"

"Indeed! A number of the congregation are on holiday, David. We're usually far more crowded—Reverend Portor attracts large crowds. He is doing a series on the ethical consequences of sinful behavior; it's quite informative. He often treats topical issues—the question of the right to vote for women, the labor movement, the effect of the Southern Rebellion on the economy—all in a Christian context, of course."

"We have some of the finest families too, don't we, Edith?" Morton added eagerly.

"Indeed."

"We're fortunate to have Reverend Portor, aren't we, dear?" Morton continued.

Edith's mouth opened, probably to explain why, then shut. She smiled at Morton. "You tell him, dear."

Edith nodded to encourage Morton. "Reverend Portor was recently offered a pulpit in a large church in New York," Morton explained, "but he prefers the vitality of Chicago and will stay on. Isn't that right, dear?"

"Exactly," Edith agreed, smiling proudly at her husband.

The quartet was in place. "I think we should turn about," Morton told Edith.

After the sermon, Julia heard Edith whisper to Morton, "Dear, ask David if he liked the sermon." It had concerned the effect of lascivious spectacles on society.

Morton turned to David. "What did you think of the sermon?"

"I'd say it was aimed more at the intellect than the spirit. But it contained some interesting thinking and my conscience was stirred. What did you think, Julia?"

"I agree. The sermon should have stirred our spirits as well as our minds."

"I disagree," Edith ventured. "We must reach the intellect in order to open the spirit."

The next morning Bridget hung laundry under a blue sky with clouds that billowed fuller than her sheets. *Saints, in Ireland they never had such blue skies as they do in Chicago*, she thought reflectively. Then she felt guilty for being disloyal to her beloved country.

"Hi." It was Mary at the hedge, her cats running behind her. Her laundry was finished. "I ain't got much laundry this week. Mrs. Cullen is out East and that cuts the laundry, I'll tell you! I wonder what she's doing out there? If you ask me, I'm worried. All she ever says is how wonderful it is out East. I hope she ain't thinking of moving back. What would I do? I ain't moving east to clean for her."

"Herself won't be leaving this fair place."

"You ain't doing a good job gettin' your whites cleaned. You should use more bluing," Mary remarked.

Bridget studied her laundry. It glistened as far as she was concerned. What a difficult best friend Mary was. Sometimes she was tempted to drop her and take up with Margaret down the street. Margaret was quiet and didn't criticize others. "If myself used more bluing, they'd turn blue."

"Well, don't be huffy. How's my bridesmaid's dress coming along?"

"I've got itself cut out, and it's pretty as can be."

Patrick was chained on his run, and Mary confined the cats on her back porch before coming through the hedge. "I gotta talk to you. Remember I said that Billy had some awful gossip. Well, he told me it. Of course, I ain't to tell no one—but I'll tell you. It's—"

"I don't want to be listening to gossip."

"This gossip you'll hear. Billy saw Mr. Gerard kissing the lady next door to where he works—Mrs. Hastings. He was just coming off work when he seen it. Mr. Gerard and Mrs. Hastings was back in the driveway, where they thought no one could see them. But Billy did."

Bridget stared at Mary, speechless.

"Ha!" Mary's eyes sparkled. Bridget knew Mary was delighted her prophecy of trouble had been fulfilled. "It's love between them two, I say—and worse!"

Bridget exploded. "Let that not be said! Billy is a liar, he is. Himself will be saying anything to have revenge on Mr. Gerard for firing him."

"My Billy don't lie," Mary spat. "Remember, Mr. Gerard gave

Billy fifty dollars. Well—he paid him off to keep quiet! You ask Mr. Gerard, I say! Just ask him. He'll tell you!"

"Saints!"

"Billy ain't got no way to earn fifty dollars by working. You're the Bible scholar. Doesn't the Bible tell you to trust your best friend and not think she's lyin'?"

"Aye."

"Do you think Mrs. Hastings is the veiled lady that once came here?"

"Myself isn't knowing." Bridget hadn't missed the tension between the Gerards. Had Julia been afraid to tell Mr. Gerard about the miscarriage because she doubted his love? Julia might suspect that Mr. Gerard had married her for her money; that was if he had. Was Mr. Gerard with Mrs. Hastings during his long hours away from home? Yet Mr. Gerard had a kindly nature, like Father Brady's back home. But where would Billy be getting fifty dollars, a fortune itself? She didn't wish to think about it. A loyal servant girl mustn't think of such things! She would be praying for the Gerards' happiness, she would. Night and day! Bridget worried that the fragile Julia would break if Mr. Gerard didn't love her. Sad, it was, that Julia was not loving Jesus and depending on Him.

Bridget avowed, "If yourself says one word to Mrs. Gerard, I'll never be speaking to you on this earth. You'll not be in me wedding!"

Mary placed her hands on her hips. "I ain't no gossip."

"Don't be telling any of the servant girls either, Mary Monahan!"

"I ain't. I only told you because I had to—you working there and all."

Bridget wouldn't cry in front of Mary—she wouldn't give her that satisfaction. She hurried from the hedge and finished hanging her laundry. Not until she had unhooked Patrick from his lead and carried her laundry baskets to the porch did she cry. Patrick pushed under her hem and nuzzled his head on her shoes, covering her feet. As she gulped back a sob, she heard the kitchen door open.

"What's wrong?" Julia asked, seeing Bridget's tear-streaked face.

"Oh . . . oh . . ."

"Can you talk about it?" Julia urged gently.

Bridget wiped her face with her apron. "Mary is upsetting me with bad gossip. All the servant girls is gossips and Mary is the worst of them. It's sorry I am that Mary is in me wedding, and that me mama's lace is on her dress."

"Was Mary gossiping about you and Michael?"

"No. Itself was gossip Billy gave her. Would yourself be believing something Billy said to Mary, and himself so mean?"

"That depends on what it is and why he said it."

"Oh, if only me mama were here—I need to be talking to her."

Julia didn't say anything for a while. Her forehead was furrowed as if she were struggling with some thought. Bridget picked up her baskets, thinking Julia wished privacy. "Wait," Julia said. "You might see your mother soon. Mr. Gerard sent tickets to your parents inviting them to your wedding. We haven't heard yet if they can come."

Bridget's eyes were amazed. "Is itself true, I'm wondering!"

"Yes."

Bridget ran into Julia's arms. "Oh, thank you! When will themselves be here?"

"We sent the tickets about two weeks ago, and we should have word in about three weeks. This isn't for certain—remember that!"

"Oh! Themselves will come!"

"Bridget, please! I don't want disappointment to ruin your wedding. I wasn't even supposed to tell you—I promised Mr. Gerard I wouldn't until we were sure your parents were coming. But you were wishing for your mother, and I couldn't help it."

Bridget regretted that Julia had broken a promise. It was another sign of trouble between the Gerards. She determined to pray for them twice as hard—but in the meantime herself must say this one little thing or burst. "Julia . . . I . . . myself is worried. Did yourself tell Mr. Gerard about the miscarriage?"

"Yes, of course. I never meant to keep that a secret long."

At least that was in the open, Bridget thought with relief.

Certainly, Mr. and Mrs. Boland would come, Julia hoped. After all, a chance to see Bridget and the United States, which the Irish esteemed, could not be refused. "Don't tell Mr. Gerard I mentioned the invitation."

Bridget stared at Julia with troubled eyes. "Excuse myself, Julia. I shouldn't be saying anything, surely, but isn't ourselves supposed to tell everything to our husbands? Myself is telling Michael everything."

"I'll tell Mr. Gerard about this when it's the right time. We have some problems in our relationship, and I must use discretion."

Julia felt Bridget's eyes follow her as she turned toward the kitchen door. She supposed Bridget thought her mistress should be above problems and secrecy.

Fifteen

$\mathcal{I}$t was the dead-center of summer, when the heat and the steamy atmosphere glued Julia to her porch chair in a delicious lassitude from which she hoped never to move. Perhaps last winter was a dream; the cold winter ahead a fable. The locusts had bawled their last chorus and it was peaceful. An ant crawled up her lower skirt and disappeared as it negotiated the underside of the flounce on the upper skirt. *Ah, there it is,* she thought, pleased it had made the journey. She wondered if today was the best day she would have, centered as it was between the past and the future. Maybe what she didn't know about David was like sweet summer and knowledge was cold winter. *And, of course, winter might be a fable*, she mused again.

As the letter-carrier wheeled past on a velocipede, she hoped he would turn back with a letter from the Bolands. Of course it was too early to hear; the round trip by steamer took about eleven days, and when one counted extra days for delivery between the port and the Bolands', one must figure on at least a month.

Julia had no plans this morning. This afternoon she and Bridget would visit Edgar. As she sat musing, she was surprised to see David and Mr. Poppy, an inside salesman, arrive, each driving a separate buggy. She walked out to meet them. Mr. Poppy, a cheerful man of an indeterminable age with long legs and a big belly, jumped from his buggy and pumped Julia's hand. David had told Julia that Mr. Poppy's cheerful personality produced sales and generated him a substantial commission.

"My dear young woman, don't you look the picture of loveliness in that cool white dress! I say, my sweet wife could learn some beauty tips from you."

"How is Mrs. Poppy's heart problem?"

His cheerful eyes dimmed only a moment. "She's doing very well. She rests when she has pain and always sits with me at dinner."

"Oh, good!"

"She is determined to have you to dinner as soon as her health is stable."

"I'd like that." Then turning to David, she said, "I'm surprised to see you."

David was looking at Mr. Poppy's buggy, the muscles around his mouth trying to suppress a smile. "I should think you can guess why I'm here."

"How can I?"

David took her hand and led her to Mr. Poppy's buggy, a phaeton with shiny plum fenders and a lighter shade of plum upholstery. The wood doors were the same shade as the body, and Julia thought it a most attractive buggy. It had a fold-back top, two oil lamps, and open sides and back. The horse was a stylish gray hackney with a black mane and tail, and she had noticed his high-stepping action when he trotted in.

"Well, do you like it?" David asked her, trying to be businesslike. "I've wanted you to have a buggy for some time."

Julia looked at him. He smiled fully, unable to suppress his joy any longer. As she realized the rig was hers, she threw her arms around him, crying, "For me! Oh, thank you, darling."

"Now, didn't I tell you she'd love the buggy," Mr. Poppy stated. "Mrs. Poppy has one like it, and, my, she's proud of it."

David showed Julia how the various features operated and accompanied her on a trial ride around the block. "Do you mind my choosing it without you? I wanted the joy of surprising you."

"No, I love it. David, I love you! It's exactly what I would have chosen. I love the color—it's dignified."

"This morning I hired a boy to groom and feed the horse for you—and my horse as well. I don't have the time."

That afternoon she drove the rig to Edgar's. Bridget sat beside her, admiring it. "Myself hasn't seen its like in Dunquin or Chicago or Queenstown, when I was there. Stop dripping," she scolded Patrick affectionately.

Edgar had requested Bridget bring Patrick, and to protect the upholstery Bridget held him so that his hot tongue dripped on her uniform. "I wish we had brought a towel for you," Julia declared.

"Myself will dry." Bridget continued her praise. "Myself feels like a queen on a throne on this soft seat. Mr. Gerard is loving you so much. Aye, itself is the grandest gift in the world."

Julia thought Bridget's extreme delight with the gift a bit odd. "Yes, yes—it's nice."

At the Gerards', Alma met them with a smile and detained them in the vestibule. "Edgar stood alone for fifteen minutes! Really it's a miracle! He has smiled at times and he enjoys the estimating. I haven't seen him like this since we were first married. I shouldn't say this—but the attack has improved him in many ways."

"Well—wonderful!" Julia was sincerely delighted.

Alma's expression changed. "Of course I worry all the time. He can revert just like that. He still has horrible moods and makes us miserable with his demands. It's like living on a swing. I don't know what mood to expect . . . Well, come—Edgar is expecting you."

Alma found Bible study boring, and she excused herself to rest. Edgar's nurse, Mrs. Reatherford, plumped up his pillows, then left to do some shopping. Julia worried about Alma, who had developed a fear of the outside world. Alma delegated the shopping to the nurses and her servant girl and went out only when it was unavoidable, and then only if dazed with chloral tablets. Her life literally revolved around Edgar.

As they entered the room, Edgar snapped, "This is a bad day for me. Hand me a cracker." Crackers were more helpful for his indigestion than stomach tonic. He ate a cracker and gave Patrick a quick pat on the head.

"Set Patrick on the floor and let's proceed with the Bible study," Edgar demanded. "I'm sitting on a keg of dynamite with this upset stomach of mine. Please present something clear-cut today. I don't understand half of what you read. Find a tale or something interesting. Don't give me any prophecies or parables. I'm not in the mood for depressing information."

"Is the story of Jonah all right?"

"Fine—fine."

Bridget read about Jonah's confinement in a large fish, ending with, " 'And the Lord spake unto the fish, and it vomited out Jonah upon the dry *land*' " (Jonah 2:10).

"Sheer fairy tale—impossible!" Edgar bellowed. "No man can live in a fish."

"If the Bible is saying it, then itself is being true."

"Impossible. Julia, do you believe such nonsense?"

Julia temporized. "I don't think it's nonsense. I think it's an allegory of how when man doesn't do what God wishes, he will end up in a dark place. When I'm far from God, I have depressed and dark feelings."Oh yes, she had those feelings to a great degree.

"That's more like it," Edgar stated. "That makes sense."

Bridget calmly met Edgar's stormy face. " 'Tis true what Mrs. Gerard is saying, but Jonah lived in a great fish."

"Ah—enough!"

"Then which part of me Bible is true?"

"I am *not* in a mood for philosophy."

But Julia thought the question pertinent. She didn't feel qualified to separate true scripture from false; could anyone?

Edgar blurted, "I've had enough. Come back soon. I'm sorry if I'm disagreeable. I don't mean to hurt your feelings."

"Aye."

Julia dropped Bridget at home, but enjoying the novelty of driving, she toured the streets in her North Side location. Finally she headed for David's lumberyard, which was also on the north side of the Chicago River. It was close to the McCormick Reaper Factory and the Rush Street bridge, a swing bridge with the bridgekeeper's house atop the trusses. Julia found David in his office. Pulling a chair up to his desk, she stated joyously, "I've been driving around for over an hour—testing the buggy. I love it!"

"I'm glad! Are you having any trouble?"

"None."

"You're my second unexpected caller. Martha just left. She returned from Virginia last night and visited Nelda this morning. Martha said Nelda glows. She found it odd."

"The last time I visited Nelda she was maniacal, not glowing. She was concerned about her book, that it had too many plots. Her thinking is muddled and she doesn't finish sentences and events. The book is hopeless."

"Will she be upset when the book isn't published?"

"Very," Julia said, daintily wiping her damp brow with her handkerchief. "She has no capacity to handle problems. Perhaps George was correct to stop her writing."

"I don't agree. She must learn to cope."

"I suppose."

Julia stood to leave. "I'm meeting a man from Iowa for dinner and won't be home," David informed her. "He's a housing contractor with a large business, and he doesn't have a quality source of lumber. If he likes what I have, he'll contract with me."

She had learned not to show disappointment. She would rather have slivers of David's time than not have him at all. Of course, she had her church and the Women's Mission Society to occupy her time. She wished, though, that she, rather than the lumberyard, could be his joy.

Yet, in rapidly expanding Chicago, men like David were the rule, men like Morton the exception.

Before she left, David gave her fifty dollars to purchase wallpaper and have it installed. She bought a cream and blue pattern for their bedroom and a beige design for the sitting room.

By the end of the week the paper was up and she was pleased with it. Once she had wished for a house that Trina hadn't lived in; now she felt differently. The iron pickets that fenced their roof were original—she didn't know another house in Chicago that had them. The four bedrooms, though small, were sufficient for them and at least one child. She enjoyed listening to the birds and insects from the side porch. She liked being near enough to David's lumberyard that he could join her for lunch, though he seldom did.

On Sunday afternoon while David worked in his study, Julia drove her buggy to Dr. Sutton's asylum. She found Nelda reading her manuscript in her armchair. Nelda wasn't allowed to write on Sunday, and her pencils and pens had been removed. The bright flush of madness was on her face, and her eyes were glittery. She wore a cream-colored dress, which emphasized her red face. Perhaps the flush and glitter were the glow Martha noticed; Martha was apt to interpret Nelda's symptoms positively.

"I'm proofreading—oh, Julia, do you think I'll ever have the book right?"

"There's a point where a work is the best it can be, and one must stop. Perhaps you're at that point."

"No! Netta has fallen in love with a painter, and they will marry in England. Netta is fond of the southern region, as it is a wealthier section, and they will marry there."

"Isn't Netta married—after all, she lost a son?"

"What?"

"Don't you remember?"

"No." Nelda looked blank and alarmed, and Julia wished she hadn't mentioned it.

"Melinda says hello."

"Where is Melinda? She hardly ever comes."

"She's working at Lakeside this afternoon." Melinda was helping George define the frequency of individual delusions at Lakeside (sight, smell, sound, taste, feel, suspicions, mutilation, grandeur, poverty, God, spirits, demons, murder, witches, bodily organs, and others). George needed the information for a meeting with experts of the mind on Monday. Julia didn't like Melinda working on Sunday; but Melinda and George had at least joined Julia and David at church.

"Tell her to come—I've got to show her my painting."

Nelda pointed to a painting opposite her bed, placed where she could see it on waking and before sleeping. It was of the Chicago skyline. The colors were peculiar: the sunlight greenish, the buildings the color of dirt. The sky was black and blue. "Do you like it?" Nelda queried.

"It's interesting. Did you do it?"

"No, I'm a writer—writers don't paint."

"Then who painted it?" Julia asked.

"An inmate. He's very nice and about my age." Nelda lowered her eyes, like a girl in love. "He's dark-haired and he limps from a wound he got in the Southern Rebellion. This gives him a romantic air, I think."

"Do you like him?" Julia questioned further.

Nelda's eyelids fluttered. She didn't comment.

"Nelda, please answer." Dr. Sutton believed romantic emotions stressed the patient and retarded progress; therefore he forbade conversation between sexes. "Where did you meet him? Why did he give you the painting?"

"You won't tell anyone?"

"No."

"We met on the piazza one day. It was fate. My attendant and his attendant started talking and forgot us—his name is Bernard. We talked about my writing and his painting. He's an artist and his family imprisoned him here to keep him from becoming a famous painter. It's quite awful—I hate to tell you. They're jealous of his talent. They've had him locked at various places for ten years."

"This isn't a prison; it's an asylum."

Her eyes lost their focus, and perspiration appeared on her face. "It is a prison—it is! He said it is and he knows! I have tried to leave and I can't. I try every day."

"Try! How do you try?"

Nelda ignored the question. "Maybe I'll go see Melinda."

"Don't do that! Melinda will come when she can. She wouldn't be able to see you if you went there. Nelda—listen! Do not try to leave! Now tell me—how did you get this painting?"

"Bernard left it outside my door. I told the attendant you brought it. Please don't tell Dr. Sutton where it came from!" Nelda gripped the arms of her chair. "Oh, please!" she begged.

Julia couldn't inflict pain on Nelda. The painting could not intrinsically produce romantic feelings. Nelda would not likely speak to Bernard again and her interest would subside. "All right," she agreed.

Julia slipped out, locking the door behind her. Just beyond the hallway, in a small anteroom, she met an attendant and an inmate, a man with delicate features and dark hair. His fingers were stained various colors. Because he stood still, Julia couldn't tell if he limped. His eyes darted from Julia back to Nelda's door. "Hello," he said cautiously. "Do you know her?"

"Yes. Are you Bernard?"

"Yes."

There was no apparent sign of Bernard's madness. He had an intelligent face, and Julia thought if Bernard and Nelda were sane, he might be a good suitor for Nelda. "Nice to meet you," Julia said.

"Come along," the attendant urged, taking his arm.

"Goodbye," Bernard said pleasantly.

When Julia returned the keys, she found Dr. Sutton weeding mums. Gardening was Dr. Sutton's hobby. He wiped his hands on his canvas trousers. "Did you have a good visit with Nelda?"

"No . . . I'm worried about her. She's somewhat maniacal again. I . . . I don't mean to question your methods, but I wonder if Nelda needs more sedation."

"I don't want Nelda stupefied. She must learn to work through simple problems. It's difficult to maintain a balance between too much sedation and too little. I watch Nelda carefully and I'm aware of her mood swings."

"She threatened to leave."

"It's unlikely she could. She's either locked in her room or with an attendant. But if she makes another threat, I'll increase her dose of bromides."

"I met Bernard in the anteroom. What is his problem?"

"He has delusions of persecution. He believes he's being martyred for his art."

She was tempted to tell him about the painting, but she had promised Nelda she wouldn't. She couldn't betray her trust. "The poor fellow," Julia commented sympathetically.

At home, the wasting sun threw long shadows as she climbed the back stairs.

To her surprise the door was locked. Using her key, she stepped into the silent house. Everyone was gone, including Patrick. She found a note from David near the sink, requesting her to meet him at Lakeside. It was hastily scrawled on a ledger sheet, she noted. Why would David be called to Lakeside? Why would she? Fear gripped her heart.

Arriving at Lakeside, she saw David's phaeton and Morton's light-bodied stanhope in the driveway. She identified the horses hitched at the posts as from the police department by their highly polished leather and brass fittings. Her father's buggy was parked near the portico, the door on the driver's side still open. Father never left his buggy door open, Julia observed. There were no attendants, patients, or police officers on the front grounds. The windows in the wings were raised behind the bars, but there was no one in sight.

The activity was on the other side. She heard it now: the murmur of conversation, the alto harmony of waves. Walking quickly across the lawn, Julia wrapped her hands around her waist to calm her churning emotions.

She rounded the north wing and saw the water—it was creased and white in the late sun. There was a crowd on the beach, and a number of small manned boats on the lake. Julia had seen a similar scene when a young boy was missing, and she remembered he had not been found. She thought she'd faint from apprehension. Then David came running to her. He was in his shirt-sleeves and had apparently left the house hastily. Looking past David, she saw Edith and Morton standing on the edge of the beach, transfixed, staring at her. She felt sick. *Oh, let me wake up and find this a dream!* she whispered silently.

David caught her in his arms and held her close.

"David!" she cried, pulling away from him. "What's wrong?" She was afraid to hear what he would say. Then she said, "Is it George?"

"No." His eyes were stark.

"Oh, David!"

"It's Melinda."

"Oh—"

"She's missing," David choked. "She went swimming."

She lifted her head, her teeth chattered. "But she and George were working."

"You know he insists on daily exercise."

"How long has she been gone?"

"Three hours."

"No—no—oh, David, not that long!"

Julia heard the sound of her voice as it screamed. She wanted to scream until her throat ripped out. She wanted to scream and follow the sound up and leave no shadow on earth, like a gull.

David held her face down on his shoulder. "Hush, Julia. Melinda's an excellent swimmer. The police haven't given up hope. She well might have drifted."

"What happened?"

"Melinda's swimming attendant said Melinda swam quite far out; then she lost sight of her. She immediately searched for Melinda in George's skiff. The attendant is quite shaken. She blames herself, and yet it's not her fault."

"No," Julia whispered, "it isn't. Melinda always swims out too far." She could not say swam; she could never use the past tense concerning Melinda.

"Darling, I'd like to join the search. Your father's out searching with George. I was waiting for you before going with Morton in his boat. Will you be all right without me?"

"Yes. Where is Miss Nancy? I don't see her."

"She left for a brief holiday this morning."

On the beach Julia found Melinda's blue swimming cape. It was in a heap, the white pointed collar on top. The attendant had evidently forgotten it. It looked soiled and sandy; the crowd had been walking on it. Didn't they care? Didn't they realize it was Melinda's? She picked it up and shook off the sand. She would dip the soiled areas in the lake and scrub them and return a clean cape to Melinda.

Julia started for the lake. Then Edith was there, pulling her close, crooning to her like a mother as Julia sobbed.

"Of course Melinda is all right," Edith obviously tried to convince herself as well as Julia. "I have declared that to the police and Morton, and I expect Melinda in shortly. There are six police boats searching, plus George and Father and others. Melinda is perfectly fine, believe me."

With all her heart, Julia wanted to believe that.

Sixteen

Melinda had been missing six hours. Her swimming attendant had just returned from Edith's house, where the servant was watching Freddie, and had reported that the boy was fine. Julia and Edith were near the shoreline, the attendant standing behind them. The air smelled fishy. The sun had set and the sky had grayed except for a blur of pink light at the horizon. Figures on the lake were pressed in one dimension, like an amateur painting. It drove Julia mad to watch the boats. She would think she saw an extra member in one until it moved and she realized the person was in the boat behind.

Julia turned her head to Edith. "It's my fault!" Julia cried. "Listen, please! It's my fault Melinda's lost. Melinda is weak from dieting. I shouldn't have encouraged her to diet. I was responsible for her. I always have been. I hate it—I hate being responsible for her. Oh, Edith—why did I encourage her to diet so strictly? I love her. I can't stand this waiting. Why doesn't a boat come in and at least report? At least Father should!"

"It is *not* your fault. No one is responsible for another person. One makes suggestions to improve an individual's life, that's all. One cannot violate another's will. Now, shake the sand from your shoes, Julia. You're hobbling around."

Julia's gray leather shoes were new, with violet tassels and lining. She thought how pretty they had looked this morning with her lavender silk stockings. "Why bother. They'll just fill up again."

"Mind the little things and the big things will fall into place."

"Edith, what does that mean?"

176

"It means Melinda might come back."

"That's like practicing magic," Julia said disgustedly.

"Shake out your shoes!"

Julia emptied out the sand. Then Edith tried to comfort the swimming attendant. Neither Julia nor Edith took her eyes from the lake for long.

"Melinda will be twenty-six in September," Julia said, fixing her frightened green eyes on Edith. "Edith! Melinda *will* be twenty-six."

"Yes, of course." Edith looked shaken—"Oh, Julia. I practically raised her and you. I was hard on her—do you think too hard? But I had to do as Mother would do. It wasn't easy, Julia. You and she didn't give me the respect you would have given Mother. Julia, was I too strict? Was I a good mother substitute?"

Julia looked at her tall, stark-faced sister. So much like herself in appearance, except the lines were more sharply drawn on Edith. "Yes," Julia said. "Yes—I had never looked at our situation from your perspective. Edith, is Melinda all right?"

"I've heard of swimmers being found hours after they've disappeared." Edith stepped up to Julia and started brushing off her dress. "There," she breathed. "Now, don't fret."

The brightest evening lights, Sirius and Venus, appeared as the sky turned dark. The lake, sky, and boats were the same color. Julia determined the boats' positions by their lanterns. The flares on the beach cast a crimson glow. The cheerful scene was a stark contrast to the tragedy before them. "How long do you think they'll continue the search?" she asked Edith.

"Not much longer."

Only the hardiest of the crowd had stayed on. The rest would read Melinda's fate in the newspaper tomorrow, Julia reasoned cynically. One who remained, a middle-aged woman, approached them. She carried a brown cloth satchel, which smelled of fruit and cheese; food for her vigil here, Julia thought. "I say they'll quit," the woman said in a jabbing voice.

"I should prefer not to have your opinion," Edith replied bitterly.

"They can't see anything out there."

"If you don't mind," Edith tried to cut her off.

"There's no hope of finding her. I've witnessed many drownings, and they have searched for her longer than most. I heard she was your sister."

Edith drew near the woman, confronting her sternly. "I would suggest that you leave. This is a private establishment and means can be found to evict you."

"Well!" the woman huffed.

"Good evening," Edith said curtly.

Julia viewed Edith with respect as the woman marched off.

Lanterns bobbed in the air as the boats advanced to shore. Julia hurried to the water. The first boat in was from the police department. Three officers stepped out, pulling the craft to the beach. "Are you related to Miss Adams?" one of the officers inquired.

"Yes," Edith answered.

"I'm very sorry, but Miss Adams hasn't been found."

"But there are other boats," Julia protested, glancing at several craft beaching nearby. "She must be on one of them."

"I'm sorry, young lady, but if she were, we would have been signaled."

"No, no—you're wrong!" She plunged toward the nearest boat, her shoes striking the water. Let it splash! What did she care!

"Julia!" It was David. He took her hand and pulled her from the water. His hand was cold and wet from beaching George's skiff. "Let me go!" she cried. "I must find Melinda."

Holding her arm firmly, he guided her toward the grass beyond the beach. Stumbling beside him, she gasped for air. She was sure she would suffocate.

When they were away from the crowd, he stopped. "The police discontinued the search," he stated. "Five square miles of water were gone over. There's no sign of Melinda. There's no hope she's alive, Julia," he finished strongly, apparently trying to get her to grasp reality.

"No. She's all right! She's just drifted off. She's all right!" Julia screamed.

"Darling, I wish she were."

"She'll come in!"

The rest of the family joined them. Morton was holding Edith's arm, her face was drained of color. Even the lantern he held failed to lend color to it. Edith stared at Julia, her eyes turned upward, vacant. Suddenly her upper body swayed, her knees folded, and she sank to the ground.

Morton knelt and placed her head in his lap. Though Edith never had fainted, she carried smelling salts in her reticule to aid others. Julia found the vial and held it under Edith's nose. "You really loved her," Julia whispered. "Oh, you loved her! Edith, it wasn't just responsibility with you. You loved her as much as I did."

Edith's eyes opened, and she reached up to touch Julia's cheek. "Let me get up," she demanded, firmly in control now.

Julia retrieved Melinda's cape from the bathhouse. "Let's go," she pleaded to David. "I can't stand it here. I never want to see this beach again. I never want to see the lake. I'll never swim in it—I'll never boat on it. I hate it!''

Julia had been standing for hours. Now it was a relief to sit in David's phaeton. "We'll bring your buggy home later," he stated.

The horse walked along, the steady clop, clop of its hooves on the road providing a monotonous background to Julia's dark thoughts. The bright stars that shone on the world since creation shone on it now; they always would, Julia thought ruefully. Didn't they know they should dim? Didn't they know Melinda was dead? Didn't God know? Didn't God care? Where was God? What kind of world was this, where tragedy brought no response from God, where everything continued as if nothing had happened?

"It's George's fault—mine too—that Melinda died," Julia uttered in despair.

"What on earth do you mean?"

"Melinda was weak from a diet and didn't have the energy to swim back in. George and I encouraged her to diet. She was too weak to be swimming. George shouldn't have permitted it. I should have insisted she quit swimming."

"Don't start that, Julia. Don't blame George or yourself. Don't put yourself through that."

She would experience what she had to, she inwardly declared.

But for now she felt death—heavy, solid, like a mountain. It was hard to breathe under the overwhelming weight. Death was black, stretching on infinitely. Death was cold, like the lake, but it had no moisture of life; and nothing warmed it, for no breeze, no sun, no human life touched it.

You could stand death in the noontime sun and sing hymns to it and flatter it and embrace it, but you'd never change it, Julia mused in her grief-stricken state of mind.

The morning of Melinda's memorial service, Julia sat in her father's parlor. Chairs, brought in from the church, had been set up in the parlor and dining room. The kitchen was laden with desserts and hot dinners from friends. Miss Nancy had returned last night and was presiding over the gifts. She planned to listen to the service from the kitchen, preferring to grieve in a familiar setting. The house had been draped with black and purple crape.

Melinda had not been found, so there was no casket. Where the casket would have been placed between the windows, there was a table with a lace cloth. A picture of Melinda decorated the table, as well as flowers from the family and hothouse orchids from George Huntly. Julia thought the orchids too exotic for simple Melinda. But she knew that Melinda would have adored any gift from George.

A tombstone had been ordered to read:

MELINDA ADAMS
BORN 1846
DROWNED 1871
NOT LOCATED

The "not located" was Edith's idea; if that were not stated, observers would suppose Melinda were buried beneath the tombstone. Edith hated deception. In addition, Edith maintained, if Melinda's grave were exhumed after the family died, there would be suspicions about Melinda's missing body. "Why risk scandal," Edith had told her father, "when the remedy is so simple? The possibility of exhumation is not so remote. The graves in the old Catholic cemetery are being exhumed to build Lincoln Park." Julia thought it unlikely anyone would care where Melinda was in a hundred years, but she didn't argue with Edith. If the information eased Edith's mind, then let her have it, Julia had told her father.

"Father is closing his office all week," Edith said. "He's quite broken up."

Julia didn't understand why her father expressed love only at marriage and death, but she was grateful at least for that. "Did you see Charlie in the dining room?"

"Yes, and I'm surprised. Doesn't he know Melinda was engaged?"

"I don't know. But either way, I'm glad he came. Melinda would have appreciated his presence."

Julia looked down at her plain black gown, trimmed with a narrow strip of black velvet at the neck and sleeves and a broad band of velvet on the lower skirt. It was the same dress she had worn at her grandmother's funeral. For months mourning clothes would remind her Melinda had died. What a cruel custom mourning was. She would rather be free to occasionally think Melinda were alive. How could she live without sharing life with Melinda? How could she even survive the funeral without Melinda!

David's hand covered hers. "Darling, is everything all right?" he asked tenderly.

"I just want to get this over with. Why doesn't Reverend Portor begin?"

"He is now," he whispered.

When the service was finished, George walked toward her. His face was drawn and his legs moved in a stiff and unnatural manner—like a wound-up toy. She looked bitterly at him. She didn't wish to speak to him. Why couldn't he make condolences to Father and leave it at that! He was intelligent; he must have deduced she blamed him in part for Melinda's death.

"It was a tasteful and appropriate service," he remarked. "I hadn't realized until Reverend Portor mentioned it that Melinda was only twenty-five. I had always thought of her as older."

"I'm surprised you hadn't discussed age."

"I assume there will be no service at the cemetery."

"None. The tombstone will be erected Friday at Fieldcrest Cemetery."

"Will you be there?" George asked.

"No. It's just being set in the family plot, so there is no reason to be there." His look of grief softened her. She gave him details to allow him to feel closer to the family. "Edith says they will simply lay a gravel foundation to set the stone in. It will take two men to raise the stone, because she ordered one weighing four hundred pounds. It will face east to catch the rising sun."

"I will be present," George said with determination.

"Then Edith will give you the name of the company engraving the monument so you can find out the time."

"I feel responsible for her death," he confided in Julia.

"What!"

"She was in a weakened condition. I shouldn't have let her swim."

"Oh, George—you shouldn't have!"

He turned white, accenting the bones on his neck. She realized he had lost weight. The shadows under his dull, listless eyes indicated he hadn't slept either.

"Forgive me," she said quietly. "We can't lay blame. It simply happened. I cannot blame myself either—though I encouraged her to diet." Julia started crying. "But, George, I *do* blame myself."

"I—I wonder what Melinda thought as she drowned."

"George, please. Why think about that!"

"I worry if she were troubled about the ring. I had made a point of being careful with it."

Julia couldn't believe he meant that. Yet his expression indicated he was serious. "I cannot believe she would think of a ring while she was drowning."

He looked at the lace-covered table. It was the picture in particular that held his attention. "This is a lot to ask, but could I have that picture of Melinda?"

Julia wished it for herself; it was the clearest image of Melinda she possessed.

"I understand it would be a sacrifice," he said.

Julia realized where Melinda would wish the picture to be. "Of course you can have it."

"I loved her," he admitted with difficulty, not used to sharing his true feelings with anyone.

She stared at him. The color had returned to his face. His eyes were intense and the veins under his thin skin were defined and pulsing. Julia hoped Melinda had known the extent of his love. Julia gave Melinda the memorial she would have wished. "There are many possible reasons Melinda drowned. Perhaps she became tangled in weeds. She might have hit a cold spot and gotten cramps in her legs. Some heavy object from a wreck might have struck her."

His eyes fixed on her as if she were a lifeline. He didn't speak. Finally he breathed a grateful, "Yes."

Fearing Nelda would have an excessive reaction to Melinda's death, Dr. Sutton advised that she not be told. Julia explained to her that Melinda was working long hours. Nelda threatened once again to visit Melinda, and when Julia informed Dr. Sutton of this, he increased Nelda's dosage of drugs.

On the first day of September Julia saw the letter-carrier peddling up her driveway and she met him outside. He jumped from his velocipede and handed her a thin, crumpled envelope. "It's from Dunquin, County Kerry, Ireland. It's in bad shape and it's a good thing you don't live on the West Coast."

He looked expectantly at Julia. He had been delivering mail only a short time and he still had his curiosity. "It's from my servant girl's parents," she explained.

"Oh?"

"My husband wrote them and they are replying."

"Well, you see the mail coming and going, and you get to wondering about the four corners of the world. When I'm off this job and don't have to work anymore, I'm going to travel."

Handing her the August issue of *Godey's Lady's Book And Magazine*, he left.

She didn't move from the stoop; it was hot, with the sun pouring down from a cloudless sky, but she hardly noticed it. She found Melinda's poem "Reflections" in *Godey's* "Arm-Chair," a melange of letters to the editor and comments on glove fashions and various facts. Julia had been hoping "Reflections" would have a page of its own, even though she had never seen a poem so honored in *Godey's*. Melinda's poem was placed between a letter to the editor and a chromos advertisement. It was separated from each of the items by a long dash and a line of space. "REFLECTIONS" was in capitals, but the text was in small print. Melinda's name was at the bottom of the poem. The poem could so easily be overlooked among the other reports, and Julia feared no one would read it. Yet *Godey's* was the predominant women's magazine in the country, with a circulation of 150,000. Surely thousands of women read every item in it. What she wanted was Melinda's life to count! It did count—yes, it did! But Julia would make certain it affected millions. Melinda had a drawer of poems in her room that Julia would submit to various periodicals. Julia read "Reflections," word for word. Though she firmly grasped *Godey's*, the paper trembled. She felt dizzy and the sun spotted the print with black dots. The last time she had seen the poem, it had been in Melinda's hand.

She became aware of the thin envelope pressing the back cover of *Godey's*. It was addressed to Mr. David Gerard, but she felt justified in opening it. If Bridget's parents weren't coming, she would have to deal with Bridget's disappointment. She slit open the letter with her finger. The Bolands were arriving September 6 at 8:00 p.m. on the New York Express! If they were delayed at sea, they hoped to inform David by telegram before the sixth.

Julia found Bridget sweeping the back sidewalk of poplar leaves, pale yellow droppings that offered no decoration to the yard. The dry summer had caused an early fall. Julia handed Bridget the letter. "It's from your mother—to David. You'll see why she wrote him when you read it."

Bridget held the letter to her face and moved her head along as she read. "Oh, oh, Julia! Themselves is coming! It's a grand thing, it is! Myself had told Michael they might. Do you mind? He isn't telling a body at church."

"You can tell anyone you wish now."

Julia noticed Mary standing by the hedge with a trash basket in each hand. The hot air seemed like street tar, and Julia thought it was that which kept Mary from falling over the hedge while she eavesdropped. "Mary, be coming here quick," Bridget called. "Me mama and papa is arriving on the New York Express in five days, and let me tell you itself is fast."

Mary dropped her baskets and joined them. "You're lucky. I ain't seen my parents since I left Ireland."

"Oh, myself is selfish to be carrying on," Bridget said contritely.

"I don't mind. I got used to missing them."

Bridget's eyes darkened, and she addressed Julia. "Michael and myself have been talking. It isn't fitting we should marry with Miss Adams passing. Me parents won't mind if I wait, I'm thinking. I could be married right before they leave."

Mary jumped forward. "You gotta get married now. Your parents are expecting it and they'll be mad."

"Let it not be said Bridget Boland's parents are being mad."

Mary's hands flashed out and she seemed about to shake Bridget. "You gotta get married right now. Billy's got to see me in that pretty bridesmaid's dress. He's been courting another girl, and he never comes by no more. The dress is my only chance to attract him back."

"Is himself coming to me wedding for sure?"

"Yes. He don't pass up good food."

"Still, Mrs. Gerard is being the one to think of."

"Please get married as you planned," Julia insisted. "I'm looking forward to your wedding. I'm not comparing your happiness to my grief."

"Yourself is really meaning that?"

"Yes, very definitely."

"Then I'll be marrying the ninth."

Julia's stable boy crept around the house, his hands jammed in his pockets. He approached timidly, with his eyes on the ground. In principle, the boy freed David's time. In reality, work-related matters claimed the time the boy freed. Julia thought it was a vicious circle at the lumberyard: more help, more sales, more work, more help—

The boy's voice interrupted her thoughts. "Hello, ma'am."

"Hello, Frank."

"Anything extra I gotta do?"

"No."

He scurried off to the stable, and Mary left as well.

Julia turned to Bridget. "Of course I'll tell Mr. Gerard I opened the letter. I'll still not tell him you've known of the invitation."

Bridget's expression was troubled, but she said nothing.

Late in the afternoon, Julia bought a copy of *Godey's* for George and drove to Lakeside. She was careful not to park where she had the day Melinda drowned. Nonetheless, she forced herself to walk the length of the wing and observe the lake. One could not avoid the lake in Chicago. The water was gray, but sparkling. She tried to think of the lake impersonally, how it was valuable for fish and transportation. Then she heard water slap the beach, the herring gulls mewing, skimming for food—scavengers. The sun seemed to glare on the water like a demon eye. She lifted her skirt and ran inside.

George's office door was open. A man with a patch of hair on the back of an otherwise bald head sat at Melinda's worktable. Julia had not seen him before, and she supposed he was a secretary. Julia spoke from the doorway, reluctant to enter without an invitation. "Is George Huntly here?"

"No, please come in."

She saw Melinda's picture on George's desk.

"Mr. Huntly's meeting with one of his advisors downtown. He'll be back in an hour, if you would like to either wait or return."

"No, I'm afraid I can't."

She handed the secretary the copy of *Godey's*. "Would you see that Mr. Huntly receives this?"

"Whom shall I say it's from?" Julia could not tell the secretary that. She could not handle the impersonal sympathy the explanation would produce. "Just tell him it's from a friend. He'll understand."

"Of course."

When David arrived home for dinner, Julia ran to meet him in the yard. Quickly kissing him, she put her hand on his chest to keep him from going inside. She was nervous, hating her evasion of the truth. "The letter came from Bridget's parents today—addressed to you. I opened it and found the Bolands are coming, so I showed Bridget the letter. Do you mind?"

"They're coming—well, good."

"Then you don't mind my opening it?"

"No, not in this case. I'm glad you did. I'm glad you gave Bridget the news."

He kissed her again and looked at her as he might a silly child who said things for the sake of saying them.

They found Bridget lifting the soup lid. On seeing David, she dropped it and ran. David set down his case of papers and opened his arms to the girl hurtling in his direction. "Sure, it's hard set I am to find words to be thanking you."

"Well—yes, well, that's quite all right," David said with moist eyes.

Bridget and Michael waited in the kitchen for Julia to finish dressing the evening the Bolands were to arrive. Bridget wished to leave an hour early in case the train was ahead of schedule. Julia hadn't convinced Bridget that trains were seldom, if ever, early. David was at a business dinner and couldn't accompany them to the depot. Julia tried to hurry, but she had been having difficulty controlling the temperature of her curling iron. She pulled her iron from the gas jet and squeezed a piece of tissue in the prongs to determine the temperature. Finally! The heated paper was the proper light tan so she could form a curl at her forehead.

She felt vaguely nauseated—unsettled was more the term. Of late, she admitted, everything pointed to her being pregnant: nausea, fatigue, no menses.

She set down the curling iron, placed her long fingers around her waist, and by squeezing tightly, she almost spanned it. If she were pregnant, it would soon be thick, she thought.

Fear of having a miscarriage almost overwhelmed her, and she saw the reflection of her face in the mirror turn white. But it was foolish to be so terrified of miscarrying; the odds were she wouldn't. Her best course was to see Dr. Scott as soon as possible.

If she were pregnant, she would do everything possible to carry the child, even stay in bed until it was born. Did David want a child? She assumed so. But his comment on the matter, "I had looked forward to the other child," was ambiguous.

Bridget's wedding was in a few days; she would get through that, then see the doctor.

She finished curling her hair, then joined Michael and Bridget. Julia followed Michael's wagon in her buggy. She would not accompany the Bolands to their quarters.

The Illinois and Michigan Central depot was erected on a narrow strip of land between Lake Michigan and a lagoon. Black smoke from a train puffed over Terrace Row, a luxurious row of private townhouses opposite the lagoon. The depot had a hemispherical roof and three entrances for trains. Bridget and Michael stood on a platform as close to the rails as safety permitted, staring at the entrance for the New York Express. Julia stood back a little. Bridget's face and neck were flushed and damp. She wore her favorite blue dress, and she had arranged her hair as her mother liked it: braided and coiled. They had been standing there for forty-five minutes.

" 'Tis lost the train is, I'm thinking!" Bridget wailed.

Julia tried to calm her. "The train's only fifteen minutes late."

Michael added, "Trains don't get lost."

"What if Mama and Papa doesn't be liking yourself? Mama was never liking any of the boys that called on me."

Michael looked patiently at Bridget. "It don't do no good to worry."

Bridget continued to fret. "What if Mama isn't on the train?"

"Then she said she'd send a telegram." Michael looked as if his patience was wearing thin.

"But what if herself is still at sea?"

"That ain't likely."

Bridget was making Julia nervous. She sighed with relief when a cloud of smoke and a screaming whistle announced the arrival of the New York Express.

The train slowed, its brakes grinding to a halt. Several cars of passengers disembarked and filed toward a central baggage depot. Julia searched in both directions for the small, dark-haired couple Bridget had described. She felt damp, nervous.

Bridget had stepped back for a wide view. "Saints!" she suddenly hollered, and Julia followed Bridget's eyes to a car to the right. A conductor was helping off a short couple wearing cotton and an air of simplicity.

"Saints!" Bridget hollered again.

The couple looked around for the familiar voice, their eyes anxious. Then they sighted their daughter and stretched out their arms just in time for Bridget to fall into them. Over Bridget's shoulder Julia saw the Bolands' teary faces. Julia choked with emotion.

Bridget passed her hand over her mother's face. Mrs. Boland had Bridget's small bones and large eyes. Her teeth were white and even, her cheeks still flushed from the Atlantic air. Julia thought Bridget had every reason to be proud of her mother. "I was afeard you weren't on the train," Bridget sighed through tears of joy. "Oh, Mama, I've missed yourself. I thought I'd be dying somedays. How is me family?"

"Fine and fit, every last one. Grandma and Grandpa Boland is staying with them, and Maury and the others are helping." Mrs. Boland studied Bridget. "But it's pasty-faced you are. What is yourself eating, daughter?"

"I eat good, surely."

"Then the food is being bad. I've heard itself is all sugar over here and the life is cooked out of it."

"Myself is cooking all that I eat."

"Then it's more teaching you're needing, daughter."

Bridget introduced her parents to Michael and Julia. They joined the crowd waiting at the baggage depot as the baggage carts were being loaded.

Mr. Boland looked at Michael. "Me wife and I are happy yourself is working for a priest."

Bridget replied, "Michael is the best janitor Father Purcell is ever having." She apparently didn't see Michael blush. "Himself was borned in this country, but his parents was borned in Ireland. Himself has been west to California and knows all about America. Himself—"

"Did you get in a good trip?" Michael interrupted. "I heard it was stormy last week at sea."

"Ourselves was being knocked around a bit, but it was nothing to complain of,'' Mr. Boland commented stoically.

Bridget looked sadly at her father. '' 'Tis sorry Michael and myself are that we didn't be asking your permission to marry. But ourselves didn't think it was fitting by letter—with yourself across the big ocean. Are you being unhappy?''

"Not at all, daughter. Himself looks a good man.''

"Oh, surely!'' Bridget heartily confirmed his opinion.

Michael again turned crimson.

Julia handed Mr. Boland a key. The Bolands were staying for six weeks, and David had rented them a cottage on Taylor Street, a few doors from the house Michael purchased. Michael had furnished the cottage with pieces from his church, and Edith had loaned curtains. Edith had told Julia, "Be sure Bridget gives them back. You know how careless the Irish are." Julia had inquired as to why Edith loaned them if the Irish were so careless. "I really don't care to discuss it if you don't mind,'' Edith said tartly. "Just return my property.''

With tears, the Bolands thanked Julia. When the baggage arrived, Michael and Mr. Boland claimed their valises.

On Saturday morning, the day of Bridget's wedding, Julia, David, Alma, and Edgar, in his wheelchair, entered Bridget's church. Edgar's two nurses accompanied him. Julia didn't think their presence necessary, but Edgar believed everything would go wrong and everyone would be needed. That he was even there amazed Julia, as he hadn't been out since his attack. He maintained that invalids belonged in their quarters. On the trip over he hadn't commented on the scenery or the sunny day—only on the various maneuvers of his stomach.

Julia and David greeted the Bolands in the narthex. Julia thought Mrs. Boland looked young and pretty in a peach dress with an embroidered bodice. Mrs. Boland shook with emotion as she hugged Julia. '' 'Tis a grand thing to be seeing my girl being married, and her me oldest now.''

"Where are you sitting?''

"In the front, as close to Bridget as we can be. Let it not be said this isn't the happiest day of me life.''

Julia introduced the Bolands to Edgar and Alma.

"I'm rather fond of your little girl,'' Edgar admitted almost shyly.

"It's happy I am that you are,'' Mrs. Boland smiled.

"How many children do you have?''

"Twelve now, and every last one of them a good Catholic.''

"Well,'' Edgar turned to David, "let's get on.''

"Where would you like to sit?''

"In the back row where I can get out quick.''

"You'll be all right, dear," Alma said, trying to reassure him.

"Quiet! Are you a prophet?"

Mrs. Reatherford placed Edgar's wheelchair between the wall and the last pew. There were twenty vacant pews between them and the guests in front. This was Julia's first visit to a Catholic church, and she looked around with interest. A crucifix of Christ was centered behind the altar. There were two side altars, one containing a statue of Mary, the other of St. Joseph. Banked before the statues were votive candles, glowing softly. Overlaying it all was the faint scent of the street brought in over the years on the shoes of faithful Irish Catholics.

"My blanket slipped," Edgar complained.

Alma straightened it. She was pale, her hands trembling from the strain of being in a crowd.

"Look, I think my foot's twisted in this contraption I'm in. I say I belong at home!"

Alma lifted the blanket. "Your foot's fine, but I moved it for you."

"The blanket, fix the blanket; you've mussed it!"

Julia blushed as heads turned in their direction.

When Bridget stood beside Michael, she looked diminutive in the thirteen yards of material draped on her. The gown was lovely, made of satin with two skirts and a bustle. Margaret, the servant girl down the street, had sewn her own artificial pearls on the bodice for Bridget, and Julia had donated a pearl pin and the satin. As Bridget looked up to Michael, Julia believed Michael would give the world for a clear look at the face beneath the veil.

After the ceremony when Father Purcell invited Michael to kiss the bride, Michael lifted her veil with a gloved hand. He had to bend far down to kiss her. The church was quiet, and Julia thought everyone heard the sob from the paralyzed man in the last row.

Bridget grasped Michael's hand and retrieved her bouquet of orange blossoms from Mary. She walked down the aisle and laid the bouquet on Edgar's plaid blanket. Julia saw the fingers of Edgar's good hand close over the bouquet. Then his paralyzed fingers extended and touched the delicate petals. He had stood often and even taken some steps, but this was the first thing his hand had reached for since his apoplexy.

Julia's eyes quickly filled with tears. She noticed David wiping his eyes also.

Edgar said gruffly, his voice filled with emotion, "I'm going home. Get me out of here!"

"But you said you'd go to the reception," Alma pleaded.

"My stomach's upset—get me out of here, I say!"

Seventeen

*I*t was noisy, crowded and hot at Mr. and Mrs. O'Keefe's, where the wedding reception was held. Julia perspired and tried to keep her chicken salad from falling off her plate each time an elbow struck her. A thin man with a cold dragged around the parlor, coughing. Julia saw him coming and turned away. Many of the guests, unable to find room inside, were eating their lunch in the backyard. There was no front yard, just a foot of space between the cottage and a high paling fence. The house contained a kitchen, parlor, and two bedrooms. Julia thought it amazing that the O'Keefes had raised eight sons in this place, each child big enough to require the space of two. The food was served from the kitchen table, which was laid with a starched cloth and brightened with a bowl of snapdragons and asters. The main attraction was the bridal cake, decorated with shamrocks and hearts, which Mrs. O'Keefe had baked.

David didn't attend the reception because he had to return to work; nor did Alma, who had already been gone too long from home. The Bolands were in the kitchen sitting behind the table. The huge O'Keefe family and the surging crowd were too much for them, and they were content to watch the reception and their daughter from a position of safety. Julia was near the kitchen doorway watching Bridget prepare to cut the bridal cake. "Myself hates to be cutting into it, and itself so pretty. Saints, I'll remember it all me life, Mama O'Keefe."

"Thank you, dear," she murmured.

Bridget addressed Mrs. Boland. "Mama, how big should I be cutting the cake pieces?"

"It's being a big crowd, daughter, and I'm thinking the cake has to go a long way. No bigger than your thumb length, surely."

Bridget held the plate containing the first piece of cake toward her mother. "Mama, is this being right?"

"Aye."

Julia smiled and wished David had been here to see this cake being cut.

Bridget had become friendly with Mr. and Mrs. Cullen over the backyard hedge. They, too, were at the reception. Like the Bolands, they were having trouble negotiating the crowd and had stationed themselves out of the way against a wall. Julia had brought them their food earlier and she now brought them cake.

Mrs. Cullen received the cake with thanks.

After she had eaten, Mrs. Cullen announced, "Did you hear we're moving?"

"Bridget told me."

"I'm from the East and I miss it—and my family. Mr. Cullen spends little time in his office, and he can travel back here occasionally for business. Frankly, I've never become accustomed to the mud or the lack of culture in Chicago. I won't be sorry to leave before the city falls apart either. Did you read the editorial in the *Tribune* about the shabby construction? Why, even the most expensive buildings are one brick thick, and when the bricks break loose, nobody's safe on the sidewalks. Cornices hit pedestrians regularly, and the cast-iron facades on buildings aren't secured well. Most buildings are wood and about to explode in flames. Frankly, Mrs. Gerard, I worry all the time."

"Have you sold your house?"

"Yes, to a family with eight children. They've agreed to hire my servants and will move into the house the first part of October."

"I haven't been East, but I hope to go someday."

"You must. One needs that exposure."

The Cullens finished their cake and left. Julia noticed Billy in the corner behind her, blocked in by Mary. "Don't go, Billy," Mary pleaded.

He picked his teeth with his thumbnail as he considered his answer. "I gotta go. I wouldn't of come if you hadn't nagged. I gotta make up the time tonight for coming. It ain't been worth it—I don't like Bridget. She's high and mighty—she ain't once come over to talk. Michael's in for a life of misery, the poor guy. Ha, ha! The food was good, though."

Julia was about to move away when Billy spoke to her. "I'm surprised you came here. I didn't know your kind of people came to this kinda place."

"Bridget and her are friends," Mary explained.

"I overheard you, Billy," Julia said; "you badly misjudge Bridget."

He looked angry, his mouth curved in an unpleasant smile. "I might as well get some sport from this party," he muttered. Billy pushed Mary aside and stepped from the corner. "I work for Mr. and Mrs. Weber on Ontario Street—next door to an old friend of your husband's."

"Old friend?"

"Billy!" Mary cautioned him.

Billy laughed and rocked on his heels. "Yeah, a real good friend—Mrs. Hastings."

Julia stared at him. She wanted to look away, but couldn't. She didn't want to hear anymore, but she had to know all Billy knew.

"Mrs. Hastings and your husband are pretty good friends from what I see. Not that I'm an expert on them, just a gardener that sees things."

There was a horrified look on Mary's face. Her hand clutched her throat.

"Yes?" Julia asked weakly.

Billy looked Julia over lewdly. "If I had what Mr. Gerard had, I wouldn't be sneaking around."

"Billy!" Mary cried futilely.

He jammed his hands in his pockets and continued rocking on his heels. "I seen Mr. Gerard kissing Mrs. Hastings. I seen it with my own eyes. I was just off work and goin' for some relaxing. I seen them wrapped around each other in Mrs. Hasting's drive. They was back by a tree where nobody could see them. I saw them, though. I happened to look at an angle."

Julia felt the blood leave her face. Was there more—she had to know! Let him say it!

"Billy, stop it!" Mary warned again.

"Your husband paid me off; that's how much he don't want the business knowed. He gave me fifty dollars in cash. Ask him—he'll tell you!"

Julia felt as if she had been kicked in the head. Little dark flecks spotted the air, like a fall of ashes.

"Leave at once!" Julia demanded. "Get out of here!"

"Suits me—it ain't my idea of fun here."

Billy had a new-looking stovepipe hat in his hand. He strutted off, shoving it on his head and looking like a cocky rooster.

Mary's face was an alarming melange of white and red spots. Her voice was desperate. "He's gone—gone. Oh, he'll never speak to me again! He'll marry that other girl now, that's for sure. Oh, oh—"

"He's nasty—horrible. You're well rid of him. You've lost nothing in him—nothing!" Julia declared.

Mary sobbed. "My life is wrecked. I shouldn't have let him go. I should have stopped him somehow."

Julia felt like shaking the girl. Didn't Mary realize Julia was desperate herself and didn't want to discuss Billy? "Mary, be sensible!" she said sharply. "He's not your type."

"I love him—I love him! What would you know about love!"

"Quite a bit!"

The girl looked struck. "I'm sorry."

"Look, Mary—I know you tried to prevent him from saying what he did. I appreciate that."

Mary nodded numbly and stared at the door.

Julia felt faint from the closeness of the room and her raging emotions. She leaned against the wall. "Mary, do you believe Billy's story?"

"Billy ain't got no way to get fifty dollars. Billy bought the hat he's got with some of the money. He ain't lying."

Julia agreed with Mary. In fact, she had burned the letter that corroborated Mary's statement.

Mary's eyes were dazed and she wrung her hands. Julia felt Mary was hardly aware she spoke. "There's been nothing but gossip since you married Mr. Gerard. The servant girls all say you and Mr. Gerard are breaking up. Why, they seen Mr. Gerard bringing a veiled lady to your house just before you married him. We all know he married you for your money."

Oh, God! So the affair had been going on for months! Julia remembered the stale box of chocolates in the parlor when she had unpacked wedding gifts. Were those Diane's? Julia choked out, "I've heard enough, Mary. You're out of line."

"Oh, oh, I'm sorry." She blinked and looked as if she would faint.

"I don't want to discuss Mr. Gerard's past with you."

"Oh . . . I'm sorry . . . I'm sorry. You won't tell Bridget what I said?"

"Leave me alone, Mary. Just leave me."

Mary stared at Julia with a white face, then stumbled off toward the bedroom that served as the women's dressing room. Julia shook so hard the wall behind her vibrated. Why was David having an affair? She had given him no reason. She had concentrated her love on him, on his parents too. She had kept David's house running smoothly. She had done everything expected—and more. No one could have loved him more. Diane couldn't have! Why? Oh, why had it happened? Had she caused the affair? She had kept some things a secret for a time. He had not liked that. But that wasn't sufficient reason for adultery. Nothing was sufficient reason! Anyhow, the affair had probably been going on for some time. Certainly Diane was the veiled woman David had brought to the house. There was only one reason to wear a veil!

The awful, terrible tragedy was, Julia thought, that she still loved David. *I need to go home and think things through*, she decided.

She found Bridget and Michael in the kitchen. The cake had been cut and distributed, and they were eating a piece. "I have to leave." Julia tried to sound normal.

"Yourself is looking famished with trouble."

"No, it's just a headache or something. I'm fine, just fine."

"Michael and myself will be leaving soon too."

Bridget and Michael were using their week off to settle into their house on Taylor Street and to show the Bolands around Chicago. "Have a wonderful week," Julia said.

At home, Julia locked the doors and windows and closed all the draperies. She was thankful David wouldn't be home for hours and she would have privacy. The osnaburg draperies in the sitting room blocked out most of the sunlight. What light did enter reflected dully from the brass gas fixtures and the glass face of the mantel clock. Julia liked this dark effect. She liked the feeling of having nothing bright or living around her. She liked the quietness. Pulling a rocker to the fireplace, she sat before the cold grate, rocking mechanically, hardly aware of the action of her foot. She thought of how her mother resided at Fieldcrest Cemetery and Melinda resided in the lake.

This is my residence, she thought, *and David's*. Julia stared at the interior of the fireplace, still stained from soot despite Bridget's efforts to scrub it clean. Julia began to wish she had another residence.

Frequently the newspaper reported suicides; recently a woman had swallowed arsenic after a fight with her husband over money. The woman had told her husband she had changed her mind about dying, but it had been too late. Julia had read in the Chicago *Tribune* about suicide by poison, by jumping from a bridge into the river, by gun, knife. Obviously it was easy to kill oneself. But she was a coward. She couldn't shoot herself or jump in the river. She had to die at the hand of something easy, less frightening.

The arsenic with which they poisoned rats was in the cellar. She had read that rats so poisoned suffered a few hours with severe gastric pain before dying. Julia wondered how long it would take a person to die from arsenic poisoning. How much would one take? A teaspoon? Just a pinch? What about the pain, the severe gastric symptoms? But surely it couldn't be too painful to die from arsenic since many people chose the method. There was strychnine in the cellar, too, she remembered. She had read about the sardonic smile one got from strychnine when muscle control was lost. No, she wouldn't use strychnine.

Though she had already locked the windows and doors, she checked to assure they were locked. When she had finished, she checked again. She felt like a mad woman, checking and rechecking. *Just once more around*, she thought. *I must be sure.* Yes—yes! They were all locked!

In the cellar she lit a lantern and set it on a box near the storage shelves. There were six shelves in all. The bottom three contained jars of preserved food, put up long ago by the last servant—and probably spoiled, Julia supposed. She remembered she had meant to throw them out. She must leave Bridget a note: "Don't use!" The next two shelves held paint and tools. The bottle of arsenic was on the top shelf. She was tall enough to reach it on tiptoe. The bottle was cobalt blue with a wide middle and narrow top. "POISON" was printed over the middle in relief, so that one would not make a mistake with it, Julia surmised.

She proceeded to the kitchen and wrote Bridget a note concerning the preserved food. Should she write David a farewell note? No. She couldn't explain herself adequately. Just let him think what he would. He would be less hurt that way.

She supposed the arsenic would taste coppery, so she looked through the cupboard for a food to camouflage it. She decided on blackberry jam, which had a strong flavor. She mixed a teaspoon of arsenic and several spoonfuls of jam in a cup, stirring until the white powder was mixed. She poured a glass of water to wash down the jam. Had she forgotten anything? No! How simple the preparations were.

Then Julia remembered she might be pregnant. But wasn't it kindest to save a child from the pain of existence? *Yes*, she thought, *oh, yes!* But her stomach heaved and her throat filled with a sharp acid taste. She leaned over the sink, sick. She couldn't murder a child. She could kill herself a thousand times but not a child.

She stared at the purple mixture in the cup. Would she have taken it if she weren't pregnant? No! She had lied to herself. She could not have tolerated the pain. Oh, where had those suicides reported in the newspaper gotten the courage! She almost admired them!

In every area, she was a coward! She didn't have the courage to confront David about his affair either. He might ask for a divorce—she couldn't live without him.

Coping was one thing she could do. She had coped with Melinda's death. She had coped when Mrs. Newton called her a fallen woman. She had coped with a miscarriage. She had coped with Diane's letters. She had *not* coped at the seminary in Indianapolis—but she had at least coped with her failure there.

Julia washed the jam down the sink and threw out the cup and spoon, then tore up the note. She returned the arsenic to the shelf in the cellar. In the cupboard she found the bottle of medicinal brandy, and as she poured herself a small amount, her hand trembled. She sipped at her glass. Warmth crept through her chest and her hand became steady. She had just put away the bottle, when the doorbell sounded.

It was Edith, attractively bonneted and dressed, clasping a prettily skirted Freddie in one hand. Julia saw Morton in the buggy, the reins resting in his lap. The blue sky and sun startled Julia; she had accustomed herself to the dark. While Edith glanced sharply into the rooms adjoining the vestibule, Julia kept clear of her. It wouldn't do to have Edith smell the brandy. She would somehow extract a confession from her.

"Why have you pulled your curtains? It's a lovely day, and the air is beneficial. Really, Julia—you aren't sensible. Morton has a back complaint and I'm accompanying him to the doctor. It's a little thing, going with him, but I've committed myself to pleasing him. Freddie is tired, and I'd rather not bring him. I wonder if he could nap here while I'm gone? Nora is shopping."

Julia wanted to say, "No, Edith! I can't watch Freddie. I have to cry! Don't you understand?" But she replied instead, "Oh—yes. Leave him."

"Thank you."

The brandy gave Julia a burst of courage. "Edith, what does Diane Hastings look like?"

"I've told you that before. I've also told you not to dwell on that woman."

"Edith!"

"She has black hair, and she's very attractive. She's not like you at all—she's very aggressive. Believe me, she's nothing compared to you."

"Please describe her facial features."

"That information cannot be helpful."

"Edith—tell me!"

"Diane has a wide mouth and large eyes, very penetrating and not quite blue, more violet."

"Yes, I can see her now."

"I advise you to forget Diane," Edith asserted. "I cannot imagine why you don't. I shall say no more. Tell me, how was Bridget's wedding?"

"Oh, I don't know." Julia didn't see the wedding in her mind; she only saw Billy.

"What? It was poorly planned, I suppose. The Irish cannot plan worth two cents." Edith's eyes examined Julia's face. "You look terrible. I suggest that you rest while Freddie naps."

Edith opened the door and waved at Morton. "Well, I can't leave Morton waiting. Our relationship is improving daily, and I can't risk it. Of course I can't elaborate, but I might just say that things are rather romantic between us." Edith bent and kissed Freddie.

Freddie carried a red wooden wagon. Julia laid him on the sitting room sofa with the toy and covered him with a light blanket. She didn't put him in an upstairs bedroom because she expected he would ransack the room.

"I'm thirsty," he said.

Julia brought him water, and he gulped down several mouthfuls.

"I'm gonna be a team driver when I'm big."

"That's nice. Will you take me for a ride?"

"No!"

Julia wondered if Freddie would ever be a pleasant child.

"You smell funny, Aunt Julia."

"It's nothing. Now be quiet."

Freddie asked, "Where did Mama go?"

"Didn't you hear her say she was going to the doctor with Daddy?"

"I want'a go."

"She'll be right back."

"I want'a go!"

Julia sat on the edge of the sofa and looked down on Freddie. His mouth puckered up and tears jumped from his angry eyes. She hated to admit how much she disliked the child. Freddie jabbed her arm. "I want my mama! I don't like it here! I don't like you!"

"Stop poking me. It hurts." She removed his hand from her.

"I want my mama."

"Yes, yes—soon."

"I'm thirsty."

Julia handed him the glass. He drank the water, his eyes staring at Julia over the glass rim. "Now lie down!" she snapped, taking his glass.

He didn't move; his eyes became distressed. "Is you mad at me?"

"A little."

"I don't like you mad."

She patted his hand. "I'm not anymore."

He suddenly hugged Julia's neck. "I love you, Aunt Julia."

"Oh, Freddie! You surprise me."

He leaned against her and she stroked his hair. After he had fallen asleep, she lifted him to her lap. He smelled like fresh soap, and it was comforting and pleasant to hold him. She was glad Edith had brought him. "I love you too, Freddie," she murmured.

When Edith returned for Freddie, she said that Morton had scoliosis, a curvature of his spine, for which he would have to wear a back brace. "The doctor isn't sure what caused it, but I know it's due to Morton's long hours at the store standing on his feet. This proves you're right, Julia—Morton shouldn't overburden himself."

"Can he be cured?"

"The doctor made no predictions, but I'm sure he can. How was Freddie?"

"Fine, very good."

Shortly after Edith left, Julia saw David's buggy driving around the back. A feverish excitement possessed her. She ran to the yard and was at the side of his buggy when he parked at the stable. Not knowing why she had hurried out, she looked up at the tall man wearing a top hat that greatly added to his height. He seemed a stranger to her. The crisp lines of his tan suit further distanced him from her.

He stepped down. "How nice to be met so enthusiastically," he smiled, lifting her face and kissing her.

"The neighbors," she warned, pulling back.

"No one's in the Cullens' yard, and the other neighbors can't see over their fence," he stated. But he left her alone. "How was Bridget's reception?" he asked.

"Lovely, just lovely! It was crowded, but just lovely."

"The food?"

"Wonderful!"

"Did the Bolands seem comfortable with so many strangers?"

"Yes, I think so." She felt her face burn, and wondered that he didn't realize she was confused. "Let's go out to dinner—to the Walnut Room, some place special. Let's have a wonderful time and laugh. Let's just leave and have fun."

He laughed. "My, you are in a gay mood."

"Yes, I am."

They went to the Walnut Room, a French restaurant with a frescoed ceiling and gilded columns and all the starched linen and gleaming silver Julia's spirit craved. The table was adorned with a silver basket of sugared fruit. To the right of her soup plate were glasses for water, madeira, claret, and champagne. David scanned the menu and ordered a seven-course dinner. After the waiter had set down the second course, clam shells filled with shrimp, Julia said, "It seems a shame the Cullens are moving just as we are becoming friends. I wish things would remain as they are. I hate things to change, don't you?"

"I don't mind change, Julia."

Julia tasted her shrimp. "It's delicious! I like the cream sauce. Isn't it lovely?"

"Yes, it's good, darling."

"If only we could always sit at this table and let nothing intrude on us again."

He smiled fondly at her. "That would be nice. But one needs to make the money to afford this."

She threw back her head and uttered a brittle laugh. She wondered again why he didn't detect her erratic behavior.

"I should have taken off work for Bridget's reception," he confessed.

"I didn't mind."

"I felt bad about it. I think I put business first too often."

"I don't mind." *How many hours a week do you spend with Diane?* she thought. *Has business ever interfered with that time?*

"I've rearranged things so we can be together more. I turned down the presidency of the Lumbermen's Association. I plan to have Mr. Werner and Mr. Luken, our two outside agents, do most of the traveling. I'll take them around to the lumber mills to train them, and from then on they can do the out-of-town purchasing."

"When will you train them?"

"We'll leave on the seventeenth and be back the sixth of October."

"David, that's so long!"

"I do business with lumber mills in several states—you know that. I need to take sufficient time to train Mr. Werner and Mr. Luken. Darling, don't you understand I'm doing this so I can have more time with you eventually?"

"Yes."

"Nothing is more important to me than you."

"Nothing?"

"Of course!"

She hoped he meant that. He did seem to be enjoying his dinner and her company. She wondered if a man could love two women at once. Yes, that was it apparently. He loved her and Diane. Well, at least he wouldn't be seeing Diane while he was out of town.

A staggering array of food followed the shrimp. David commented on Julia's light appetite. "You've hardly eaten anything." He shook his head and smiled. "I suppose I don't understand women."

"No, you don't. But I love it here—it's exactly right for me."

Cherry ice had been served. "At least eat a little ice; it's light," David encouraged her.

"All right." She dipped her spoon into the ice. It tasted both tart and sweet. She liked it and ate it all.

Sunday morning in church before the service, David chatted with Julia's father. Julia's eyes were riveted on the third-row pew. Mrs. Newton sat on one side of Arthur and Nancy Smith, Julia's friend who was a volunteer at the historical society, sat on the other. Nancy was short and her saucy gypsy bonnet slanted at quite an angle as she looked up at Arthur. Julia hadn't known Nancy was the type to go in for saucy clothes, though she should have guessed it from the way she cinched in her waist. There was no extra space between Arthur and Nancy. Julia was the last young woman who had sat with Arthur, and she hated Nancy having her spot. Not that she had anything against Nancy. Nancy taught the third grade girls' Sunday school class and did an excellent job. It was just that Nancy continually discussed the historical society, and Julia would think that would bore Arthur, who liked to talk about finances. Nancy was rather pretty, though; she had a dainty mouth and naturally curly brown hair.

Edith turned in her pew and followed Julia's gaze. "It's rumored that Arthur is smitten with Nancy."

"How long has this been going on? I've never seen them together." *At the bazaar, Arthur still cared about me*, Julia thought in despair.

"A few weeks, I suppose. He's been taking Nancy to the theater— you know how Arthur loves the theater. And Mrs. Newton has had Nancy over for tea. Mrs. Newton is fond of Nancy, finding her quite refined."

"I suppose she is."

"Of course she is. The Smiths are one of the best families."

"I don't think Nancy is Arthur's type."

"I think she's exactly his type."

"Nancy shouldn't marry. She's too devoted to her work at the historical society."

"I didn't mention marriage," Edith said. "I was speaking of compatibility." Edith glanced at David, who was still talking to Mr. Adams, then adjusted her pince-nez to better study Julia. She lowered her voice. "You're jealous."

"I am not!" Julia snapped indignantly, but her face blazed. She changed the subject. "How is Morton's back?"

"Much better."

While the quartet of voices sang, Julia watched Nancy and Arthur exchange little glances.

The temporary servant Julia hired to replace Bridget was impossible. She was lethargic and weepy. Every last suggestion Julia offered was received with tears. Hardly able to bear her, Julia spent a great deal of time with Edith.

Toward the end of the week Julia visited Dr. Scott and he stated that, though it was a bit early to confirm pregnancy, it was almost certain she was. She left his office in a daze. She shouldn't be stunned; after all, she had suspected pregnancy! As safeguards against miscarriage, Dr. Scott advised mild exercise, rest, and nourishing food. "Of course," he said, "I can't guarantee you won't abort. That's in God's hands."

Stepping into her buggy, she sank back on the seat in tears as she pondered what the impact would be on David if she miscarried. He couldn't go through that grief again; that would be one too many losses. He'd blame her and never be able to love her fully. Yes, even if he knew intellectually it wasn't her fault, he'd charge her. He'd seek comfort from Diane—oh, Diane would be so glad to give it! Dr. Scott had said her pregnancy was in God's hands. Well, didn't God realize she shouldn't be pregnant at all?

One thing was certain: she couldn't tell David until she passed the most likely period to miscarry. She'd suffer a miscarriage in secret if that were her fate. She'd get through it somehow! She absolutely refused to provide David with a reason to seek Diane.

When was the danger period over? What a fool she was not to have asked Dr. Scott. She looked back toward his office. She could return, but there had been a full waiting room and the wait would be long. She would ask him next visit. She would rather forget her fears for now. She would just follow the doctor's instructions and be hopeful. But in spite of her determination, she began to shake. She noticed an old woman in a black kerchief staring at her. Tapping the horse with the whip, she left for home.

Sunday evening David left on his trip with his agents. On Monday at 7:00 a.m. Bridget bounced into the kitchen, her eyes starry, her face flushed. Julia couldn't tell if it was love or a fever. She hugged Bridget. "Are you sick?"

"Just a wee cold." Bridget set her bag and gloves on the table and appraised the kitchen.

"The woman who took your place was terrible—an emotional wreck, and not much good at cleaning."

"Aye," Bridget agreed, frowning at the greasy sink.

"I don't know how you do the laundry, ironing, cooking, and cleaning. It's far too much. Now you'll be traveling to work besides, and that will take extra time. Mr. Gerard and I would like to hire a part-time girl to help you."

Bridget widened her stance. "No! Myself can do it. The girl would be in me way and doing everything wrong!"

Julia sighed. "The offer is open if you should change your mind. How was your honeymoon?"

"Lovely itself. Myself was living with Michael and loving him and him loving me, and us the only people in the world—except when ourselves was seeing Mama and Papa. Me mama and papa loved seeing Chicago, though Mama is afraid of the traffic."

Bridget tied on her apron and opened the firebox door. She poked the fire and set the kettle on to boil. "Papa will be helping Michael part time and the priest is paying him, and Mama is cleaning at the church part time and herself is getting paid too."

"Wouldn't they rather rest while they're here?"

"Themselves don't know how to be resting. And they can be using the money at home."

While Bridget spooned coffee into the coffeepot, Julia told her David would be out of town until October 6. "Myself would be dying, and Michael gone so long."

"I don't mind—in fact, it's best."

At first Bridget looked queerly at her. Then Julia read sympathy in her eyes. Julia wondered if Bridget knew that Billy had blackmailed David. Surely Mary had told her; Mary was not one to keep secrets. In fact, Mary's request that Julia not tell Bridget she had gossiped indicated that Bridget had warned Mary to be quiet. Yes, Bridget knew. But of course the girl wouldn't tell tales. Julia was tempted to throw herself in Bridget's arms, cry it all out—have Bridget comfort her. But she couldn't bring herself to disturb Bridget's newlywed happiness.

"David's father has missed you." Julia forced herself to control her emotions. "We should take time to go see him this afternoon."

They arrived at Edgar's after lunch. The yard faced La Salle Street, a main thoroughfare, and the dust kicked up by horses had settled on the trees and plants, giving the yard a desert atmosphere. A good rain was needed. The grass was patched with brown, and the flowers along the foundation had wilted.

Alma answered the door, blinking in the sunlight. Julia supposed Alma hadn't been out, or even near a window, for some time. She ushered them in, smiling at Bridget. "You look as happy as any new bride."

"Myself is!"

"I was happy with Mr. Gerard before he stopped trusting people and became bitter. Of course, Mr. Gerard was never what you would call agreeable, but he was more pleasant when I married him."

"Why did he stop trusting people?" Julia wondered aloud.

"Years ago his business partner cleaned out their banking account and left town. Edgar never recovered the money. But it wasn't just that. So many people cheated him. He'd give a customer credit and the customer wouldn't pay. He'd contract for a certain grade of lumber and get a lesser grade."

"Does he worry that David will be taken advantage of? Is that why he's so exacting with David?"

"Maybe, but Edgar is hard on everyone—it's his nature. You see how hard he is on me—his own wife." Tears filmed her eyes. "It hurts, Julia—it eats away at me, little by little!'"

"I'm so sorry, Alma."

Alma dried her eyes. "I'm getting used to it. Julia, I can't say another word. I hate to talk against Edgar and I shouldn't have now."

In the back parlor they came upon Edgar batting cigar ashes into a dish on his bed tray. He had missed and ashes littered the tray. Edgar's face lit up when he saw Bridget. "I'm trying a Russian cigar—a mild type," he explained. "Harsh tobacco bothers my stomach." He placed the cigar in his mouth, then lifted his damaged arm to adjust the cigar forward.

"Saints! Look at that arm moving itself!" Bridget exclaimed.

"The first time was at your wedding."

"Me own wedding! What an honor itself!"

Mrs. Reatherford excused herself for their visit. Edgar motioned to a straight chair. "Pull up, Bridget. I've missed you. You'll have to bring Michael around soon. He's a nice chap."

"Himself is that!"

"You are obviously very happy," he observed.

"Remember when we were first married," Alma reminisced. "In thirty-three. We honeymooned at the Sauganash Tavern on the river. Why, Chicago was just a frontier town then and everything was plain. You could see the prairie on three sides and nothing blocked the lake. We had no jail or schoolhouse, and roads went every which way, according to the land or the river. The most important people in town were the fur traders."

"I remember." Edgar's expression softened. "The beach was mostly swamp and sand dunes then."

"We walked along it, holding hands."

He smiled at Alma. "You had the prettiest smile in Chicago—the way it flashed out dazzled me."

"Do you remember my mauve and pink flowered dress with the wide sleeves? I wore it the first time you called on me."

"I remember—yes, I remember it very well."

She had lost no love for him, Julia realized; nor had he for her. Edgar looked at Bridget. "Where's Patrick?"

"At me own house. Himself couldn't be coming to work on the horsecar."

"Have you brought your Bible?"

She took it and some Irish soda bread from her satchel. At the appearance of the Bible, Alma started toward the doorway. "Stay, Alma," Edgar coaxed. "I'd like you to be here for a change. The Bible is actually very interesting."

Alma joined Julia on the sofa. "I've been doing some deep thinking since your wedding," Edgar confided. "I've come to the conclusion that God sent you to me, as He sent Jonah to Nineveh."

" 'Tis true, I'm thinking."

"You got to me all along with your preaching, Bridget, just the way Jonah got to Nineveh."

" 'Tis because yourself is a sinner and knowing you're needing the grace of God. Ourselves is all being sinners and yourself is not being the worst of the lot in Chicago. Yourself is needing to give your life to Jesus. Himself died for your sins."

"You can have faith in God, Bridget, because things are simple for you. It is more complicated for me."

Yes, it is with all you've suffered, Julia agreed inwardly.

His head bent and an expression of sadness came to his face. Alma was shaking her head slowly back and forth in bewilderment, but Julia noticed she didn't take her eyes from her husband.

"I've made life difficult for you, Alma," Edgar confessed miserably.

"Yes," Alma admitted honestly, "but I'm used to it and I don't mind most of the time."

Edgar shook his head, "It wasn't right—I'm sorry."

"Really, it's all right now."

"Is yourself wanting to give your life to Jesus?" Bridget asked him simply.

"Look, how should I know that for sure? I'm a man that's used to getting my own way. Maybe I'd do that just to get my way with God. After all, I'm not a man anymore—I can't do a day's work. Maybe I'd just be after special favors from God. Maybe only women do this kind of thing."

Bridget placed her hands on her hips. "Jonah was no woman!"

Edgar nodded.

"Being a Christian isn't being less a person; itself is being more." Bridget looked gently at him. "Mr. Gerard, would yourself give your life to Jesus?" Bridget recited John 3:16. " 'For God so loved the world, that he gave his only begotten Son, that whosoever believeth in him should not perish, but have everlasting life.' "

Julia looked up to see tears running down Edgar's face, and she looked away. She was deeply moved. She had never taken such a step herself—she felt humbled and as much a sinner as Edgar. She felt troubled.

Edgar slowly raised his head. "What do I do?"

"Tell Jesus yourself is sorry for your sins and ask Him to forgive them. Then give Him your life."

"I'm sorry—I—" His voice broke as he struggled to speak. "Jesus, forgive my sins—come into my life—please. I give myself to You."

Bridget leaped up and threw her arms around Edgar. He gasped. "Itself is a wonderful thing you have done, and ourselves will be in heaven all through the ages, I'm thinking."

"Well," he smiled tentatively.

"What have you done, Edgar?" Alma exclaimed in alarm.

"You saw—I think you *do* understand," he asserted.

"But is it best for you?"

"Aye," Bridget answered for him with confidence.

A large crash downstairs shattered the peace in the room. Edgar made Helga so nervous that, though she was a good servant, accidents were common. Alma had told Julia she had lost an heirloom china tureen and several pieces of her best china lately. "We'll have nothing left to serve dinner on," Alma worried. "Do you mind if I leave, Edgar?"

"No, fine."

Edgar requested of Bridget, "Please find my wallet in the top bureau drawer. Buy me a Bible like yours."

"Aye."

"Now go—I'm tired." His lips trembled and Julia thought he didn't want to shed tears again in front of them.

As Julia and Bridget drove home, Julia confessed, "That's the first public religious confession I've heard. We don't do that in my church. We live a good life. We are kind and we please God by helping others."

"That isn't having salvation."

"I think we probably all have salvation if we aren't evil. I think we'll all go to heaven if we wish to. Melinda didn't commit herself to Christ, as Mr. Gerard did. I must believe Melinda *is* in heaven. I'm not sure that what Edgar did is necessary."

But Julia knew she was not kind and good. She was as selfish as Edgar, more selfish, in fact. She grasped for David's love, not for God's sake, nor for David's, but for her sake. She was a sinner. Yet she did not have the courage to relinquish her sin.

Bridget spoke hesitantly. "Herself could have given her life to Jesus at the last minute."

"While she drowned! Bridget, I doubt she'd think of that while she drowned!"

Bridget tucked her hands in her lap and proceeded to stare at them.

"What does your mother think of your religious views?" Julia inquired.

" 'Tis fearing I'll become a Protestant, she is. I told herself I'll always be a Catholic, but herself is thinking I'm converting soon. It's me Bible reading that is having her upset."

"Well, I don't blame her for being skeptical—after all, you *have* changed your religious practices quite a bit." Julia smiled. "Yet, I find your faith appealing," she said.

Bridget smiled quietly and said no more.

Eighteen

"I don't know—I just don't know," Julia said, touching the cream-colored satin nightgown, a Paris original in a white box. The saleslady behind the counter stepped to the side so she wouldn't interfere with Julia's examination. Julia smiled nervously at her. The nightgown was beyond her means, and the clerk knew it. "Do you have something else of a similar design?" Julia inquired.

"This is French satin and a bargain at the price. It's an original design as well."

"Well. . ." Julia was in the lingerie department of Field, Leiter & Co. at Washington and State Streets, a Chicago showplace, six stories high and constructed of white marble. The aisles were wide and beautifully lighted. The clerks were well-trained and dignified. The voices of the women shoppers were hushed, like voices in prayer at church. Julia wished she had some of her knipl left, but she had used the last of it to purchase a telescope and a gold cigarette case for David's birthday next month. The rest of it had gone for various items this year. "I'd like to see what else you have."

The clerk lifted two boxes from beneath the counter and opened them. "The satin, as you see, isn't quite as nice. Neither gown has Valenciennes for trim."

Julia had a similar quality nightgown in her bureau. "I see that. Is there something else?"

"There are some less expensive gowns in the next department." The clerk indicated an area in the back of the store.

Julia hesitated.

"You might wish to examine the nightgown from Paris in the dressing room."

"Thank you." She would do so and then return it to the clerk and leave.

In the dressing room she stood before the mirror with the gown held over her dress. She would love to wear this for David's homecoming in eleven days. She imagined his admiration as she walked across the bedroom, the folds swishing, the fitted waist and low neckline revealing her figure. Diane certainly wore gowns like this!

She left the dressing room.

There wasn't sufficient cash in her household allowance to buy the garment. Before this trip, David had arranged a joint checking account in case of an emergency. She could write a check for the gown. Of course this was no emergency! Yet David had said his business was doing well. Certainly he'd want her to have nice clothes, she thought, justifying herself. Hadn't he bought her a rig? But this was an extravagance; fifty dollars would buy a wagon or a parlor carpet. She placed the nightgown on the counter. "I'll take it. My checks are at home. May I have the nightgown delivered and pay for it then?"

"Fine."

The clerk folded the gown in tissue.

At home Julia lifted the day's mail from the hatrack table and tore through it. Ah, finally there was a letter from David—the first. She had visited the wives of the agents traveling with David yesterday, and they hadn't yet heard from their husbands either. She ripped open the envelope and read the letter. So he and the agents were in New Orleans at the Smithton House—a dreary place with bad food. He missed her. Longed for her. Loved her. Oh, she missed him desperately. Wait until he saw the nightgown!

She went to the kitchen for coffee. Bridget was at the worktable mixing batter for gingersnaps. "Could yourself be coming to dinner tomorrow?" Bridget asked. "I'm wanting you to see me house."

Bridget's eyes were red and watery. Purplish circles had formed beneath them. "Your cold is worse. You shouldn't be entertaining. In fact, you should be home in bed."

Bridget coughed. "Sure, 'tis on the mend I am. Myself doesn't have a fever. Mama and Papa is coming. Mama is bringing the meat and dessert, and all myself is doing is peeling some potatoes. I won't be fixing dinner here, and it isn't being any trouble."

"Well—all right. I'd love to see your house."

When the nightgown arrived the next afternoon, Julia wrote a check on the small hatrack table. She filled it out slowly, for she hadn't written a check before. "Whom do I make it out to?"

"Field, Leiter & Co. Use the *and* symbol please," the delivery man said politely.

"Do I sign my name or my husband's?" She was embarrassed and wished she had received instruction from David.

"Your name."

"Is this all right?" She handed it to him.

"Fine."

She placed the checks and receipt on David's desk and the nightgown in her bureau.

That evening Julia sat in Bridget's parlor while Bridget and her mother finished fixing dinner and the men walked Patrick. Bridget had proudly shown Julia the cottage, which had a kitchen, parlor, and bedroom. The parlor was brightened with Bridget's embroidered pillows and samplers. A rag rug, in which Julia recognized scraps of her material, lay on the rough board floor. The main attraction of the room was the drop-front desk Michael had built for Bridget on which to write letters home.

"Saints, the potatoes is being done!" Julia heard Mrs. Boland exclaim. "Now sit yourself down and I'll be mashing them. Yourself is whiter than the potatoes."

"Hush, Mama. Mrs. Gerard will be feeling bad."

"Sit!" she commanded as she began mashing the potatoes.

Michael called Julia to dinner, and they gathered around a small table. The table and chairs took up most of the floor space, and Julia had difficulty squeezing into her chair. After Michael took Bridget's hand and blessed the meal, bowls of food were passed. Bridget coughed and the attack lasted some time. Mrs. Boland shook her head. "What is itself I'm hearing again?"

"Mama, please stop talking about myself."

The conversation turned to Michael's plan to add a second bedroom for guests, and someday, children. Bridget ate very little, and while dessert was served, Michael's eyes sought Julia. "I got something on my mind. I ain't happy to tell you it."

"Please go ahead," Julia said.

"Workin' and doing her own housework is too much for Bridget. Could she work part time? If that ain't too much trouble for you."

"It isn't. Mr. Gerard and I think the house is too much for one person. I need a full-time and a part-time servant." *Especially if I have a child,* Julia thought.

Bridget looked unhappily at Michael.

"I'm sorry, darling, but I gotta take care of you."

"Myself can't have another girl in me house. She won't be putting enough starch in Mr. Gerard's collars. She'll be sweeping crumbs under me carpet."

"I ain't gonna have you falling apart."

"I'll get someone you can work well with," Julia promised.

Bridget sighed in resignation.

It would be difficult to find a satisfactory servant, Julia knew already, remembering the temporary servant who had replaced Bridget. Edith was on her sixth servant in just ten years, and only reasonably happy with Nora at that. In fact, many couples in Chicago boarded in hotels to avoid the servant problem. Julia considered Mary. She did think the girl had a good heart and that her gossip might be controlled.

"Is Mary still planning to work for the people who will move into Cullens'?"

"No. Herself is looking for another place. She says having eight kids around will be worse than watching cats."

"Is Mary a good worker? If she is, I might consider hiring her."

"Aye."

"Is she still going with Billy?"

"No, Billy's engaged and Mary is hating him. Herself said she'll die before talking to his like."

"If I hired Mary, I couldn't have her gossiping about David and me."

"Myself wouldn't be letting her."

"Would you recommend Mary?"

"Aye. Mary will be holding her tongue. Herself is tired of living in an attic itself, and her cold as a snowball in the winter. Herself will be grateful to have a nice room. She won't gossip."

"I'll offer her a job. If she accepts, I'll hire her on trial."

Julia didn't expect Bridget to appear in the morning, but she was there and looking better. Her face was pale, but with a tint of natural pink. She didn't cough as frequently. "Michael said myself is to come home, if you once say I'm ailing." Bridget peered earnestly at Julia. "But myself is all right, I'm thinking."

"We'll see."

Julia saw Mary in the yard with the cats, and she joined her. Julia hadn't spoken to her since Bridget's reception, and Mary blinked nervously, apparently afraid Julia was on the attack.

"Bridget told me you're looking for a job?" Julia began.

"I ain't found one yet. I ain't working for a family with eight kids. I'll go to the factory first; though I hate them places. I can go because I've got a girlfriend that can get me on."

Julia offered Mary a position and explained the terms: no gossip, the hours, etc. Mary's hand crossed her chest. "You're good, real good, Mrs. Gerard, and I'll be faithful like Bridget. I'd love working with Bridget, and I won't cause no trouble and you'll not be sorry one minute."

Julia smiled; she believed Mary. "You'll have Bridget's old room."

Mary gave a little leap of delight. The Cullens were moving out Saturday, and she said she would sweep up after them and move in that evening.

The Monday after Mary moved in, Julia saw Bridget coming up the drive, her step not as quick as usual. She covered her mouth, and Julia assumed she coughed. Julia went to the back porch steps to meet her. It was chilly, but clear, the sky just shaking the morning mist and coming forth blue. Since July 3, there had been only two and a half inches of rain. A breeze sent a shower of leaves from the maple, and Julia picked one up. It wasn't as flexible as she would expect; it felt rather dry. The air was faintly smoky and Julia supposed there had been another fire. They were a daily occurrence, and this weekend a warehouse on the South Side burned, receiving six hundred thousand dollars damage. The drought affected Michigan, Wisconsin, and Minnesota as well, causing forest fires on a large scale.

Bridget was scheduled to work Monday, Wednesday, and Friday. Julia would pay her six dollars a week, plus thirty cents for transportation. (Bridget would either take the horsecar or be dropped off by Michael, depending on Michael's schedule at church.) Bridget thought the salary too high, but Julia believed her work warranted it. She hoped David would agree. Mary would receive three-fifty a week plus room and board, and Julia would give her a fifty-cent raise if she proved capable.

Bridget entered the porch coughing—a deep, racking sound. Her cheeks flamed and her breath was shallow and rapid. "Why did you come to work in this condition?" Julia scolded.

"Michael dropped me off. I promised him I'd go to the doctor after I'm telling Mary what needs doing. Sure, I'm afeard of going, though."

"Why?"

"I'm afeard of doctors. Me Bible says to not be fearing, but I am."

"I could have trained Mary."

"Myself should be giving her directions. Herself is working for me."

"Oh!" Julia hadn't known Bridget considered herself Mary's boss. "I'll take you to Dr. Scott's."

They joined Mary in the kitchen, where she was peering in the cupboard. Mary looked neat in a dark pin-striped uniform with a white collar and cuffs. "I can't find anything," Mary told Bridget. "Where do you keep the juice glasses? Mrs. Gerard wants juice for breakfast and there's nothing to put it in except water glasses. Mrs. Cullen never puts juice in water glasses.''

Bridget reached behind the water glasses and lifted out a juice glass. "Ourselves is using more water glasses than juice glasses, so I keep the water glasses out front.''

Mary opened her mouth as if to suggest another method, then closed it.

Bridget sat in a kitchen chair. "There's being paper in the first drawer in the cabinet. Bring me a piece, Mary, and I'll be giving yourself orders.''

Mary brought the paper. "Is yourself liking your room?'' Bridget asked.

"I ain't never had anything so pretty. Except for mass, I spent all of yesterday in it.''

Bridget wrote the list for Mary.

Dr. Scott's front parlor served as his waiting room. Julia had told Bridget Dr. Scott's back parlor had been converted into an examination room. Bridget stared vacantly, careful not to look at the others waiting, who might think she was studying them. She was too frightened to read. There had been no doctor in Dunquin and this was her first visit to one. In Dunquin, the midwife helped a body into the world and the priest helped one out, and in between, a body did the best one could. Bridget wouldn't have come, but Michael had insisted. She had heard about doctors cutting their patients open and removing things. Bridget O'Keefe wasn't letting any doctor take anything!

Dr. Scott appeared in the doorway and looked around the room. "Next?''

Bridget didn't speak. "Bridget O'Keefe is next,'' Julia offered.

The doctor's eyes brightened as he looked at Julia. "How is the nausea?''

Julia glanced nervously from him to Bridget. "Oh, the nausea— well, I still have it.''

"It'll pass soon, I expect.''

"Yourself is sick?'' Bridget asked.

"I'll tell you later.''

"Come along,'' Dr. Scott told Bridget.

Bridget stared at the strange instrument around his neck. It had two prongs, like an ice tong, which were attached to some kind of mouth-piece. She was terrified of the apparatus and stood there trembling.

Julia looked at her with concern. "Are you all right?''

"No!"

"Shall I come with you?"

"Aye."

Dr. Scott said firmly, "No, Miss O'Keefe will be all right."

"Mrs!" Bridget corrected him in spite of her fears.

She followed him into the examination room, a regular looking parlor except it contained a high bed and a cabinet with medical equipment on top. The windows were covered with attractive curtains. "What is your trouble?" he questioned her.

She had to protect herself. "Itself is being nothing," she began, but a vigorous attack of coughing gave her away.

He indicated she should sit on the high bed. "Don't be nervous. I won't hurt you. How long have you had the cough?"

"Fearful long."

He looked kindly at her and smiled. "I expect you're from Ireland."

"I'm from Dunquin, County Kerry."

"Is it on the ocean?"

"Almost—just a short walk, and me papa has a boat for fishing. And seaworthy it is."

"Will you unbutton your dress please and slip it back? I need to listen to your chest." He put the prongs of his instrument in his ears while she prepared herself. He then placed the mouthpiece on her chest. It was cold, but it didn't hurt.

"What is itself that's on me skin?"

"A stethoscope. I can hear the fluid in your lungs with it."

"Saints!"

He held the mouthpiece over her back and chest. He then thumped on her back with his fingers. "There's quite a bit of mucus in there. When did you become sick?"

"The last day of me honeymoon—about two and a half weeks ago."

"You should have come in much sooner."

Bridget had the sudden hope of the new bride. " 'Tis pregnant I am, surely—and itself is causing me to be weak and ailing."

A faint smile appeared. "You might be pregnant of course, but that is not the issue here. You have pneumonia, and you'll need care and rest. You're a very sick girl. You must drink plenty of water and stay warm." He took a brown bottle from a cabinet. "Take one tablespoon four times a day for your cough. I'll visit you tomorrow. Do you have someone to care for you?"

"Me mama. Herself is working part time at me church, but she can be taking off."

"Have her put hot camphor packs on your chest and rub it with guaiacum. I don't want you out of bed."

After Bridget told Julia about Dr. Scott's diagnosis, they drove toward Bridget's church to pick up her mother. Julia became quiet and didn't comment on the cause of her nausea. Saints, it would be fearful if Julia were getting pneumonia too! Bridget worried. Yet Dr. Scott hadn't seemed alarmed about the nausea, so it wasn't that. "What is yourself ailing with?" Bridget finally asked.

As Julia turned to Bridget, tears dropped to her cheeks. "I . . . oh, Bridget, I think I'm in the family way. Mr. Gerard doesn't know about it, so don't say anything. I'm waiting until I'm sure before I tell him."

"Wouldn't himself want to know so he could think joyful thoughts?"

"No—and remember—don't tell anyone. Just forget this conversation."

Bridget nodded; then a coughing attack took her attention. When it passed, she wondered at the lack of communication between the Gerards. If only themselves could be happy and talking all the time like her and Michael.

After they picked up her mother, the two women settled Bridget in bed. Now that she was in bed, she didn't want to move. Oh, the bed felt soft—the pretty white and red quilt she had made felt comfortable on her body. Patrick leaped up and laid his head on her chest. "Scoot!" Mrs. Boland screeched. "Get off the bed."

"Mama, leave himself be."

"Daughter, no dog belongs in the bed I'm nursing."

Mama couldn't be argued with, Bridget had learned. "Get yourself down," Bridget conceded.

She closed her eyes. She might have slept. Then she smelled the hot camphor pack and felt someone kissing her forehead. She opened her eyes. "Is yourself leaving, Julia?" Bridget whispered.

"Yes—now sleep."

"Mary is needing me. She can't be finding anything."

"She'll do fine. You couldn't find everything when you were new, either."

"But myself is quick."

"So is Mary."

Bridget heard footsteps and the front door shutting.

Nineteen

Julia wandered into the kitchen the evening David was due home. Restless, she couldn't sit or stand still. Mary turned over the dishpan and hung her apron on a hook. "I wonder all the time how Mrs. Cullen is doin' with her cats. I had a nightmare about them last night. I can't tell you how many times them things jumped in my clean laundry baskets and muddied my clothes. I hated them cats. It's a secret, but I don't mind telling you. Mrs. Cullen slept with them cats, and poor Mr. Cullen slept in a separate bedroom."

Though Julia found the fact interesting, she shook her head. "That's just the kind of thing you shouldn't be saying about your employer."

"But Mrs. Cullen did sleep with them cats."

"Mary!"

"I'm sorry. I forget sometimes."

"Don't forget again."

"No, ma'am."

Mary did try hard, Julia reflected, and was doing a good job cleaning. And though she had little opportunity to cook at the Cullens', she did a fine job in the kitchen as well.

"Is Mr. Gerard still coming in?" Mary asked.

"Yes," Julia answered. His train was supposedly due in fifteen minutes. He had written that the Michigan Central was badly off schedule, and rather than hang around the depot, she should wait at home. She should have gone. She was so restless here. But it was too late to leave; if the train was on time, they would cross paths.

"I'm going to Bridget's tonight," Mary informed her, "and then

I'm going to visit Margaret. I made Bridget some chicken soup. I seen her last night and I say she ain't getting no better. She's coughing and she breathes like it's her last breath."

"It takes a while for pneumonia to clear up." But Julia was worried about Bridget, who wasn't rallying as fast as Julia would like.

"Is there anything I can do before I go? I could add a log to the fireplace, I could light the furnace. I learned how at Mrs. Cullens'. Let me tell you that wit—I mean that lady had me do everything."

Julia smiled. "Mr. Gerard will light the furnace tonight. Go on."

It excited Julia to think that David would take care of the furnace, and the routine of their life would resume. That she would wear the nightgown. That it would be the agent to heal her marriage.

"You look like a picture, even though you got to wear that ugly black," Mary commented as she was finishing up her work.

"Thank you, Mary," Julia said with a smile.

Mary emptied the slop pail and left.

The doorbell rang, and Julia jumped. So David was home early! Why had he rung the bell? Had he lost his key? As she ran to the door, she patted her hair and bit her lips to give them color. But it was Alma in her usual distraught state, her eyes teary, her chins trembling. Alma's big frame swayed, and fearing she would faint, Julia led her to a chair in the parlor. "Edgar sent me."

"Is he all right?"

"Yes, but I'm not. It hit me on the way over how upset I am."

"Would you like a cold drink?"

"Yes, please."

Julia gave Alma a glass of ginger beer. "You're my only friend except Martha," Alma said. "She's visiting Nelda. I suppose you knew that. Nelda's depressed now, but I suppose you know that too."

"Is that what's upsetting you?"

"No. It's Edgar. Suddenly he wants me out doing everything. Having friends, having fun, going to church—laughing, smiling, all the things I've forgotten how to do. I just can't, Julia. I've done everything for him, but I can't do this." Alma's lips quivered. "His religion has changed him. I wish Edgar weren't a Christian. I wish he'd revert to how he was. I knew how to live that way."

"You do need to be out. You need more friends."

"No, I don't. A woman from the Illinois Street Church called this morning. She's about my age; her husband has a bad heart. We have a lot in common, and I suppose I like her. She wants Edgar and me to visit her church, and Edgar is eager to go. She said Mr. Moody is a charter member of the church—a deacon and a frequent speaker. I don't like his strong religious views, and I don't want to go."

"You should at least try it once."

"No! Why do you suppose that woman visited? I didn't invite her, nor did Edgar."

"Bridget said she wrote Mr. Moody about Edgar."

"Then that's it."

"I still think you should visit the church. It's important to support Edgar."

"I don't know—I just can't think."

Julia nodded sympathically. She agreed that Alma's position was difficult. "Why did Edgar send you?"

"He wants to see David tonight. He says it's important. I know David will be tired, but could you bring him?"

"Yes." Thinking of the nightgown, she hoped Edgar wouldn't keep David long. She hoped the train would not be too late.

David's train was late. It was fully dark when he arrived. She went out to meet his buggy at the stable. The air was dry and cool, the sky starry.

She ran the last few steps and climbed up beside him, falling into his arms. "Oh, I missed you! I started out the door every time a horse passed." She ran her hand over his face. It was thinner and there was slack in his frock coat. He had lost weight on his hotel diet. "How was the trip? Darling, I've been so lonely. Thank you for writing often— that helped. Did you get my letters? I tried to follow your itinerary so that you would. I—"

His lips interrupted her. Time passed. She had no idea how long, nor did she care. "I love you, my darling," he said. "I received your letters—in fact, I memorized them."

He helped her from the buggy and lifted his valise from the backseat.

"Did Mr. Werner and Mr. Luken learn the territory?" Julia asked.

"Yes, I think they'll represent me well."

"I read that the drought is causing forest fires up north. Were you near any of them?"

"No, but the fires are extensive. There's been a great loss of timber, and undoubtedly lumber prices will rise. I bought rather heavily at a good price. I hope to sell the lumber quickly enough to make the deal profitable. There should be no problem, as there's a demand for lumber. But my cash and credit are tied up, and I have to ask you to be thrifty for a while."

She told him about her household arrangement with Bridget and Mary, and that Bridget had pneumonia. "Bridget will make six dollars a week and Mary three-fifty. Can we afford that?"

"Yes."

Julia wondered if she should return the Paris nightgown. "Can we afford a few luxuries?"

"We aren't in financial straits. I simply meant be careful—don't go overboard."

Then she could keep the nightgown.

They were standing beside the buggy. "Let's go in," David suggested. "I want to unpack and relax."

"David, we can't stay. Your father wants to see you."

"Why?"

"He's had a religious experience. It's probably about that."

"I hope he hasn't stopped doing the estimating. That was doing him good."

"No—if anything he's working harder. Your bookkeeper has been keeping him well supplied."

Julia noticed the tense lines on David's face as he entered the back parlor at Edgar's. She had never seen David relaxed in his father's presence. The bed tray that bridged Edgar held a Bible and pen. David lit a cigarette and regarded the Bible with surprise.

Alma spoke to Mrs. Harper, the night nurse. "Perhaps you could take your break."

Mrs. Harper gathered up her knitting and left with Alma.

"Should I leave?" Julia asked.

"No," Edgar said. "You're David's wife and you should hear what I have to tell him. Before that, how is Bridget?"

"Not too well."

"I'll go see her tomorrow."

Julia looked fondly at Edgar, knowing how much he hated going out. Edgar then asked David about his trip, and David described the forest fires, but omitted telling him about his large purchase of lumber.

Edgar commented, "I noticed your surprise at seeing me with a Bible."

"Julia said you'd had a religious experience."

"You knew Bridget had been coming to read Scripture to me?"

"Yes."

Edgar's hand nervously fingered his Bible. "I . . . I hope you won't doubt my sincerity. I've committed my life to Christ. That's . . . why I asked to see you tonight. I . . . I need to ask you to forgive me. I've been hard on you. I caused you deep problems at the lumberyard. I'm sorry—very sorry."

"Of course," David said matter-of-factly. Julia didn't see a sign on

David's face to indicate he had heard anything extraordinary. David's lack of reaction amazed Julia. Then Julia remembered David had long practiced hiding emotion from Edgar. Didn't he know Edgar had just laid his pride on the line?

"David . . . I . . . I didn't allow you free rein . . . I realize I was a tyrant."

David's mouth relaxed, and his hand moved forward on his knee in the direction of the bed. He was looking at his father, not taking his eyes from him. But why didn't he say something? Julia wondered. "David—" Julia said tentatively.

"Son, I care deeply for you."

The angle of David's body moved forward, and his breath drew sharply in. Julia felt the impact of David's emotion. He stood slowly, approached the bed, and looked down at his father.

"I never meant to hurt you," Edgar explained. "I was trying to make a man of you—the wrong way. David, you are a man; you've done a better job with the business than I."

"Father—I—" David's voice broke. He leaned over his father, lifted the bed tray, and set it on the floor. His arms circled Edgar, pulling him up and holding him to his chest. A rough sound came from David's throat.

Finally, David spoke. "Of course I forgive you."

David released his father, but remained at his bed, looking down at him. Julia wiped her tears as she looked at the love on David's face.

"Do you remember when you were three or four very young?" Edgar asked.

"Yes."

"I would take you to the yard. Give you a ride on a lumber wagon."

"I remember. That's what got me interested in the lumber business. There was something special about the fresh scent of lumber—its solid feel."

"We were close then."

"Yes."

"I've asked your mother to forgive me too. She doesn't really understand the change in me. She's upset—she doesn't understand her position in my life."

"She will—she needs time."

"I wish I hadn't wasted my life. I plan to do something for God— I'm not sure what. But I'll spend the rest of my life making your mother happy. I promised myself that the day I received Christ."

While Julia and David were driving home, David said, "Have you ever given your life to Christ?"

"Not in the way your father and Bridget have. I tell myself that I'm a Christian, but I don't know if I am. I don't like thinking about it, because of Melinda. She never committed her life to Christ."

"You don't know that."

"Yes, I do! I was closer to her than anyone. She would have told me." Julia turned to the fact that haunted her. "I can't accept her death. I'll never understand why God let her die!"

"Maybe God was sparing her from a difficult life."

She turned her face sharply to him. "What!"

"It's possible. I do think God controls the universe."

"I know He does, but I don't exactly understand what effect God has on events," Julia stated. "Have you ever considered giving your life to Christ?"

"No, but I'd not mind having a strong vision for God. I'd not mind having Father's faith."

In their bedroom, David set his valise on the bed and removed a clean nightshirt and dressing gown. Julia closed the valise and left it for Mary to unpack. David changed and carefully scrubbed his teeth, taking forever, it seemed to Julia. She paced the room, glancing at the bureau drawer that contained her nightgown.

When David rinsed his brush, Julia said brightly, "Will you leave me alone a minute? I've a surprise for you. I'll call you when I'm ready."

His eyebrows raised; she supposed he was thinking that it wasn't her personality to be playful. But she would like to be playful more often, have things fun and light between them.

"Well—all right," he agreed hesitantly.

She locked the bedroom door after him. By his footsteps, she realized he was heading for his study. Would he examine bills and checks and be irritated by her fifty-dollar purchase? Certainly he was too tired to look into the accounts. He probably meant to relax in his armchair. Why hadn't she sent him to the kitchen to get her a cold drink? Oh, how was she to know he had purchased all that lumber! *Stop worrying!* she scolded herself. *He said we aren't in financial straits.* But she felt uneasy. She wished he hadn't told her about his lumber purchase. Should she return the nightgown? She couldn't! Too much depended on it.

Julia slipped on the nightgown. The satin felt cool. She liked the way it swept the tops of her bare feet. She brushed her hair, then scented herself with rosewater to sweeten the air while she walked to him. She looked into the pier-glass. Her cheeks were flushed, her eyes brilliant as emeralds. Her nightgown tucked into all the right places. She unlocked the door. "David."

"Just a minute."

Five minutes passed and Julia paced the floor. She wiped damp hands on her gown.

Then his footsteps sounded in the hall. He entered the room. A flick of appreciation crossed his face. Then he held out the receipt. "Julia, I don't understand this—a nightgown for fifty dollars. Certainly this is a mistake! Nightgowns don't cost fifty dollars."

"Can't we talk about this later? I'll explain it then."

"I told you to be thrifty."

"I didn't know that when I bought the nightgown."

"Will you please explain this receipt."

She pulled at her skirt. "It's for this. This!" He had ruined it, ruined it all. Why must everything she did fail!

"You spent fifty dollars on *that*?"

"I bought it for you!"

"Fifty dollars!" He looked amazed.

"Yes! Yes!"

David's finger jabbed the receipt. "Julia, I have debts to contend with."

"What? I bought that nightgown days ago—before I knew about your debts!"

"You have an extravagant streak in you."

"I don't! When have I been extravagant? When—when!" she screamed.

He glared at her. He hated her, after all—that's what this attack meant. She meant nothing to him. It was only Diane he cared about.

"You had money from your father—why didn't you spend that?"

She refused to tell him about his birthday gifts, on which she had spent thirty-five dollars. "I've spent it—mostly on little things. That was what it was for."

"You should have saved it."

"Saved it—why?"

"For reasons of thrift."

"That's crazy."

"You never plan ahead."

"I do too."

"No, you don't. You *are* impulsive!"

Julia looked at him in horror. "David—stop this!"

He looked taken aback. He put the receipt in his dressing-gown pocket.

Hot tears ran down Julia's face. "I only bought the nightgown for you. I hoped for a . . . a . . . Oh, forget it!"

She tore from the room, lifting her skirt so she wouldn't stumble.

She noticed that no light shone under Mary's door. She hoped Mary was asleep. It would be awful if Mary were now coming in from Margaret's and Julia met her. Mary would think her mad, streaking through the house in a skimpy gown and bare feet. She heard David behind her and ran faster.

She flung open the cellar door and dashed down the stairs. Running to the corner by the coal bin she dropped to a wood box. Her breath came in gasps. She heard David coming down the stairs. Oh, she never wanted to see him again. If only she could get away from him!

She buried her face in her hands and rocked back and forth. The air was cold and clammy and the floor like ice on her bare feet.

"Julia, look at me!" David demanded.

"I can't—just go away. I can't talk now. Just leave me alone."

"I shouldn't have attacked you. I'm under pressure, and I let it get to me."

"I know that! But that's no excuse!"

"I'm sorry—please forgive me."

She heard the movement of his body and she knew he knelt by her. His hands clasped her shoulders, warm on her cold skin. She shivered and wished to be upstairs in warm clothes. She raised her head. "I don't know why I bought the gown. It was a silly, female thing. I'll return it tomorrow."

"I hate you to, but it would help if you did. Perhaps next month you can purchase it."

Julia wondered if the saleslady would be surprised. After all, the clerk had thought Julia could afford the nightgown. Would the clerk try to sell Julia another? What reason could Julia give for returning it? Would she break down and cry while the clerk looked on in disdain? Perhaps she would have Edith, who handled these things with aplomb, return it. Julia stood. "I'll take it back tomorrow."

"It looks exquisite on you."

"Do you think I care?"

He looked stricken; she knew he wished to take back the last minutes. But he had put her through too much. She could not sympathize with him.

"Julia, just as soon as I can afford it, I want you to have another."

Suddenly, she felt cheap. She had tried to lure David with the nightgown; she had behaved like a woman of the street. She had been wrong about Diane. Diane had too much dignity to wear such garments. "I don't want another. I'm cold—I'm going upstairs. I forgot to mention earlier that we probably need the furnace lit."

"Darling, please. I don't want you hurt."

"I'll be all right. I accept your apology—we all say things we'd rather not. David—I *will* be all right. Just leave me alone!"

Julia didn't meet Mary on the way to her bedroom—thank heavens! She jerked the gown over her head and slipped into a sacque nightgown. She fought back her tears. If she cried David would apologize again and she would become hysterical. She placed the gown back in its box. Her habit of saving boxes had come in handy. She placed it on the bureau, where it sat—white and ready for the next customer.

Julia didn't cry until David was asleep.

You could try and try, and what did it matter, she decided ruefully; everything was wrecked in the end. You could not try and you would do as well.

In the morning Julia woke to David's kiss and sunny, cool weather. Her head felt heavy, as if she had been drugged. She was amazed that she had slept. David was sitting on the side of the bed in an undershirt and long drawers. His face was clean-shaven.

"I didn't hear you getting ready for work," she said.

"I was quiet. I knew you were tired from last night."

"It's strange, I didn't hear a thing."

He kissed her again. His eyes showed concern. "Am I forgiven for hurting you?" he asked again.

Let him believe he was forgiven, she thought. *Just leave me alone.* "Yes," she responded distantly.

"You don't need to get up for breakfast," he said. "I shouldn't have wakened you."

"No, I will." She felt slightly nauseated but could probably manage a glass of juice. It was important to be with David at breakfast; that was one time Diane couldn't be with him.

"How is Mary's cooking?"

"Good, very good, really. Bridget might disagree."

"Julia, you look so hurt."

"Like I said, I'm fine." *Tell him you're not fine,* she thought. *Tell him everything. Tell him you know about his affair. Tell him you're pregnant. Time confirmed that fact. Tell him you're terrified you'll miscarry. Let him be terrified too. Be honest! Maybe you'll have peace then.*

He leaned over and kissed her, and she placed her arms around his neck. Tears streamed down her face.

"Julia, you're crying."

"It's nothing—nothing!"

"Darling, what is it?"

"Nothing!"

She avoided his questioning eyes. He stood and finished dressing.

Later in the morning, Julia buttoned on her gloves, put on a light jacket, and picked up the white box. Convinced she would break down in Field, Leiter & Co., Julia planned to ask Edith to return the night-gown. She would also invite Edith to lunch. Edith should be free today; it was Freddie's day to be at the store with Morton. It was Edith's idea that Freddie experience the business one day a week. Edith fluctuated between ignoring Morton's sewing-machine business and managing it. Julia thought that for Edith not to domineer Morton would always be a goal.

Julia stopped in the kitchen. "Mary, don't fix lunch for me. I'll eat downtown."

"All right."

"I'm stopping to see Bridget this afternoon." Mary had reported at breakfast that Bridget had not improved.

"Tell Bridget them new people is moving into Cullens' today. I ain't met them, but I talked to some of their kids. They're chattery—and jumpy. I'm glad I ain't got to put up with them. I met the servant girl that's takin' my place and she's pretty nervous about being around all them kids."

"That's understandable."

"Tell Bridget I counted fifteen wagon loads of things coming in so far. Land, them people is rich."

"Mary, that's rather gossipy, if you ask me," Julia said and left.

Edith accepted Julia's luncheon invitation. As they climbed in the buggy, Julia decided to ask her to return the nightgown after they ate.

"What's in the box?" Edith asked, her curiosity aroused.

"I'll tell you later."

"Why the secrecy?"

"Edith, please wait. I promise to tell you later."

They went to the Tremont House, Edith's favorite restaurant, and were seated in the lady's section. Julia recalled that ten years ago when the buildings in Chicago were raised several feet from the marshy ground, George Pullman installed 5,000 jackscrews around the Tremont House and lifted it so smoothly the guests were unaware they were going up. Julia ordered ham croquettes and Edith prairie chicken. The box leaned against the wall.

"Well, what's in the box?" Edith asked again.

Hoping not to have to explain too much, Julia chose her words carefully. " I . . . It's a Paris nightgown. I paid fifty dollars for it and David can't afford fifty dollars this month. He asked me to take it back."

Edith's eyebrows rose. "Why?"

"He's purchased a lot of lumber."

"That's not what I mean. I mean, why can't you take it back?"

"I had a bad experience wearing it, and I don't want to face the clerk. It would be too difficult."

"You'll have to explain more than that to me!" Edith snapped.

Julia stared at her. Maybe she would feel better if she confided in her. Maybe she should tell it all. "All right then," Julia blurted. "David's having an affair with Diane Hastings. I bought the gown to win him back."

"Diane Hastings!" Edith's fork clattered on her plate.

"Yes."

"So that's why you've been morbidly interested in Diane! How did you find out?"

Feeling breathless, Julia tugged at her neckline. "From Billy Williams, an eyewitness." Julia related Billy's story. "As I said I . . . I bought the gown to win David from Diane. I love him, Edith. I have no pride. I'm desperate and I tried to lure him! Yes, I did! I couldn't help it. I suppose you can't understand—you and Morton are so stable. But I can't attract David—that's the awful thing! I felt so cheap, displaying myself in the nightgown. I never want to see it again. He loves Diane and me—both of us. It's—it's incomprehensible, but it's true!"

The waiter appeared and set soup bowls on their service plates. The bowls made no sound as they touched the plates; it was a practiced movement from a professional. What did he think of her looking so distraught? Did he think she was sick? Or emotionally unstable? His face was impassive. But certainly he was thinking: What a pathetic woman!

The waiter left and Julia continued. "Knowing what was ahead, I would marry David again. Edith, do you understand? I love him! I know you think I'm ridiculous, that I have no pride."

"Have you spoken to David about this affair?"

"No."

"Well, why not?"

"He might ask for a divorce."

"That's conjecture."

"You don't know the situation, Edith."

"I'm wise enough to know he might not have had an affair at all. Is this Billy trustworthy? It seems to me you jump to conclusions; you always do, Julia."

"But Billy said David gave him fifty dollars—blackmail money."

"Billy might have gotten the money a number of ways. Speak to David."

"I can't."

"Conjecture can be fatal. Facts are easier to deal with than conjectures."

"I can't confront David. Will you return the nightgown? Just forget the conversation!"

"Diane isn't David's type—you are. I never liked her at all. She has always been grasping. She attracted every man in high school. She even went after Morton and had him spellbound. Morton saved for weeks to buy her some candy, and he found her passing it around at school to several young men. You'll find no good word about Diane from Morton."

"Then why is David in love with her?"

Edith took Julia's hand. "I say he isn't—I've seen his tenderness toward you. Confront him. I could be with you, if you wish."

"I don't think I dare," Julia whispered.

"Why?"

"He might choose Diane."

"That's foolishness. I've just told you she isn't his type."

"I can't. Edith, I know Diane lives on Ontario Street. Do you have her address?"

"You aren't going to speak to Diane!"

"No, but I might drive by sometime. I want to know what her house looks like. I want to see the drive where Billy saw them embracing."

"That will not be helpful."

"Tell me!"

"No."

"I can find out this information from Mary."

"Take my advice and stop dwelling on Diane. Speak to David. Now let's eat. Our soup will be icy."

Later at Field, Leiter & Co., Julia tied the horse to the iron ring in the pavement while Edith left to return the nightgown. In fifteen minutes Edith marched to the buggy without the box. "Did you have any trouble?" Julia asked.

"No. I simply told the clerk you were dissatisfied."

"Which clerk did you have?" Julia asked.

"A compact woman with gray hair."

"That's the one I had. Thank you, Edith."

"I didn't mind."

But Julia didn't like being a coward. She wished she had returned the gown. She didn't like asking Edith to mop up after her. Yet Edith always had. Julia couldn't remember a time when Edith hadn't helped her. "I wish I had returned it myself."

"I wish you had too."

"Do you?"

Edith's eyes were soft. Julia felt deep warmth for Edith. Julia knew the feeling was more than warmth, that there was a reason she could always turn to Edith. "Edith?"

"Yes."

"I—I love you."

"Of course," Edith said crisply. But Julia saw the moisture in Edith's eyes.

"Well," Edith said decisively, "let's go—I have several projects at home that need attention."

After Julia dropped off Edith, she headed for Bridget's by way of Dearborn Street. She approached the Chicago Historical Society, where Nancy Smith volunteered.

In fact, Julia saw Nancy Smith on the walk. She was talking animately to Arthur. He squarely faced Nancy so Julia could only see his back. But she knew it was Arthur. She'd recognize his erect posture anywhere. She had seen that gold-headed cane at the bazaar. He had worn that brown suit before.

Nancy tugged on Arthur's arm. He turned and they waved.

"Hello," Nancy greeted her.

"Nice day," Arthur added politely.

"A little cool," Nancy commented further.

"Yes."

"See you at church tomorrow," said Arthur. His hand reached for Nancy's.

As Julia passed, she heard Nancy say "Arthie."

Arthie! Julia thought with disgust. Julia had never called him Arthie. Arthie! What a silly name! Oh, but it was as personal as *darling*! She surmised Arthur would hate the undignified title. She thought Nancy was too refined to use it. Suddenly the sun was too bright and the air too thin for her lungs. Her head swam. Why were they outside the historical society? Nancy didn't work on Saturday, did she? Was she giving Arthur a special, private tour? Or had they accidentally met as Nancy left the building? Or were they meeting there and about to go somewhere? Oh, what did it matter!

But it did matter. *Arthur is my backdrop*, she thought, *and my backdrop is gone*. She'd better face it. The curtain was up, the view infinite, and frightening.

Tears streamed as she drove in a daze. She didn't want to think. She wanted to forget Nancy and Arthur and David and Diane. She wanted to be young and happy. She was twenty-two, but felt ninety. It wasn't fair that one blow after the other had hit her. She wanted to forget everything. She felt dizzy and disoriented. What street was she on? She wiped her eyes and squinted to see the street name on the lamp-post glass. It was too distant. Drawing closer she saw she was on the right street. She had automatically turned onto Kenzie and hadn't noticed.

Julia had time to compose herself before arriving at Bridget's house on the West Side. Mrs. Boland ushered Julia in and described Bridget's condition in a nervous burst of speech. "Herself is feverish and is breathing bad. Me husband has gone for Dr. Scott. Herself is propped up with pillows so she can be breathing easier. Mr. Edgar Gerard was just here, and herself not even knowing it."

Julia peeked into the dim room. Bridget's breathing was rapid and shallow, the little puffs hardly able to supply the oxygen of one healthy breath. Her eyes were deeply set between thin cheeks. An asafetida bag (folklore had it that the fetid resin prevented disease, Julia recalled) hung around her neck, giving off a pungent, rotten odor.

Julia tiptoed back to the parlor.

"Would yourself like coffee?" offered Mrs. Boland.

"No thank you." Julia felt too tired and depressed to comfort Mrs. Boland. "Is there anything I can pick up for you?"

"No, me husband has been getting what I need. Neighbors is bringing food, and Mrs. O'Leary brought us a jug of fresh milk just now."

"I'll stop by again this evening," Julia decided. "Try not to worry too much."

In her bedroom, Julia flopped on the bed. She didn't take off her shoes or loosen her clothes. Her head felt heavy, her thoughts confused. Finally, she slept.

A knock woke her. "Come in."

Mary peaked in. "It's Mrs. Gerard and she wants to talk to you. She ain't looking happy. I told her you was resting, but she said I should get you up."

"What time is it?"

"Five o'clock."

"Then I certainly slept long enough." Julia thought this was as good a time as any to ask Mary. "Tell me, what is the address of the Webers', where Billy works?"

All interest, Mary jumped into the room. "Are you gonna go see him?"

"No, I just wanted to know where he works."

"Oh, then you're gonna see that lady that—"

"Mary, why I need to know doesn't concern you! But for your information, it's another reason entirely."

Mary gave the address.

"Thank you," Julia said. She would figure out which side of Billy's Diane's was on when she got there. She would survey her house and the driveway where David and Diane had had their clandestine meeting. She might even catch a glimpse of Diane.

Of course she would not confront Diane. She simply wanted correct images for her mind.

Julia joined Alma, who sat by the center table in the parlor with her jacket on, visibly upset. Julia supposed she had suffered another disappointment with Edgar. She kissed Alma's cheek.

"I need water, dear—I must take a pill."

When Alma had the water, she swallowed two chloral tablets. The pill bottle was on the table, and Julia saw through the glass that the bottle was almost full of small, white tablets. How easy they were to take, she mused. How close at hand relief was. Oh, she would like one of those! One would help her cope! Her life seemed a complete failure. Chloral pills were inevitable. "Mother Gerard, could I—"

Alma stared at Julia.

Julia remembered that Edith had said facts were preferable to conjecture. Perhaps reality *was* easier to face than avoid. Mother Gerard avoided reality, and when it finally prevailed on her, she was helpless. And this effect was continual for her—or for anyone taking chloral tablets. You could join Mother Gerard now, Julia thought.

"I—never mind," Julia changed her mind.

Alma put the bottle in her bag.

"Shall I ask Mary to make tea?" Julia asked.

"No. I couldn't enjoy it. Nelda's gone, Julia," she finally related, "and it's my fault—all my fault!"

Julia recalled that whenever Dr. Sutton decreased Nelda's sedatives, Nelda threatened to leave. Nelda was convinced Melinda would help her start a new life.

"I'll never forgive myself," Alma groaned. "I—I visited Nelda this morning, took her some of the currant muffins she loves. Nelda was better than usual—on light sedation and handling it well. She seemed almost normal. Nelda wanted to go to lunch, and I thought that would be pleasant for her. When I asked Dr. Sutton's permission, he advised against it. He said Nelda's moods were too unpredictable. I said, 'Oh, let her go.' The outing will do her so much good. I'll watch her closely and if there's the slightest change, we'll return.' I coaxed and of course legally he can't insist she stay. We ate at the Arcade Dining Hall."

Alma breathed roughly. "Nelda seemed all right on the way to the Arcade, though she was quiet. We both ordered the special, chicken and noodles. She didn't eat, though. She didn't even pick up her napkin. Then she started to cry. I thought: *Oh, there's something on her mind, but I'll help her through it and then she'll eat.* I should have taken Nelda back then and there. But I asked, 'What is it, Nelda?' Nelda was looking at her lap and didn't speak. Then she seemed to draw herself up. There was something different about her. At that point I should have suspected she had a plan."

"Did she mention Bernard?"

"Who is Bernard?"

"You've met him at Dr. Sutton's, I'm sure—he's a patient. Nelda's in love with him. He gave Nelda the painting opposite her bed." Julia filled Alma in on the details. "I wish I had told Dr. Sutton about the painting."

"Why didn't you?"

"I promised Nelda I wouldn't."

"Julia, you should have told Dr. Sutton! You should have told me! I wouldn't have taken Nelda out if I had known she was lovesick."

"I know—I'm sorry. If only I had!"

"Well, let me tell you the rest. Nelda's eyes got bright and peculiar. Suddenly she jumped up and ran from the restaurant. You know how slow I am. By the time I found my bag and got outside Nelda was gone. I ran up and down the street like a madwoman. I notified Dr. Sutton and Martha, and of course the police have been searching. Anything could happen to Nelda—she's in no condition to be out. Martha is hysterical. She's convinced when Nelda's found, the police will make her undergo a trial and she'll be committed to the asylum in Jacksonville."

"Have you told David?"

"I stopped by, but he was out. Julia, will they find her?"

"Of course—of course!" Julia hugged Alma. "Just go home and stop worrying."

I am the guilty one, she thought. *Let me worry!*

Twenty

hough Julia felt sick about Nelda's disappearance, she managed to sit across from David at dinner. But she felt choked up, and to release the pressure on her throat she unbuttoned the top button on her dress. Dishes clattered in the kitchen.

"Have you noticed that Mary is noisier than Bridget?" David asked, his voice edgy.

"Yes, I have."

David had been upset at the news about Nelda. He ate quickly, planning to check on Martha and his mother immediately after dinner, then search for Nelda.

"David, it's my fault that Nelda's missing." Julia told David about Nelda's fixation on Bernard. "I'm the only one who knew about Nelda's feelings for Bernard. If Alma had known, she wouldn't have invited Nelda to lunch."

"Don't worry about it. I would have kept quiet also."

"Would you have?"

"Yes. I would have made the promise to Nelda and kept it. I believe in keeping promises."

Oh? Julia questioned in her mind. *To whom? Are you trying to tell me something, David?* She stared at him. He wore a brown frock coat and tan waistcoat. He looked his best in earth colors, the colors that were like the lumber he loved. How she loved him! How she loved his large frame. His wide-boned face. The solid footstep. The black hair. She knew every line of his body. If only she knew his mind. Edith said she should confront him about Diane. If only she could. But what if he

231

chose to continue seeing Diane? Yet how much longer could she handle her mental anguish.

She wished she had the nerve to confront Diane, ring her doorbell, stand eye-to-eye with the dominating woman and not flinch once. She wanted to tell her, "Leave my husband alone. Stop issuing him invitations! Do you hear me! Things can be done about women like you!" *What things?* Julia wondered. She could think of nothing. Women like Diane got whatever they wanted. They crushed people like Julia.

"Darling, try to eat," David coaxed. "It's going to be a long night between searching for Nelda and checking on Bridget."

"I can't. Do you think Nelda would have been better off at Lakeside?"

"I don't know. I don't guess about such things. We placed her at Dr. Sutton's and thought it best. I'm comfortable with that."

It was cool, and after dinner while David stoked the furnace, Julia changed to a wool suit. She was trying on a bonnet when Mary announced Mr. Boland.

He stood near the front door, clutching a blue cap. His eyes, large and blue like Bridget's, were frightened. There could be only one reason for him to be here, she realized with fear. "I was just about to come," Julia said weakly.

"It's hard set I am to be telling you."

Julia supported herself on the wall.

"It's terrible ailing Bridget is, and she's asking for yourself."

"Then she's alive?"

"Aye." Mr. Boland explained that Bridget's pneumonia had advanced to both lungs. She was often delirious and had an incessant cough that made rest difficult. She had severe chest pain. Mr. Boland wiped his eyes with a handkerchief. "I'm afeard to be worrying yourself, but Dr. Scott says Bridget might die if she isn't fighting hard."

"She'll fight! I know Bridget."

"Dr. Scott is saying the only hope is a favorable crisis. Ourselves is all praying for it. Mama is kneeling by the bed doing her rosary, and Michael is making up prayers like a Protestant."

David appeared, and Mr. Boland described Bridget's condition to him. "I'll do what I can about Nelda and meet you at Bridget's as soon as possible," David told Julia.

Julia went to the kitchen to inform Mary about Bridget. Mary turned white. "I ain't never treated her good, and now it's too late."

"It's not too late. Don't even think that."

"Should I come with you?"

"No. There'd be too much company. I'll give you a report when I get home. Pray, Mary."

Mary signed the cross on herself. "I'll get my rosary just as soon as I get the dishes done."

Julia followed Mr. Boland, who drove Michael's wagon. The courthouse bell tolled, announcing another in the long series of fires the drought initiated. There had been twenty fires since September 30, just a week's time.

The extent to which pneumonia must be accommodated struck Julia as she entered the parlor. The shades were drawn and the windows shut to keep drafts from Bridget. The lack of ventilation exacerbated the fetid odor of asafetida and illness. There were two cots in the middle of the floor and the sofa was piled with bedding. Through the kitchen door Julia could see various bottles of tonic on the table.

Mr. Boland indicated the bedding. "Me wife won't leave with Bridget being so sick." The house David had rented for the Bolands was just three doors away; nonetheless, Julia understood Mrs. Boland's desire to be constantly with Bridget.

Michael came from the bedroom. He walked slowly, as one does when he is stunned. "Dr. Scott just left and he says Bridget ain't improved. Her lungs is plugged and she coughs almost all the time. Dr. Scott wants her to rest and he says only two people can be in the room at a time. She don't rest too good, though. She gets delirious sometimes and rambles on. Mama Boland's in there prayin', and she won't leave for nothing."

"Did you want me to go in now?" Julia asked quietly.

"Yes."

"I'll be going after your parents now, Michael," Mr. Boland said.

Julia tiptoed into Bridget's room. Patrick, curled at Bridget's feet, looked up and wagged his tail as she entered. It was hardest on Patrick, Julia thought; for he couldn't understand Bridget's lack of response.

The wick on the oil lamp was turned low, and from the shadowy figure at the bedside came the click of rosary beads. " 'Tis a terrible thing having a dog in a sickroom bed," Mrs. Boland said, "but when Bridget wakes up and Patrick isn't in it, she starts crying. Herself is quiet now. She's been sleeping, thanks be to God."

Bridget was propped up with pillows to aid her breathing. Her skin was gray, her nostrils pinched. The veins in her eyelids were frighteningly prominent. She breathed in shallow puffs and perspired profusely. Julia remembered reading of the pneumonia sweats.

"Her sweats come and go. Oh, saints preserve me little girl," Mrs. Boland whispered. "Itself runs in me family to die of pneumonia. Me mama died of it and two of me ten sisters."

Julia didn't comment. It could do Mrs. Boland no good to discuss that. "How long has Bridget been asleep?"

"About a half hour."

"Does she eat?"

"Only bites. She had a bite of Mary's soup. She keeps asking for yourself."

"Does she say why?" Julia had a sudden fear that Bridget intended to will some possession to her. She prayed Bridget hadn't given up to that extent.

"No."

Several minutes later Bridget stirred. "Is you being thirsty?" Mrs. Boland asked Bridget.

"Aye," she whispered weakly.

Mrs. Boland held a glass of water to Bridget's lips. "How are you feeling, darling?"

"Ailing."

Bridget had a coughing spasm that threw her into the depths of the pillows. Perspiration broke out afresh on her face. *This is awful!* Julia thought, gripping her hands. Finally Bridget stopped coughing and perspiring. Her nightgown was soaked, and Mrs. Boland changed it for a fresh pink one.

"Thanks for coming," Bridget whispered to Julia.

"Don't talk," Julia urged, brushing back Bridget's wet hair.

" 'Tis sorry I am to bring you out, and yourself with nausea from—" Sick as she was, there was a trace of chagrin on her face. "I'm after forgetting not to say anything about that."

"Shh, that's all right. I'm feeling fine. Is there some special reason you wanted me?"

"I just wanted yourself here with me."

"Oh, Bridget! Of course, I'll be here. I'll be here as long as you need me!"

"Myself isn't afeard of dying," Bridget declared calmly.

"Don't talk about death," Julia said.

"Michael would be missing myself. Himself is wanting children. 'Tis hard it would be on Michael if myself is dying."

Yes, Julia thought. *Just keep thinking that. Will yourself to be well.* "Don't give up," Julia commanded. "I'm praying for you. Everyone is."

Abruptly, it was as if a charge of lightning passed through Bridget, and she threw back her head. Her hands tore at her nightgown. Her voice was rapid. "Oh, I'm hot. Mama, get me out of the sun. Ah—get

Mary. Mary! I do be thinking yourself should dust Mrs. Gerard's furniture with a dust brush. Use old silk on the center table. Be using a painter's brush on the ledges and crevices. Be doing the ornaments and fine books with feather brushes—Mary, do you be hearing me? Mary! Be cleaning the hearth with redding and milk. Mary—"

"Shh," Julia said, trying to quiet her, but to no avail.

"Mary, be scalding the sink with hot lye every evening after dinner. Be turning and airing the mattress every Wednesday and—"

" 'Tis nothing you can do but let it pass and keep her quiet," Mrs. Boland told Julia.

"Why don't you take a rest and I'll watch her awhile?"

"Aye. We haven't had dinner and we'll be eating. Dr. Scott will be coming by later."

When the delirium passed, Bridget slept lightly. The O'Keefes arrived and Julia and the family took turns sitting with Bridget. When eleven o'clock arrived and David hadn't appeared, Julia figured Nelda had been found and he was dealing with whatever that entailed.

Dr. Scott arrived shortly after eleven. He had been delivering a baby.

Julia waited outside Bridget's door with the Bolands and O'Keefes, while Michael was in the room with Dr. Scott. Mrs. Boland was white and jittery, and Julia wondered that she wasn't calmer, considering the many illnesses she had witnessed in her large family.

Dr. Scott palpated Bridget's chest and back. "How are you?" he asked.

"Ailing bad," she answered, coughing.

When he finished the examination, he told Michael. "Just keep her warm and quiet. We'll continue to wait for a favorable crisis. She's not any worse."

"Is she any better?"

"No."

"I gotta do something more for her. There's gotta be something I can do."

"There's nothing you can do, I'm afraid. Come for me if you need me."

Julia exchanged a bleak look with Mrs. Boland. She prayed they would not need him.

After Dr. Scott left, Julia stood on the stoop looking up the street for David. She breathed deeply to expel the sickroom air. The courthouse bell had rung earlier, and a neighbor had reported there was a fire at Lull and Homes Planing Mill, a wood-working factory. Julia looked at the large crimson swath to the north and figured the fire was extensive.

A small man in work pants stopped at Bridget's fence. He, his wife, and three staring children, nightshirts creeping from under their jackets, had obviously been to the fire. "I'm Barney Codd, from down the street. How is Mrs. O'Keefe? We're all worried. She's a nice little lady."

"About the same."

"We was just at the fire. It's burning out a few blocks."

"Then it's out of control?"

"No. We got a modern fire department and seventeen steamers. They'll get her out. If my wife or me can help ya, let us know."

"Thank you."

She saw David coming and ran to him, stumbling over her skirt in her haste. He had parked on the street, and as he stepped from the buggy, she buried her head in his coat. She heard pedestrians passing, but she didn't care. He was here! Her extreme tension dissipated when she felt his arms around her.

"I'm worried." She described Bridget's condition. "She's very bad. I'd like to stay the night."

"I'll stay with you."

"Oh, would you?"

"Nelda's still missing." David took Julia's hand as they climbed the stairs. "The police believe she will return to Martha's or Dr. Sutton's. I told them about Bernard, and they think it most likely Nelda will be found around Dr. Sutton's, because she'll want to be near him. They're making regular checks of that area."

"Why were you so long?"

"I couldn't break free from Martha. She's hysterical. Mother was with her and she's just about as bad."

"Would you like some coffee?"

He smiled. "Very much."

"Be quiet going through the parlor. Mr. Boland is resting. The O'Keefes are in the kitchen and Michael and Mrs. Boland are with Bridget. We're taking shifts in her room."

She squeezed his hand before entering.

Twenty-one

Sunday morning as the first rays of light appeared, a rooster crowed, breaking the stillness of the night. The fire at the planing mill had been extinguished. Julia and David were at Bridget's bedside, Julia particularly noting the fetid air. If Mrs. Boland weren't set against having the window open a crack, Julia would let in fresh air; surely it would be healthier for Bridget.

"Help me, Julia. Be taking me off this hot place I am." Bridget stared ahead, her eyes focused on the place in her mind. Bridget lay still now, too weak to thrash about. That was frightening, for it meant she was worse.

"Would you like some water?" Julia asked in a soothing voice.

Bridget sipped from the glass. "Oh, Julia, take me from this place."

Julia was severely alarmed. "I think Michael should get Dr. Scott."

"No. Look. Look closely," David urged.

At first Julia saw nothing different. Then she noticed that Bridget's eyes were more focused. Her face appeared a more natural color. There was perspiration on her forehead as if the fever had broken. "Go get the family," David advised.

When Julia and the family returned, Bridget's face had lost the look of the dying and appeared nearly normal. So she would be all right! Julia rejoiced at the thought. Patrick knew it also. His tail thumped against a foot post on the bed. Michael fell over Bridget, his wide chest hiding her, and held her in his arms. "Oh, Bridget—oh, darling! Thank heavens, my little one."

Bridget's arms moved up around his neck. The open sleeves of her nightgown dropped back and Julia saw how frail her arms were. But they were in the air. Moving! Alive!

"Would yourself be liking some cake and milk?" Mrs. Boland was apparently eager to see Bridget regain her strength.

"No, Mama," came a voice softly from beneath Michael.

"How do you feel?" Michael asked tenderly.

"Fine itself." She looked distressed. "Was yourself famished with worry?"

"Yes, little darling." He smoothed back her hair. The Bolands were staring at their daughter, seemingly unaware of their tears. Julia wiped hers.

"Then you're feeling all right?" Julia supposed Michael needed to hear her say it again.

"Aye," came the soft reply. "Like loving yourself. Oh, Michael! I love you!"

They left Bridget and Michael alone.

When Julia and David arrived home, Mary flung open the kitchen door. In the morning light, Mary's plain face was sallow, her eyes shadowed. The odor of coffee indicated what had been keeping her awake. "She's dead!" Mary blurted. "I got a sixth sense. Holy Mother! She's dead! I ain't never thought she'd make it."

Julia caught her arms. "She's *not* dead. She's much better."

"What? Oh, I knowed deep down Bridget would be all right."

"Have you slept at all?" Julia asked.

"I prayed my rosary, and I worried, I'll tell you. Can I see her today?"

"I think so."

"I ain't going to mass until late so I can sleep. I'll see her after that."

Julia and David went to bed exhausted. Later when Julia woke, she reached sleepily over to touch David and found, instead, an empty spot. There was a note on the night table: "Darling, I hope you sleep late. I'm going to Martha's. I'll also be looking for Nelda. David."

She regretted that he had slept so briefly. She would like to sleep the entire day, but with Nelda missing, Alma would need her. She dressed hurriedly, had a glass of juice and a biscuit, and was rinsing her dishes when Edith entered the kitchen. Julia supposed Edith had used her key because she was too impatient to wait to be admitted.

"I became alarmed when I didn't see you at church," Edith announced. "Why didn't you notify me you wouldn't be there and spare me the worry?"

Julia told Edith about Bridget.

"Well—that's good news! I'll make something light for Bridget to eat," Edith volunteered. "She mustn't eat heavy food at this point. That Irish bread those people eat is lethal."

Julia smiled.

"Is David home?"

"No."

"Good. I must talk privately with you. Can you drive me home afterward? Morton and Freddie are outside, and if you can, I'll send them on."

"I'll drive you. I'm going out anyhow."

After dismissing Morton, Edith joined Julia. Mary had laid a yellow cloth on the kitchen table, making the area cheerful. Julia poured Edith coffee. "I'm not staying long—I've a roast at home, and Morton and Freddie are hungry."

Edith peered steadily at Julia. "Well, did you confront David?"

"No. I'm tired. I don't even want to think about our relationship."

Edith calmly drank her coffee. "I won't leave here until I have your promise to speak to David. I've examined my reasoning and I know it's imperative you do so."

"I have other problems." Julia told her that Nelda was missing. "I'm not in any frame of mind to—"

Edith interrupted. "You would have far less problems if you would rid yourself of your main problem. You need to talk to David."

"All right—all right! I will." Giving one's word was not *always* binding, Julia thought. If only Edith understood that Julia could not risk losing David. It had been lunacy to confide in Edith.

Edith finished her coffee and put on her gloves. "Let's go." But Edith did not move to leave. "Do you think David will join the church?"

"Yes. He's attracted to Christianity because of his father."

"This indicates he's not a philanderer. Philanderers aren't usually religious."

When Julia returned from taking Edith home and checking on Alma, who was heavily sedated with chloral pills and asleep, David was heating coffee. He poured her a cup and they sat at the kitchen table together.

"I have encouraging news from the police," he declared. "The janitor at the St. James Protestant Episcopal Church reported seeing a distraught woman on the property early this morning. He sleeps on the premises and noticed her when he unlatched his shutters. The woman ran off, but she left a reticule that Martha identified as Nelda's. Nelda probably slept in the churchyard."

"I hope so. It's at least safe there."

"The janitor has been given a photograph of Nelda and he will be on the lookout for her. The police will make periodic checks there."

David added cream to his coffee and drank it quickly, obviously needing the stimulant. His eyes were bloodshot and he wearily leaned his elbows on the table.

"Darling, please go back to bed," Julia pleaded.

"I can't. I've got to continue looking for Nelda, and Martha wants to go with me."

"I'll wait at your mother's. I was just there and she was asleep—but surely she will be waking soon."

"Good."

During the afternoon, Edgar studied Martin Luther's *Commentary on the Epistle to the Romans* in his bed; theology had become an absorbing interest for him. He had improved physically, so he could now cross the parlor aided by his canes and his nurse. Alma woke and reclined on the front parlor sofa, where she blamed herself for Nelda's disappearance. Too distraught to dress, she wore a wool dressing gown with a fringe of little balls and satin slippers with rosettes. There was a dish of cashews by Alma's side, into which she regularly dipped her fingers. A wet cloth covered her forehead. "I'll not be sane until Nelda's found," Alma declared. "I should have known she'd run from the restaurant. I should have stopped Nelda."

"It's just a matter of time until Nelda turns up," Julia encouraged.

"Chicago is full of disreputable men. I have read—"

"Why can't you think the best? That's what I do."

"Do you, Julia? How do you?"

Julia couldn't answer, for she realized she thought both the best and the worst about matters and was, in her way, as unrealistic as Alma. Would she someday end up on a sofa, her feet propped on a pillow, rosettes hanging over her toes, her mind as uneasy as Alma's? Julia leaned back in her chair and stared at Alma. She felt like saying, "Move over, Alma, and I'll join you."

"Well, Julia?"

"I'm not the one to ask."

"Nelda could be anywhere now. I hate to think where she could be. I've heard of abductions tha—"

"Please stop!"

The afternoon passed and Alma found another worry. "Where are David and Martha? They should be back by now."

"I don't know."

"They might have had an accident."

How did Mother Gerard's system take it? Julia puzzled, her own stomach churning.

At dinnertime, David and Martha returned. Julia moved the pan of leftover chicken and gravy she was heating to the back of the stove and joined them. David explained, "The janitor at the Episcopal church saw Nelda in the yard again, but she disappeared before he could detain her. The police check periodically at the church. They expect she'll return tonight."

"Oh, no!" Alma cried. "Then where is she now?" she moaned. Though troubled, she went on to eat dinner without difficulty. Alma had, however, ruined Julia's appetite.

Julia drove her buggy through whirls of leaves and debris about 8:30 that evening, heading for Bridget's. David was continuing to search for Nelda. A gust lifted the brim of Julia's bonnet. She guessed the wind at fifty miles an hour. Looking up, Julia searched the sky for signs of the fierce weather, but the sky was clear, starry. The moon had not yet risen.

Engrossed in her thoughts, Julia passed Taylor Street, where Bridget lived, an easy mistake. All the streets looked alike to her—all were narrow as alleys, all contained wood shanties. On some of the lots two shanties were coupled back-to-back, like railroad cars. With the outbuildings poking between the shanties, the area seemed an artificial forest to Julia.

Because she couldn't turn in the narrow road, she drove on to De Koven Street, planning to drive around the block. She heard a fiddle playing a polka in a shanty, the front of two shanties on the lot. A man with a peg leg stood across from the merrymaking, tapping his peg to the music. Julia thought he looked lonely; perhaps he wished to be inside. It would appeal to her to be, laughing and dancing. Dust from the street blew into the man's face and he coughed. He looked curiously at her, probably wondering why a woman of her class was in this neighborhood. "Hello," he called.

"Hello."

"Some wind."

"Yes," she said and passed him.

In Bridget's bedroom the first thing Julia noticed was that Patrick had been relegated to the floor. He jumped up and licked Julia's hand. Bridget was wearing a white bed jacket with a velvet bow, and she looked frail but pretty in it. Her dark hair was brushed out to her shoulders. Julia hugged her, saying, "You look so much better."

"I'm feeling good enough to be up a bit, but Mama won't be letting me."

"Saints forbid! It's sick yourself would be then—and myself having only ten days to be nursing you back to health again."

"Can't you and Papa be staying a wee bit longer?"

"No. Sure the little ones have worn Grandma and Grandpa out."

"Aye."

"I passed your street and went down De Koven," Julia said. "Do you know the man from there with a peg leg?"

"Aye, he's being Pegleg," Bridget related. "Himself is a friend of Kate O'Leary, who's been bringing milk. I don't know how he lost his leg."

"Where are Michael and your father?"

"Themselves is helping a neighbor make his pigsty double strong. The pigs broke out and went in the road." Bridget glanced at her bed jacket. "Your sister was giving me this today—and some good-tasting cheese dish for supper. She's a lovely one, she is. But myself was being afeard of her once."

"So was I."

"Yourself is sure Mary is keeping up the house good?"

"She tries very hard. Nobody could be as good as you, though."

Mrs. Boland fixed coffee and buttered Irish bread, just the kind of fare Edith wished Bridget to avoid. While they ate, the wind hummed at a constant pitch. Then suddenly it changed intensity and tore at the house frame, rattling the walls and windows. Julia's cup shook and drops of liquid soaked into her black dress.

"Itself will be blowing the roof off," Mrs. Boland stated in alarm. "It's being windier than in Dunquin, and itself near the sea."

But it was more than wind that Julia heard; she heard voices and banging. She raised the shade and looked out. Flames leaped from a structure near where she had seen Pegleg. A couple in nightcaps ran outside and joined others milling around. There was a spray of sparks over Bridget's street, like red rain. "I had better see if we're in danger," Julia said.

She was putting on her jacket when Michael and Mr. Boland arrived, their boots muddy from work in the pigsty. Mrs. Boland looked askance at the boots.

"I was just going to check the fire," Julia said, relieved to see them.

"It's in Patrick O'Leary's barn." Michael looked worried. "Pegleg found it—he was across the street from O'Leary's when he seen flames. The fire's spread to the house next door. Papa and me helped neighbors pour water on the O'Leary barn, but it's a goner. The *American* hose cart just came and the steamers are on the way."

" 'Tis a terrible thing," Bridget remarked.

"I ain't happy to move you out, Bridget, but the fire's blowing this way. We'll bundle you up good in the buffalo robe I got out West. We ain't got time to take much—that wind is hard and there's lots of sparks. Remember how quick the fire at the planing mill spread last night."

Mrs. Boland threw aside Bridget's covers and started pulling stockings on her. "What do you want to take?" Michael asked Bridget. "We'll get a few things now and come back for the rest if we can."

Bridget jumped from bed, stumbling over a sock half on. "No fire is burning me house! Let's throw water on itself."

Michael grasped her shoulders and spoke firmly. "Bridget, there isn't time. What do you want to take?"

Bridget gave a sigh of acceptance. "Me Bible. Itself is on the bureau—and me pretty pillows and embroidery in the parlor."

Michael set about collecting the items as Julia packed two satchels with clothes. Mr. Boland attached a rope to Patrick's collar, and the dog stood uncommonly still for it, obviously sensing danger. Julia smelled smoke and a rancid odor that might be burning rubber. Mrs. Boland put sturdy boots on Bridget, then tied a kerchief around her head and a bonnet over that. She handed Bridget a long coat to put over her night clothes. "Mama, myself will smother."

"Yourself will be warm and no arguing, surely."

Michael wrapped Bridget in the buffalo robe and lifted her up in his arms. As Julia followed Michael through the parlor, she watched how Bridget stared at the objects she might be seeing for the last time. Bridget cried, her hand quickly wiping her tears. Michael comforted, "Darling, we're in God's hands."

"Myself isn't minding losing me things too much."

"It ain't things that are important, but the meanings in them. We got our minds to remember them."

"Aye." She tightened her arms around his neck.

Outside, they were greeted by a roar of wind. The air was smoky and Bridget coughed and retreated into the folds of the buffalo robe. The fire on De Koven Street had spread, and Julia believed three dwellings now burned. As the fire's agent, the wind delivered brands and sparks to Taylor Street, Patrick nipped at the glittering air, then yelped as it stung him. He pressed against Michael for protection. A few of the houses on Taylor smoldered. The steamer *Illinois*, a shiny machine with a boiler shaped like a milk can, was hosing them down—and exuberantly tossing up clouds of smoke and cinders. A few spectators chopped fences and sidewalks to supplement the steamer's fuel. Julia studied Bridget's house and thought it appeared untouched by fire. Residents were carrying their possessions to the street and sidewalks, but Julia thought their things would be safer inside, away from the burning debris landing on them. Wagons were being loaded and livestock tied to the back. All the houses were lighted; no one slept. A rooster strutted past as if he owned the street.

Bridget leaned close to Julia's ear and whispered, "Will smoke be harming the little one?"

"I think babies in the womb are protected from external influences."

"Yourself must be careful."

"I will be."

A woman raced wild-eyed from her house next door and grabbed the arm of a man on the sidewalk. "Help me get out my dining table, sir—my husband's at work!"

"No—let go! I'm busy."

She tugged desperately at his sleeve. "Sir, it's my best piece of furniture!"

He shook her off roughly, snapping, "Go! I've got to help chop firewood!"

Julia knew the entire neighborhood was doomed. She saw on Bridget's pale face that she knew it too. "Please stay at my house," Julia offered. "I've plenty of room."

"All right, and thank you," Michael accepted the invitation. "Tomorrow we'll go to my parents'." Mr. Boland went after Michael's wagon, and Mrs. Boland hurried to her house to pack clothes.

Bridget continued to cough. "The smoke is bothering Bridget terribly," Julia asserted. "If you'd like I can start on ahead in my buggy with her."

"I'd appreciate that, Mrs. Gerard," Michael said.

Julia looked to where her rig had been hitched. It was gone, in its place was a smoking sofa. "Michael, where is it?"

Michael set Bridget on the stoop and ran to the street to look for it. People, animals, and vehicles jammed the roadway. Julia hoped the crowd had blocked the progress of her vehicle. Barney, the workman who had spoken to Julia about the fire at the planing mill, appeared. His family was with him, their eyes stark with fear. One boy carried a canary cage with the cover tightly drawn to protect the bird, and a girl clutched a doll.

"Are you feeling all right?" he asked Bridget.

"Aye."

"Do you know how the fire started?" Julia queried.

"I ain't sure, but some say Kate O'Leary's cow kicked over a lantern in her barn. Others say that ain't possible because Kate was in bed and didn't have no lantern lit out there. Kate is running around in a fright, they say. She don't have insurance and has lost four of her cows. She says her milk route's ruined."

Mr. Boland parked Michael's wagon out front and went on foot after his wife. Michael returned and said, "I'm sorry, Mrs. Gerard, but your buggy ain't anywhere. I think it got stoled by somebody needing a ride."

Julia shook her head angrily. "How can people do that? How can they just take what they wish!" She had loved the plum phaeton and the horse with the high-stepping gait.

"I don't know." Michael looked up and his jaw dropped open. Julia followed his gaze to the curl of smoke on the roof. The house was burning! Michael lifted Bridget and they hurried to the safety of the sidewalk.

"Oh, look at itself!" Bridget cried.

Horrified, they watched the flames prick the roof and spread like syrup over the flammable material. In a short time, the flames slipped over the side and entered the house through the dry siding. Julia was amazed at the speed of the fire.

Bridget and Michael stared at the fire. Julia wondered what was going through their minds. Then they looked at each other and their gazes held. He bent his head and kissed her. Her arms were around his neck and she was crying.

"Oh, sure yourself is all I'm needing," Bridget assured him.

"Little one," he murmured.

"There's nothing in all of Ireland worth yourself."

"Darling," he said, "I've got you and I got my health. I can earn the money for another house." He carried her and their few possessions to the wagon, and they picked up the Bolands.

As they slowly progressed through the crowded street, no one looked back.

The T-shaped Chicago River dissected Chicago into three sections—the West Side, South Side, and North Side. It wasn't until they crossed the Madison Street Bridge to the South Side that Julia looked behind her. Sparks, brands, and fireballs sailed through the West Side. Some of these objects had tremendous flight and speed, traveling 300 to 500 feet in the air. Julia supposed the brands exploded into flames on landing. Julia readjusted her estimate: it wasn't only Bridget's neighborhood that would burn, but the entire West Side.

Julia watched the road for David's phaeton. It was likely that David knew of the fire and was driving to Bridget's house to check on her. They never went in the same direction, she thought despondently, never!

Twenty-two

What Julia noticed first about the North Side as she crossed the river was the clear air. She hoped David was home. The experience on Taylor Street had exhausted her, and she wanted him to help her settle in her guests. But it wasn't just that. She wanted him. She wanted him to say, "It's all right, Julia. Everyone's safe and it's all right. Come, darling, let's sleep." And he would hold her in his arms all night.

David's phaeton wasn't in the drive. Julia jumped from Michael's wagon and tugged at the stable door. It dug into the ground, causing her to jerk it open. The sweet smell of hay in the loft and sawdust greeted her. She stared in disappointment at the empty stalls and parking area. Undoubtedly, David had learned the location of the fire and was at Bridget's, looking for her. She prayed he hadn't been injured unloading someone's furniture, or that he hadn't volunteered to help the fire department. No, he wouldn't linger on Taylor Street. He would be concerned about her and return home. Oh, if only she could be with him right now, wherever he was!

Michael carried Bridget to the kitchen chair. She was limp, her eyes only half open.

Mary appeared in a nightcap and wrapper, rubbing her eyes in amazement. Julia explained that Bridget's house had burned and a fire raged on the West Side. "That's terrible!" Mary exclaimed. "Are you all right, Bridget?"

"Aye."

"You look like a dead woman."

246

"Sure, I'm fine," she assured, leaning her arm on the table.

"Are you sure, daughter?" asked Mrs. Boland.

" 'Tis only time I'm needing to find me strength."

"Did you lose everything?" Mary asked. "I got friends that lost everything in a fire once. Their cookstove even melted."

"We got out a little," Michael said. "I ain't got no insurance on the house. It looks like we've got to rent awhile until we save up for another house."

"Mary, have you seen Mr. Gerard?" Julia asked.

"No, I ain't seen him. But he could of been by. I was asleep."

Michael and Mr. Boland carried in a few satchels of clothes, while Mary and Julia settled Bridget in the guest bedroom and brought cots to the study for the Bolands. Mary was eager to help, which Julia appreciated.

When her guests had retired, Julia lit the back and front lamps for David. From her back yard she could clearly see the crimson area in the southwest. The spot was definitely brighter, wider, and higher, as if a hand had turned a colored lantern up full wick.

The couple who had moved into Cullens' joined Julia. They were in their late thirties and well dressed. For the first time, Julia noticed her dress was muddy and ripped at the hem. After they exchanged names, Julia explained, "I've wanted to call, but I've had a lot of problems. One of my servant girls has been near death. Did you get moved in all right?"

Mrs. Owens answered, "Yes, though I wouldn't wish to try it again with our eight children."

Mr. Owens looked at the western sky. "Have you heard a recent report on the fire?"

"I just came from there," Julia answered, giving them the details.

"It'll be hard to put out," he ventured. "I'd say the wind's at sixty miles an hour."

"The wind is the big problem," Julia agreed, then turned to Mrs. Owens. "Do you like Chicago so far?"

"Very much. The shopping is good, every bit as good as in Philadelphia."

"If there is anything I can do, let me know," Julia offered.

Julia perked coffee and was pouring a cup when David arrived. He stared at her from the doorway, from her head to her feet. Not moving, he just stared, his faced wreathed in relief. His overcoat was pitted with burn holes, his mustache singed on one side. So he had been terrified—searching frantically for her! Julia flung herself across the space between them and into his arms. His coat smelled smoky and the material felt gritty. "Then you saw Bridget's house?" she asked.

"Yes. Julia, it was scary as the devil. When I arrived, there was nothing left of Bridget's or any of the houses on her side of the street. I wasn't sure which lot was hers. There wasn't a tree or a fence—nothing. Everything was burning at ground level. I could barely make it up the street for the smoke. I hollered for you. Yelled! Nothing, no one was on the street. It was like hell! Finally, in the next block, I met a man. He said he thought everyone was safely out of Bridget's neighborhood. But I didn't know if I could believe that. Or if I should." David's bleak eyes didn't leave her face. "I've been out of my mind until I saw Michael's wagon and then you." He held her head down on his chest, pressed it—crushed it to him.

"Are you all right, darling?" she cried, gently touching his face.

"Yes. Are Bridget, Michael, and the Bolands all here?" he asked.

"Yes."

"How is Bridget?"

"Weak, but all right, I think. She's accepted everything. Everything! She only cares that she and Michael are uninjured and can start over again."

"Where's your buggy?"

"It was stolen in front of Bridget's. I'm sick about it—I'm worried that the horse will be mistreated."

"I'm sorry, darling. I'll buy you another rig as soon as I have the cash."

She moved her fingers over his face. "Are you really all right? Are you burned anywhere?"

"No." He smiled. "I'm fine."

"How far has the fire spread?"

"It was at Ewing Street when I left. Several blocks are blazing. I saw my friend, Chief Fire Marshall Williams, on Ewing. He looked exhausted. His men are tired from last night and seemed to be working in a daze."

"Has Nelda been found?"

"No. But the police are confident she'll turn up at the Episcopal church." He looked at the coffeepot. "I could use a cup of that."

They drank their coffee in the kitchen. She was past exhaustion and felt a strange nervous energy. David said, "Sparks and brands are crossing the river to the South Side. Unless the wind dies or it rains, the South Side will burn too."

"Then your parents and Aunt Martha should be brought here."

He nodded. "I've been planning to go after them."

"I'm coming with you. Mary's here, if anyone should need anything. I'll go crazy if I'm separated from you again tonight."

They crossed to the South Side on the State Street bridge. The river was jammed with tugs pulling brigs and steamers to safety on the lake. The street was jammed with traffic. The farther south they traveled, the more sparks and brands they encountered, the brighter became the southwest sky. They stopped at a corner for traffic and David asked a police officer, "Are any buildings burning on the South Side?"

The officer cupped his hands to be heard over the wind. "The Parmelee Stage and Omnibus Company building is on fire. (Julia had read that the $80,000 structure had been scheduled to open in three days.) I believe the South Side Gas Works is burning too."

They made slow progress to the Gerards' and arrived at a dark house. David opened the door with his key and yelled hello as they walked to the front stairs. Alma and Mrs. Harper appeared at the top landing, Alma's bare feet showing beneath her nightgown. Alma's face turned white as she realized the import of having visitors at midnight, and the timid face of Mrs. Harper mirrored Alma's emotions.

They hurried downstairs. "Is something wrong?" Alma cried breathlessly. "Is it Nelda? Is she dead—oh, no!"

"No—no." David informed her of the real problem. "There's a fire outside, a rather bad one. It started on De Koven Street in a barn and it jumped the river and is heading this way."

Alma's eyes were terrified. "What?"

"I'm surprised you haven't heard the commotion."

"I don't pay attention. This is a noisy area and we have all kinds of things going on."

"Just pack what's most important. The fire is spreading fast, and I'd like to be away in half an hour. I'll go to Martha's and bring her here. We'll use her buggy, yours, and ours—and we should be able to manage quite a few boxes."

Julia woke Helga, Mrs. Reatherford and Mrs. Harper. The nurses dressed Edgar and set him in his wheelchair, then rolled him into the front parlor to wait for the others.

When Alma had dressed and tottered into the parlor, perspiring under a load of clothes, Julia noticed Edgar found it as impossible as she not to stare. Judging from the bulk and various materials showing at her neck, Alma had on at least six dresses. Her head was adorned with two bonnets, and her neck and wrists spangled with jewelry. She carried a fur coat with bulging pockets. But it was all too much for Alma, ingenious as her packing had been, and she swayed into a chair, panting with heat and nerves.

"Look at me, Edgar! Aren't I a fool?"

"No, not at all."

"I couldn't think of any other way."

"It's fine, very smart of you."

"Julia, get the silver—and whatever else you think of. I can't think any further. We just aren't ready for this. Oh, it's terrible! I'm just too old for it. Do you really think we'll burn?"

"I hope not," Julia answered, "but we need to be prepared."

Alma looked at Edgar. "Can you think of anything Julia should get?"

"Our marriage license and the strongbox. The strongbox is in the closet in my study and the marriage license is in a leather case beside it—just bring the case."

Alma was crying. "I wouldn't have thought of the license."

"There, there, dear."

"Get my pills, Julia—I need one. This house, Edgar—it contains our lives."

"No, Alma, our lives belong to God."

Alma gazed at him, and beyond the tears that streamed and the earrings that bobbed, a look of understanding came into her eyes.

David and Martha returned, and Martha remained outside to guard her possessions while David carried out his parents' boxes. Helga tied a rope around her trunk handles. She hugged Alma and cried out something in a heavy German accent that Julia couldn't understand. Julia held the door open for Helga and watched her bump down the stairs and into the crowd, the trunk tagging behind like a dog.

"Poor Helga!" Alma cried. "Will she be all right?"

"She has strong legs and will have no trouble getting to her friend's home," Edgar reassured his wife.

Because Martha disliked driving, Julia took the reins. Martha clutched a jewelry box and whimpered, her frightened eyes blinking out tears. "Of all nights for Nelda to be lost. I can't stand to think of it. What do you do when you can't stand your thoughts?"

Julia touched her hand. "We'll look for her again when we get to my house."

Martha shook her head. "If only Wilbur were here—Wilbur would know what to do."

"Try not to worry too much."

"Look!" Martha cried.

Julia's eyes followed Martha's hand toward a flat brand directly overhead. It landed on the Gerards' roof and flamed. The fire spread over the wood shingles so quickly the dry material didn't have a chance.

The Gerards' buggy was in front of Julia, and she saw Alma gazing up, her hand over her mouth. Edgar kissed her cheek, then followed

David into the road. This was the first time he had driven since his apoplexy.

They made slow headway through the downtown area. Property inside establishments was being emptied outside, and the animate and the inanimate fought for space. Wagons loaded with household goods and stock from stores pressed through the streets. Everything was being trampled on: valuable-looking oil paintings, bolts of silk, cheap toys. Screams and cries punctuated the air. Some awnings and signs burned, but no buildings were yet on fire. A dark-haired woman knelt on the sidewalk, praying over a large crucifix. A little girl with streaming blond hair screamed for her mother. A procession of men carried an under-taker's caskets from the area. A thief swaggered from a jewelry store, his pockets bulging, gold chains dangling from his hand. No one de-tained him. People dragged trunks with ropes, but Julia didn't see Helga among them. Several men ran from a saloon with casks of liquor, prob-ably stolen. One of the men ran after Julia's buggy and tossed a slug of cold liquor in her face. She shut her mouth, but not before some of the liquid entered. She spit it out and wiped her face on her jacket sleeve. With a cocky smile the man waved his cap and yelled, "Happy fire!"

"You pig!" Julia screamed. "You awful fool!"

"Ha, pretty lady."

Julia snapped her head forward. If she were a man she'd wring his neck off. Why hadn't she at least slapped his face?

"Oh, I just can't believe it!" Martha exclaimed. "Where is Nelda? Is some drunk throwing liquor at her?"

"No."

"You don't know."

"You're right," Julia admitted. "Where is she? Chicago is an awful place to be. It's going to go—all of it—up like a torch. The courthouse—everything."

"Julia, don't say that."

"I'm sorry. I was reacting to everything that's happened tonight."

They arrived at Julia's at 1:30 a.m., and before unpacking the bug-gies, David climbed to the roof to see if the fire had reached the North Side. It was quiet upstairs and Julia assumed the O'Keefes and Bolands were asleep. Julia made a fresh pot of coffee, and she served her guests coffee, cheese, and crackers at the kitchen table. The coffee lifted her energy level and she was able to plan accommodations with a clear mind. She would put Alma and Edgar in her bedroom, Aunt Martha on the parlor sofa. She and David would sleep in the sitting room, one on the sofa, the other on the floor. She looked at Alma and Martha, drinking from their cups in nervous sips, and hoped they would hold up. Then Julia's head nodded, and she refilled her coffee cup.

David entered. "I can tell by your face you've got bad news," Alma pronounced dourly.

He stood by the table and Julia handed him a cup of coffee. "There's a blaze near the lake—near Lill's Brewery, I think. It's in an isolated spot and I doubt it'll spread for a while. Julia, you'll need to pack though—it's just a matter of time for us."

Alma turned to Edgar. "Certainly the fire won't come this far."

"It has jumped the river twice; it can come here."

"Where will we go?" Alma looked panic-stricken.

"We can decide later," David responded. "I would like to get out of town, a place where the fire won't spread."

"David! We can't go until we find Nelda!" Martha cried.

"I'll check with the police and see if she's been found."

Julia longed to go with him. But who would pack? She glanced at Alma's trembling hands. Certainly Alma couldn't be counted on for that. "All right, but don't be long," Julia conceded.

"I won't. Wake the others. Ask Michael to put carpets on the roof and haul up buckets of water to wet them down."

Julia walked David to his buggy. "Will it be too much for you to pack and manage everything?" David asked, concerned.

"Yes, but hurry back."

She heard the faint sound of the courthouse bell. The courthouse, situated near Edgar's, was the heart of Chicago; with fear she realized she might be hearing its last peals. A mixture of leaves and sparks eddied in the strong wind. Some neighbors were loading vehicles. "Hurry!" she shouted.

Julia knocked on the guest room door and Michael opened it. As she explained why they must prepare to leave, she looked sympathetically at Bridget's sleepy face on the pillow. "Bridget, don't get up yet," Julia advised. "We'll come for you at the last minute. Can I bring you some tea?"

"If yourself is having time."

Julia woke the Bolands, and Michael and Mr. Boland went to protect the roof. Julia returned to Bridget with a cup of tea and found her standing in her petticoat. "Myself will come down on the sofa. I couldn't stand lying up here and wondering what was happening."

"But are you strong enough to dress? We could wrap you up again."

Bridget's shoulders raised in determination. "Sure I'm feeling fitter every minute."

"Then let me help you." Julia found a warm brown dress in Bridget's satchel.

"Is yourself all right?" Bridget asked. "Yourself is looking terrible worried."

"Am I?" Julia's hand touched her face. Yes, it felt very dry and gritty. She hadn't looked at herself or combed her hair. She didn't care about her appearance. She just wanted to get through this night without collapsing. What bothered her most was that she had lost control of events. However, she reasoned, she should be accustomed to that. But one could be without footing only so long. "I wish I had your faith—nothing shakes you."

"Yourself can have faith."

Julia knew the way. She should ask Christ to come into her life. She was almost tempted. Oh, what a relief that would be. Oh, dear God, how she needed to surrender to Christ. But could she ever give her all—entrust her love for David to God, entrust Melinda's death? "This isn't the time."

Bridget's eyes pleaded with her to take the time.

"Let me help you with your dress," Julia urged, slipping it over Bridget's head and buttoning the back. "Are you going to Michael's parents'?"

"Aye. Michael is thinking it's out of the line of the fire."

Mrs. Boland entered to get Bridget's satchels.

Julia walked downstairs and entered the vestibule as Edith was coming in the front door. There wasn't a fold of cloth out of line on Edith, despite the wind. There was no sign of the calamity on Edith's composed face. Julia took comfort in Edith's orderly demeanor; if Edith could be orderly, then the world would follow suit.

Edith handed Julia a square tin box. "I shouldn't be out alone; it's sparking and my horse is shying. This is Melinda's poetry. I went to Father's for it. Of course, we will all burn out, and we might as well gather up what's important." Both Edith and Julia's Father lived a few blocks north.

"I never thought of it. Thank heavens you did!"

"You look quite awful, Julia. I hope you're not falling apart. Please guard Melinda's poetry. I can't watch it and Freddie and Morton as well. I have quite enough to do."

"Of course I will."

"What's all that noise?"

"I have a houseful—David's parents, Aunt Martha, Bridget and Michael, Bridget's parents, Mary. I'm responsible for them all. Nelda's missing and David's out checking on her."

"Then I'll take the poetry."

Because Julia had been closest to Melinda, she felt she should have it. "No, I'd rather. David will be back to help soon."

"Where are you going to stay?" Edith asked.

"I'm not sure."

Edith spoke with exasperation. "I need to know exactly where to find you."

"I'll find you—where will you be?"

"At Uncle Albert's. I suggested it to Morton. Evanston is some distance from the fire and we'll be safe. Father is going with us."

Edith looked at Julia. Her eyes were hard and at first Julia thought she was angry. Then she saw her tears and realized Edith was memorizing her face. Edith reached for Julia. "Don't leave me wondering about you. Contact me as soon as you can."

"I will," Julia said, crying.

"Hush, enough of this. Don't dodder—see to your guests. Be strong and you'll be all right."

— Twenty-three —

ichael and Mr. Boland had laid the sitting room and parlor carpets on the roof. Now Julia heard a dull sound as water from the buckets struck over the bedroom ceiling. Mary had helped her lug a Saratoga trunk from the cellar, and though the trunk was large, Julia thought the backseat of David's buggy would hold it. She had packed the silver, and she now added jewelry and clothes. She packed the heirloom shawl and her mother's daguerreotype. Before closing the lid, she added David's birthday gifts.

As she looked in the mirror, her tired, dirty face stared out from under matted hair. She filled the washstand bowl, worked soap over her face to the hairline, and scrubbed with a facecloth until her skin tingled. She leaned over the bowl and splashed on cold water. Changing into a clean black dress, she then brushed her hair and pinned it into a bun to secure it from the wind. After she tied on a warm bonnet, she laid a cloak and gloves on the bed. Yes, a person did feel better when one's clothes and appearance were in order.

Mary knocked and entered, carrying two valises and two satchels. She batted her lashes nervously at Julia and bowed her head. "I hope you don't mind me going, but I ain't able to take no chance on this fire. Margaret says it has got itself on State Street, and it'll be here any minute. The sky is all yellow and red in the south, and I'll bet some of them flames is two hundred feet high. I got a friend out by the prairie, and Margaret and me is goin' there." Mary looked up. "You ain't mad?"

"No, we'll all be leaving soon. Good luck."

"The house is a goner. There's all kinds of flying things and sparks out there. Mrs. Gerard and Mrs. Boland is out there swatting them off the horses right now."

"My house might not burn!" Julia said sharply. "The wet carpets might save it! The wind might change direction and blow the fire out to the lake. It might rain. Mr. Gerard isn't back. He won't leave me alone while our house burns. You hear me? He—" Julia realized her urgent need for David to return was making her hysterical.

"I shouldn't of said nothing. I speak too much. I'll get hold of you through Bridget tomorrow."

"Fine."

"I'm real sorry for what I said."

"I am too. We're all tense."

When the carpets on the roof were drenched, Michael and Mr. Boland watched the horses, and Alma and Mrs. Boland came in. Julia joined them in the sitting room. The room was not smoky, but the smell of smoke was in the air. Bridget coughed and struggled for breath. Julia thought it imperative that Bridget be in clean air and in bed.

"What time is it?" Aunt Martha asked nervously.

"It's twenty to three," Julia informed her, reading the mantel clock. Aunt Martha sat facing it, but she was too distraught to observe it. Alma was flushed like an apple from her overload of clothes. Both women continually wrung their hands.

"Why's David taking so long?" Aunt Martha wondered aloud.

"I don't know," Julia answered, "but I don't want you to wait any longer. This is too hard on Bridget—on all of you. Mary says the fire is almost on us."

"You *do* mean to come, too, Julia?" Edgar inquired.

"I've got to be here when David returns. I don't want to lose track of him. He'll be back—he wouldn't stay away at a time like this."

"No, he wouldn't," Alma said, her jewelry clanking as she fluttered in her chair. "He's had an accident!"

"I'm staying with Julia," Aunt Martha decided. "I have to be here for Nelda."

Julia shook her head. "It'll be too upsetting for you. If Nelda is with David, we'll bring her to you." Julia couldn't cope with Martha and her worries about Nelda, and she prayed that Martha would leave with the others.

"Julia is right," Edgar agreed.

Martha sighed, but nodded. Julia supposed Martha knew she was at her emotional limit. "Where will we go?" Martha asked submissively.

"To Alma's cousin in Oak Park."

Alma wrote out the address for Julia. In the event David didn't return, Martha's buggy was left for Julia. Michael loaded Julia's trunk in it. After Bridget was seated in her wagon, Julia reached up and pressed her hand. "Go right to bed when you get to the O'Keefes'."

"Sure and you be doing the same when you can."

"Pray that David is all right," Julia said softly. "I *am* worried he's had an accident."

Bridget nodded. "It's sad I am to be leaving you, and I wouldn't if I had me health."

Julia gazed after them until they disappeared into the crowd. It was a relief to have everyone safely gone.

Trees and bushes smoked in the Owens' yard. Their lights were out and Julia supposed they had left. Two houses at the other end of the block were burning. Many of the neighbors were loading carriages. The man across the street was digging a hole, evidently to bury possessions in. A large brand sailed overhead and landed on the area covered by her wet carpets; it didn't ignite. She looked up to the roof area. There was no smoke or fire. It was safe to wait for David a little longer, she thought. Julia entered the house and turned on every light. When you had on all the lights, you could hope the house was invulnerable, she thought irrationally.

She closed the front door and sat on the stoop, the tin box on her lap. At least Melinda was spared this night. Melinda didn't have to see Bridget's and Alma's houses burn. But that omission didn't justify her death; it was only a small comfort within a nightmare. Nothing justified Melinda's death. But she'd drive herself mad if she dwelt on that. Maybe she would have to blindly trust that God was just. Certainly Bridget would applaud that.

Oh, how she longed to trust God entirely!

Julia began to cry. She had never cried like this. It was as if something within her were breaking apart. It was very painful; her lungs and throat felt raw. She buried her face in her hands and rocked back and forth. She realized she was a very jealous, very superficial, very sinful woman. She remembered that jealousy had caused her to burn Trina's picture. At the time she hadn't cared that she was jealous; her only concern had been that David would fault her for jealousy. That's how she was—always fearing another's reaction. Always wanting to be loved. Always aiming to please to get love. Placing what others thought of her before what God thought—or she thought. Grasping for David's love. Oh, God must hate her. She had erected a facade—hidden behind a sweet smile and pretty hat, like many of the women in her church. She hated that kind of woman. She hated herself. She hated her horrible dislike of Diane. She was tired of feeling it. She was drained of it. She knew hate and jealousy and fear had made her wish to commit suicide. Over and over, jealousy ruled her life. She was even jealous of Nancy Smith's relationship with Arthur. How could she begrudge them happiness just because she was unhappy—just because she hated Mrs. Newton. *Yes,* Julia admitted, *I hate Mrs. Newton with a passion. How dare Mrs. Newton have intimated I was a fallen woman!* Oh, but Julia had the capacity to be one! Yesterday, if Arthur had invited her to meet him, she would have accepted. She felt the absolute truth of that. Let her not fool herself, she was furious with Nancy for stealing Arthur. She was no better than Diane. Or David. She evidenced all the wrong instincts.

Julia trembled and tightened her cloak around her. She had even tried to place her faith in coping rather than God. How long could a person cope before he gave in? She had almost broken many times—at Riverview Young Lady's Seminary, after Billy's exposé of David—and the next event might truly break her. She had thought confronting David about Diane was the answer, but she knew now that it wasn't. If he admitted he was having an affair, she couldn't live with the stark reality. That would be the breaking point. She had no idea how to manage her life. She had craved David's love to the exclusion of everything. Somehow she had confused passion with caring, sexual attraction with love. If she really loved him, she would want his happiness. Even if that meant he must be separated from her. She hoped God would give her a chance to talk to David. She prayed to God he wasn't dead. Oh, God, not that! Not some accident, not any event that would prevent her from talking to him.

She was a liar, too. She had done nothing but lie—about the miscarriage, about the child she now carried. Not telling David had been lying. He had a right to know about the child. After all, it was half his. Whether or not she miscarried wasn't an issue. Her scenerio of David's reaction to a miscarriage wasn't the issue either. Truth was the issue.

She looked above her. There was smoke now behind the pickets on the roof, but no flames. Oh, how tired, defeated, sorry she was. She couldn't continue this way—not another minute. She had no strength left to try. She observed the smoke and activity on the street, but it blurred and another street appeared in her mind, one she knew she had been approaching all her life. There was no confusion on this road and no obstacle blocking entrance to it, except herself. She was ready for that road; Bridget had known that.

"Oh, Jesus," she prayed. "Please take my life. I'm so sorry for my many, many sins. Oh, dear Lord, please forgive me!"

There was a rush of tears that she wiped with her gloves. Then joy sprang up in her. She smiled, amazed to be smiling in this mess. Oh, she knew that church would never again be a nice hat; it would be Christ.

There was an explosion of smoke around her, obliterating her view. She coughed and jumped up, waving aside the smoke. She saw flames poking through the wrought-iron railing on her roof. The lights still glowed invitingly in the house. She remembered the family Bible in the parlor and wondered if it would be safe to go after it. She also remembered Trina's seascape. She would love to give that to David.

She opened the door, and seeing no indication of fire inside, she entered the parlor. She clasped the tin box; she had been afraid it would disappear if she left it on the stoop. Streamers of smoke floated in the air. There was a wood smell, as if friendly logs burned in her fireplace. She covered her mouth and nose with her handkerchief. Lifting the Bible from the center table, she noticed a thread of fire along the cornice, on the wall partitioning the parlor and sitting room. Judging the fire too small to be a threat, she proceeded to the sitting room for Trina's picture.

After placing the Bible and tin box on the floor, she lifted the wire holding Trina's picture. She was startled by a cracking sound. Terrified, she saw flames dart along the cornice, in a far wider line than they had in the parlor. Then in one fast action the fire burst through the entire wall and part of the ceiling. A section of the ceiling dropped to the floor, scattering plaster.

She jumped back and furiously brushed the hot material from her skirt. Thank God she had her gloves on! Thank God the ceiling hadn't fallen on her! What a fool she had been to go after the picture. She lunged for the Bible and tin box and fled the room. The box was warm. Her eyes burned and tears flowed. She plunged through the kitchen, her eyes half shut against the smoke, and didn't stop until she was on the back sidewalk. Clutching her belongings at her waist, she stood trembling. How close she had come to dying! Oh, dear God, let my child be all right! Where was David? How could he leave her in this situation? Or would he have expected her to leave when fire struck the neighborhood? Had he in fact died? Surely many had. Where, oh, where was he!

She followed the sidewalk to the front. Several houses burned on the street, smoke plumed from the houses on either side, but no fire was apparent. Popping and shattering sounds came from above, and she looked up just as her bedroom window exploded. Glass rained over the yard and fire poured from the window. Her head reeling, she noticed how quickly the fire spread. Yes, it would have the house, and whatever of the contents it wished.

She fled to Aunt Martha's buggy. The trunk took most of the space, and she had to set the picture on top of it. She would hold the picture down as she drove, she thought.

She raised her foot toward the step, then lowered it. The bay horse was nervously dancing around on his feet, snorting and whinnying, and she doubted she could drive him. Suddenly he reared back and broke the bridle. He shook his head in freedom and galloped into the road, the buggy swaying behind him. The picture flew to the street, the Bible and tin box followed. The trunk tottered and crashed to the ground. The buggy hit a carriage and she heard a splintering sound.

Julia started to cry; oh, this was too much! Everything was ruined— gone, everything! She would never find the tin box in the littered, smoldering street.

Julia ran to the accident site. The coachman for the carriage was freeing her horse from his harness. "Oh, I'm sorry," Julia said. "Is your carriage ruined?"

"No, but I'm afraid the shaft is broken on your buggy."

"Then I can't drive it?"

"No."

As soon as her horse was free, he moved to the side of the coachman's horse and seemed a little calmer. But he was still trembling and skittish. "You'll have to leave him," the coachman advised. "He'll follow us to safety. I'll return him tomorrow."

"Yes," Julia quickly agreed. The offer was kind, and she couldn't manage the horse at all.

"Have you other transportation? You can come with us if you haven't."

"I'll be all right." She could walk; she might see David on the way out.

She believed the items in the buggy had fallen out near the junction of her driveway and the street. Lifting her skirts high to keep them from catching fire, she looked through the litter. The trunk was intact and smoldering at the bottom. She caught sight of a gleaming object and recognized it as the tin box.

"Thank goodness!" she cried in relief. She would give all she owned for that one item. She kicked through the rubble and unearthed the Bible and seascape. The Bible was open and burning from the middle outward. The frame on the seascape was cracked and most of the picture burned. She cried over these ruined items; they symbolized all she was losing.

A solid hand clasped her shoulder. She wheeled around and faced David and Nelda. "David. Oh, David!"

While he restrained Nelda by the wrist with one hand, he slid the other around her. She pressed to him, feeling security.

"Darling, you're all right!" he breathed with relief.

"Yes. Thank God you have Nelda. Where have you been? I tried to save Trina's seascape for you, but it's ruined. The family Bible is burning and the shaft on Martha's buggy is broken—her horse bolted. The trunk is ruined, I think. Everyone is off safely, though." She told him where they had sought refuge.

Julia embraced Nelda. Nelda trembled, clung to Julia like a child to her mother, gasping with emotion. Between them was a tattered folder of papers. Julia supposed it was the manuscript of *Trouble on the North Side*. Nelda's dress was filthy and torn, the hem trailing after her. Julia ripped it off so that Nelda wouldn't trip. Nelda's hair was tangled—but worst of all, she had that mad look in her eyes. "Nelda, it's all right—everything's all right."

"Bernard!" Nelda cried.

"What about him?"

"He's dead!"

"No," David corrected her. "That's not true, Nelda. I'll tell you later, Julia. We can't stay here."

They looked at the house. The fire was wrapped around it, melting it down. You could not tell where the bedroom had been, or any of the rooms, Julia observed with grief. "Where should we go?"

"Our exit is blocked in every direction but east. We'll have to go to the Sands."

The Sands was a forty- or fifty-acre area on the lake. At one time the Sands had been a gambling and prostitution district, but a former mayor had burned the establishments. Now the land was vacant, except for a bathhouse and a few out buildings. "Nelda can't sit out on a beach all night," Julia stated.

"There's no choice."

"Where is your buggy?"

"I had to leave it at church—I set the horse free. He was nervous and would go no farther." David's eyes were bleak. "We have nothing, Julia—nothing!"

"David, I don't mind so much—really. You're here. That is what's important. But what kept you?"

"I'll tell you after we're settled."

They arrived at the Sands, succeeding thousands of others. The bizarre sights on the beach shocked Julia. People camped on dining room chairs, bare mattresses, blankets, even velvet sofas. Possessions were stacked around the camps. Animals of all kinds were held on ropes or left to wander at will. Many people camped on the cold sand; *as I will*, Julia thought with a shudder. The usual drunks staggered around, and Julia doubted they would remember the fire in the morning. But the lake was the most unsettling sight of all, because it reflected the rose color of the fire. Yes, she would expect the lake to have a rosy top, a deception.

They found a spot next to a couple who had laid a blanket between two chairs to make a tent for their children. Julia saw six little feet peeking out and was touched at how the father diligently brushed sparks from the tent.

Nelda tried to shake free of David. "I want water—I want a drink. Let me go to the water and get a drink. Let go of me, I say!"

David borrowed a cup from the couple beside them. "I'd better restrain Nelda," David told Julia. "She's strong when she has a mind to run. Will you get the water?"

After Nelda had drunk, Julia asked, "Where did you find Nelda?"

"At church—she had just arrived when I came. The janitor had left. It's a good thing I arrived when I did. She was hysterical, saying that she had seen Bernard on the Sands. She said he was darting around, quite out of his mind. She had tried to catch him, but couldn't. She pleaded with me to search for Bernard, and I told her I couldn't. She kept dancing around in front of me—I reached for her but her arm slipped through my hand. I didn't catch her until we were on the Sands. Nelda isn't rational—I wonder if she imagined seeing Bernard. I'm certain Dr. Sutton is carefully guarding the patients tonight. It was a nightmare to me. I was worried to death about you, but I had to find Nelda."

Nelda's eyes suddenly shot to David. "I saw Bernard—I said I did!"

"You can see we need to drop this subject," David told Julia.

"I did—I did!"

"Then he's all right," Julia assured her. "Somebody will have helped him by now. Nelda, why did you run away?"

"To see if I could find a new life for Bernard and me. I thought I could publish my book and we could have a house. He could paint pictures and my writing would support us until he was known."

"Maybe that can work out someday. But you need to get well first."

"I am well!"

"Oh, Nelda!" If Nelda couldn't understand she needed help, was there any hope for her?

"Take me to Melinda; she'll help me!"

David looked at Julia with sympathy, obviously understanding Julia couldn't handle a discussion of Melinda tonight. "Stop it, Nelda—right now!" he commanded.

"Melinda! I—"

Nelda broke off and looked down at her lap. When she looked up, her eyes had lost their glitter. Julia felt relief, but she was wary. For it wasn't uncommon for Nelda to pass from lunacy to sanity and back to lunacy in the space of an hour. "Is Dr. Sutton upset?" Nelda asked.

"Yes, of course."

"Maybe I shouldn't have gone."

"You certainly shouldn't have."

"Is Mother all right?"

"Yes. She's at your second cousin's in Oak Park. Of course, she's worried about you. Did you sleep in the churchyard?"

"Yes, in the stable."

"Then no men troubled you?"

Nelda shook her head. "Will you look for Bernard—please? I did see him!"

It sounded to Julia and David as though Nelda spoke the truth. They each took one of her hands and proceeded to search for him.

Twenty-four

After a long, futile search for Bernard, they sat down on the beach.

"Tired, darling?" David asked.

"I'm all right."

Julia had given the answer relative to her circumstances. In reality her eyes burned and her back ached. She placed her hands in the sand behind her to brace her back. The sensation of having her back warmed by the city's breath and her face cooled by the lake's was unpleasant. She searched the smoky sky for a sign of the rising sun, but could find none. She thought that when this one natural light appeared, she would feel hopeful that the fire would soon burn out.

Julia shifted her hands. They had just learned the waterworks was burning. So the fire had another advantage on its list, Julia thought. Now the steamers, unable to use the hydrants, had to rely on the river and the lake. Much of the fire was now out of control. "I'm afraid the fire will spread to the prairie," Julia speculated. "The grass is dry—the fire could go on and on."

"It's possible. Don't think the worst, though."

Julia nodded. "At least Nelda's quiet now."

After Nelda had cried bitterly for Bernard, she pressed her manuscript to herself and slept with her head in Julia's lap. Julia envied Nelda her madness—or whatever it was that allowed her to sleep in this environment.

A tug had just pulled up and carried off a group of people. Julia asked, "Should we move nearer the water? We'd have a better chance of being rescued there."

"I don't want to wake Nelda. Only a few have been rescued out of thousands. Even if we were up front, our chances of being where a boat beaches is dim. Here, lean your head on my shoulder—you'll be more comfortable."

Julia leaned on him and the pressure on her back was relieved.

She had asked God for an opportunity to speak to David. Nelda was asleep and there was nothing but the fire to interrupt. "David," she blurted, "I have so much to tell you. I hardly know where to start. I hope you can forgive me. I—I'm pregnant, almost three months, I think." She exhaled deeply in relief; the hardest part had been said.

"Pregnant! Why *didn't* you tell me sooner?"

"I . . . oh . . ." *Tell the truth,* she thought. "I was afraid I might miscarry and it would be too painful for you. I was afraid you'd go to Diane Hastings for comfort. Yes, I know about Diane! But I understand—really I do—"

"Julia!"

His face was crimson in the light of the fire, a frightening color. "Please, don't interrupt. This is *hard*! I've kept so much from you. I . . . I tried to commit suicide. I almost killed myself and our child."

"Suicide—good Lord, why!"

Oh, she shouldn't have stated it so bluntly. Why, when words were important, were they so difficult? "I'll tell you, but you must realize that I forgive you. I want your happiness. At Bridget's wedding Billy told me he saw you and Diane Hastings embracing in her driveway. He said you paid him fifty dollars to be quiet about it. I was stunned. I couldn't think sanely. I just wanted to die. I . . . I found the arsenic in the cellar, and I didn't remember the child until I had almost swallowed it. Then I realized I couldn't kill the child or myself. I decided I would cope with your affair somehow."

"Julia! I didn't—"

"David, please listen—please don't interrupt!" She felt breathless, dizzy. "You remember the night I wore the Paris nightgown? I had bought it, hoping to lure you from Diane, and when you asked me to return it, I was crushed. I felt cheap about trying to entice you. I was confused and desperate to have love. Yesterday I saw Arthur Newton and Nancy Smith outside the historical society. I became extremely jealous of their relationship. I'd have given anything to attract Arthur. David, I'm no different from you! I've just never had the chance for a lover. I understand about you loving Diane—I understand it's possible to love two women at once. I honestly do."

"Julia, stop this!"

His eyes blazed. She thought that he must be furious. "No! Let me finish! I'm telling you all this so you'll understand I want you to be happy. If you can't be happy with me, you're free to leave. I just want what's best for you, whatever that is. In the past all I thought about was getting your love, and that is selfish. I never considered your best interests. I never cared that you missed Trina or that you were hurt over Diane's marriage. I would have done anything for your love—lied, cheated, anything! I was desperate and jealous. I even burned a letter Diane sent you recently."

She took a ragged breath and sobbed. Of course he didn't understand! She had pushed him past his limit of understanding. "I . . . I've sinned against you. You're kind, David, and you've been loving and sweet—and I appreciate it. I—"

"Sinned!"

"Yes."

He looked struck. "My God—oh, God!"

Julia had to be open—about everything. "When we moved in, I found a packet of letters from Diane. They disappeared before I could read them. David, I would have read every last one if I had found them."

"Darling, stop this—please be quiet! How much I've hurt you. I burned those letters a long time ago—but they shouldn't have been saved in the first place. I'm deeply sorry for all I've put you through. I don't love Diane—I love you! I wondered what had happened to the letter Diane wrote this summer. I thought perhaps I had thrown it out at work. When I received it, I was alarmed. Diane is persistent, and I was afraid it was the first of many invitations. I decided to speak to her and put an end to any designs she had on me. I went to Diane's one day after work, and she arrived in her carriage as I pulled up. We met in her driveway. I told her to stop writing me, that I no longer loved her or cared to hear from her. She threw back her head and laughed, and a determined look came in her eyes. Before I understood what she was about, she was embracing me, kissing me. This is what Billy saw. After I left Diane, Billy threatened to tell you I was having an affair, and I idiotically let him blackmail me. I was afraid you would believe Billy, not me."

He shifted his legs on the sand, then continued. "You had reasons to believe Billy. I . . . I don't want to hurt you with this; but of course you knew my feelings were ambivalent toward you at the beginning of our marriage. You knew I was still attracted to Diane then. You knew I had stopped at Diane's the night Charlie was over. Also you were jealous over Trina. I've been watching your reactions for months, Julia. So many times you've seemed strained, and I'd think you were comparing yourself to Trina."

He looked intently at her, compelling her to understand. Oh, she did! She did! "I remember the night we ate in the Walnut Room—after Bridget's wedding reception. You acted so strangely," he said, "rather brittle, too gay. You hardly ate. I felt something was wrong, but I couldn't bring myself to press you as to what. If only you had told me about your suicide attempt. If only you had told me what Billy had said." There was a deep look of pain in his eyes.

He leaned very near. "The night you wore the Paris nightgown, I behaved terribly, and I've not forgiven myself for it. I shouldn't have complained about money—fifty dollars is nothing compared to your feelings. I was a fool. You looked lovely, darling—breathtaking, and I'm so afraid I've prevented you from giving me another such surprise."

"I'll buy another nightgown like that," Julia promised.

His eyes were like fire, burning with love. She allowed it to fully dawn on her: David didn't love Diane at all. All her suffering had been for nothing. She would never lose him to Diane!

"Julia, you're precious to me. You're a lovely wife. You've cared for my father and mother as if they were your own parents. Mother relies on you. You've devoted yourself to Nelda. You're kind to Bridget and Mary, and Bridget loves you like a sister. You've put up with my traveling and long hours. I can only imagine how my ambivalent attitude toward you hurt the first few months of our marriage. You are very fine, Julia. I thank God for the day I married you. Darling, if I could kiss you now, I would not stop. If I could take you in my arms, I would not let you go."

"David!" she gasped in boundless elation. "Oh, David, you have!"

His long arms reached for her over Nelda. His eyes were brilliant, not a shade of darkness in them. She could read love in them. It was the same light and love she had seen on her wedding day. Yes, it had always been there for her.

Nelda stirred. He lowered his hands. He said, "I hope this night hasn't hurt the child."

"I don't know, David—I've been through so much strain tonight. But let's not worry. Let's just leave it with God." She smiled. "David, I finally can do that. I finally can trust Him. While I waited for you and Nelda, I gave my life to Christ." She looked closely at him. "You look surprised."

"I'm glad you have. I love you—I will love any stand for Christ you take."

"Have you ever thought anymore about being a Christian?"

"At times. Father's changed nature is a miracle. He couldn't be that way in his own power. Yes, I have thought about it, but when I take such an action, I want to be sure of my sincerity. I don't want to do it for ego reasons—to receive a spiritual lift. I've sought enough ego satisfaction in my life."

Eventually the sun rose and the slight mark it made on the smoke depressed Julia. The buildings along the Chicago River were blazing, including David's lumberyard and the huge grain elevators. The conflagration threw cinders, smoke, and miserable gales of heat at them.

"It really looks like all of Chicago will burn," Julia said, brushing a cinder from her skirt.

David's eyes were on the area where his lumberyard burned. There were no buildings standing nearby to mark it, and Julia estimated where the yard was by its distance from the mouth of the river. She reached for his hand. "Darling, I wish it weren't burning!"

"Yes," he said tightly.

"Oh–yes!"

He looked down at Nelda. She was still asleep but breathing with difficulty, her face moist with perspiration. "Are you having trouble breathing, too?" he asked Julia.

"Yes, and with the heat."

"We'll have to move into the water." In the last hour, hundreds of people had taken refuge in the lake, bringing along their vehicles and animals.

Julia didn't want to enter the lake, where Melinda had died. But the alternatives were grim: they could wait it out here or they could bury themselves to their necks in the sand. She looked at those partly buried in the sand and wondered how they stood their confinement. The family next to them was seeking protection there. While the father dug a hole, his boy ran a handful of sand through his fingers, apparently believing his father was playing.

Julia shook Nelda awake. Nelda brushed sand from her skirt and combed her hair with her fingers. These little signs of sanity relieved Julia. "I'm thirsty," Nelda announced.

"We have to move from the heat," David said. "We're going to stand in the lake—you'll feel better there."

"The water's cold. I'm not going!"

"We have to, Nelda—it's necessary."

Nelda didn't argue further, and they entered the water. Julia lowered her hand to raise her skirt, then thought, what's the use? It will be thoroughly soaked in a minute. She felt the cold water seeping into her shoes. For a moment that felt good.

They walked until the water was around their knees. Julia thought only about Melinda. As she gazed toward the smoky horizon, she felt as though she might reach out and touch Melinda's round face, see her brown hair bouncing. It was as if Melinda would appear and say, "I've been on a trip, Julia, and here I am. I'm so sorry for having worried you. A boat picked me up, and one thing led to another, and I just didn't get around to writing. Julia, I should have sent for you and David—you would have loved that place."

Julia sobbed. David touched her shoulder. "Darling, what is it?"

"Melinda."

"You can't look back—not tonight."

"I know, but—I—hate this lake. I hate being in it."

"It *is* protecting us."

"I know! I wish it weren't!"

"Julia, calm down for Nelda's sake."

"I will. I just needed to say it. I'll be all right—I know the lake is protecting us. I know God is with us."

"I don't like it here," Nelda complained. "I'm thirsty!" Nelda cupped her hands to lift water to her face.

"Don't," David warned. "The water is filthy from the animals."

Nelda whined. Julia and David wrapped their arms around her, David trying to shield them with his coat. Nelda struggled, but finally laid her head on his shoulder. *At least she's quiet*, Julia thought—*at least that! Oh, dear Jesus, please keep Nelda sane.*

Later that morning the buildings surrounding the Sands were substantially destroyed. The air was cooler, and they returned to shore. The fire had moved north of the Sands. Julia's legs were numb, and she was amazed that she was able to walk.

They headed north, toward the walls at the northern limit of the Sands, hoping there to find a vehicle to drive them west. Julia's water-soaked dress was heavy and cumbersome, but the warm wind from the city promised to dry it quickly. She longed to collapse on the sand. Anywhere would do. She stared at every vacant area they passed. She didn't look up at all—just clutched Nelda's hand and followed David's feet. Nelda was rational, but just barely so. Poor Nelda. She had been outside since yesterday and was certainly the most spent of them all.

"I'm hungry and thirsty," Nelda whined.

David said patiently, "Please try to hang on a little longer."

"I'm tired."

"I know—I understand."

"I wish I had stayed at Dr. Sutton's. If I had, I'd be all right and Bernard wouldn't have left to find me."

"Yes," Julia agreed. It would not be helpful for Nelda to know that Dr. Sutton's place had most certainly burned. Nor that Bernard probably had other reasons for leaving.

They joined about fifty people waiting to leave the Sands at the walls on Superior Street. Superior Street and the streets surrounding it weren't passable until late that afternoon. In the meantime they had to stand; hot embers on the ground ignited the clothes of those who tried sitting. Nelda whined and Julia spent hours rocking her in her arms. Finally, vehicles emerged from the smoke still enveloping the city and rescued some of the refugees. Heading toward them was a coal cart, the driver waving. "Need a ride?"

"Can we hire you to take us to the West Side?" David asked. They would go to Michael's parents and ask Michael to drive them to Alma's cousin's in Oak Park.

"I ain't taking pay for helping somebody out. I come to see if anybody needed a ride. My wife and grandkids is safe and I'm grateful to God." The driver's slight frame wasn't garbed like a saint; rather, he wore work pants and a cap so battered it likely had topped his head many of his numerous years. He had the kindest blue eyes Julia had ever seen.

"Thank you," David said humbly. "How widespread is the fire?"

"The downtown is burned up. Most of the North Side is burnt. The fire's up north—somewheres nearby Lincoln Park, I heard. Though don't quote me on it."

"Have many died?" Julia asked.

"I ain't sure how many, but I know it's quite a few."

They climbed into the coal cart, a dirty and cramped box with high sides and bits of coal on the floor. David swept the coal to the side. The cart wasn't wide enough for all three, so Julia and Nelda sat across from each other and drew up their legs. Nelda closed her eyes and Julia leaned against the high back, relishing the support it gave. Even the folded position of her legs was a relief from standing. David put his arm around her.

The driver pulled into the street. Nothing of much height stood, just an occasional cookstove or stubs of chimneys. In the rubble twisted pieces of metal gleamed—strange things, unearthly. The few trees that stood were stripped of bark and most of their limbs—charcoal skeletons in the smoke. She hoped she would never again see a sight like this. The loss! The bleakness! The desolation! It would take years to grow a mature tree. And all of the trees gone in a night!

But it doesn't take long to construct a building, Julia thought.

David was looking at her. His eyes were searching her—not judging in any way, only loving her. She looked fully at him. That they could gaze at each other with nothing hidden between them was a miracle. If not for Christ, it wouldn't have been possible, she reflected.

"Nothing matters, except we've made it through together," he said. "My insurance probably won't cover the loss of the lumberyard and house. Most insurance companies won't have the capital to cover all of tonight's damage. I'll likely have to be content with a percentage—probably fifty percent. I would give the fifty percent an infinite number of times to have you safe. Nothing—nothing matters except you."

"Oh, David!"

He continued to look at her, his eyes still intense, loving. "There is Someone, though, who is more important than us."

She knew what he would say. She stared at him in wonder.

"Christ, darling. He is Christ."

Epilogue

The sky clouded and a light rain started at about 11:00 p.m. the day that Julia and David were rescued. The Chicago fire burned out about thirty hours after it began. It destroyed 3.32 square miles of property and left 98,500 homeless. It was estimated that 300 people died.